A LIFE REMOVED

A NOVEL

JASON PARENT

ISBN 13: 978-1-940215-92-1

ISBN 10: 1-940215-92-7

Red Adept Publishing, LLC

104 Bugenfield Court

Garner, NC 27529

http://RedAdeptPublishing.com/

Cover and Formatting: Streetlight Graphics

PROLOGUE

Fall River, Massachusetts. A new millennium.

THE NIGHT WAS COLD, FAR too cold for her to be out on the streets. Early fall in New England was a crapshoot—hot one day and blistered ass cheeks the next. The opposing temperatures had blanched the leaves, a holocaust of swirling colors.

Fall was a pleasant time for most New Englanders, but for Eliza, the season meant the coming of winter and harder times. Cold or not, work beckoned.

She'd been pretty once. Eliza's parents had encouraged her ambitious dreams of modeling, but that was before they'd thrown her out, before she'd fallen into bed with cocaine. Those dreams of modeling had turned into a reality of stripping. As the addiction wore her down, she'd turned to a life of whoring. With every snort, she looked a little more beaten and strung out. At twenty-seven, she was fruit gone rotten, her core porous and withered. Her oversized fake tits hung awkwardly against her frail body. Her eyes were sunken, and her mouth was spoiled by crooked fences, courtesy of her last boyfriend.

In the right light, Eliza was still beautiful, a fleeting reminder of an earlier, more innocent day. But after five years, a thousand lines, three abusive boyfriends, and more johns than she could ever hope to forget, Eliza's pinup days were over, as gone as her money and her self-respect. She had a need to fulfill. Her body was a means to an end.

Eliza preferred to work Bedford Street. People only went to Bedford Street after hours for two reasons: alcohol and pussy. Fewer cops patrolled Bedford than Plymouth Avenue, so her odds of spending the night on her back were far better than passing it in a holding cell. She would probably run into Lexi or Carla, but otherwise, her competition would be slight. On Bedford Street, Eliza could earn enough to get her off later, picking up a regular or hustling a drunk exiting one of the countless dives.

Prostitution wasn't exactly rampant in Fall River. The decaying city full of downtrodden people had once been a bustling textile city. The mills had long since closed, leaving a generation jobless. Unlike that of a big city, serious crime in Fall River was limited mostly because there was nothing to do and no reason to go there, except for those unlucky enough to live there. Just fifteen minutes outside Providence, it had a few wannabe gangs, a noticeable drug problem, and the occasional murder.

Eliza called it home. She'd been born in Fall River, and she would die there, her chances for escape as dead as her dreams.

Still, she scraped by. Occasionally, tricks turned out to be a bit rough, but she hadn't experienced anything she couldn't handle. So like so many nights before, she walked along Bedford Street in short heels and a shorter dress just before closing time. It was her need, not the cold weather, that made her shake.

"I said, how are you doing tonight?" a voice called from behind.

Eliza whipped around, startled. She hadn't noticed the van pull up or the man calling to her from its passenger-side window.

Bingo. Eliza's nerves quickly settled. Her thoughts were well past the callous sex, focused on her next fix. She approached her first customer of the night, and by the look of him, it would be easy money. The man resembled a fifties crooner in some silly doo-wop band. Pat Boone meets Buddy Holly, only much more handsome and minus the nerdy, thick-rimmed glasses. He was well dressed, clean-cut, and chiseled like a Greek statue.

It can't be for him. The driver must be a pig. Eliza couldn't make out the driver, whose face was hidden by shadow.

"Are you looking for some company?" she asked, knowing they wouldn't be talking to her for any other reason.

6

"Actually, we were looking for you." The man's smile and his voice's velvet tone oozed with charm.

Eliza grew suspicious. "You a cop?" She'd been with her share of lonely men, but even the decent-looking ones lacked his confidence, his seductive stare. Although she was a whore, the man's charms were not wasted on her. But they did make her question his intentions.

"No, nothing like that. We'd like to hire you."

New to this. Eliza grinned. *I'll make it easy for him.* "Thirty for head. Fifty for pussy. No anal." She knew she would blow the guy for a cigarette, but it never hurt to negotiate.

"Sure, sure." The man's smile was unwavering, his poise unflinching. "Can we go someplace more private?"

"Where'd you have in mind? I have a spot I use around the corner." By "spot," she meant "alley."

"How about the back of my van? It's much more comfortable than it looks. Come on, get in."

She was no fool. She'd heard all the stories about hookers who'd gone with the wrong guys. *You get a bad vibe, you run.* But she got no bad vibes from that guy. His eyes were kind and soft, almost angelic, and she briefly imagined him as her Richard Gere, her savior, come to take her away from her life on the streets. Eliza was too smart to cling to that hope. Not that she had a choice. Her shakes were getting worse by the hour. It could be a while before the next business opportunity presented itself. She was definitely getting into the van.

"All right. But I don't do groups. One at a time."

The man opened the door and stepped out of the vehicle. He was dressed all in black, except for a silver chain looped around his neck and tucked into his shirt. His eyes, like soothing springs, invited her in, and for the first time, she felt afraid, not of imminent danger but of not being in control. She feared she would do anything he asked, anything he wanted. She was his for the taking. She might not even ask for the money up front. He was a gentleman going about ungentlemanly business, and she liked the façade of chivalry.

When he slid open the van's side door and took her hand, excitement tingled through her body, a sensation she'd never felt from her work. The back was empty, and she slid into the middle seat. The man closed the door and returned to his spot up front. The driver remained silent as he pulled away from the curb.

"So, who's fir—"

Someone put an arm around her neck from behind. The assailant's grasp came quickly and was unrelenting, so fierce that she bit deeply into her tongue, clenching hard against the sudden force. Her head throbbed. Pressure built around her neck, blocking the flow of blood to her brain. She tried to scream but had no voice.

Even in her terror, she knew what was happening. Her heart knew it, too, pumping feverishly, speeding along her unconsciousness. Her eyes rolled back. She dug her nails into the arm around her neck, but her assailant wouldn't let her go. Her vision blurred as tears began to flow.

As her need for air became vital, Eliza's eyes shot open. She reached out to the man in the passenger seat in front of her, the man in whom she'd foolishly placed her trust. *Please stop this.* She clung to the hope that in those last waking moments, he could still be her savior.

He stared back at her, flashing that charming smile.

CHAPTER 1

Aaron Pimental woke feeling as though he hadn't slept at all. His muscles ached. His tongue lolled, dry like a slug on hot pavement, a film that tasted like broken pills coating it. The alarm clock flashed 7:00 a.m. His shift started in an hour. He eased out of bed, trying not to disturb Arianna, who didn't need to get up for another half hour. Looking down at her long dark hair curving around her ear and under her chin, he envied her that half hour.

After six years with her, he still found her beautiful, still loved her. But they had been spending less and less time together of late, and he was beginning to wonder if she still loved him. Something or *someone* had infected their former bliss, spreading like a cancer through all aspects of their relationship.

Or maybe just through me.

He stared at her, wondering how long it had been since they'd last had sex. Listening to the air whistle through her nose as she snored, he couldn't even recall when he'd last wanted to.

She shifted and moaned, and he slid away. He headed to the bathroom to begin what would be just another long day in a long, sad string of them. *The definition of living.*

After his shower, he stuffed his close to two hundred pounds into his navy-blue uniform pants. They had fit him so much better only a year ago, and he had to wonder if tedium made a man idle. Even so, he was in decent shape for a twenty-eight-year-old. He dried and combed his mostly still-pepper hair, trying to remember his last good night's sleep. Beer helped, but it wasn't helping his uniform issues, his sex drive, or his relationship with his girlfriend. He blamed it for the disappearing trick his abs had pulled.

Once dressed, he stepped out into the hallway, which was lined with photos of a once-happy couple. He stopped before his favorite and sighed: a simple shot of Aaron, looking tall and lean, smiling, his arm around Arianna as snow-capped peaks shot up like arrowheads behind them. He didn't smile like that anymore, not that big and bright and genuine. And Arianna...

She looks as good today as she did then. Allowing himself the memory, Aaron did smile, if only just a little.

He fed, walked, and brushed his dog then headed to work. *Wonder where the captain will stick me and the radar gun today? Four years... I've been doing this for four years, and I haven't gotten anywhere.*

Just as he'd guessed, his shift began with speed control during rush hour on Plymouth Avenue, where the chances of speeding were next to nil. Fender benders, though, were a regular occurrence, and they meant paperwork.

Fun, fun.

Aaron was sitting in the lot of a small café, sipping piping-hot coffee, when a call came over the radio. A woman's body had been discovered in a dumpster behind a sandwich shop on Plymouth Avenue, not more than three blocks from the café. He would have been fine letting someone else take it, but the dispatcher knew his cruiser's location. With a groan, he headed toward what he prayed wouldn't end up being a shit show.

When Aaron got to the sandwich shop, the shift manager was hysterical. Aaron sat the man on the curb and waited patiently for him to calm down before taking his statement. During a spot check before opening, the manager had found a bigger mess than the usual litter. The body lay atop a mound of garbage bags, naked and exposed. Flies had already started laying eggs in her wounds. Whoever had placed her there obviously didn't care if the body was found.

Aaron cordoned off the crime scene and walked over to take a look at the body. The deceased was the first murder victim he had seen and only the second dead body he'd ever encountered. His first had been in an open casket at a relative's funeral, and that alone was enough to creep him out.

But the body in the dumpster filled him with sadness. A life wasted.

Aaron shook his head in disgust. He knew nothing of how the woman had lived her life, but the mutilated corpse painted a dreadful picture of how she had died. It hit him like a punch to the gut, and he choked on his Adam's apple. He covered the body with a blanket, much like a father lovingly tucking in his child, then waited for the cavalry to arrive at the front of the restaurant.

Perhaps her slashed wrists had affected him most, bringing back the pain from years long past. His own scars were physically faded but emotionally irremovable. He looked at his wrists, where a horizontal line of raised whitish flesh crossed each. When he thought about them, they itched. Despite the scars, the Fall River Police Department had welcomed him with open arms.

I guess they figure time heals all wounds. Or they were desperate. He sneered. But he knew the truth: his decent grades, the years past, and the fact that he had only harmed himself had little to do with his rise in the academy. His girlfriend's lawyerly connections—she had graduated with half the scumbags who controlled the city politics—had secured him the position, though he often wondered if she had offered *them* a few positions of her own. Whether she hung that over his head consciously or not, it was always a debt he felt he owed her. It made him feel small.

He shrugged it off. Times had been worse. He scratched his scars. *Vertical slits, you dumbass. Everyone knows that. You couldn't even do that right.* Running fingers across the marks brought to mind the same stinging sensation he'd felt while carving them. His mind drifted back to their inception.

"You're such a prick!" The words had shot from Ricardo Jimenez's mouth like bullets from an AK-47. "Why? Because of a fucking girl? If you want a near-death experience so badly, why don't you just try skydiving, like most people?"

Shame washed over Aaron. He couldn't even look his best friend in the eye. "It wasn't just because—"

"Shut up, man. Just shut the fuck up. I don't want to hear your melodramatic bullshit. You don't know how lucky you are. You have friends, family, and a good future ahead of you. You're such a fucking ingrate. You don't appreciate what you've got."

Aaron shuddered. Wallowing in his own self-pity, he'd forgotten that some people had it rougher. People like Ricardo. "Your vision's still getting worse?" Aaron asked.

"It sure as hell isn't getting better. In a few more years, I'll have to walk with a cane."

Ricardo had been born with a degenerative eye condition. He'd been from doctor to doctor, specialist to specialist. Each told him the same thing—he was going blind. Aaron imagined that being born blind, never knowing what it was like to see the world in all its color, was hard enough. But Ricardo had been forced to sit by helplessly as his vision deteriorated.

He'd always handled it with poise and strength... until the night Aaron had slashed his wrists. Along with himself, Aaron had dragged down the only person who gave a damn—a real damn, not that superficial Hallmark brand—about him.

Aaron stared into space, still feeling the shame even after all the years that had passed, still not appreciating all that he had. He didn't notice the detectives until they were standing right in front of him.

"Where's the victim?" a gruff voice asked.

"Huh?" Aaron shook himself out the memory.

A gaunt, narrow-faced man with slicked-back black hair tapped his tattered brown loafer. His entire body, from his blue blazer to the cuffs of his Levis, seemed to vibrate with impatience. One look at the guy's smug grin and those glasses that seemed to hover over his beak-like nose made Aaron feel as if he'd just swallowed something bitter. *Oh, great. Detective Marklin. This should be fun. I hope I didn't fuck anything up.*

No one liked Detective Bruce Marklin. He was a hard-nosed, arrogant prick, but for a Fall River detective—hell, for *any* detective—he was pretty damn good. And smart. *Too* smart. Aaron had heard he'd graduated *summa cum laude* from Harvard but had shirked a more lucrative future for the thankless work of public service. Rumor had it that his choice had something to do with a murdered family member—or girlfriend or boyfriend, depending on who was telling the story.

Regardless, Bruce Marklin was the best damn detective in the state outside of Boston, and maybe inside of it, too. Unfortunately, he knew it. He was a loner and generally always pissy, which made it all the stranger when he had taken on a partner a year ago. Aaron figured the guy had just been trying to get laid.

Detective Jocelyn Beaudette was an ambitious woman only a few years older than Aaron but light-years ahead of him on the force. She was every bit the opposite of her mentor: polite, approachable, and soft but not weak. Genuinely likable. She tied her shoulder-length blond hair back then flexed her fingers as if readying for battle. With her lanky build, like a not-so-ugly duckling that never quite transformed into an elegant swan, she ought to have been clumsy. But Aaron knew she was deft when she had to be: he had seen her take down more than a few overzealous recruits in the self-defense courses she taught at the academy.

Aaron's eyes lingered. Even in her unflattering jeans and flats complemented by a schoolteacher blouse that hung on her small, flat-chested frame, something about Beaudette made him tingle. Maybe it was her social awkwardness that he found appealing; her self-doubt often cast a shadow over her competence and determination. Never overconfident or overbearing, she hid all that under a long wool overcoat. He wondered what else she hid under there.

His eyes lingered too long. Heat rose from his cheeks as she caught him staring.

"Well?" Beaudette crossed her arms and faked a smile. When she smiled for real, she was striking, despite the seriousness that lingered in her piercing blue eyes. Those eyes, sharp and predatory like an eagle's, belied her strength. Though more blundering in her movements, Beaudette's results suggested she might become as shrewd as Marklin, but she was half his age and one-tenth the prick. She'd been working with Major Crimes for only a year when she was assigned her first homicide. She already had a few murders under her belt, mostly open-and-shut cases, when Marklin decided to take her under his wing.

Aaron swallowed, his mind frazzled, all his training and even rudimentary thinking momentarily forgotten under the detectives' examination. The two seemed to work in tandem. As if sensing the glare her partner was giving him, Beaudette shifted to business mode, lips pressed flat. *Detective Robot and Detective Asshole reporting.* The thought was unfair to Beaudette, who, unlike her partner, was more than a stereotype. She could exhibit normal human emotions without having to look too hard for them. Still, Aaron wondered what she would be like if she just let loose, kicked back with the boys, maybe unbuttoned a few buttons...

Beaudette cleared her throat then stared at him with a steely glare.

Aaron looked at Marklin, who twitched as if he were just waiting for the chance to earn his *Detective Asshole* moniker, and shivered. Warmth spread across his cheeks. "She's in the back. In the dumpster." He motioned for the detectives to follow.

Red and blue lights and lines of yellow tape filled the parking lot. No one would be getting their steak-and-cheese subs that day. The detectives surveyed the lot as they strolled.

Before they reached the body, Marklin exploded. "Who the fuck fucked with my crime scene?"

Aaron knew immediately what had set Marklin off. The large navy-blue police-issue blanket was an eyesore. "I covered her," he said sheepishly. "She's naked."

"Do you think she gives a fuck? If you fucked up any of my evidence, you can kiss your ass goodbye." Marklin's clenched teeth and steady glower made clear that he meant every word.

Even Detective Beaudette gave Aaron an inquisitive stare.

"Do you have anything worthwhile to add to this investigation?" Marklin asked.

"Dispatch sent me in first. No one's seen nothing. No sign of a struggle in the immediate vicinity. No blood spilled anywhere I could see. I already talked to the shift manager, and he—"

"We already know that much." Marklin scowled. "Don't you worry about the shift manager. We'll talk to him ourselves. Can you give me an ID on the girl?"

Aaron shook his head. He knew better than to open his mouth again.

"No? Then get the fuck out of here. Go help keep back any nosy civilians, employees, and press. And don't go doing another stupid thing, like making a statement."

Marklin had made his order. Aaron had no choice but to comply.

14

Still, his heart ached for the deceased woman he'd never known. Aaron couldn't understand what she could possibly have done to warrant such a brutal death, to have her body lifelessly tossed aside like garbage.

He ambled to the crime scene's perimeter. At the tape, he turned back to watch Detective Marklin peel off the blanket.

"Jeez, what a way to start the morning, huh, Jocelyn?" Marklin asked. The victim was nothing more than a dead body to him, just another lifeless part of his job.

"Do you think it's the same guy?" Beaudette asked.

"Looks like it, or a good copycat. Two kills in less than a week. The press is going to have a field day drawing wild conclusions."

After donning a pair of latex gloves, Beaudette cradled the woman's hand in her own. "Same markings on the wrists."

Marklin nodded. "I see them. Thin slits. Looks like they were made by a razor. Surely, the killer wasn't trying to disguise this as a suicide?"

Aaron couldn't help but chuckle. *A difficult task. I doubt she could have lived long enough to remove her own heart.*

"You never know," Beaudette said. "Criminals can be so stupid. Just the other day, a masked couple robbed a local convenience store. When the woman saw a contest entry form near the counter, she filled it out before leaving. Sometimes, they make our job so easy." She shrugged. "Anyway, the cause of death seems to be the same."

Marklin chewed on the end of a pen. He shook his head. "Heart carved out? I'm not so sure. What are these bruises on the sides of her neck? Possible strangulation? We'll need an autopsy report immediately. Where is that M.E., anyway? Christ, we haven't got all day."

"The other victim had been dead for days before we found him. Assuming the same person did this, do you suppose there are more bodies we haven't found yet?"

Aaron gasped. Beaudette's question provoked another, more horrifying question. *A serial killer in Fall River?* It would be a first in his lifetime. The thought brought a chill to his spine.

Marklin didn't flinch. "Who knows? But if there are, it will only make him that much easier to catch. The more bodies we find lying around, the more evidence we'll have to work with. He's bound to have left evidence somewhere, if not here."

"She's naked. What about semen samples? We can't rule out the possibility of a sex crime."

"Possible, but unlikely." Marklin scanned the parking lot. "Damn it! Where the hell is Dr. Hawthorne? Do I have to do her job for her?" He slapped his thigh then used his pen to poke through the garbage before returning it to his mouth. "Anyway, assuming that the murders are linked, Fernald was naked, too. I don't think there's a sexual motive here. But you're right. We should have the team do a full sweep for fingerprints around the dumpster, dust what and where we can. I'm sure our absent M.E. will do a full examination for genetic material, hair follicles, and anything else that doesn't belong here."

"Fernald was dumped into the river," Beaudette said. "Why do you think this one was displayed so openly?"

"Maybe he needed to get rid of the body fast. We'll ask him when we catch him. For now, all we've got is a dead girl with her heart ripped out and another heartless body down at the morgue. We won't know much more until Dr. Hawthorne and the lab guys do their thing." Marklin turned to leave.

That's it? That's it, you bastard? That's all you're going to do for her? Aaron flexed his fingers. The way Marklin was just leaving her there, piled atop garbage, didn't seem right, though he still wasn't quite sure why he cared so much. Aaron had seen enough. It wasn't his case to solve, but he'd hoped somebody would step up to the plate. He let out a long breath, realizing he was overreacting.

"We got lucky with Fernald," Detective Beaudette said. "He was in the system, imprisoned for sodomizing preteens. People at the department recognized him." She gestured at the body. "Maybe she's in the system, too."

"We'll let the officers on the scene have a look before she's moved," Marklin said. "Seems we have all the time in the world. Come on. Let's talk to the manager. There's not much else we can do but wait."

Days later, Aaron still couldn't get the dead woman out of his mind. Something about her face haunted him. Those soulless eyes stared at him, filled with accusations, as if wondering how he'd let her murder happen. *As if there was a damn thing I could have done about it.*

He shrugged and rubbed his wrists, trying to massage out the pins and needles. In the mirror across the bar, his reflection stared back at him. *Funny.* His eyes looked just as dead as hers. He took a long draw from his beer. "I tell you, man, this city has gone straight to hell."

"It certainly has," a bald man with bushy eyebrows and a five-o'clock shadow replied as he leaned forward on the stool beside Aaron. A red-and-white cane, his tool to see beyond where his eyes could not, was propped against the bar near his leg. "Hopefully, someone will do something about it, sooner rather than later." He finished his beer, signaled the bartender, then gestured at Aaron's bottle. "You want another?"

"Nah." Aaron patted his stomach. "I'm getting too fat for my uniform. And if I come home drunk again, Arianna will toss me right back out. Man, Rick, I don't know how you do it. We're the same age and eat and drink the same shit, but you're still the same weight you were ten years ago, while I'm shaped like a grape."

"Grapes are healthy." Ricardo chuckled. "But seriously, it's stress. Your paranoid crap with Arianna, your problems with your job, your feeling that somebody else's grass is always greener. You're doing it to yourself. Always have—"

"Let me stop you there. I know where this is heading."

"Oh yeah? Where's that?"

"You were going to tell me that if I just let God into my life, all my burdens would be lifted."

"No, I wasn't." Ricardo laughed. "Okay, maybe something like that. I'm just saying, you've got a lot to be thankful for, including a girl who loves you. Don't let all those crazy, confused thoughts up in that head of yours screw up the life you're making for yourself."

"Okay, okay. I got it."

"Hey, I'm just looking out for you, man. That's what friends do. And you're the last person I'd trust looking out for yourself."

"Maybe I will have one more." Aaron shifted on his stool and peeled the label off his bottle. "So… how's Brittney?"

"She's good. We're good. But if you don't believe me, ask her yourself this Sunday."

"We're still watching the game?"

"Yeah. Why wouldn't we be?"

Aaron stared down at his beer. "I don't know. Seems like I hardly see you anymore."

"You're seeing me now."

"I know, but…" He shook his head. "I guess we're just getting older, man. You've got your things, and I've got mine."

Ricardo smiled. "Anytime you want to be part of my things, you're more than welcome."

Aaron scoffed. "Yeah, I'd fit right in with that group."

"What? Everyone likes you. Come for a reading. Who knows? You just might learn something."

"I'm afraid I'm already too set in my ways. Are you going there after this?"

"Yep. Doug's picking me up."

"What's tonight? Judo or Jesus?"

"It's jiu-jitsu, and we don't really separate the two. Both faith and martial arts take discipline. Maybe a little discipline is all you need to get rid of that beer belly you're growing. Maybe clear your head. Come on. At the very least, you'll get a good workout. I guarantee you'll lose some weight."

"I'll pass." Aaron ordered another beer.

CHAPTER 2

DON'T KNOW IF I CAN do this. Jocelyn stared at the body. Not since she'd shot and killed the first of a handful of armed assailants had she felt so inadequate, so grossly unprepared to do what was expected of her. She could handle the violence. She could deal with the gore. She could even deal with that dead man's accusatory look, the way his eyes seemed to say, "Where were you when this was happening to me? Where were you when my life was taken away?"

Yeah, *that* shit Jocelyn could handle. At least she thought she could. Crime had been easier to deal with before she'd started working homicides. *That* shit was the nature of her job, her tragic misfortune to only be involved after the bodies had chilled. She was like a janitor, called in to clean up the mess. For once, she would have liked to arrive and find a body still warm. Maybe then she would see two fewer dead eyes when she closed her own at night.

But she could handle a few nightmares if that meant knowing she was making her family safe. What she couldn't handle was the shit that made no sense. No matter what angle she approached her case from, no matter how she twisted it in her head, she couldn't conceive of a single reason to extract a man's heart then hang the naked body like a Christmas ornament from hell above the stone steps of City Hall. *If the killer's trying to make some sort of statement, why couldn't the son of a bitch just tape a note to the victim and be done with it?*

She sighed, thinking of her daughter, Caitlyn, who was just learning to crawl. How she wanted to shield her from the horrors that ordinary humans inflicted upon others on a daily basis. How she wanted to be home in her chair, Caitlyn cradled in her arms, safe from the outside world. *Is this the world I've brought you into? Can I make it a better place for you?* She smiled, twisting her wedding ring around her finger. She'd married a good man, one who would keep their little girl safe while her mommy worked.

Under the umbrella of the Fall River Police Department's Major Crimes Division, Jocelyn had worked Robbery and Vice and anywhere else a short-staffed precinct required. She spent most of her time down in the dirt, turning caught crooks into confidential informants and surveilling nightclubs and projects. She'd seen her share of shit: Columbian neckties, severed genitalia stuffed in all sorts of orifices, tweakers so strung out that they mutilated themselves or others with razor blades or machetes, and babies who had died from neglect. She saw the kind of stuff regular people only saw in torture porn, except there, it wasn't real. Those things kept her up many a night, sweating and screaming, not knowing if she'd found her place in the world, wondering if bringing another into it had been selfish.

But no matter how crazy the crime, the motives always made sense. They were always the same: Person A wanted or stole something from Person B. Person B took issue. Mayhem ensued. Any ancillary craziness was easily explained away by the fact that the victim, the perpetrator, or both were higher than the ceiling of the Sistine Chapel or more desperate than a fox in a trap.

This crime scene, however, was a brand of crazy all its own. As she studied the man hanging from the white column gallows, his feet a few inches from the step, Jocelyn wondered if she'd ascended the ranks too quickly. Her stomach gurgled with butterflies beating their wings as if trying to start a hurricane in Asia, and they were breeding, multiplying. A chill ran through her. Doubt plagued her every action, stalled her every word. Her mind was more shaken than a 007 martini.

On the outside, she took a deep breath and managed to fake being as cool and calm as 007 himself. *Never let them see you sweat,* her father used to say. She smiled the slightest smile. *You got this, Detective.*

On a police force that was ninety-eight percent male—*thank God for Officers Reilly and Cusack*—Jocelyn was hard pressed to find a friend at work. Most of the guys she'd upstaged at the academy resented her—her barreling her way up the food chain threatened plenty. Anyone who didn't know her thought she was "just a girl," and those who did know her blamed their own inadequacies on affirmative action, because someone as clumsy and weak as Jocelyn Beaudette couldn't possibly be a good detective. And almost all of them began every conversation by staring at her nearly nonexistent tits.

Her dad had been like that, minus the tit staring. He'd been a chauvinist old prick until the day he died from a heart attack four years ago. Still, the old dog had surprised her by supporting her decision to join the academy. At her graduation, no one had cheered louder than he did. *I miss you, Dad.*

Perhaps that was why she liked Bruce. In spite of all his chauvinism, sexist remarks, and testosterone-laced dick swinging, Bruce, of all people, treated her like a person. *No. Like a cop.*

But Bruce hadn't arrived yet, and the scene, one of the busiest intersections in the city, was hers to commandeer. With the clock nearing eight on a Wednesday morning, Jocelyn had no way of shielding the scene from public view. She'd managed to keep spectators and reporters back, cordoned off the front entrance, coordinated with the mayor to have government employees start work at ten, and arranged for traffic redirection to limit the chaos.

She had just set about the real reason she'd been called there—to solve a murder—when Bruce strolled up the steps.

He smiled at her. "Looks like you've got everything under control."

"No thanks to you." Jocelyn smirked.

He handed her a Styrofoam cup filled with hot black coffee and kept one for himself. She mumbled a quick thanks before taking a sip.

Bruce grinned. "Someday, you'll be standing in my shoes. Then you'll appreciate what it means to be near the top of the pecking order. Except... wait a minute... aren't *you* supposed to get the coffee?" He set his coffee down on the cold step then polished his glasses with his hot breath and the end of his untucked shirt. "So," he said as he adjusted the earpiece of his glasses behind his ears then bent over to pick up his coffee. "What brings us here—" He stopped to gape at the body. "Christ, is that—"

"Yep. Benjamin Reinhart. Age forty-seven. Corporation counsel for the city. List of potential enemies probably a mile long."

"Yes, but none with this MO. Shit, Beaudette. The city's top attorney? This investigation is about to become a shit storm. Everything we do is going to be under a fucking microscope." He took a gulp of his coffee then held up the cup. "We're going to need a lot more of this."

Jocelyn had rarely seen Bruce as jovial as he had been a moment prior, but she'd *never* seen him as frazzled as he suddenly became.

He walked down a few steps and waved over one of the boys in blue. Handing the officer the empty cup, he said, "Toss this for me, will you?" Without waiting for a response, he hustled back to Jocelyn. His face was deadpan, his eyes soft, then he managed a slight grin. "Just focus on the case. I'll handle the press conferences."

Jocelyn pressed her lips flat. *How did he know I was stressing it?* She poked him in the arm. "Looking for some face time with the media so that when we crack this, you can use it to launch your political career? I'm sorry to tell you this, but you're not likable enough for politics."

"You ever meet a politician who is? Speaking of which…" Bruce peered up at the body. "Any thoughts?"

"Our killer's now into still life. Putting his work on exhibition. Why the sudden change?" She pulled on a pair of disposable gloves and peered into a cavity the size of a grapefruit, the shredded muscle resembling pulp flecked with bone-shard seeds. "Chest wound appears identical to the last victim's." She grabbed the dead man's right hand and turned it palm up. "Similar markings on the wrist. The fingernails appear to have been scrubbed. The rope's new, though."

"I'll be sure to include everything in my report," Dr. Rosetta Hawthorne said, walking up behind them. She turned to Bruce. "I'm going to have him cut down."

Bruce just shrugged. The medical examiner took over, ordering her assistants to cut the rope holding up the body.

Jocelyn went over Reinhart's life and the details of his death in her mind. "What did you make of the markings on his head?" she asked no one in particular as she chewed the end of her pen. When she realized what she was doing, she stopped. *Am I picking up Bruce's habits?*

"Markings on his head?" Bruce asked. "I thought they were just scratches." He stopped the gurney that two of Hawthorne's staff were using to jackhammer the body down the stairs. After unzipping the body bag, he squinted at Reinhart's forehead.

Jocelyn came up beside him. She pointed at the lines that had been scratched into the dead man's skin. "See? Numbers."

Bruce leaned in closer. "I'll be damned."

"What do you suppose they mean?"

"Not sure. Looks like a time. Maybe the killer though it would be cute to announce his victim's time of death? Maybe it's a date?"

Frowning, Jocelyn rubbed her chin. *6:21.* Those numbers meant something to her. She was drawing a blank, but it would come to her.

CHAPTER 3

Snow glazed the peaks but not yet the trails. The air was fresh and revitalizing. Aaron had found a hideaway untainted by the stench of exhaust, pollution, and decay. The only sounds were the crackling of leaves under playful footsteps and the solitary squawk of a winged predator in flight. Along the skyline, rolling hills led to grander summits, a far cry from the usual decadent apartment complexes and mill stacks casting malformed shadows like a grimy darkness blanketing the Fall River streets. The tranquil lake below, as still as glass, refracted the setting sun's rays into a prism of muted colors.

"I'm so happy we decided to come here." Arianna peered off the balcony of their four-hundred-dollars-per-night suite. Their hidden resort was one of the dozens nestled deep within New Hampshire's White Mountains.

Seeing her smile like that, Aaron was happy, too. It had been too long since he'd last seen Arianna so radiant, so full of life. He had read in the increasing lines on her face, her blotchy skin, her quick temper, and their nonexistent sex life that she'd needed a retreat from her bustling law practice, the clients who didn't stop calling, and the partners who didn't stop piling on the work and the bullshit.

Day in and day out, she was always hustling, seemingly as miserable as Aaron was. He wondered if they could just forget everything and be like they used to be, if only for a day or two. Drawing her into his arms, he felt affection and serenity. They were real. He was sure of it, if only for the moment, even if the problems they were ignoring were real, too. It was nice to pretend, to just be happy, whether real or illusion.

"They're waiting for us." She pulled away.

Aaron's fantasy of perfection evaporated like morning dew under a hot sun. The quiet moments he treasured were times Arianna seemed to care little for, her overactive mind requiring constant activity. *Constant attention. Always "me, me, me."*

She twiddled her dark flowing hair, a sign of her unrest. Aaron sighed. The moment spoiled, he peeked into the adjacent room.

"Let's play some cards!" Ricardo yelled.

"Deal it up," Aaron called back as Arianna took his hand and led him back into the other room.

They took their places at the table where Ricardo and his girlfriend, Brittney, sat. The games began, and with them, Aaron's gradual descent toward the bottom of a bottle.

Aaron had found shuffling the Braille deck a little odd at first since the cards didn't lie flat, but he'd gotten used to it and was grateful he could still play cards with Ricardo. They would all be drunk by the end of the evening, and he readily welcomed that state of mind. Like Arianna, he also needed a retreat, from a life that was becoming increasingly dissatisfying.

Again.

"Did you hear about the fourth body?" Arianna asked. "This one was found lying in the middle of the street. Talk about subtle."

"Hey, Aaron, do you have any inside info?" Brittney asked.

The killer had left his work out for public display twice since Aaron had seen that poor woman tossed in a dumpster. People in the city and neighboring suburbs were getting home early and double-checking their dead bolts at night. The streets of Fall River were like a ghost town after eight o'clock. With the fourth victim, the death toll had rung outside the city, in the lily-white town of Somerset, where middle-class families thought they were tucked safely away from the groveling insanity of their impoverished city-dwelling neighbors.

"You know I'm not supposed to talk about it. Plus, I don't *like* talking about it." Aaron stifled a hiccup. "But yeah, I know a few things."

The others perked up. *Tell us!* their faces shouted.

Aaron leaned forward. "Everything I say stays here."

Most of what he could tell them had already been covered in the newspapers. The first two victims were, as far as the general public was concerned, loners and lowlives no one would miss. No one had even come forward to identify the dumpster body. The press had been inordinately slow to connect the two slayings. Media coverage outside of Fall River was sparse at best. The third victim changed everything. That unlucky lot fell to Fall River Counsel and outspoken gay rights advocate Benjamin Reinhart. His death had spawned a sensation not seen in Fall River since Lizzie Borden's chopping spree.

"You know how Reinhart was strung up outside city hall, his heart cut out and his wrists slit like the two priors? Well, the detectives on the case have been canvassing the area, and of course, nobody's talking. I don't care how late you do it; if you hang a dead body outside city hall, somebody's gonna see something. He was a political figure, for fuck's sake. Somebody's gotta know something."

"Don't cops patrol that area, too?" Arianna asked.

"All the time. I wouldn't be surprised if the killer was a cop at this point, because we certainly aren't getting the full story. Plus, the victims and disposal sites have been metibulously... *meticulously* cleaned. We'd have better luck lifting fingerprints from a snake." Aaron realized he was drunk and should probably shut up, but he couldn't help but enjoy the attention.

"So you think the killer is a cop?" Ricardo asked.

Aaron threw up his hands, splashing his drink on his shirt. "No, no, I'm not saying that. Jesus H. Christ, man! Don't go around saying something like that. I'm just saying it could be anybody."

"Well, that's reassuring," Brittney said. "You cops have done a great job of limiting your suspects. You're now down to anybody."

"Everyone's a smart ass." Aaron slumped forward, feeling a bit drowsy. He took a deep breath. "Anyway, profiling has limited it some. Given the strength involved and the violent nature of each homicide, they're pretty sure it's a man. Also, the displaying of the bodies, the similarity of the kills... it all adds up to some kind of plan. I mean, the killer has gotta have a reason for doing this, something more than that he just likes killing people."

"Yeah, he's insane," Arianna said.

"Then again, who wouldn't want to kill a lawyer?" Brittney winked at Arianna.

"Well, as long as he's not a rapist or child molester, I'd defend him." Arianna laughed. "I've got standards, you know."

"And that's what makes us such a great couple, huh, babe?" Aaron smirked, trying to hide his frustration. "A cop and a defense attorney—not exactly a match made in heaven." *Fucking doomed right from the start.*

Arianna glared at him.

He looked away. "Anyway, with this fourth guy, I heard they found somebody who might know something."

CHAPTER 4

DETECTIVE MARKLIN'S OFFICE SMELLED OF old-man aftershave, his coffee breath, and whatever hair products kept his hair so stiff and unnaturally black. Yet it was the smell of the woman sitting in Marklin's office that made Jocelyn's nose curl, the stench of primping and properness even in the face of impropriety.

Bruce seemed to share her distaste. "You came to us," he said. "You'd better have something."

He'd already lectured the new witness—Maura Fleurent, a bored housewife who'd shown up of her own accord—about how people were calling in every day, claiming to be the killer or saying that a neighbor, lover, cousin, friend's nephew's dog-watcher, Eric Clapton, the Russians, or the president of the United States was either the killer or somehow involved in the murders. He'd rambled on about how people were blowing up their phone lines, wasting their precious time with ridiculous allegations that the killer had murdered everyone from Hollywood starlets and religious figures to pets. Each would-be informant had an excuse, a motive, or a justification for the killer's actions.

Jocelyn studied the back of Maura's head. She knew the type: easy life, easy lay, always getting whatever, or whoever, she wanted. Maura was the kind of girl who picked on shy, awkward girls like Jocelyn. The low-cut blouse and cherry-red lipstick had given all the insight the detective needed into the life Jocelyn hadn't been pretty enough or confident enough or promiscuous enough to have. Not that she had ever wanted that kind of existence. Women like Maura set their gender back a half century.

Jocelyn took a seat atop a cabinet behind the witness, where she wouldn't have to look at her. Jocelyn knew she was being unfair—she didn't even really know the woman—but she couldn't help resenting Maura for the gifts she had evidently squandered. *And with a married man.*

Maura seemed smart enough. Smart enough to know better. She worked as a waitress at a local diner—probably only when she felt like it—but spoke as if she were well educated. Her voice was quiet, and she presented a meek posture, her head hung low.

As Bruce stared at the witness across his desk, his gaze lacked the hint of desire Maura's long legs, slender hips, and luscious lips likely garnered from most men. He seemed annoyed and skeptical, and his tone failed to mask his contempt.

Still, Maura was trying to help them, but they weren't making it easy for her.

Jocelyn released a breath, letting the resentment blow out with it. "What do you know?" she asked.

Maura jumped as if she had forgotten Jocelyn was behind her. She didn't turn to face Jocelyn; instead, she looked up at Bruce as if to ask if it was okay to respond.

"Well?" Jocelyn pressed. "What do you know about Garrison Huntley?"

Maura finally looked over her shoulder. "Who?"

"Garrison Huntley, the fourth victim." Crossing her arms, Jocelyn went to sit on the corner of Bruce's desk. "Damn, Bruce, another one wasting our time?"

Maura frowned. "Garrison who? He… he told me his name was Steve Austin." No sooner were the words spoken than Maura's face reddened as she no doubt realized the married man's deception. With knowledge came sullenness. She buried her chin into her chest.

Marklin smirked. "Stone Cold or the Six Million Dollar Man?"

The witness looked away. Jocelyn sighed, letting a tinge of sympathy for the woman breach her otherwise-impregnable wall. It vanished quickly, and she reset her face into her usual on-duty mask that lacked pity, understanding, friendship, or anything else remotely amicable.

After all, Maura was married, and so was Huntley—and not to each other. One of the biggest laws in the book addressed that particular crime, and its rule was absolute. She shot Marklin a look meant to suggest he lay off a bit.

That didn't stop him from continuing. "His name was Huntley. His wife already identified the body, their two kids crying in the hall. They couldn't understand why their father was still here since he was supposed to be away on business. You did know he was married, right?"

Maura shrank in her chair. "I... I saw the indentation around his finger."

"So you were screwing him?" Jocelyn hadn't intended to sound harsh. She just wanted to get that settled so they could all move on to the questions that really mattered.

"Yes, for almost six months. And yes, I knew he was... we were both married." Maura scowled.

Jocelyn looked to see if Bruce, the senior officer in the room, had any objection to her taking control of the questioning. When he nodded, she pulled a small notebook from her breast pocket and flipped it open then uncapped the slender pen she kept inside the spiral rings. "Were you with him on November third?"

"Yes."

"Care to elaborate?"

"We met for dinner at Colafranceschi's in Providence," Maura said.

"Just the two of you?"

"Yes."

"Did you make reservations?"

"He did."

"Under what name?" Jocelyn asked without a hint of sarcasm.

Maura blushed. "Austin, I suppose."

Jocelyn didn't miss a beat. "What time was dinner?"

"Seven. We finished around eight forty-five."

"And after?"

"We went to watch the WaterFire."

"What time were you through there?"

"About eleven. We had a few drinks at one of the cozy places nearby, an outside bar. We were surprised it was still open because of the cold weather. I guess with the city putting on the WaterFire show longer this year, everyone stays open longer. Afterward, we walked back to Providence Place, where we'd parked our cars. I'm separated from my husband, so I live alone." Heat reddened her cheeks, and she sat a little straighter. "I invited him back to my place."

"On Everett Street in Seekonk, correct?" Jocelyn asked.

"Yes."

"Huntley was from Somerset. Where did you meet him?"

"Online."

"Of course." Marklin rolled his eyes. "How long was he at your place?"

"Until about one thirty in the morning. He got a call on his cell phone about one fifteen. I knew something was wrong. Steve—*Garrison* looked so worried. I asked if everything was okay, but he refused to talk about it. A short while later, a white van pulled up in front of the house. I asked if he wanted me to go with him, but he said no and ran out the door. He got into the van, and it drove off." Maura shivered. "That was the last time I saw him. His car's still parked in my driveway."

Marklin rocked back in his office chair, absently tapping the end of a pencil on the chair arm. "Did you see who was in the van?"

Maura shook her head. "No. It was dark, and my street is poorly lit. But there were at least two people. The driver, I couldn't see, but the passenger... he smiled and waved when he saw me at the door."

"Caucasian?"

"I think so, with dark hair, short. I can't remember much more about him. They were only there for a moment, then they were gone." Maura gasped. "You don't think I could be next, do you?"

Detective Marklin waved a hand dismissively. "I don't think so. Doesn't seem to be his MO."

Maura's eyes narrowed on the detective. When Bruce didn't say anything more, she glanced up at Jocelyn.

"*Modus operandi,*" Jocelyn clarified.

"Oh."

Maura still looked confused, but Jocelyn didn't feel the need to explain further. "Can you tell me any more about the van? Did it have a sliding door? Was it a minivan?"

"Yes, it did have a sliding door, but it wasn't a minivan. I only saw the front and some of the left side while it was parked in front of my house. There was no front plate, which I only noticed because I thought that was illegal. Nothing seemed unusual about it. It looked like most vans, like those a friend of mine uses for her catering business, except it didn't have any markings that I could see. I didn't bother to watch it drive off."

"Can you think of anything else that could help us find Mr. Huntley's murderer?"

"Not really." Maura's knee began to bounce.

Jocelyn looked at her partner. "Bruce, do you have any more questions for Ms. Fleurent?"

"Not at this time, but I'm sure I'll think of some later. Ms. Fleurent, thank you for your assistance. We'll keep in touch. In the meantime, let us know if you think of anything else that could help us, no matter how trivial it may seem." He held out a business card.

Maura snatched it from his hand as she popped out of her chair. She hurried out of the office without so much as a goodbye.

Once the door shut, Jocelyn took the chair the woman had vacated. "A bit rough on her, weren't you?"

"I'm just sick and tired of people wasting our time."

"Are you sure it's not because you're a sexist prick who hates women?"

"My two ex-wives might agree with that assessment."

"It's hard to picture Bruce Marklin in love. Bet you were a different guy then."

"I was. But you talk to me after twenty years doing this job. We'll see how your marriage holds up. Now, can we get back to work, or would you like to pour some more salt on old wounds?" He smirked.

"Jerk." She laughed, but the thought of her and Gabriel not lasting had made her uneasy. When she'd said her vows, she'd meant them. Shaking it off, she delved into her work and the one question that had to be as prominent on Bruce's mind as it was on hers. "Are we dealing with more than one killer here?"

Bruce wagged a finger at her. "Let's not get ahead of ourselves. First, let's examine what we know. Only from facts can we extrapolate a rationale, motive, and method."

Before interviewing Maura, Jocelyn had been beating herself up for finding so little to go on. Now that they had something to work with, she was eager to let the wheels of her mind roll. But her partner and mentor was right: jumping to conclusions wasted time and cost lives. "Okay. According to Dr. Hawthorne's reports, the bodies were sterilized and dried, stripped of almost all evidence that could be used to identify their killers, before they were put on display. The victims were wrapped up, likely in cellophane, given the imprints on the skin, for transportation purposes. Whatever the killer used, it kept the bodies preserved."

"Yes," Bruce said, "but Hawthorne found no foreign substances on the bodies: no hair, no skin, no blood, no dirt, no dust, no chemicals. Nothing. The more people involved, the more likely some DNA evidence would be left behind."

"Are you forgetting the skin cells under the dead woman's fingernails? You don't get much more damning evidence than that, assuming we can find a match."

"There are questions about whether that sample is contaminated, and there's no guarantee it belonged to our killer."

"No guarantee!" Jocelyn huffed. "Come on, Bruce! The incidents of pre-mortem injury are slight. These victims were taken unaware and overpowered. The amount of strength it would take to hold someone down and carve open his chest with a freaking serrated knife? The autopsy reports were clear: the cause of death for each had been the ritualistic carving. The victims were still alive when the killer began cutting and would have likely been thrashing and kicking like crazy! No way one person could do it alone."

Bruce tapped his pen. "The medical examiner found bruises on the woman's neck and rope burns around Fernald's wrists. Perhaps they were bound, drugged—"

"Hawthorne conducted a litany of tests for controlled substances. She didn't find a thing."

"Not all drugs are traceable."

"You're just trying to make me second-guess myself."

Bruce smiled. "You know me better than that."

Jocelyn crossed her arms and pursed her lips. "They sawed through all four victims' chests and removed their hearts like scooping the pulp out of a jack-o'-lantern. It must have taken tremendous strength and a wickedly sharp blade to chisel and grind through the ribs. The metal chips that broke off the weapon and the bone fragments prove a considerable effort went into each crime. No one man could have pulled this off once, never mind four times. And now, we have an eyewitness who puts two men at the scene of the abduction."

"We only have a single witness. No corroboration."

"That's horseshit, and you know it. We have two killers here, maybe more."

"Statistically speaking, do you know how unlikely that is? Contrary to popular belief, not all serial killers are loners, but they do tend to kill alone." He held up a finger. "Even so, I agree. We can't rule out the possibility."

"*Probability*. One of the gangs around here could have raised its bar for initiation. Some of the more hardcore, big-city gangs consider murder a prerequisite to joining up, one hell of a membership fee." She shook her head. "Then again, most of Fall River's gangs are poorly organized and, well, too stupid to get away with something like this."

"That's a possibility but also unlikely. And just because the murders have taken place around here doesn't mean we can rule out a murderer who doesn't shit where he eats." Bruce sighed. "We're getting way ahead of ourselves here. We don't know who drove the van or even if the van is linked to the crimes. Maybe the killer met Huntley later in the evening."

"But the autopsy report approximated the time of death between one and three a.m." Jocelyn was sticking to her theory, but the interplay between her and Bruce always brought out the most logical conclusions. Unlike most in her department, she could tolerate Bruce and knew they made a good team. Her questions were met with sincerity rather than his usual sarcasm. "You don't think feeble little Maura could have done this, do you?"

"I'm not ruling her out," Bruce said. "Where was her husband that night? He could have killed Huntley and made it look like our guy."

"A copycat? No way. You read the autopsy report. All the victims were killed in exactly the same manner. The only way someone would be able to copy these murders is if he had access to our investigative reports. The weapon information was kept from the press. The inox steel alloy is, fortunately for us, uniquely high in chromium, corroborated by particles found in each wound. Our killer's weapon of choice wouldn't be easy for a stranger to duplicate."

Bruce stroked his chin, his thumb and forefinger tugging at two white hairs that grew from a mole at the jawline. "Every lead must be looked into. All theories are possible until proven otherwise."

"I agree with you there." She knew him well enough to know that he was just playing out every scenario in his computerlike brain, but some scenarios were highly doubtful. Often, he pushed the role of devil's advocate into the realm of implausibility. When Jocelyn had a theory she could wrap her fingers around, she wanted to run with it, letting each piece move where it may. Being wrong meant wasted resources and the need to pursue another avenue. Being right, though, meant fewer people died.

But Bruce understood the politics and strategy elements of investigating better than she did. She'd learned not to question him in that regard the first time she'd ended up tasting her foot. But procedure required that all possible leads be investigated. Jocelyn would just check up on the most promising first, and if she needed the rest, she would get to them when she got to them. The numbers on Reinhart's head seemed of lesser importance, since he'd been the only victim with those markings so far. For fear of appearing foolish if she were wrong, she hadn't even mentioned to her partner that she thought they could be a Biblical reference. It wasn't the first time her lack of confidence kept her mouth closed. She wanted to research it herself first.

She leaned forward in her chair. "Okay. What do we have to follow up on? We need to corroborate Fleurent's story: her reservations, the bar, the parking garage. Any video surveillance? There should probably be some at the mall. We need to get officers checking into all of that, including whether a white van was spotted at these locations. We also need Fleurent's and Huntley's phone records and those of their spouses." She raised an eyebrow. "Huntley's wife is not going to like learning about her husband this way, but if we have to rule her out as a suspect, so be it."

Bruce nodded. "Also, let's not forget the specifics of the van. It has a sliding side door. Is that common? We need to have a researcher look into makes and models of vans with sliding side doors. It may be useless if there are a lot, but if not, it could limit our search." He sighed. "I hope we can keep this information out of the press. I don't want the killer to think we're getting closer, if we are getting closer. Do you think calling Fleurent back in for a police sketch would be useful?"

"Probably not, but it couldn't hurt. Fleurent has been helpful, but I wish she had more to give us—a name, a license plate. Anything. Maybe we'll get lucky with the phone records." She thought about the victims.

"What's wrong?" Bruce asked. "You look aggravated."

She felt responsible for letting a murderer remain free. "I can't understand why no one, myself included, has any clue why the victims were chosen. I can't see any connection between the four."

"They could have been chosen at random. What about the woman? Any update there?"

"I showed her pic to some of the guys here the other night. Officer Lambert recognized her as someone he'd brought in on possession. Her name was Eliza Ramirez. She had four arrests, two for prostitution and two for possession of cocaine. Lambert doesn't recall her being any trouble. He said he felt sorry for her, thought she had a rough life."

"Oh, please. 'My daddy abused me, and my mommy never loved me, so I turned to a life of hooking and drugs.' Is that the story? Lambert should save his swan songs for someone who gives a shit."

Jocelyn pushed down her righteous indignation. She hoped that when she had as many years on the force as her partner, she wouldn't dismiss human life the way he did. "Actually, Ramirez came from a well-to-do family with no signs of a troubled childhood. Her parents told me they threw her out when her addiction became too much for them to handle and rehab wouldn't take."

Bruce waved a hand dismissively. "Well, that gives us a hooker, an attorney, a diddler ex-con, and—what did the fourth guy do again?"

"Antiques dealer and appraiser. Yeah, if these four are somehow connected, their employment doesn't seem to be the common link."

"The whys aren't nearly as important as the whos and hows right now. Let the psychiatrists determine the whys later." He tapped the folder on his desk. "Except this one. Why would Huntley run out on his fuck-pal to get into that van at one thirty in the morning? I mean, assuming, for the sake of argument, the van's occupants are our killers or could somehow lead us to the killer, the question we need to answer is how did they get Huntley into the van willingly?"

"There was obviously a lot Huntley wasn't telling Fleurent, so there could be countless reasons why he'd get into the van. Most likely, though—and this is only if Fleurent's story is to be credited, mind you—Huntley would have gotten into that van for one of two reasons: he was threatened or he knew and trusted somebody in the van."

"Or both," Bruce added. "It's a hell of an assumption. Have an officer contact Huntley's family and find out if any of his friends, relatives, co-workers, or acquaintances own a white van."

Jocelyn grinned. "Finally, we have people to question and facts to investigate. Our luck is starting to change."

"Let's just hope one of our leads hits."

CHAPTER 5

PETER ROBILLARD WAS NOTHING IF not consistent.

Every morning, after a cup of coffee and a bagel with cream cheese from the doughnut shop down the street, he arrived at the Swansea PetPro Clinic where he worked as a veterinary technician promptly at eight o'clock. The clinic didn't open until nine, but he was tasked with opening up, caring for the animals that had stayed overnight, and cleaning up after the human animals who'd worked the night before. His digital watch beeped, signaling the beginning of the eight o'clock hour as he turned the key in the entranceway's lock. Smiling, he stepped inside and locked the door behind him.

He had barely flipped on all the lights and fed Moogle, the clinic's housecat, when someone pounded on the glass door. Walking toward the entrance, he saw two men standing outside. One was of average height and build, with an immaculate appearance, as if every hair on his head was exactly where it belonged. The other, though, made Peter slow in his steps. The guy was freakishly huge. *He belongs in a carnival. If not as the strong man, then as the elephant.*

"I'm sorry!" he shouted through the door. "We're not open yet."

"Could you let us in, please?" Clean Cut asked. "It's an emergency." He held up some sort of animal wrapped in a blanket, either a cat or a small dog, maybe a bunny.

Peter glanced at his watch: 8:12. Georgia wasn't due in until half

past the hour, and she was never on time. *Still, an animal in need...*
"What's the emergency?"

Clean Cut shifted the blanket, revealing the head of a kitten. The animal was shivering and looked terrified. With a delicacy unbefitting one his size, Circus pulled the blanket away from the kitten's front paw.

Peter gasped. The leg was unquestionably broken, bent at such a wrong angle that it was a wonder the animal wasn't screaming.

"Oh my God." Peter unlocked the door with trembling hands. "Come in! Come in!" He stepped out of the way to let the two men into the building.

"Thank you," Clean Cut said.

The bigger man just stared at Peter with stone-cold eyes, not the eyes of a concerned pet owner.

Clean Cut smiled. Pete barely had time to wonder why the guy would be smiling before the man yelled, "Catch!" and tossed the bundle at Peter.

"No!" Peter managed to catch the poor feline but dropped it when the big man's fist slammed into his stomach. With the wind knocked out of him, he couldn't get enough breath to scream for help.

Mighty hands encircled his neck and squeezed. Circus lifted Peter off the floor then pressed him down on the reception desk. Pens and paper clips scattered. Peter flailed his arms, searching for anything he could use as a weapon. His fingers curled around a small chain dog leash. He whipped it into Circus's face. The metal clip on the end hit Circus squarely in the left eye.

The big man yelped and released his grip on Peter's neck to bring his hands to his face. Peter raised both legs, planted his heels on the man's stomach, and pushed off. He fell to the floor behind the desk. He jumped to his feet and ran for the back exit.

A man and a woman stood in front of the door. "Oh, thank heavens!" He almost sprinted to hug the couple before his mind could process that they had no business being there, between him and the exit.

At the last moment, he changed his trajectory and dove into a small examination room. He slammed the door behind him and locked it, panting like a dog under the hot sun.

"Monsieur Robillard!" Clean Cut howled.

Peter pressed his ear against the door and listened, hoping they would just take what they came for and leave. He figured they wanted drugs. Fall River was loaded with their type, junkies willing to do anything for their next fix. Sometimes, the city's neighbors had to deal with its runoff. The addicts would leave as soon as they realized the clinic didn't keep narcotics on hand, at least not any that would be worth the time and effort to steal.

Unless they think the good stuff's in here with me.

"You should have knocked him out," Clean Cut said. "You had one fucking job to do, Doug. One fucking job! Why couldn't you do it right?"

The other man grunted. "I shouldn't be choking him anyway. We need a better way of doing this. I could have killed him."

"I have a stun gun."

"What? You could have told me that sooner."

Clean Cut huffed. "The weak need to be led. The sheep need their shepherd. How many weeks did we spend planning this one? Well, let's get our heads out of our asses and do what we came here to do. Take down that door. Kelly, bring the van around back. We should be gone in less than ten minutes."

"Oh shit." Peter backed away from the door. He scrambled to pull his phone out of his pocket, but in his panicked haste, he dropped it.

With a thunderous crash, the door broke off its hinges. The lock splintered through the frame just as Peter was picking up his phone. He jabbed at the buttons to call 9-1-1.

"Now, now, Mr. Robillard," Clean Cut said, sounding almost motherly as he stepped through the door with Circus and the couple behind him. "We can't be having that now, can we?" He thrust out his hand, and something shot toward Peter.

A horrible jolt coursed through his body.

"9-1-1. What's your emergency?" a woman said on the phone. "Hello?"

Dazed, Peter tried to speak, but all that came out was drool. Clean Cut bent over, and Peter realized he was lying on the floor. His attacker reached out and plucked the phone from Peter's hand.

"What do you want from me?" Peter's words were so slurred, he wasn't sure if the man understood him.

Clean Cut stared back at Peter with a smile as big as the Cheshire cat's. "Your soul."

Peter awoke in a strange place. A blinding light overhead forced his eyes shut again. He winced and squinted but saw only a white flare. His other senses worked fine, though. He lay flat on a cold, hard surface that felt like metal. *An operating table?* He had laid so many of his own patients delicately, *kindly*, upon a similar table.

Moist air hung heavy around him, thick with mold. It stank like the inside of an old refrigerator kept in a cellar then finally opened after years of disuse.

He tried to bring a hand to his nose, but he couldn't move his arm. He looked to the right and saw that his wrist was tied around a metal pole. *An operating lamp?* He swallowed hard as he raised his head a little. His other wrist and ankles were similarly bound. He tried to scream, but his mouth had been gagged and duct-taped shut. A muffled gargle was all he could manage.

In the distance, he heard a man's voice, then a woman responded. They were arguing. A door slammed. Footsteps came closer. Another door opened nearby. He shuddered violently, his body rattling against the table. He opened his eyes wide, but all he saw were hazy purple shadows on the peripherals of a wall of light. The door slammed, and his heart leapt into his throat. Tears crept from the corners of his eyes. His bowels let go. The stench quickly filled the room.

"That's disgusting." Clean Cut's smiling face appeared above Peter.

Peter couldn't see anyone else, but he could hear their whispering. *Where the heck am I?* He tried desperately to piece together all that had happened. The overhead light shone relentlessly on his face. Slowly, his eyes adjusted until he could see rust-colored walls. He turned his head, and a moldy, water-damaged tile floor came into view.

A shadow flickered on the rotted wall. *Candlelight?* He wanted nothing more than to be home with his wife, Charlotte.

Three or four different voices began speaking in unison. They spoke softly, as if reading a children's bedtime story. He couldn't quite make out the words. In any other setting, Peter might have found the sounds comforting, harmonic even. There, they made him want to vomit.

Clean Cut disappeared then returned wearing gloves. They were of the same powdered Latex variety that Peter was allergic to. A rash was the least of his worries at the moment.

The man held a gruesome knife that looked like something out of a *Mad Max* film, medieval in a way but definitely made in modern times. If he looked closely enough, Peter was sure he'd probably find "Made in Taiwan" stamped on its stainless-steel blade, which was curved like a shovel that had been split down the middle, but sharper. Much sharper.

The way the weapon gleamed in the glow of the operating lamp made Peter want to piss and shit himself all over again. The metal table creaked and rolled an inch as the knife-wielding psychopath leaned against it.

Clean Cut stared down at him. "Do you have anything you'd like to confess before we begin?"

Peter couldn't speak around the tape, so he nodded and tried to groan out a yes, attempting to delay the inevitable. He wanted to explain to the man that they had the wrong guy, that he'd done nothing to deserve... whatever they were going to do to him. He wanted to beg for his life, barter for it if he could. His mind grasped for ideas, the magical act he could perform that would keep him alive.

"No?" the man asked, his bared teeth glistening devilishly. "You sure, now?"

No? What do you mean, no? Peter screamed silently. Yes—the word came out incoherently, but surely his nodding made his desires known. *Are you blind?* Looking up into the man's bright, feverish eyes, Peter could tell it didn't matter how much he nodded. He was already dead.

He closed his eyes and braced himself. *What have I done to make these people hate me so much?* He whimpered as he felt his captor draw a line from his sternum to his belly button. The blade didn't break the skin, but the sensation of the cold steel was agonizing, all the same. The feel of the knife left him, and Peter almost opened his eyes, but he decided he was better off not seeing what came next.

As the blade entered his chest, Peter's eyes flew open involuntarily. The metal seared inside him, his every nerve ending screaming their torture into his brain. The blade pierced flesh and bone until its hilt rested against Peter's chest. He felt it tugging at his insides. His ribcage put up some resistance before it yielded. He squealed as his life slipped away.

Numb with shock, Peter stared up to see his killer was still smiling.

CHAPTER 6

SUNDAY AFTERNOON, AARON WENT TO Ricardo's apartment in Somerset to watch the game. As he walked up to the door, he turned off his phone. *It's not like people are getting their hearts ripped out,* he thought, slipping his phone into the pocket. *At least not for almost two weeks.* He let himself into the house.

He glanced into the dining room and smiled at Brittney, who was sitting at the table. She politely smiled back then returned to her magazine. She always spent weekends with Ricardo. Aaron felt awkward interrupting their private time, but he knew Ricardo would be watching the game no matter who was around. It would be silly not to watch it with him.

"You ready for this game?" Ricardo asked as Aaron entered the living room. "The Colts are going down! Beer?"

"Do you really have to ask?" As Ricardo started to rise, Aaron said, "I can get it—"

Ricardo walked toward him, leaving his cane on the floor beside his chair. He could maneuver around his own apartment with his eyes closed, but he usually used the cane in case he or Brittney had left something out of place. He made a beeline for the refrigerator, only deviating from the most direct path to step around Aaron. As he reached into the fridge, he said, "Oh, by the way, I invited Doug and Craig. I don't think Doug can make it, but Craig may show."

"I didn't know Craig was in town."

"Got back last night. Some of his show's tour dates were cancelled." Ricardo closed the refrigerator door and turned to face Aaron, holding two cans of beer. "Heads up."

Realizing Ricardo meant to throw him the beer, Aaron's eyes widened. "I don't think that's such a good—"

The beer was in his hands before he could finish his sentence, a perfect throw. Aaron frowned and stared at the can for a moment, then he shrugged and plopped down on the couch. "I haven't seen Doug in a while, either. What's he been up to?"

"He got a new job working for the Department of Environmental Protection as some kind of inspector. It takes up most of his time. I'm not sure what he does, but he seems to like it."

"I never pictured him as the tree-hugging type."

"He's not. I think he goes around to where there's been an oil leak or something else hazardous, fills out reports, and hands out citations. Isn't that the same thing you do?"

"Tell me about it. Being a cop is nothing like it is in the movies, except the part where they make fun of officers eating doughnuts. Seriously, I walk into Dunkin' Donuts in uniform, and the snickers don't stop. Meanwhile, the whole town is going to Dunkin' Donuts. Do you realize Somerset has four Dunkin' Donuts within a mile of each other? That's counting the one inside the supermarket. The town is only seven miles long. I also read that Rhode Island has more Dunkin' Donuts stores per person than any other state. There's a claim to fame. We're all a bunch of doughnut-gorged fatties."

"You done?" Ricardo asked.

"I guess."

"Good iced coffee, though."

"Damn straight."

"And doughnuts."

"The best."

Ricardo sat in his chair several feet back from the TV. Usually, he positioned it inches from the screen to see what he could. Aaron wondered if his friend's eyes had deteriorated so much that he had stopped trying, but the way Ricardo was moving so confidently, coupled with his dead-on throw with the beer, contradicted that conclusion. He studied his friend. Ricardo's eyes were glued on the screen, following the action. *He's watching it. Has his sight improved?*

He thought back to all the times they used to throw around the football or play stupid video games together, neither of them worrying about the future or caring about what would come. Their bond was strong and had evolved over time. Their friendship had survived both their failings, Ricardo's physical and Aaron's mental.

Funny, it was Ricardo who'd wanted to become a cop. Aaron had wanted to be a veterinarian. *When did I give up on that dream? Maybe I could look into taking some courses part-time or at night or something.*

Ricardo's apparent partial recovery hinted that things could someday get back to the way they used to be, back when they both thought of life as something they'd beaten, not something that beat them down.

Aaron had no time for pipedreams, though, or the kind of false hope that wore down the soul. He had to know if his friend's improvement was real. He had to know if *they* could be healed. "Can I ask you something?"

"Sure. What's up?"

"I noticed you haven't been using your cane. Did you have something done?"

"You know my eyes can't be surgically corrected," Ricardo said, sounding uncharacteristically chipper. "I can't say what it is, but lately, my eyesight's been better. I haven't gone to my doctor for an explanation because I don't think he'll be able to give me one. I don't want to get ahead of myself here, but for the first time in my life, my vision is improving. There's no scientific explanation for it. It must be—"

"A miracle?" Aaron scoffed. "Why is it that everything good not immediately explainable must be a miracle?"

Ricardo was Christian, but of what faction, Aaron didn't know for sure. Ricardo had grown up Catholic and had always believed in God, but it wasn't until his failing eyesight had become unmanageable that he'd found new religion and been "born again" or "spiritually enlightened." *Or whatever the hell he calls it.* Ricardo had started going to Bible class once a week, then twice, and sometimes more often. Aaron had asked him a ton of questions about it at the outset, thinking Ricardo was playing some kind of joke. But the fervor with which Ricardo had spoken about it and begged Aaron to go had eventually convinced him that his friend was serious.

"It's a load of crap, void of anything resembling the scientific process," Aaron had said the first time the topic had come up. Trying to sound smart, he rambled on about carbon dating and the scientific method to an immovable audience, not completely unaware that he'd been equally immovable. His ranting had ended in a stubborn deadlock between what Aaron perceived as one rational and one religious mindset.

After that, Aaron tried not to talk about it. He would hang out with Ricardo and his fellow God groupies from time to time, but he stayed away from anything that involved reading from the Old or New Testaments. *Too much excitement for my blood,* Aaron thought, rolling his eyes. Ricardo's group took the words literally, and Aaron had to bite his tongue whenever Christian "scientists" tried to prove the Earth was formed in seven days or that dinosaurs had existed four thousand years ago.

My best friend... brainwashed by Jesus freaks. He sighed. *It could be worse. He could be a Scientologist.*

Winning the argument would only come at the expense of their friendship. And Aaron had to concede the change he saw in his friend—as if his faith had made him healthier and happier—so he kept his mouth shut. Still, he didn't like to be preached to. Since as far back as he could remember, he'd remained neutral in the great spiritual debate, mostly because he had no clue what to believe. He'd seen no miracles, and life hadn't been much of a blessing. Certainly, the man upstairs hadn't done him any favors. If God was real, he didn't believe in Aaron.

Ricardo snickered. "Do you have a better explanation, oh wise one?"

"Come on, Rick. Go get it checked out. This is great news. Maybe a doctor can help advance it."

"Doctors don't know shit. I've been seeing doctors for nearly thirty years, and what good have they done? They fill you with false hope, only to crush it the next time they see you." Ricardo shook his head. "Like you should talk, anyway. When was the last time you went to the doctor?"

"It's been a while." Aside from annual mandatory physicals, Aaron intentionally avoided all members of the medical profession. His philosophy was simple: if it ain't broke, don't fix it. And as far as he knew, he wasn't broken. Well, not physically.

"Come to class with me, Aaron. One time—that's all I ask."

Aaron sighed melodramatically. "How many times are you going to ask me to go with you?"

"As many times as it takes."

"Do you think that if I go to class with you, I'm going to suddenly see the light? You know I'm not religious. I know that you are. Let's just leave it at that."

"One time," Ricardo said. "I wouldn't have thought it a month ago, but yes, I do believe one time may be enough. I've been shown something, something amazing... something I know is a miracle. I can show you one, too, if you'll let me."

Brittney rustled the pages of her magazine. Aaron could see her from his seat on the couch, and he knew she was listening. Every now and then, she would peek over the pages. She shared Aaron's lack of faith, and it had been a source of some uncivil debate between the couple.

It wasn't Ricardo's beliefs that bothered Aaron so much. He'd always thought of Ricardo as open-minded and independent. Then Ricardo had started taking jiu-jitsu with a few of his friends, and all of a sudden, he's attending Bible study with his sensei, spewing sermons about the power of Christ. Long gone were the days when they would head-bang to death metal.

"Come on, Aaron. I don't push it with you." Ricardo turned his head, and although several feet of empty space stretched between them, Aaron could have sworn his blind friend was looking him right in the eye. "But I do have to try and save you, and one time is all I ask." Ricardo's face was deadpan, but he sounded only half serious. The silence almost became awkward before Ricardo laughed. "After all, I owe you one."

"Dislodging a fast-food hash brown from your throat doesn't compare to the soul cleansing you've got in mind for me. Besides, there aren't enough cleaning products in the world to wash away my sin. Not to mention, you got lucky. I had no idea how to do the Heimlich maneuver." He, too, was only half joking. He hadn't done anything great with his life. Maybe he deserved to rot in hell. He thought most people believed in God for fear of the consequences if they didn't. Aaron chose not to believe in God for fear of the consequences if he did. The scars on his wrists were constant reminders of where he would be going if certain Christian denominations were right.

Or maybe that's only if you succeed in killing yourself. He made a mental note to look up the answer to that.

The doorbell rang.

"That's probably Craig," Ricardo said, standing to answer the door. "I bet he wants to get food."

"No way I'm taking that bet," Aaron called after him.

Ricardo returned with Craig Sousa, a black-haired, dark-skinned man with thick stubble and a cleft chin. Craig wore Bermuda shorts and a sweatshirt in sizes sold at GAP Kids.

Craig smiled, flaunting coffee-stained teeth. "What's up, Aaron?" Without waiting for a response, he asked, "Who wants Taco Bell?"

"After the game," Aaron said.

"I can't," Ricardo said. "I have plans tonight."

They watched the Patriots trounce the Colts thirty-four to ten. When the game was over, Aaron and Craig said their goodbyes, got into Aaron's car, and headed to the nearest Taco Bell.

"So is Rick still in his Jesus-freak stage?" Craig asked.

Aaron cringed. The insult sounded worse when spoken aloud. He was ashamed for thinking it earlier. "Come on, man. It's not like he's going door-to-door, trying to convert all us heathens like those Jehovah's Witnesses." *Except me. He's still trying to convert me.* "He's harmless."

"Harmless?" Craig dropped his beef burrito, feigning disgust. "Oh yeah? Listen to this. Last time I was here, we were all watching reruns of *The Office.* It was me, him, Doug, Mikey, and Doug's girl... what's her name?"

"Kelly."

"Right. Anyway, *The Office* was over, and that old movie with Christopher Walken where he's like Gabriel or some shit was coming on next. I wanted to watch it, but Rick turned it off. He said we couldn't watch it because it had bad angels in it. It was fucking weird. Soon, the only thing we'll be able to watch over there is Barney—as long as Barney's not a Jew, that is. That's not harmless? A marathon of Barney the big purple asswipe dinosaur? He's your friend. Set him straight."

"I don't think Barney has been on TV for… never mind. He's your friend, too, last time I checked. You ever think maybe he didn't want to watch that show because it sucks?"

"Ha, ha. Laugh it up, dick."

"Anyway, there are a lot worse monsters out there than Barney the big purple asswipe dinosaur. And Ricardo just isn't one of them. He's the best guy I know, way better than you or me, and you know it. When has either one of us ever done any volunteer work like he does? All the time he puts in trying to help others who are going blind, all the other causes he sponsors and donates his time and money to? He's trying to save the world, while we sit on our asses, eating pancakes. We don't even hold a candle…" Aaron sighed then smirked. "But I guess it's all relative. Even we look good compared to this new guy I'm investigating. Well… *helping* to investigate. You picked a bad time to come back to this neighborhood. We got ourselves a serial killer on the loose."

"Yeah, I know. My mom wrote me about it. She's scared shitless. Actually told me not to come." His brow crinkled. "I *think* that was because of the murders. Anyway, I know about four kills. Have there been more?"

"No. That's it. Hopefully, that will be all. The killer's been quiet for two weeks now. We've been making progress on the case. Maybe the killer decided to lay low or, better yet, leave this area altogether. People are scared. We get so many calls day in and day out. From Providence to New Bedford, everyone's on edge. My precinct is not a fun place to work right about now."

"What progress have you made?"

"I can't say." Actually, Aaron didn't know any details. But a large number of fellow officers had been diverted off their regular assignments to work on the case. Rumor had it that the FBI might be called in. Aaron was already averaging fifteen more hours per week than usual. Something had gotten Detectives Marklin and Beaudette motivated. Aaron was sure he would hear about it soon enough from somebody at the department. *Nothing stays quiet for long. Even cops can't keep their mouths shut.* "Honestly, though, I don't know too much. I haven't done anything on the case since the second victim, unless you count all the false alarms I've had to respond to."

"I never thought something like this could happen around here."

"No one ever does, Craig. No one ever does. But it's like I always say: there are good people and there are bad people wherever you go. We just happen to have one of the worst pieces of shit right here, right now." Aaron leaned forward and slurped the last drops of soda from his super-sized cup then blew out a burp. "In other words, watch your back, *amigo*. Around here, nobody's safe."

CHAPTER 7

THE TASTE OF METAL IN her mouth made her want to retch. She couldn't pull the trigger. Not yet. Not until she tried to make him see.

Sharon Henderson had known Douglas Fournier for years. In secret, she loved him. Always had. Always would, it seemed, considering her final breath was near.

She'd met Doug and his wife, Kelly, at a tent revival outside Houston back when they were still kids, young and impressionable. Kelly had made a heck of a first impression on Doug, one of blissful bewilderment, while Sharon was shy and unable to understand what she'd been feeling, never mind find a way to express it. Still, her bond with Doug had been true, outright, and everlasting, an unshakeable friendship.

They'd known it was fate when their parents joined up with the good, pious folk at the compound in Waco soon afterward. Kelly had been ordained to become the seventh wife to the Great Prophet, and Doug couldn't have been happier for her. Sharon was happy, too, albeit for more selfish reasons.

But a Satan-maneuvered government was out to destroy the wonders set before them. As the Great Prophet foresaw, the government's power eventually became too mighty for their small band, who'd fought the powers of evil until the Lord's Rapture had taken them all—except three children too young and too frightened to fight. They'd lost everyone that day twenty years ago but survived it by sticking together, always struggling, clawing their way back into God's good graces, vowing never to fail him again.

Under their new prophet, they were almost there, back in his light. They'd come so far. But while Kelly was the rock at Doug's side, Sharon spent her nights alone. Rebuilding had to be harder on her than on them. He should have been there for her more. She knew it was sinful to resent Kelly for her good fortune, to covet what her friend had. Perhaps her resentment had blinded her and allowed her to be led astray so easily.

None of it mattered anymore, though. She had committed the ultimate sin, and neither Doug nor Kelly were to blame. She needed to let her love know the truth. She had to tell him he was damned.

So it seemed that fate had interceded again when her phone rang in her lap. Doug's name appeared on the screen. She pulled the gun from her mouth and answered the phone.

"Sharon?" Doug said. "You there? We're all worried about you. I've been trying to reach you since—"

"I'm… I'm here."

"You okay? It sounds like you're crying. I'm coming over."

"I saw him," Sharon cried. "I saw him when he Tasered Robillard." She closed her eyes, searching for a moment's peace in the dark, but peace had become an illusion, a lie like all the others *he'd* tricked them into believing.

"Sharon, please calm down. Let's talk about this."

"No, Doug. You're not listening to me. He… he was smiling. He actually enjoyed stunning that man, even after Robillard was already unconscious."

"He had to be sure he was out and not just pretending again." Doug let out a long breath into the speaker. "Look. He *does* enjoy it. I've seen that, too. But that's because he feels the light inside him, knows he's saving yet another lost soul. We all are, Sharon. We're doing so much good."

"And what about the cat?" she blurted. "Why did he have to kill the cat? We were at an animal hospital! He could have left it there alive. When I confronted him about it, he said he didn't want to set it loose with a broken paw. He said it was a humane death. I think he got off on it. It's funny, five redeemings, and it takes the death of a cat to make me realize how wrong I've been… how wrong *we've* been. And not just now, Doug, but all those years. That's the worst part. All of it, all it's ever been is one giant lie."

"Is that what this is all about? A cat? What we're doing is so much more important than that. Do you really want to just lay it all aside over some stupid cat?"

"What's the expression? 'God is in the details'? Well, there was something seriously wicked in those details, Doug."

"Sharon, where would we be without him? He's helped us all so much. You know how we were before. You know it better than any of us. Me, you, all of us. We have purpose now. We're stronger. We're doing what others are afraid to do."

"Has he helped us? Look at me now: depressed, afraid… alone. I'm right back where I started when we left the compound."

"Let me come by. We'll talk in person."

"No, I don't think so. I think I'd rather be alone right now."

"Don't lose it, Sharon. He's shown us something you can't ignore. I know you felt it like the rest of us. You can feel it again. We need you, and we all love you. Don't walk away from us."

"He's brainwashed us. Don't you see? I don't know what causes that feeling, but there's nothing miraculous about it. He doesn't kill them for their sake; he kills them for his own sake. You can see it in his eyes. I watched him kill the last one. I watched him closely. When he brought down the blade, his eyes were horridly delighted. His smile was dark and twisted like something straight out of *Psycho*. And that's us, too, Doug!" She sobbed and tried to catch her breath. "We're psychos!"

"The prophet has—"

"Prophet?" Sharon sneered. "He didn't look like a prophet to me— that's for sure. He looked like a demon. He's a *false* prophet, Doug, and he's led us all astray."

"Sharon, we save them."

"No, Doug. We *kill* them. We're murderers, we're sinners, and we're all going to hell. I left a full confession for the police. You should get out of here. I have to go now. Take care, Doug, and give Kelly my love. Goodbye."

"Sharon, don't hang—"

She tossed the phone onto the bed. Then she put the gun to her temple so she wouldn't have to taste it.

CHAPTER 8

THE SKY DARKENED WITH FAT clouds threatening rain on a cold day so close to Thanksgiving. Those in attendance had less to be thankful for that holiday. Some had lost a relative. Some had lost a friend. A few, however, had lost something more. They'd lost a kindred spirit, one of their own.

Aaron was bored. Death was already starting to get old.

He'd driven Ricardo to the funeral out of respect for his friend, not for the dead woman he'd barely known. He'd only met Sharon once or twice. She'd seemed nice enough, maybe a little dull. But she was dead, and life went on for the rest of the world. He wondered why he should pretend to care just because the rest of the world was pretending. *Because he's your friend.*

Reason enough. "Is it an open casket?" he asked as he pulled into a parking spot in the funeral home's lot.

Ricardo frowned. "How could it be?"

"What do you mean?"

"You don't know? Aren't you a cop? Don't you read the paper?"

"Know what? How she died? I guess I just assumed it was drugs or something."

"She blew her freaking head off. If anyone should show a little sympathy and understanding for her, I would think that would be you."

"I'm sorry, Ricardo. I—"

"Doug found her like that. He got there before your friends could. He had to see..." He covered his mouth and pretended to cough.

"I..." Aaron didn't know what to say.

Ricardo opened the car door and got out. His cane was in his hand, but he didn't unfold it as he started inside.

"I'm sorry!" Aaron called after him. "Stupid," he muttered. "That was so stupid." He ran a hand down his face and groaned.

Real swift, Aaron. He stayed in the car, hoping to let his gaffe blow over. He laughed nervously. *She shot herself. I've never even had the balls to do that.*

He rested his forehead against the steering wheel, recalling the last time he'd tried to kill himself.

The container held fifty tablets. "Do not consume more than six tablets in twenty-four hours," its label said. Aaron had known he wasn't supposed to mix the pills with alcohol. For most people, aspirin was fairly harmless. But Aaron was supposed to be allergic to it.

As a child, his mother had once given him half a pill, and his neck had swelled like an over-inflated bicycle tire. The swelling blocked his air passages and nearly suffocated him. The doctors were considering a tracheotomy, but fortunately for little Aaron, the swelling had subsided rather quickly.

Since then, Aaron had always wondered if he was still allergic to aspirin or if it was merely a childhood hypersensitivity he'd outgrown. *Guess we'll answer that question.* He took a handful of pills, rolling the dice with his life on the pass line, then chased them with Jack and Coke. He wrote Arianna a note. He cried. He crawled into bed, guessing he probably wouldn't be crawling out of it in the morning. Arianna slept beside him all night, never the wiser.

As the fates would have it, Aaron woke up fine. The aspirin left no side effects, save for a chalky taste in his mouth. He got up, flushed the note down the toilet, and went about his day.

The morning would have been uneventful and his second suicide attempt would have gone unnoticed if he hadn't left the near-empty bottle of Jack Daniels sitting on the counter. Arianna apparently still found Aaron's drinking on a weeknight peculiar, though he'd been doing it more often, and the amount of whiskey that had disappeared from the bottle would have raised the most oblivious person's suspicions.

"How many did you take?" Arianna asked when she found the empty aspirin container on the bathroom sink and marched it over to him. Aaron knew he would have to answer for what he'd done.

She seemed outraged at first. He worked the pity angle as best he could with sad, puppy-dog eyes. It calmed her, but only a little.

"How much, Aaron?"

"Enough. We ran out." *You should have bought the hundred-count bottle.*

Teary-eyed, Arianna looked as though she might collapse into Aaron's arms. Instead, she slapped him hard across his face. "Why would you?" She slapped him again. "Why would you do such a thing?"

"I don't know." *It seemed like a good idea at the time.*

"'I don't know' is not acceptable. Is it because of me?"

"No." *Shit!* He'd paused too long before answering. She must have noticed. *Not* just *you, anyway.* He tried to recover. "I'm just so tired of everything. It's not even that I'm depressed. It's that I don't see a point. I go through life, day in and day out, doing things I hate, and for what? I have absolutely nothing to show for it. Yet every day, it's the same old miserable bullshit routine."

"Nothing to show for it? What the hell am I?"

"You know what I mean. With work and... stuff."

"Do you still love me?"

"What? Yes! Of course!"

"You'd better." She slumped in the chair across from him. "So if it's gotten this bad, quit your job. Do something else."

"That's just it. I can't quit my job, start over, and work for less somewhere else. I need every cent of every paycheck. I spend each one before I can even deposit the damn thing. I'm stuck where I am, and there's nothing I can do about it." He decided not to mention the part where his girlfriend making twice as much as he did made his balls shrivel. "I had so much ambition but never any direction. It makes a lot more sense to kill myself than to go through a lifetime of endless monotony. Even the weekends suck because I can't afford to do anything.

What's the point? I racked up all that college debt to pay for something I hate doing. Life's a cruel joke."

"We will get through this. Together. It will get easier."

"When will it get easier? I've been telling myself that same lie for years. Death seems like my most rational option."

"There's nothing rational about killing yourself, you stupid, selfish little man."

That hurt. *Selfish? Ricardo said the same damn thing...*

She crossed her arms over her chest. "Is this about the abortion? You're not still upset about that, are you?"

"Well, I wouldn't say I'm happy about it."

"That was months ago. Get over it already. What right do you have to tell me what to do with my body? You know I don't want children. Not now, anyway."

"It's *your* body, but it was *our* baby. I just wished you had talked to me about it first."

"What was there to talk about? Combined, we're over two hundred grand in debt, we live in a small house in a bad neighborhood, and we barely have enough time to show the dog enough affection. A baby was not something we need right now."

"I know that. We made a mistake, and we're usually so careful. Still, did we do the right thing?"

"*We?*" Arianna exploded out of her chair. Her stare was accusatory as she leaned toward him. "*We* have nothing to worry about because *you* were too dumb to notice. So don't worry about it, Aaron. It's my cross to bear." She pushed past him, heading for the door. "God, you sound just like Rick. Get off your fucking high horse." She stormed out of their home, slamming the door behind her.

Aaron jolted awake as Ricardo closed the car door. "Have a good nap?"

"Sorry," Aaron said, rubbing his eyes. "Haven't been sleeping well." *Two years ago, and not a thought about suicide since. Why have I been dreaming about it so much lately?* He shook it off and turned the key in the ignition.

"I just don't want to lose her, man."

"What? Who? Arianna? Because I know you aren't talking about Sharon."

"Yeah, Arianna. I'm sorry. This really wasn't the best time—"

"Well, you are going to lose her," Ricardo snapped, "if you don't pull your head out of your ass. That girl's stood by you, put up with all of your bullshit, because she remembers the guy you used to be—the guy I remember. Sometimes, I wonder, though. Was that guy ever real, or was he just an act? 'Cause lately, you're so stuck in this 'woe is me' funk that you don't even recognize how good you've got it. Smarten the fuck up and show that girl a little appreciation."

"I want to. I just... I just don't feel like she wants to be with me anymore."

"Sometimes I don't know if *I* want to be with you anymore." Ricardo slumped and sighed. "I shouldn't have said that. You're right—this is not a good time to talk about this. Just know this: you're crazy. That girl loves you. The only way you're going to lose her is if you push her away. So don't be stupid and push her away."

Shaking his head, Aaron pulled the car into the small funeral procession. They rode to the cemetery in silence. When he parked on the path three cars behind the hearse, Aaron got out and walked with Ricardo toward the gravesite.

"I'm going to hang back," Aaron said, stopping to lean against a monolithic tombstone. "I didn't really know her, but I'll be right here."

"Suit yourself." Ricardo finished walking the thirty feet to where the dozen or so other attendees had gathered.

From his vantage point, Aaron watched and waited. Another person his age had beaten him into the grave despite his earlier efforts to win that race. It almost seemed unfair. Had the sun been out, the cemetery might have been beautiful, a well-manicured landscape of stone-walled fields and fertile earth.

Ricardo stood beside Doug and his wife as the casket was slowly lowered into the ground. Doug—six feet ten inches, and two hundred ninety pounds of muscle—crumbled like a baby into Ricardo's arms as his wife cried beside them. Ricardo was a rock, but Aaron knew his friend was in pain. Kelly's mascara ran down her cheeks, creating grotesque streaks, while Brittney attempted to console her. Aaron wondered if anyone would cry for him at his funeral. *And who would cheer?*

The four mourners, and Aaron, by default, stayed long after the priest had said his final words and all the others had gone. After a while, the gravediggers asked them to leave so that they could fill in the grave and be on their way.

Ricardo started away then spun back and tossed his cane onto the snapdragons, carnations, daisy mums, and gladiolus flowers covering Sharon's casket. Aaron heard it thud against the hard cedar. He gasped as Ricardo turned to walk toward him. Brittney moved to his side, but Ricardo shook off her arm.

Ricardo walked straight up to Aaron. "Brittney will take me home. Thank you for the ride."

"Rick... your cane... I..."

"I don't need it anymore."

That night, Aaron dreamed he was back at the cemetery. Only *his* body was in the casket, dressed in a fine black suit and being slowly lowered into the grave. Blood gushed from the scars on his wrists. His heart pumped feverishly, draining him faster and faster. Above was a bright-blue sky, then shadow, then his own face smiling down, laughing. His other self slammed the coffin lid closed.

He thrashed awake.

"Another bad dream?" Arianna laid her head on his chest. The melon scent of her shampoo wafted into his nose as her thick curls tickled his chin.

"Yeah, sort of." His scars itched. "Maybe I just need a vacation."

She sat up and straddled him. Her arms squeezed her breasts together in a way he found tantalizing. She leaned down and kissed his cheek. "We just had one."

What's gotten into you? Aaron didn't know what had brought about the sudden display of affection, but he liked it. Ricardo was right. He did need to show her a little more appreciation. Maybe their problems were all in his head. Smiling, he stroked her soft arms. "How about a whole week this time?"

"My boss would love that. But seriously, with your snoring and bouts of insomnia, maybe you should do us both a favor and see a doctor. I have bruises all over my legs from your kicking. People are starting to wonder if I'm a victim of domestic abuse. It's not healthy for either of us. You could have sleep *eepnea*."

"Apnea."

"What?"

"Forget it. At least I have the morning off. My shift doesn't start until four today." He pulled her down closer and whispered into her ear, "Maybe we could—"

"Actually, I didn't get a chance to tell you last night." Arianna slapped his chest and jumped out of bed. "My brother's home, and I volunteered you to help him move back in."

Aaron groaned. "Aren't you a sweetheart?" *So much for my morning off. I should've known she was being nice for a reason. Ricardo doesn't know shit about it.* "How long is he back for?"

"At least a couple of months. He's helping my dad out with the landscaping and snow-removal business, then it's back down to Deltona, if I can't convince him to stay this time. I'm glad you woke me, because we've got to get ready."

"Now?"

Arianna gave him a good whack with her pillow. "Yes, now, silly."

He knew if he didn't get up, she was going to keep hitting him with it. He couldn't determine if her intent was to be playful or irritating. Either way, it worked. "All right, all right. I'll get in the shower."

Less than an hour later, Aaron pulled up beside an overstuffed U-Haul with an equally overstuffed man standing beside it. Seth Medeiros had always been heavy, but lately, he was pushing four hundred pounds. He was kind of egg-shaped, like those toy people that rocked back and forth but didn't fall down. He fit the fat-guy stereotype well. He consumed massive amounts of food and beer and always smelled like he was hiding pepperoni between his third and fourth spare tires. And he was always jolly, a regular Portuguese Santa Claus.

Aaron and Arianna climbed out of the car and walked over to the van. The lazy, fat bastard hadn't unloaded a thing, apparently content to wait for Aaron's help. Arianna went inside to visit with her mom.

Aaron was pretty sure he faked friendship with Seth convincingly enough. Occasionally, they would even go on a fishing trip or casino run together. Aside from drinking, fishing, and gambling, the two had only their love for Arianna in common. Seth was always protective of his sister. Aaron had never received the you-better-treat-her-right-or-I'll-kill-you speech, but a glance from Seth would imply it from time to time. Aaron wasn't perfect, but Seth seemed to respect his sister's choice.

"How have you been, Seth?" Aaron asked as he approached the rear of the U-Haul.

"Can't complain. Both Miami and Tampa Bay suck this year. I guess I'll have to root for the Patriots again."

"I knew you'd come around eventually."

"Hey, man, no bullshit. When are you going to marry my sister?"

"Well, you don't waste any time. No 'Hi, Aaron. How's the family? Is your dog still crapping on the rug?' Right to the hard-hitting questions, that's your style." Aaron had expected the question, so he wasn't as surprised as he let on. Seth was always quick to bring up the subject.

"Seriously, Aaron. I only mention it because my parents ain't getting any younger. Everybody likes you. Why not make it official?"

"I will. I'm just waiting for the bills to lighten so that I can afford the ring." Aaron had been giving that same excuse for seven out of the eight years he and Arianna had been together. He wondered if it made him sound cheap.

"If you need to borrow some money, I could—"

"No. I'm fine. Thanks, though."

Seth stared at him as though he'd been expecting a different answer. After a moment, his shoulders drooped. "Well, let's get this done. I'm starving."

CHAPTER 9

Bruce Marklin drove up to Charlotte Robillard's house, knowing he looked as though he'd just gotten out of bed. The dark circles around his eyes, a deeper purple than usual, were a sure tip-off that he hadn't slept well. He hadn't gotten much sleep in weeks. He never did when he had a case he couldn't solve immediately. His second wife, Marie, had always been able to distract him from his overactive mind. He'd thought about calling her, even had the phone in his hand, but decided against it. He didn't know how to apologize for being distant, for never being there, despite being right beside her. *How does one apologize for something he can't change?*

And so the Rubik's Cube in his mind had twisted and reshaped all night long, all month long. Try as he might, he couldn't get its damn colors to align.

The flashing lights of the cruisers parked outside the house hurt his eyes and sent a stabbing pain into his forehead. He winced and pulled over before taking in the rest of the scene. The street had been blocked off at both ends, yet the news vans had somehow gotten there first.

He grabbed his coffee cup, got out of the car, and pushed his way through reporters. He had a statement he would have loved to give each and every one of their parasitic kind, making their livings off the misery of others.

One hell of a way to start the morning, he thought as he traveled the walkway up to the house where Officer Temple waited to give him the rundown. He half-listened to the officer's ramblings as he sipped his coffee, waiting for his partner to arrive so they could conduct a proper investigation.

A pang of guilt carried with it a wave of heartburn. He swallowed the coffee that threatened to come back up. *I could have done more for these people. I should have done more. I should've been smarter.* He'd visited the Sycamore Avenue home three days ago when the department had finally decided he should be alerted to Peter Robillard's abduction. If not for the 9-1-1 call from the veterinary clinic, no one would have investigated Peter's disappearance until he was officially classified as a missing person after forty-eight hours. Even then, the department probably would have given the case the cheating-spouse treatment and made it a low priority.

Bruce's instincts told him that Peter's disappearance was related to his investigation. It certainly wasn't every day that people were kidnapped in the suburbs. On the rare occasion it did happen, it was usually a child in a custody dispute, not a thirty-eight-year-old veterinary assistant. Peter's body, slumped across the threshold in front of Bruce, confirmed his instincts.

"Number five, I presume?" Jocelyn asked, also looking as though she'd just rolled out of bed. But with youth on her side, she somehow pulled it off, a classic beauty without all the trappings.

"What took you so long?" he asked, only half-serious. Her bedhead made him think of her in a light he shouldn't have, since he was old enough to be her father. He twisted the wedding band on his finger, where it had been for the last decade he'd spent separated from a wife who'd probably loved him only half as long. Not that he could blame her.

"A girl's got to do a lot more to get ready than a man. Plus, Caitlyn's teething. She was fussing all night. Steven and I took turns, but…"

"Ah." Bruce smiled.

"Oh, shut it." Jocelyn slapped his arm. "You have no idea what it's like to be a parent."

"Just because I don't have any kids doesn't mean I can't sympathize with your ordeal. Then again, you did *plan* to have the little monster."

"And I wouldn't unmake that decision for all the money in the world."

"You sure?" Bruce laughed. "You're going to need that much to put her through college. Should I start a college fund now?"

"Well, not everyone needs to go to *Harvard*, Bruce."

Bruce stiffened. "You know about that, do you?"

"I am a detective, trained by the best. Come on, partner. There's a story there, and we're not supposed to have any secrets…"

"Some other time."

"Come on. At least tell me what you majored in."

"History and social sciences." Bruce smoothed the wrinkles out of his shirt then waved toward the front door. "Now, if you're ready to work… shall we?"

"Relax. It's not like he's going anywhere." Jocelyn eyeballed the naked body stretched halfway into the Robillards' living room. "Who found him?"

"The wife. Apparently, he'd been propped against the door, and when she opened it, he fell into the room like a zombie out of those horror flicks you like so much. A neighbor heard her screams and called it in."

Jocelyn shuddered. "That's just plain cold." She crouched beside the body, her gloved hand pointing at a circular hole in the man's chest, about six inches in diameter. "Definitely our guy."

Bruce nodded. The meat and bone hadn't been cleanly removed like a scoop out of soft ice cream. *More like rock chiseled away with a pickaxe.* He looked away. His stomach had hardened over the years, and his mind along with it. Still, he didn't want to see just how terrible humans could be any more than he had to.

Jocelyn stood. "Looks like you were right about that 9-1-1 call."

Bruce grinned. "I knew it." His heart beat a little faster. "I knew that call was about our guy. We're getting closer."

"Calm down. You almost sound like you're happy about being right. I'm sure the Robillards are none too happy. Where's the wife?"

"She's inside. Don't bother talking to her, though. She's a vegetable."

Jocelyn crossed her arms and frowned. "You're so insensitive."

"It's the job. It does that to all of us… eventually."

Charlotte Robillard was sitting on a couch in the living room, looking as pale and lifeless as her husband. Unmoving, she stared into nothingness. Her robe hung open, exposing much of her left breast. A large metallic emblem rested in her cleavage.

"What's that around her neck?" Jocelyn asked.

"I'm not sure." Bruce waved an arm, ushering Jocelyn into the house. "Let's go see. We need to try and get some sort of statement out of her, if she's well enough."

"Bruce, I know you. Don't push too hard."

He frowned. "Even I'm not that insensitive."

As they approached Charlotte, Jocelyn seemed to lose her compassion. Her eyes scrolled over every inch of the woman, examining the mourning housewife not as a person but as a piece of evidence, perhaps a material witness, taking in every detail. He smiled. He'd taught her that.

"Mrs. Robillard?" Jocelyn said softly. "Charlotte?" She kneeled in front of the woman and took her limp hands into her own. "Charlotte? Is there anything we can get you? Anything you can think to tell us that may help us get the son of a bitch who did this?"

Charlotte looked straight ahead, not even blinking. She seemed to be staring straight through Jocelyn at something only she could see.

"Come on," Bruce said. "She's going to need time. Probably doesn't know anything useful anyway."

Jocelyn pointed at Charlotte's necklace. "That looks like a pentagram. Is she a Satan worshipper?"

Bruce signaled for her to follow him back toward the door, where they stopped inches from the corpse. "She's not a Satan worshipper, though that might have given us a motive here. Mrs. Robillard is a witch, a follower of the Wiccan faith. Pentagrams are generally worn for protection. Some believe they ward off evil spirits."

"What, like Samantha on *Bewitched*? I loved that show. The movie... not so much."

"You're kidding, right?" Bruce scowled. "Her faith is actually quite interesting. Witches believe that all entities have a spirit. Each spirit is connected to all others and to nature, and nature itself is divine. Satan is a Judeo-Christian and Islamic concept. He doesn't exist within Wiccan teachings, nor does God, at least not in the form we're familiar with. The pentagram represents the five basic beliefs of Charlotte's religion, the perfect human." He shrugged. "Long story short, it's not an evil symbol. Pentagrams are only symbols of evil and the devil in the movies."

Jocelyn stared at him. "How do you know all this crap? I can't believe that's what they're teaching at those Ivy League joints."

Bruce smirked. "I asked Charlotte about it last time I was here. Then I did a little research. It's amazing what's on the Internet."

"Was her husband a... what? A warlock?"

"I believe males are still called witches, but I'm not sure. So for all intents and purposes, yeah, he was also a witch."

Jocelyn frowned. Then her face cleared, and she nodded. "A cult!"

"I already told you, the Robillards are not satanic."

"Not them and not satanic. A Christian cult. 'My son, keep thy father's commandment, and forsake not the law of thy mother: Bind them continually upon thine heart and tie them about thy neck.'" She groaned. "Why didn't I realize this sooner?"

"What are you talking about?"

"Don't you see? It was staring us in the face with Reinhart... literally *written* on his face. Look at our victims. An adulterer, a prostitute and drug addict, a child molester... I'm sure one of the Ten Commandments or the seven deadly sins has to apply to that. And please, spare me the priest jokes."

Bruce had a half dozen good pedophile priest jokes on hand, but none had come to mind until Jocelyn mentioned it. Her theory had caught his interest. "A homosexual," he added.

"And now a witch. I'm not too up on my Bible, but I vaguely remember something about pagan gods and false idols and how worshipping them would lead to damnation. The wrist slits always reminded me of Jesus. For Roman crucifixions, nails were actually driven through the gap between the radius and the ulna, medial in relationship to the wrist, unlike all those figurines where the nails are through Jesus' hands. I may be stretching here, but the slits could represent stigmata, Christ's crucifixion wounds." She paused for a moment. "But then why weren't there any other markings to represent the crown of thorns, nail marks on the feet, or a wound in the side?" She blew an errant bang out of her eye and shrugged. "Maybe I'm reaching."

Bruce chuckled. "How do *you* know all this crap?" Jocelyn's sharp mind, so young yet so capable, never ceased to impress him. She would become a finer detective than he could ever be, if her oversized heart didn't get her killed first. She tried to hide that, but he saw through her as if she were glass. Still, he let her have her ruse. "Your theory does make sense. Do you remember the voice we heard when we cleaned up the 9-1-1 recording? When Robillard asked what he wanted, the guy said, 'Your soul.' Maybe the killer wasn't being a smart ass. Maybe he was serious." Bruce let Jocelyn's theory play out in his mind for a second. "Yes, I do believe you're on to something. Jocelyn, you're a genius."

Her face reddened, and she smiled sheepishly.

"Killing for one's beliefs is hardly a rare concept," he said. "At this point, it's safe to rule out the usual motives. We'll have to talk to some experts. So we think we have a cult of maladjusted do-gooders riding around in a white van, looking for sinners. That reminds me of *Scooby Doo*, except their van was green and blue."

"And they would have gotten away with it, too, if it weren't for us meddling detectives." Jocelyn smirked. The mischievous smile suited her, made her sapphire eyes sparkle. "Anyway, let's let the medical examiner do her thing. She's late... again. I instructed some of the officers to patrol the neighborhood and question everybody."

They made their way back to the threshold. Bruce looked down to step over the victim's body. He squinted. "Wait a second."

In the hole where a heart had once been, something shiny reflected light. He crouched and peered into the cavity.

Jocelyn kneeled beside him. "I see it. Probably just another chip from the killer's blade. We'll know for sure when we get the autopsy report."

"No, it's bigger." Bruce snapped on a plastic glove and reached into the wound.

"We shouldn't—" Jocelyn began to protest but cut herself off.

When Bruce tried to pick up the shiny, orb-shaped object, he discovered that it was attached to something much bigger crammed under Robillard's ribcage. He couldn't pull it free from the broken shards of bone. He quit trying and wiped away some blood from the orb. Encircled by some sort of fabric covered in gore, a convex, yellow surface of glass or clear plastic enclosed a smaller black circle that looked like—

68

An eye?

"Fuck this." He plunged his hand into the wound, feeling squishy material, which resembled dense seaweed at red tide, around the glassy object. Wrapping his hand around the entire thing, he yanked it out.

Bruce held it up, and he and Jocelyn stared at it, speechless. The blood-covered object warranted no place in their crime scene, never mind in a human body.

"He's fucking with us." Bruce clenched his jaw. If it hadn't been covered in blood, the stuffed kitten might have been adorable, complete with a bandage tied around its tattered front paw.

CHAPTER 10

AARON PARKED HIS CRUISER ON a side street and aimed his radar gun at Plymouth Avenue. *Make your move.* Staring down its plastic barrel, he wanted to feel like a gunslinger with a futuristic weapon. Instead, he felt like a kid with a toy. *Another lame night writing tickets.*

The quarter-mile strip on Plymouth was a favorite racetrack for local teens. He had already seen a Trans-Am, two WRXs, and a Mitsubishi 3000 GT. A Pontiac Fiero slid past, looking more like a bright-yellow sled than a car.

The thirty-miles-per-hour speed limit was clearly posted, but Aaron had let a few drivers escape justice, passing him at forty-five, some even pushing fifty. Sixty was his minimum that night. He was already in a pissy mood and was looking to haul somebody's ass off to jail, if not for any other reason than to get out of the cold. Reckless driving was easy to pin on drivers going double the limit.

His cell phone lit up on the seat beside him. *Go away.* He squinted down the barrel of the radar gun. *I'm busy here.* The caller was persistent. Aaron could have let his voicemail pick it up, but the ringing became an annoyance. "Yes?" he answered.

"What's up, bro?" Craig's always overly exuberant voice came through the speaker. "What are you up to?"

"I'm working." At that moment, a Mitsubishi Eclipse with what looked like a giant spatula attached to its trunk sped by, clocking in around seventy. *Great timing, Craig.* "What do you want?"

"Dude, I've got to tell you something. When are you off tonight?"

"Twelve."

"Want to get some IHOP?"

"Wow, branching out from Taco Bell, are you?"

"The Bell closes at midnight on weeknights."

Aaron shook his head. "I should have known better. All right, then. I'll meet you at IHOP at a quarter after. Bye."

"Cool. Lat—"

As Aaron hung up the phone, a yellow Fiero whizzed by at seventy-four miles per hour. Aaron smiled, turned on his siren and lights, and pulled out onto the street.

Before he could catch up, he heard a loud clunk ahead, followed by the sputtering of a car engine. *Aw, shit. I hope that clown didn't hit someone.* An accident wasn't the kind of action he wanted—too much paperwork.

A couple of blocks up the road, the Fiero was sitting at a light that had turned green. *Gotcha!* Aaron smiled. *I hope he's not wearing his seatbelt.* "Put your hands on the steering wheel," he said through his cruiser's loudspeaker. People didn't like cops in Fall River, at least not the people joyriding on Plymouth Avenue. He got out and approached the car with his hand on the butt of his pistol. At the driver's-side window, he twirled his finger.

As the window lowered, Aaron thought he might get a contact high from the cloud of weed that permeated the interior of the car. Before Aaron could ask for his license and registration, the driver, a kid in his early twenties, exploded into a tirade about how he hadn't done anything wrong and that the police were out to get him. "What was that sound, Officer? I was just trying to neutral drop at the red light, but I accidentally kicked it into reverse, and now my transmission is fucked."

Still smiling, Aaron just nodded then told the driver to step out of the vehicle. The driver's eyes were bloodshot, and Aaron found a dime bag in his pocket. By the time Aaron finished his report, he had to rush to get to the restaurant to meet Craig.

He strode in and joined Craig after spotting him at a back table. "So what's so important that you needed to see me?"

"Nothing important." Craig smiled. "I was getting stir-crazy and knew you'd be up for something."

Aaron rolled his eyes. "Some of us do have people to get home to." He shook his head. "Ah, forget it. Arianna's probably fast asleep already."

"Problems?"

"That's none of your business."

"Damn. That sounds serious. Not getting laid, huh?"

Aaron glared at him. "I do carry a gun, you know."

"Oh, relax. I'm just busting your balls." Craig shrugged and slouched in the booth, his head resting against the back of it. "Anyway, I do have some fucked-up news."

"What?" Aaron asked, expecting something stupid. With Craig, it usually was. Still, pancakes sounded good, so the visit to IHOP wouldn't be a total loss.

Craig picked up his menu. "Let's order first. I'm starving."

When the waitress came, Aaron ordered pancakes and coffee. Craig ordered some kind of fancy omelet with extra salsa and sour cream.

After the waitress left, Craig sat back again. "Well, you know how I do capoeira, karate, aikido, and some other martial arts?"

"Yeah."

"And you know how I like to try out all the other martial arts?"

Aaron unwrapped his silverware. "Yeah."

"And you know how some people even say I could be the next Bruce Lee?"

"No one says that. Are you coming to a point?"

The waitress returned with their drinks. Craig grinned and took a long swig from his orange juice. After emptying half the glass, he made that annoying gasping sound that kids and assholes in commercials made when they found a beverage overwhelmingly refreshing.

Craig wiped his mouth. "I went with Rick to his jiu-jitsu class last night."

"So?"

"So they're all fucking whacked!"

"What are you talking about?"

"We were going over a leg-lock, and Rick was my partner. Everybody in the class, about six people and me, had gis on. Underneath their gis, most of them were wearing silver chains with crosses around their necks. So I think, 'Okay, fine, whatever.' I know they're religious and whatnot, so no big deal. I said to Rick, 'Don't you want to take your chain off so it doesn't break?' He told me that he never takes it off. So I said, just joking around, 'You'd better be careful, or your cheap metal Jesus could turn your neck green.' Granted, it wasn't the best joke, but I thought it was at least somewhat amusing. You know how cheap necklaces can—"

"I get it." Aaron snorted. "You're right. It wasn't the best joke."

"Well, I guess Carter, the sensei, heard me. What a freaking attitude he gave me! He started reciting some verse, a passage from the Bible, I guess. While he talked, he just stared at me with this blank face. The others stared, too, like I'd served them up some great insult. Oh no, how horrible. I made fun of their cheap metal Jesuses. Not exactly the end of the world." Craig laughed. "Anyway, I told them it was just a joke, to lighten up. Then Carter asked me to leave. Do you believe that? I looked at Rick, expecting some support. You know what he did?"

"What?" Aaron had to admit he was mildly interested.

"He apologized to Carter for inviting me. I mean, how long have Rick and I known each other? And he's known Carter for—what? Three weeks?"

"He's been going to that class for more than a year now, but I do see your point."

"So I left, and I assume Rick got another ride home." Craig leaned forward and lowered his voice. "The way they all stared at me, it was like those creepy kids from *The Village of the Damned*."

"Don't you think you're overreacting a bit? I'm sure I'll hear Rick's side of the story tomorrow, and it will go a lot differently… except for the part where you ditched him at the dojo with no ride home."

"Whatever, man. Mark my words: Rick and his Jesus-freak friends aren't right."

"Rick's harmless. Doug is a pretty good guy, too. That whole Bible class stuff isn't my thing, either, but I get along with both of them just fine. I've never met Carter, but they speak highly of him."

"I bet they do. Anyway, don't say I didn't warn you. Next time you hang out with them, be sure to steer clear of the red Kool-Aid."

"I prefer Tang anyway."

CHAPTER 11

BRUCE STUDIED HIS PARTNER AS she studied her notes. He could almost see her mind cranking out cold, precise logic. That wasn't something he could teach her. She'd brought that to the table herself. And yet, unlike him, she could turn it off and be a mother, a spouse...

Jocelyn sat back. "GMC, Chevrolet, and Dodge each made a model of white van with a sliding side door at one time or another." She sighed. "There are over four thousand currently registered in the Commonwealth alone, and who knows how many come in and out of Massachusetts on a daily basis? Many are registered for commercial use, but we have no way of knowing whether they're marked or not. Just driving here from the station, I saw four on the road."

"Well, that doesn't help us much," Bruce said. "We could cross-reference all registered owners with our criminal database, isolating those who live in or near Fall River and have a history of violence. Also, we should double-check if any vans have been stolen recently." He watched her frown grow and reached over to pat her hand. "We'll get him, Jocelyn. This guy is getting cocky."

She scowled. "More like rubbing our faces in it."

"He's bound to make a mistake sooner or later."

"True. But that doesn't mean he won't get a few more kills in first. And knowing the motive here might not be much help, either. Let's face it: if the motive is to kill all sinners, most of the world's population is at risk. I know I'm a target, and no offense, Bruce, but you sure as hell are, too."

"Gee, that's a comforting thought. Well, we still can't be certain that we have multiple killers or that he, she, or they are using a white van. But it does seem to be the most probable theory, especially since it would be hard to lug around someone Robillard's or Reinhart's size alone. A group could have hung up Reinhart or carried Robillard to his front door quickly and easily enough. The other three victims could just as easily have been solo jobs. Fernald was probably thrown overboard from a boat or dumped off a pier. Ramirez was so petite, *I* could have chucked her into that dumpster. And from the markings on Huntley, he was apparently thrown from a moving vehicle, left to rot naked in the middle of Route 6."

Jocelyn scratched the side of her head. "God, it's like they're showing off." Her phone rang. "Sorry, Bruce. I'll just be a second." She moved a few feet away to answer.

Bruce figured it was her husband. He tried not to listen, but she suddenly raised her voice.

"What? Slow down... a reaction? You're not sure?" After a short pause, she said, "Okay, calm down. If you're not even sure there's swelling, there's no reason to panic. Keep an eye on her, and if it gets any worse, text me, and I'll meet you at the doctor's. How is she taking it?" Pause. "Wait, Steven. I'm in the middle of a meeting. Don't put her—"

Bruce chuckled.

"Hi, baby. Mommy will be home soon. I love you." She made kissy noises into the phone. "Okay, Steven, I really have to go. Keep an eye on her—and text me." She hung up and walked back over to Bruce. "Sorry about that."

"Everything okay?"

"Yeah. Steven's just overprotective. I swear he wants to call in the National Guard every time Caitlyn so much as farts."

"Wait until she's old enough to date."

"Oh God. Let's not rush that." She ran her hand through her hair and plopped into her chair. "I'm sorry. Where were we?"

Bruce cleared his throat. "One thing's certain: the killers may have been secretive at first, but now they want to be noticed."

"Not so gung-ho on my cult theory anymore?"

"Assuming they do have a religious motive, why the stuffed cat? Someone is enjoying his work. And there's still the question of why they're mutilating the bodies. The wrist slits may signify stigmata, but that doesn't explain the removal of the heart. If we're correct in believing that the victims were chosen for their anti-Christian conduct, then why give their bodies the markings of a saint? Why take their hearts? I can't think of anything remotely Christian about that."

"No." She shuddered. "This is more like human sacrifice. If the victims are meant to be seen, then they serve a purpose. The missing hearts, or maybe the holes in their chests, are symbolic, but of what? Or do you think the killers are doing something with the hearts themselves?"

Hot acid burned in his chest. "*Using* the hearts? For what?" Bruce had no idea, and he surely didn't want to think about it. But it was his job to think about it. "Maybe they're selling the hearts on the black market. Someone's always willing to pay top dollar to move up the transplant list. The wrist slits and theatrics may be a diversionary tactic." He shook his head. "In any event, we should keep our speculation quiet. If the media gets wind that a cult may be at work here, their attention to the murders will only fuel the fire."

She ran a finger across her mouth. "These lips are sealed. Are you ready for our crash course in Christianity?"

"As ready as I'm ever gonna be."

A manila folder tucked under his arm, Bruce followed Jocelyn out of the precinct office. They got into his car and drove the few blocks to their meeting. Jocelyn had arranged for them to meet with Father Cedric Shanahan at the Church of Saint Francis of Assisi. The church had been built in another time. Its exterior was all stone, with pillars at each corner and a green dome at its center.

Bruce had done his homework. After the diocese had passed around vermin like Father Porter, he'd found it hard to trust the local white collars. He'd searched for dirt on Father Shanahan but found none. Shanahan had a Master of Divinity degree from Notre Dame and had been fast-tracked for Cardinal-ship, but he'd turned down many opportunities for advancement, apparently preferring his Fall River diocese to the grander stage. A favorite among the flock, Father Shanahan was well suited to his job and seemed eager to help the detectives catch a killer, particularly one using the Christian faith to justify his twisted hobby.

As he got out of the car and ascended the steps to the tall doors artfully carved to depict various verses of the Bible, Bruce felt as if the air itself weighed heavier on his shoulders. He held the door open for Jocelyn then followed her inside.

"Good morning, Detectives," Father Shanahan said as he met them in the hallway. The slender man carried two large books beneath one arm. Both looked centuries old, but so did the priest. "We can chat in my office." He turned and strode toward an open door on the right.

Bruce marveled at the simplicity of the room. While the church was adorned with fine candelabras, ornate sculptures, and beautiful stained-glass windows, the priest's office was as dull and drab as the priest himself. A simple wooden desk, its surface bare, sat in front of two rickety wooden chairs that seemed to grow out of the hardwood floor. Bookshelves in need of a good dusting lined the walls. The room's only source of light poured in through a small window unadorned with any shade or curtain. *The holding cells back at the precinct are more cheerful.*

The priest cleared his throat as he sat behind his desk. "I know you're busy, so rather than waste your time with an unnecessary lecture, I'll try to answer your questions directly. Jocelyn told me little about why you're here, but I can put two and two together. Your names are all over the news. Everyone knows what case you're investigating. So the two of you coming here leads me to only one conclusion: you think our fine city's serial killer is acting in the name of God. Either that, or I am a suspect." He smiled cordially.

No use in denying it. "Very perceptive of you, Father."

"With that in mind, I've anticipated some of your questions."

"Thank you, Father," Jocelyn said.

Bruce shifted uncomfortably on the hard wooden seat, happy the door was nearby so he could make a break for it in case God got angry at his presence. He felt awkward just acknowledging the priest's title. His only reasons for going into a church were weddings and funerals. He guessed he could add investigating serial killers to that list. "Let's start with something basic," he said. "Did any of your parishioners confide in you about the murders?"

"Detective, you know I couldn't tell you if they had. But if it helps ease your mind, I can tell you that nobody has. Many have talked with me about what they've seen on the news, parishioners scared for their own lives or the lives of their loved ones. These are good, God-loving people who come here. They all want you to succeed in your investigation." Shanahan sighed. "Of course, our first concern is for the lives of those this murderer selects, but your coming here worries me about his impact on this church. We've had our fair share of dirtiness to make amends for. We don't need this piled on top. And believe me, whatever the killer is doing, it's not Christian in any sense of the word. At best, it can be construed as a fanatical denomination, like Islamist is to Islamic, certainly not recognized by Rome or any other Christian authority."

"Has there ever been a situation where someone has killed in the name of God?" Bruce mentally smacked his forehead, but it was too late to take back the stupid question. Any history class in any language in any country was loaded with examples: the Crusades, the Inquisition, 9/11, and so on. *All you have to do is turn on the evening news to see someone blowing somebody else up in the name of their god.* "Let me rephrase that. Assuming our killers are Christian, is there any instance in the Bible that lends support to their actions, where God instructs his disciples to kill somebody?"

"Bruce, come on." Jocelyn shook her head. "I'm Catholic, you know. God is merciful."

"That's correct, Detective Beaudette, but Detective Marklin asks a valid question. In King James's Bible, the New Testament preaches God's benevolence. But the God of the Old Testament takes on an altogether different quality. Some see him as vengeful or destructive, but others, like myself, believe that what we mistake as vengeance and wrath is God's divine plan, making order out of chaos, employing methods beyond mortal comprehension. For example, people read the Book of Job and see the hardships placed on Job as cruel and unnecessary, ignoring the fact that Job failed to heed God's word. And when all was said and done, Job made out quite well, not that the ends necessarily justify the means. Who are we to question the Lord's devices?"

Father Shanahan paused, stroking his close white beard. "To answer your question more precisely, yes, God has instructed his followers to kill. The first one that comes to mind is Joshua."

The name rang no bells. "Who?"

"The Book of Joshua is the story of Moses's replacement, so to speak." Father Shanahan opened one of the two volumes he'd been holding. He flipped through it for a second, then putting his finger on one page, he read aloud: "Be strong and of a good courage: for unto this people shalt thou divide for an inheritance the land, which I swear unto their fathers to give them. Only be thou strong and very courageous, that thou mayest observe to do according to all the law, which Moses my servant commanded thee: turn not from it to the right hand or to the left, that thou mayest prosper whithersoever thou goest. This book of the law shall not depart out of thy mouth; but thou shalt meditate therein day and night, that thou mayest observe to do according to all that is written therein: for then thou shalt make thy way prosperous, and then thou shalt have good success. Have not I commanded thee? Be strong and of a good courage; be not afraid, neither be thou dismayed: for the Lord thy God is with thee whithersoever thou goest."

The priest looked up at them. "That was Joshua, Chapter One, verses six through nine. The text recites God's first instructions to Joshua, who was charged with the task of leading the Israelites over the Jordan River to take possession of the Promised Land." He flipped back a few pages. "In the previous book, Deuteronomy, God was more explicit in his instructions to the Israelites." He put his finger halfway down the page and read aloud again. "Thou shalt utterly destroy them; namely, the Hittites, and the Amorites, the Canaanites, and the Perizzites, the Hivites, and the Jebusites; as the Lord thy God hath commanded thee: That they teach you not to do after all their abominations, which they have done unto their gods; so should ye sin against the Lord your God."

Bruce listened intently and refrained from acting on the urge to push Father Shanahan along. The place, the preaching, the whole atmosphere of piety made his skin crawl, and he thought that if he did have a soul, it didn't belong there.

"God's first order to Joshua," the priest continued, "is to conquer Jericho, and he tells Joshua how to do it. This means invading the land and killing the people of several tribes, but in particular the Canaanites.

On God's orders, Joshua marches his army into Jericho and kills everyone but a prostitute and her family who had given his spies refuge within the city's walls. He then continues on to other civilizations, slaying all in his quest to rid the Promised Land of its indigenous peoples."

"So Joshua was a murderer under orders from God?" Bruce asked.

"If you consider it murder to kill someone when the Almighty orders you to, then yes. Historically speaking, the Book conveys a version of the Hebrew conquest of Palestine, from an obviously Hebrew perspective. Many religious theorists have suggested that the Canaanites were involved in pagan rituals, including human sacrifice and other anti-Christian and immoral conduct. So they view Joshua more as a crusader, spreading justice and God's law throughout Palestine. Certainly, they were pagan, but perhaps the Palestinians' only crime was to be non-Christians residing in Christian-coveted land. They say history is written by the winners."

Jocelyn leaned forward and whispered, "Have you lost your faith?"

Father Shanahan gave her a gentle smile. "I'm afraid you misunderstand me. I believe in both the Old and New Testaments in a non-literal sense. I believe in Jesus Christ and his spreading of the word of God. I believe Joshua was a disciple, and he had a divine role to play. The Good Books convey stories, embellished versions of historical events, inspired by God, but written by man. Each book has both divine and mortal influence. And although the stories are historically based, it's their allegorical parts, the divine parts, that are truly important."

"God instructs Joshua to annihilate civilizations?" Bruce asked, attempting to steer the conversation away from the philosophical.

Father Shanahan shrugged. "I see no other way to construe the text. Yes, God commands the destruction of all native inhabitants of the Promised Land."

"But isn't that incompatible with the capital vices, the seven deadly sins?" Jocelyn asked.

Bruce hadn't known Jocelyn was devout. He regretted some of his past jokes and anti-religious comments. Funny, he thought, how he'd just assumed she was atheist like him. If what she saw on the job didn't rattle her faith, he was sure watching those she loved die around her as she aged into a cynical old crone would probably do the trick. The job had that effect on people.

"Yes and no. The seven deadly sins were made famous through fiction, Dante's *Divine Comedy*, an interesting read. You probably know them as *luxuria, gula, avaritia, acedia, ira, invidia,* and *superbia.*"

"I assure you, Father," Bruce said, "I don't know them that way."

"Excuse me. I like to show off my Latin every now and then. Does that make me guilty of *superbia*, or pride?" Father Shanahan chuckled. "Sorry, the priesthood isn't known for its sense of humor, and I can see you two are focused on getting the job done, a good thing given the circumstances. The other sins are lust, gluttony, greed, sloth, wrath, and envy. These concepts are so broad, they can be exploited to encompass any immoral act, as well as quite a few moral ones." He opened the second book and flipped through it. "These six things doth the Lord hate: yea, seven are an abomination unto him: A proud look, a lying tongue, and hands that shed innocent blood; an heart that deviseth wicked imaginations, feet that be swift in running to mischief; a false witness that speaketh lies, and he that soweth discord among brethren. My son, keep thy father's commandment, and forsake not the law of thy mother: Bind them continually upon thine heart, and tie them about thy neck."

"Proverbs Six." Jocelyn gave Bruce a wink. "We're familiar with that one."

"Yes," Bruce muttered. "Reinhart."

"These are the real seven deadly sins, or cardinal sins. The last one, 'he that soweth discord among brethren,' is as broad as any of Dante's literary takes."

"Doesn't wiping out entire civilizations fall within those sins?" Jocelyn asked.

The priest nodded. "That's one way to read it. But if you kill those who regularly practice that which is an abomination unto God, then which is the lesser evil? Killing sinners on the Lord's behalf, ridding the world of evil and immorality, or allowing heathens to continue to practice their pagan and ungodly rituals? The answer lies in Proverbs itself. Capital vice number three is 'hands that shed innocent blood.' One who kills sinners only is not shedding *innocent* blood. Thus, he commits no sin. Given the concept of original sin, none are innocent." He frowned. "So you see how these concepts could be manipulated to justify just about any murder."

Bruce sneered. "Sounds like an explanation Hitler might have given for slaughtering Jews. It's amazing what people are capable of doing when they think they're in the right."

"And if that wasn't enough to absolve the killers of their crimes, they could be forgiven through the sacrament of confession or through perfect contrition," Jocelyn added.

Father Shanahan nodded. "Precisely, at least according to several Christian denominations." He lowered his voice. "That's twice you have pluralized 'killer.' You may want to be less loose-lipped with that information."

Jocelyn's face reddened. "Duly noted, Father."

Bruce opened the manila folder and pulled out several photographs. "I'd like to show you the markings left on the victims, all done post mortem."

The priest flipped through the photos. He never so much as flinched. "They don't seem to have any Christian significance, aside from the possibility of stigmata. This church was named after the first known stigmatic. The marks are signs of devout piousness, a relationship with God at a level far beyond that of the average believer. However, the concept of stigmata is generally a Catholic one, and Catholics view God as merciful. God wouldn't want us to kill for any reason. I don't see these killers as Catholic. Maybe you should try the Baptist church over on South Conway." He winked. "It's all hellfire and brimstone over there, I hear."

"We're not certain we're dealing with a religious sect," Bruce said. "We could be barking up the wrong tree here. It's possible we're dealing with someone who happens to like ripping out hearts and slicing wrists." He took back the folder.

Jocelyn extended her hand to the priest. "This certainly has been an informative lesson. Thank you for your help, Father Shanahan."

The priest shook her hand then Bruce's. "Please don't hesitate to contact me if I can be of further assistance. I share my parishioners' fear and would love to see your investigation brought to a successful conclusion." He cleared his throat. "Let me impart one more thing upon you, for whatever it's worth. Many read the Old and New Testaments as separate and distinct works, taking bits from each to suit their own purposes or message. But both must be read together to understand God's purpose. Some religious historians refer to Joshua as a robber and a marauder. The Palestinians of the era likely shared that view. But Joshua was many different things to many different people. He had a few different names in the Old Testament. Oshea, Jehoshua… regardless, his name always means the same thing: *savior*. In Greek, as well as in the New Testament, the word for savior is *Jesus*."

"Great." Bruce scoffed. "Our killer thinks he's Jesus."

CHAPTER 12

AARON WAS NODDING OFF IN his patrol car when his cell phone rang. The ringtone was Arianna's, so he snatched the phone off the passenger seat. "Hi, hon. What's up?"

She let out a long sigh. "I won't be able to make it for dinner tonight."

Aaron groaned. "Big surprise." He had planned a quiet dinner out at a fancy restaurant, and Arianna was blowing him off yet again. He knew the excuse she was going to give him, the same one she always gave, the one he wasn't sure he believed. *Does she even remember it's our anniversary?* He sighed into the phone. "Whose work do you have to do this time?"

"Walter's, that slithering son of a bitch. I have to depose a witness tomorrow on a case I don't know anything about. Sometimes I wonder… maybe I should quit."

"You could always call in sick."

"Yeah, that would get me fired in a hurry, though it might be worth it just to hear him squirm. God, I hate this job sometimes."

"You could kill him."

"You're such a mo."

"What the hell is a mo?"

"You."

"Okay… thanks. I'm just saying that if you kill him, I doubt anyone would care. You might even get a medal for it. You know, one dead lawyer sounds like a good start."

"Ha, ha. How original. Everyone bitches about lawyers, but we're the first people they run to when they need their problems resolved."

"No, those are cops."

"Ha! Everyone hates you guys, too. But when you need a dispute resolved, you ask a lawyer for help. And by the way, you're a butthead."

"That's because our legal system forces people to get lawyers. What's that old adage? 'He who represents himself has a fool for a client,' or something like that. Anyway, I thought I was a mo."

"You've been downgraded."

"You're too kind. So... can I reschedule our plans for tomorrow night?"

Arianna fell silent then said, "I don't know. The deposition could run late, and then I'll have to catch up on—"

"Gotcha."

"Hey, my brother was looking for something to do, and since I have to cancel our dinner plans..."

"Don't say it."

"Come on! He's harmless. I'll call him and let him know. What time should I say you'll pick him up?"

"When hell freezes over," Aaron muttered.

"What's that?"

"Six. I get off at six. I'll swing by after that."

Aaron wasn't happy with dinner: greasy Chinese food loaded with MSG. He was fairly certain he would shit his pants later. The food was bad, but the conversation quickly turned worse.

"So, did you get the ring yet?" Seth asked five minutes into the meal.

This guy's a broken record. "I'm working on it," Aaron replied, flashing a cubic-zirconium smile.

"Whoa, check out the dumpster on that waitress. Nice."

"Seth, I'm dating your sister."

"What, so you can't look? Please. Do you think she don't look?" Seth asked in his Rhode Island accent, some bastard child of New York and Boston. Everything about Seth screamed "thug." He'd been born and raised in upscale Bristol but lived like a redneck in Deltona, all the while remaining a full-blooded Portuguese gangster. To top it all off, he was a Yankees fan. No doubt his biggest fault.

"I'd rather not think about Arianna checking out other guys. Whether she does or doesn't, I don't need to know about it." *And if she's doing more than that, I'll—*

"No reason to get your panties in a bunch. Geesh."

Seth finally shut up for a few minutes while he gorged on his pupu platter for two. The way he threw crab rangoons and chicken strips down his throat reminded Aaron of Shamu's feeding time at Sea World. When Seth licked the last drop of duck sauce from his greasy fingers, he let out an enormous belch. "So I hear you're going down to Florida in a few weeks."

Arianna, Aaron silently cursed. *Why did she have to tell him about that? Now he's going to want to meet up with me down there.*

As if he could hear Aaron's thoughts, Seth said, "I won't be able to show you around, though. I'll still be up here. Where are you heading?"

"The CEO of Taser is having a demonstration for the company's new products. There'll be a shitload of vendors, all geared toward police, military, and guys who like hunting with assault rifles. It's at the Orange County Convention Center in Orlando."

"That's on I-Drive. You'll be in the heart of the tourist area, close to Universal Studios and Sea World."

"Ha! Shamu," Aaron blurted.

"It's near Disney, too," Seth continued, "like ten miles out. You'll have plenty to do. Why are they sending you?"

"It kind of fell on me. The precinct offered one free ticket. Most of my co-workers have wives or families and didn't want to go to Disneyworld without them. The department could have at least splurged for a second ticket. Cheap bastards. So I was semi-asked, semi-volunteered to go. That makes me the sole representative of Fall River's finest. Oh well, at least it's a free vacation at the taxpayers' expense."

"I'm surprised Arianna isn't going with you. I'm sure she'd pay her own way."

"I asked her, but she has a trial scheduled the following week and will need the time to prepare. I doubt Taser will reschedule the entire convention for us."

"I'll bet she's jealous."

"Probably."

"Don't let that stop you from having a good time. Orlando's great."

"Trust me. It will be nice to get away, especially at this time of year. I'm sure I'll spend those days basking in the sun, relaxing, and having the time of my life."

CHAPTER 13

CRAIG COULDN'T DECIDE WHICH VIDEO game to buy, the latest *Halo* or the best-selling *Resident Evil*—one of the tougher life decisions he'd faced. A moment of perfect clarity came over him, and he smiled. *I'll buy both.*

He grabbed the games, satisfied with a decision forty minutes in the making. Best Buy was the nectar of the gods to Craig, a gamer geek and proud of it.

Now, what movies do I want to pick up? As Craig headed straight to the action video section, out of the corner of his eye, he spotted Carter Wainwright. He ducked his head and started to turn around, but he was too late.

"Hi, Craig. How are you?"

With an inward sigh, Craig looked across the aisle. "Hey, Carter."

Beside Carter stood his faithful steed, Douglas Fournier.

"What's up, Doug?"

"I'm glad I ran into you," Carter said. "I've been meaning to apologize for the other night."

"It's no biggie," Craig replied, not meaning it. He faced the shelves and ran his hand across the DVDs. *Just stay away from me. You guys are freaks. Can't you just* pretend *to believe in God like most people?*

"Well, I feel bad about it. I definitely overreacted. We take our faith seriously." Carter's reassuring smile and sickening politeness screamed, *I'm going to kill you with kindness.*

Craig couldn't stay mad long. In fact, he was already starting to feel guilty for being upset in the first place. "Like I said, no biggie. I'm over it."

Carter frowned. His jaw tightened as he shot a glance at Doug. *What did I do now?*

Whatever Carter was feeling, it passed in an instant. His composure returned. "Well, let me make it up to you. Ricardo says you like all forms of martial arts. I'm putting together a mixed martial arts class this Saturday afternoon. Some of the guys from the other night will be there, along with some new faces. If you'd like to come, the lesson would be free. I'll even give you the whole first month free. Sound fair?"

"That's more than fair, but I'll have to think about it." Craig was willing to forget the other night, but he still wasn't keen on buddying up with a group of Bible thumpers. Still, most of his hometown friends had moved or married. Just Aaron and Ricardo were left, and all they ever wanted to do was eat.

"Well, I'll give you my number, just in case you do want to come by."

Craig pulled out his cell phone. Carter rattled off his number, and Craig typed it into his contacts list.

"The class won't be in Somerset," Carter said. "It'll be at my house in Rehoboth. I have my own dojo."

"You should come," Doug added. "It'll be fun. If you want, call Rick and let him know you're coming, and I'll pick you both up."

"Well, I may have to leave early, so if I go, I'll take my own car." *You must be crazy if you think I'd put myself at your mercy for a ride out of there.*

Doug smiled. "Suit yourself. Just let Rick know."

"All right, see you guys later." As Craig walked to the register, he could feel their stares on his back. *Wholesome or not, they still creep me out. I think I'll pass on their little weekend retreat. Anyway, I still have a few days to find better plans.*

Wearing nothing but his boxers, Craig stood in his kitchen, waiting patiently for his microwave to ding. As he watched the Tupperware bowl spin, the contents sure to remain frozen in the middle no matter how long he cooked it, he thought about the van he'd spotted in his rearview on the way home from Best Buy three days ago, again yesterday down the road from his house, and just that morning when he'd gone out for coffee. He was still trying to convince himself that it hadn't been the same van every time when his phone rang.

"Hey, Craig. It's Rick."

"I know. You have your own ringtone. I picked a really gay one for you."

"Gee, thanks. What are you up to?"

Craig scratched his ass. "Not much. I was about to eat lunch."

"Want to go to the mall?"

"Which one?"

"Silver City Galleria."

"Sure. What do you have to do out there?"

"Just pick up a few things."

"Yeah, I'm game. It'll get me out of the house and take my mind off things for a while."

"Everything okay?"

Craig let out a breath. "Nothing. I just feel like getting out of the house. I was beginning to feel a little... confined."

"C'mon, Craig. What's up?"

"Okay... no, actually. I think maybe—I know this is going to sound crazy—I think I'm being followed."

"Craig—"

"Just hear me out. I see this van almost everywhere I go. I saw it on my morning jog, outside Best Buy, at the dry cleaners, at IHOP... everywhere."

"This van, what does it look like?"

"It's white and a little beat up. It's the same kind of van you see—"

"Everywhere?" Ricardo finished. "I know what it is. The government is spying on you. They know all about that sick porn you downloaded. Destroy your hard drive before they get all your dark secrets. They probably already have recording devices in your teeth."

"Very funny. Seriously, the news said that killer might drive a white van. Maybe it's him."

"Let's think about this one for a second. What would the killer want with you? Can you think of a reason why anyone would want to kill you? For that matter, can you think of any reason why anyone would want to spy on you? You're not all that interesting."

"You guys seemed pretty pissed at me the other night," Craig said.

A long, slow breath sent static through the receiver. "Come on. That was nothing. Besides, you're the one who left me stranded, and I'm not mad about it."

"I'm sorry about that. But I do think somebody's following me."

"Could it be the cops? You didn't go back to your ex-girlfriend's house again, did you?"

"I haven't talked to her in nearly three years. And no, the cops have no reason to be tailing me."

"You're being paranoid."

"I knew you were going to say that."

"Pick me up in a half hour. I'll be ready by then. We'll see if your van follows you to the mall."

"All right. See you in a few."

As the timer went off on his leftover Tuna Helper, Craig couldn't stop his thoughts from returning to the van. He vowed to keep a closer eye out for it from then on out.

CHAPTER 14

AARON FOCUSED ON THE DROP of sweat rolling down Officer Brian Temple's forehead.

"Can you come with me?" Brian asked. "I need your help with something."

This doesn't sound too promising. Aaron tapped a pencil against the top of his desk. "I'm sort of busy."

"With what?" Brian pointed at the computer. "That thing isn't even on."

"Um…" Aaron sighed. "Okay, you got me. What's up?"

"Just…" Brian's eyes darted nervously. The material of his shirt was darker under his armpits.

"Are you okay?"

"Y-Yes. Just come with me, will you?"

Aaron stood and followed his coworker a short distance to a nearby office. "Oh no," he said as Brian knocked on the wall beside the open door. "I didn't sign up for this."

"Come in, Temple," Detective Marklin called. "Pimental."

Fuck. It was too late to escape. How Marklin had seen him from behind the mountains of paperwork on his desk and through Brian and the wall between them was anyone's guess. *What the hell did I just walk straight into?*

Brian swiped at the sweat on his forehead. Aaron could feel it starting to bead on his own. His stomach roiled. *I shouldn't have drunk all that coffee. No one comes here willingly. Is Brian begging for punishment? I don't even know what this is all about. Marklin's going to look at me like I'm stupid and have something nasty to say, and the next thing I know, I'll be writing up everyone's reports for a week.* He scowled at the back of Brian's head.

The young, squeaky-clean kiss-ass was fairly new to the force, but he should have known enough to fear talking face-to-face with Detective Marklin, especially while the man had a serial killer on his hands. He and Brian had no business stepping into that office, a needless interruption of the murder investigation Marklin was trying to solve.

Brian cleared his throat. "Good morning, sir."

"What do you want, Temple?" Marklin asked.

Aaron rolled his eyes. *Here we go.* By his count, Brian had already wasted sixteen seconds of the detective's time.

"Well, I was thinking—"

"Is that something new for you?"

Brian's face reddened. "I was thinking that maybe we could try another angle on the van, sir."

Aaron swallowed hard. His and Brian's job consisted mainly of arresting shoplifters or handing out speeding tickets, maybe breaking up the occasional bar fight. They were supposed to leave homicide investigations to more qualified cops.

"Oh yeah?" Marklin sat up. "What's that?"

"Well, my friend works for the highway department, and he says that they have several unmarked vans available for employee use. Every time an employee takes one out, he has to sign for it. They can take the van out for days or even weeks at a time. The vans all have government plates, blue like ours, and none of them have any commercial-type markings. They're plain white."

"We don't know if the van in question has government plates."

"I know. If it does, though, we have a ready-made list of potential killers. Most of the state's departments have similar systems. My friend estimates that the Commonwealth has no more than ninety of them in use at any given time, but that's across the state. There would probably be only ten to twenty of them in this area. We could check out the highway department's list and do minimal surveillance on each person. It shouldn't take long to rule most of them out. I only suggest this because almost every one of the unmarked white vans I've seen belongs to the Commonwealth."

Marklin scrunched up his nose. "Do you have gas?"

Aaron studied his reflection in his polished boots. He wondered if the detective had heard a word Brain had said.

"Yes." Brian's face turned a dark shade of red. "S-Sorry. My stomach keeps turning."

"Do you think using our limited manpower to acquire these lists and spy on those whose names appear on them is worth the department's time and energy?"

"Me? Um, I think so."

"You don't sound too confident."

Brian's teeth dug trenches into his lip. "Yes, I think it's worth a shot, sir."

"And you, Pimental?"

"I-I-I—"

"How eloquent."

"Yes," Aaron managed then added, "sir."

"Good. Then get to it. Have Stravenski help you if you need an extra hand. Good work, Temple. Showing initiative like that is how cases get solved." He shot a glance at Aaron that was easy to read: *You should take a page from your fellow officer's book.*

"Thank you, sir." Brian turned to leave.

"Oh, and one more thing. Clean your pants."

When they left the office, Aaron retreated to his desk. Fifteen minutes later, Brian came over with a faxed list of all Highway Department vehicles in use. Aaron nodded and got up to go with him, thinking that a chance to do some real police work for once might be a good thing. They signed out a squad car, and Brian set the GPS for the first address on the list.

"So who's up first?" Aaron asked. "And thanks for picking me to help you with this."

"Don't mention it," Brian replied. "You were just in the right place at the right time. I needed some backup going in there. First up is Gabriel Torres."

At that moment, Aaron's phone exploded with light and sound.

Brian shook his head. "That has got to be the most annoying, God-awful ringtone ever to disgrace a cell phone."

"Tell me about it. Just give me a second." Aaron put his phone up to his ear. "Hello?"

"What's happening, bro?"

"Craig, what do you want?" Aaron asked.

"Rick and I are heading to the mall. Wanna come?"

"Unlike you and Rick, I have to work. I'm in the middle of an assignment."

"Sorry, dude. I won't take up much of your time. One question, though?"

"What's that?"

"How can you tell if someone is following you?"

"Jesus Christ, Craig! I don't have time for this."

"I know. I'm sorry. It's just that I see a white van just like the one they say the killer drives everywhere I go."

"You and half the city who calls in useless tips every day. Don't you think you're being paranoid?"

"Yeah, that's what Rick said. I guess you guys are right. Sorry to bother you."

"No problem, but I have to go." Aaron ended the call and stuck his phone back in his pocket. "Sorry about that," he told Brian. "My friend thinks the killer's after him."

"I heard. Your friend sounds like a wuss." Brian laughed and pulled over to the curb. "We're here."

"What do we do now?"

"I guess we wait until he leaves the house then follow him."

"Oh. Which house?"

Brian smirked. "The one with the white van parked in the driveway." He pointed at a van two houses down and across the street from their position. The house was a modest gray single-family ranch.

Aaron nodded then tried to sound official. "The van's the right color, no markings, sliding side door. It fits the description. How long do we wait?"

"As long as it takes. Haven't you ever seen a stakeout in the movies?"

Aaron stared at the house. A couple of times, the shade on one of the front windows moved, but he couldn't make out who or what was causing its motion. Nearly fifty-two minutes passed before the front door opened.

An elderly man rolled his wheelchair down the driveway and straight up to Brian's car window. "Why are you two officers watching my house?"

"We're investigating a crime. Sir, please... move away from the vehicle and keep your hands where I can see them." Brian's hand was on his sidearm as he exited the patrol car.

Aaron got out and walked around the car. "What's your name, sir?"

"Gabriel Torres. Who's asking?"

"I'm Officer Pimental, and this is Officer Temple."

"Can you tell your idiot partner to relax?" Torres snapped. "He looks like he's about to pull that gun on me. I'm too old for that shit."

Brian's gun hand dropped to his side, and he pointed with the other. "Do you drive that van?"

Torres rolled forward, almost on top of Brian's toes. "You're damn right I do. It's handicap accessible, shit for brains."

Aaron eyed the van and spotted the handicap hanger on the rearview mirror. *Way to pay attention to detail.*

Torres shook his head. "You mean to tell me you didn't notice the handicap plate staring you right in your stupid faces? Good police work, fellas. You do those uniforms proud. Oh, and next time you want to spy on somebody, perhaps you should do it a little farther away—and don't be so obvious. Probably lose the police car, too, jackasses."

Aaron said, "Let's go, Brian. I think we can cross Mr. Torres off our list."

"But he could be faking—"

"Don't go there, Brian. Let's just leave." Aaron flapped a hand at the wheelchair. "We're sorry to have troubled you, Mr. Torres. You're free to go."

"No wonder you guys haven't caught that killer yet." Torres cackled. "With morons like you keeping the peace, it's a fine time to be a criminal."

Brian looked as though he wanted to respond, so Aaron gave him a nudge toward the car. Brian got behind the wheel, and Aaron went around and climbed into the passenger seat. Hell, the old man was right. They were in way over their heads. But he could learn. "Let's get my car before heading out to the next one."

Brian nodded. "Sounds like a plan."

———————————————•·•—————————————

The next name on the list was Dennis Norton, a machine operator for the highway department. Aaron pulled up to Norton's house in his almost-paid-off Subaru. The driveway was empty, so Aaron and Brian got out to look around.

"Maybe he's not home," Brian said, peering into the garage window. "No van in there, either."

"Well, I'm not going to wait this time. Let's just ring the doorbell."

"Think we should?"

"Fuck if I know, but it sure as hell beats standing around with our dicks in our hands."

"You had your dick in your hand?"

Aaron rolled his eyes. "It's a figure of speech, man."

He walked right next to Brian as they headed toward the door, drawing strength from the other's support. If they were any closer, they would have been arm in arm.

No repeats of the last screw-up. Aaron stood up straight, trying to look dignified and poised. *We couldn't possibly fuck up that badly again.* He rang the bell.

The behemoth of a man who opened the door took one look at them, yelled, "Oh fuck!" and slammed the door in their faces.

We got him! Only the guilty run, Aaron thought, though he knew Arianna would disagree. She'd argued that many people run from the cops simply because they're afraid of them—cops who would plant evidence, abuse their power, and arrest people for no other reason than their being a minority. But Norton was Caucasian, and for a big guy, he could move.

"Go around back!" Aaron shouted. He took a step back from the door, grinning. *I always wanted to do this.* He kicked the door beside the knob, but the hard wood won the battle. The force made him stumble backward, and he would have tumbled down the steps if his flailing hand hadn't caught the railing. Angry and embarrassed, he regained his balance and slammed his shoulder into the door. It took two more attempts to break the lock. *Not bad for a first try.*

Pulling his gun from the holster and holding it in front of him, Aaron entered the residence. A creaky screen door at the back of the house closed slowly, and he hustled toward the sound.

He ran out the back door and into the yard, where he heard the wails of someone in serious pain. He looked around but only saw Brian, who had climbed halfway up the six-foot wooden fence and was peeking over it. The screaming was coming from the other side. Aaron holstered his gun and started to climb up beside Brian. His partner's face had gone ghastly white.

"What's wrong?" When Aaron's hand touched the spiked tip, he grabbed something with the texture of a smashed cherry. *Gross.* He wiped his hand on his pants and started over.

Brian grabbed Aaron's sleeve and gulped. "Careful. H-He's seriously hurt. H-He got caught… I saw him when he went over…"

Aaron shrugged him off. When he got one leg over the top, he spotted a large man curled up in the fetal position and moaning on the ground. He assumed it was their suspect.

"What do you see?" Brian asked.

Aaron twisted around and whispered, "I think it's Norton, the guy who lives here. He must have fallen and hurt himself when he climbed the fence."

"That's what I'm trying to tell you, he—"

"Just jump over and help me, will you?" Aaron couldn't draw his weapon while perched on a fence. The guy hadn't looked up while he was talking with Brian, so Aaron decided to just jump down there.

Once he landed, he noticed a reddish splotch darkening the inside of the guy's pants leg. The man's hands were covered in blood as he cupped his groin.

Aaron felt a bit nauseous when he realized the guy must have come down on one of the spikes as he straddled the fence. He felt an impulse to reach for his own crotch and check his balls. When he realized just what it was that he'd gotten on his hand and wiped on his pants leg, he gagged.

Brian landed beside the man, who had stopped screaming and was sobbing. "We've got to get him to a hospital."

"What? In my Subaru? Forget it. He won't fit anyway."

The injured man looked up at Aaron. It was definitely Norton. A machine operator needed a lot of strength to do his job, and Norton certainly had it. He looked as though at any moment his shirt would rip, his skin would turn green, and "Hulk, smash" would become the full extent of his vocabulary.

"Guess we should have stuck with the patrol car," Brian said.

"Yeah, well, hindsight's always twenty-twenty. Call for an ambulance."

Brian walked a few feet away and used his handheld to radio dispatch to send support.

Aaron glared down at Norton. "We got you, you sick son of a bitch."

"I'm sorry." The big man whimpered like a little girl, still clutching his crotch, probably to prevent his remaining testicle from falling out. "I'll never grow it again. Just save my balls, please."

Grow? Aaron looked around, and his mouth fell open. He'd stumbled on the mother lode. The big guy was lying at the edge of a field in which a familiar plant grew in amounts far too great to have been natural, not that *any* amount of ganja was indigenous to Fall River. A poorly camouflaged greenhouse off to the left probably housed the chemically enhanced shit.

He whistled. "That's one hell of a stash." He and Brian would surely receive accolades for this bust. The department didn't have to know it was all shit luck.

Finally, things are starting to go my way.

CHAPTER 15

FRIDAY MIDAFTERNOON AT THE SILVER City Galleria was like a goth teenybopper festival. Craig knew it would all change in an hour, when half-crazed parents got off work and ran out to do their Christmas shopping.

"See? The only killers here are the ones playing on the Muzak at FYE," Ricardo said.

"You'd think with a name like The Killers, the band would be a lot less whiny." Craig studied his surroundings. He didn't see anybody following him, not that he knew what to look for. He imagined men in sunglasses, with index fingers holding in earpieces, saying things like, "The suspect is on the move," and "Shadow him, but not too closely." But the scene at the mall was more appropriately likened to what The Who might call a "Teenage Wasteland."

The Who—now there's a great band that most of these dumbasses probably never heard of. Ah, it's not their fault they're here. What else is there for teenagers to do before they can drink and drive? Whatever happened to bowling?

"Hey, Ricardo, want to go bowling?" Craig asked.

"We can't. It's a league night. Anyway, I have plans."

"Oh, right, Bible class." Craig hoped his verbal eye roll hadn't been too obvious. "What time do you have to be there?"

"Seven thirty. We have time for Bertucci's if you want."

"Yeah, pizza sounds good." As they walked through the mall to Bertucci's Brick Oven Pizzeria, Craig felt much more relaxed. No one was spying on him there. *No one is spying on me at all,* he reassured himself.

But something in the back of his mind made him second-guess his more rational side. He didn't want to be home alone that night. He was staying with his parents until his tour picked up again after the holidays. His parents, already needing a vacation from him, had gone to visit friends for the weekend, leaving Craig there alone until Tuesday. "Carter mentioned that you guys are having a workout tomorrow."

"Yeah, why? Are you interested?"

He gave what he hoped was a nonchalant shrug. "I don't have anything better to do."

"You want us to pick you up?"

"No, I'll drive, just in case I want to leave early. Can I follow you and Doug there?"

"That shouldn't be a problem. I'll ask him and let you know."

------ •••• ------

Saturday morning was cold, quiet, and peaceful. As Craig prepared for his morning jog, he felt more at ease than he had in over a week. Only a few cars passed as he ran. Not a white van in sight. Sweaty but relaxed, he strolled back into his parents' driveway at ten.

By eleven, he was getting restless. He flipped through TV channels, stopping briefly on a cartoon he'd never seen before, then on several reruns. *Saturday mornings suck for TV.* He decided to call Aaron, always his best shot at getting out of the house, to see if he was up for lunch. Aaron didn't answer.

I guess I'll be going over to Carter's house today. He gave Ricardo a call.

"Hello?" Ricardo answered.

"It's me. You hungry?"

"Doug and I are eating now. We're at Ponderosa."

"When did you start?"

"We've been here for a while now. I had to get out of the house. Brittney was being difficult."

"And then you marry one. Damn, I need food. You should have called me. I would have come with you guys."

"Sorry. Are you still going with us today?"

"Yeah, yeah. What time are you coming by?"

"How's twelve thirty?"

"That works. It will give me time to hit the Pizza Hut buffet."

"They only have the buffet on weekdays."

"Damn! Well, I guess I'll see you when you get here."

"All right. Later."

"Bye." Craig flipped to Comedy Central and dozed off during a Larry the Cable Guy special.

When the doorbell woke him, he rolled off the couch and went to the door. He was surprised to see Ricardo and Doug standing there since he hadn't realized he'd slept so long. He grabbed his keys and hopped into his car to follow them.

It was only a twenty-minute drive. Although he'd lived in the area as a child and his parents had always lived there, Craig had never known his home existed so close to such places—hard to get to, beautiful, secluded realty, scarcely corrupted by man. Outside of Dighton, the houses became scarcer. Most of them were gorgeous but deserted, their wealthy owners probably hibernating the winter away in Florida or some other tropical climate.

Ahead, Doug's truck veered sharply off the roadway. The growth was so thick that it hid the turn. Craig carefully followed the F-150 as it wound down a forest trail, then another, before hitting a paved driveway.

Who would actually live out here? There's nothing but farmland, then woods, then farmland and woods all over again. Country folk and woodsmen—where am I, West Virginia? They probably still shit in holes in the ground out here. Craig sighed. *I doubt I'll be able to find my way back.*

His Rabbit struggled to climb the steep driveway, almost stalling in the process. At the top was an elegant Victorian-style house. The property abutted a small lake and was surrounded by woods on its other three sides. He took in the crisp, clean air. *God, I hate the rich. They get everything good.*

The house was enormous, with a four-car garage and a large three-tiered building attached that resembled a Japanese pagoda. Some might have found the culture clash somewhat gaudy or forced. Craig found it fascinating.

I didn't know Carter was so well off. He couldn't possibly have afforded all this just from teaching jiu-jitsu. Maybe I'm in the wrong business.

Craig climbed out of his car and joined Ricardo and Doug.

Carter came out of the house, dressed like a preppy playboy. "Hey, guys. Welcome!" Even though it was less than forty degrees outside, his sweater was tied over his shoulders, and he was wearing a Polo pullover, khakis, and brown loafers, without socks.

Craig did his best to hold back his goofy smirk as Carter walked toward them. "He looks straight out of an Old Spice commercial," he whispered to Ricardo. "He would have gotten his ass kicked for dressing like that at school back in my day. Heck, he should probably get his ass kicked for dressing like that now."

Ricardo let out a strained laugh and shifted away.

Carter approached Craig with his hand extended. "Hello, Craig. I'm glad you could make it."

Craig reached out to shake but recoiled when he saw a wet black smear across the back of Carter's hand.

Carter looked down at his hand. "Oh, sorry," he said, pulling his hand back. "It's blood. It turns black when I mix it with preservatives."

Not certain how to respond to that, Craig chuckled uneasily.

Carter grinned, showing off his perfect teeth. "I'm just messing with you. I thought you liked jokes." He rubbed the smear on his hand. "It's just paint. I'm touching up a room in the house. I've been at it all morning."

Craig frowned. "You're painting a room black?"

"No. I meant the furniture in it. The room itself is gray. It's my favorite color."

Craig gazed up at the house. "You could paint this place any color, and it would still look amazing."

"You think so? It's quiet, private. I like it. But it's not the type of place you want to be in when you lose power in a winter snowstorm. Fortunately, I have a generator."

"It's good to be prepared."

"Isn't that the Boy Scouts' motto? Or the army's? I forget which one. Anyway, did you bring your gi?"

"It's in my car. Do you have some place where I can change?"

"Right this way."

Craig retrieved his gym bag and followed the others into the house. The inside was as tasteful as the outside. Candles sat evenly spaced on the mantel of a fireplace. No mirror or painting had the slightest tilt. All wood was polished; Craig couldn't spot even the thinnest layer of dust on anything. Every room seemed straight out of a package, as if they had been set up for the sole purpose of fooling visitors, or maybe Carter himself, that the house was actually lived in.

But what Craig found most odd was the complete lack of photographs. He wondered if Carter had a girlfriend, family, or anyone besides his students and fellow Bible-reading bumpkins.

Carter led him to a bathroom the size of a bedroom. While Craig changed, he heard the guys talking just outside the door.

"Where's Kelly?" Carter asked.

"She's at the mill," Doug said. "Getting things ready."

"I thought I told her to be here."

"She didn't want to do this one. She felt she'd only be in the way. She knows him, and it made her a little uncomfortable." Doug paused. "She didn't want anything to cloud her judgment."

"You'd better get her on a shorter leash. Who's wearing the pants in your relationship, anyway?"

"It'll be fine, Carter. We can handle this without her."

"All right. Go get changed."

I didn't know Doug and Kelly owned a mill. Craig frowned. *Is everyone rich but me?*

Carter knocked on the bathroom door. "Craig, when you're done changing, just walk around back to the dojo. You can leave your stuff on the kitchen counter."

"Okay," Craig called.

When Craig finished changing, he opened the door. Looking around the empty room, he realized he had no idea where "around back" was. He turned right and walked down a long corridor that he hoped led to a back door. But when he opened the door at the end, he discovered a six-car garage.

"Cool!" He hurried down the few steps.

In addition to the array of power tools neatly organized along the wall and a workbench, he saw a collection of big-boy toys that made him salivate. Two four-wheel ATVs, a snowmobile, a dirt bike, and a jet ski, each one top of the line, called to him from one corner. He hopped aboard one of the ATVs and nearly squealed when he saw that its fuel tank was full and its keys dangled from the ignition. How he wanted to turn those keys and hear the beast purr, but he talked himself off the seat to check out the street vehicles Carter's garage had to offer—three cars: a cherry-red 1987 Corvette Stingray, a black 1969 Chevelle Supersport, and a black Chevrolet 3500 van.

This guy's got the coolest shit. Craig ran his hand along the Stingray's oversized hood. *He should lose the eighties van, though, unless he's trying out for the A-Team.*

Craig moved toward the snowmobile. He kicked something that rolled beneath the van. Bending over to look, he saw that it was a paint can. The floor was covered with newspaper. He figured Carter had been painting his furniture in there.

Craig turned to leave and slammed right into Carter. "Oh, sorry. I got lost."

"That's okay." Carter's expression briefly hinted at impatience, but his tone was calm. "It's this way." He pointed over his shoulder. "Follow me."

"You got a lot of cool stuff in there. I always wanted a four-wheeler. Maybe I'll steal one of yours when you're not looking." Craig laughed.

"There are lots of paths for them around here. If you want, we'll take them out after class."

"Sounds cool," Craig said, trying not to seem too eager.

He followed Carter back down the hallway. When he saw where they'd be practicing, he actually felt his penis throb. Carter's exercise area was world-class. Made up like an authentic Japanese dojo, it even had paper-thin partitions on three sides. That would have made it pretty cold in there, since they were technically outside, but space heaters took out some of the chill in the air. Doug and Ricardo, already in their uniforms, stood in the center of the sixty-foot-square matted floor.

"Upkeep on this thing must be a pain in the ass." At the threshold, Craig kicked off his shoes and bowed, then he stepped out onto the mat.

Carter did the same. "Yes, the weather does a number on it, but it's a small price to pay for the inner peace this place brings me."

"Are we it?"

"Looks like it," Carter replied. "Let's begin. If there are no objections, I thought we'd start with a chokehold. Doug, why don't you come here so I can use you to demonstrate?"

"Sure." Doug moved to stand near Carter.

"Ricardo, I'll walk you through it with Craig after I show it once. Doug, get on all fours."

Doug complied without hesitation.

"Okay. So you and your opponent have gone down to the mat in a typical judo or jiu-jitsu match. This is my favorite judo choke. It's a version of Hadaka Jime, or 'rear naked choke.' It's called this because you execute it from behind your opponent and don't have to use any portion of the gi to do it properly. Cops use it often, or at least they did until it was protested by hippie Democrats."

Carter looked over at Craig. "Did you wrestle in high school or college?"

"One season." Craig never could stick with one thing for too long, even when he'd been fairly good at something.

"If you have your opponent in this position, you may want to lock in what's referred to in wrestling as a double grapevine. Like this." Carter straddled Doug's back, curling his feet around Doug's inner thighs. "This would be a whole lot easier if Doug here wasn't so big." Carter looked as though he were attempting to ride a horse, except the horse he'd chosen had the girth of a buffalo.

Craig watched as Carter more-or-less bear-hugged the bear beneath him then rolled Doug on top of him. "That—" Craig stopped himself from saying that the hold looked kind of gay.

"Did you have a question, Craig?"

Craig shook his head. "No, I see what you did now."

"Okay. Once you get him on top of you, make a knife with your left hand. Dig it under his chin and across his neck—like you're trying to slice his throat with your hand first, then your arm. You want his Adam's apple to rest on the inside of your elbow. Once you're through, squeeze. How's that feel, Doug?"

"Tight," Doug said with a gurgle in his voice.

"Good. Now, I haven't even used my right arm yet, other than to keep him pinned. My left arm applies the choke. My right will lock it in. Take your left hand and put it on the inside of your right elbow... higher if you can. Now push the back of your opponent's head forward."

Doug gasped. His head looked like a Munchkin on top of a pretzel.

Carter grinned and applied more pressure. "After that, you should have him locked into place. Try to get out, Doug."

Doug struggled, shifting his weight around. He couldn't escape.

"See? If you get it in good, there's no getting out of it, no matter how big your opponent is. I'm stopping blood flow to his brain by putting pressure on his carotid arteries with my left arm, while pushing and holding him in tight with my right arm. The pressure should be on the sides of the neck, *not* on the Adam's apple. Doing that would hurt like heck, but it's not a chokehold."

Doug slapped his hand on the mat several times, signaling submission. His eyelids hung low over his eyes. His face was strained and plum colored.

Carter released his hold. Doug coughed, wheezing for breath.

"Sorry, Doug. I didn't realize I'd held it that long." Carter smiled and patted Doug's thigh. "You'll be fine." He stood and approached Craig and Ricardo. "Okay, Ricardo. Show me what you got. Craig can be your opponent."

Craig got down on all fours. Ricardo performed all the steps Doug had demonstrated. And once Ricardo had everything in place, he squeezed... hard.

Craig instantly felt pressure mounting in his head. *What the fuck! This is supposed to be just practice.* Craig winced, uncomfortable and breathless. He tapped Ricardo's arm to signify that it was time to let up. Ricardo squeezed harder.

Carter was staring down, smiling like a hyena over a carcass. Craig slapped the mat as hard as he could, flopping wildly. *Fucking let go already! This isn't funny!*

Ricardo wouldn't release him. Craig became light-headed. The room spun. With his remaining strength, he rolled onto his stomach, got up on his knees, then climbed to his feet. *This is for real.* Ricardo was trying to… *What? Knock me out? Kill me? Why?* He had to get free.

Ricardo clamped around him like a boa constrictor.

"Should I help—" Doug began.

"No. Ricardo's got this," Carter interrupted.

Through blurry eyes, Craig saw Carter smiling broadly, his eyes gleaming with approval. Doug looked concerned. Craig reached out to him. *Why won't you help me?*

Craig could feel his eyes bulging from the pressure, and his sight was fading. *No!* He fought back the darkness. In a final, desperate act, he reached around Ricardo's legs as though he were giving him a piggyback ride. Craig jumped as high as he could and tilted backward, sending all his weight careening down on Ricardo. The flimsy walls shook as they crashed to the floor. Ricardo's head ricocheted off the mat and into Craig's. The pain jolted him back to full consciousness.

"Block the door," Carter ordered.

Doug scrambled to obey.

Ricardo's arms fell away from Craig's throat, and Craig seized the moment. Wheezing, he leapt to his feet. Glancing at the Doug-blocked door and at Carter moving in on him, he dashed in the first open direction he saw. Each stride was a burden on his lungs, which desperately needed oxygen. He crashed through the wall, and it tore like dry paper around him. Once free, he ran into the woods.

CHAPTER 16

"**D**OES THAT GUY EVER SLEEP?" Bruce heard an officer say to another as they passed his office.

An accurate reflection of its possessor, his workspace was as disheveled as the rest of the department. Bruce had good reason to be disheveled. Nearly two months had gone by without finding hard evidence linking any suspect to the murders. Five victims were dead, leaving their families and friends with questions he couldn't answer. He'd never failed to solve a homicide case, but he'd also never worked a serial. A double homicide, a few heat-of-passion murders—husbands with cheating wives, parents who couldn't afford or stomach their children—and several armed robberies or drug deals turned fatal were the worst Bruce had faced. Still, he'd always managed to put all the clues together in a matter of weeks. But the new killers weren't sloppy, and despite their appetite for gruesome displays, they seemed to lack a desire for public notoriety.

"The more bodies, the more evidence, wouldn't you think?" he asked Jocelyn, who was slumped in the chair on the other side of his desk. She was the only person he couldn't intimidate with mere bravado, and he respected her for it. In addition, despite their greater number of years on the job, few other detectives shared her level of competency. The department needed more Jocelyns. Too bad she was one of a kind.

"It doesn't always work that way," she said. "You know that. These guys are good, or at the least, they're careful."

Bruce chewed the end of his pen, which was already a misshapen sculpture of plastic. "I don't think I could deal with something like those poor detectives in San Francisco, working the case for so many years and never catching the Zodiac. I can't handle losing."

"It's only been like eight weeks. We haven't lost anything yet. Stop being so pessimistic. Besides, I don't think these guys are going to stop. People are calling in every day with potential sightings of our van and our killers. It's just a matter of time before one of the calls is from a credible witness. You need to have patience, Bruce."

It took a moment, but Bruce realized his walls were down, not something he cared to show anyone. He couldn't believe how comfortable he'd become with his partner in such a short stint, and making matters worse, *she* was trying to comfort *him*. Her youthful optimism, the kind that time and experience sucked dry, made his skin crawl.

"Shouldn't I be the one telling you that?" He straightened and snapped back to his old self. "Any luck with the phone records?"

"For number four? Not yet. The call to Huntley was made via a disposable phone. Those things have identification numbers. We're seeing if we can pinpoint when and where it was sold and then, hopefully, to whom."

"Good. I need some coffee. When I get back, we can go over the autopsy reports one more time. You want anything?"

"No, thanks."

Bruce strode to the break room. *How long has this coffee been sitting here? What is that crap on the bottom?* He stared at the semi-liquid, semi-plasma substance pretending to be coffee. A tired old man stared back at him from the liquid's surface. He'd seen those sunken eyes, that sallow skin, the crow's feet that reached out to his temples, and the thinning mat of hair many times, and every time, he thought, *I should retire.* But he never would, not until they made him. Retiring meant sitting at home, alone in his apartment, waiting to die.

As Bruce fiddled with the coffee machine, Officers Brian Temple and David "Sven" Stravenski passed in the hall, heading toward Aaron Pimental's desk. Both were smiling, and they walked with a bit of a bounce in their steps. *What the fuck are they so happy about?* He kept one ear on their conversation while he brewed a fresh pot of coffee.

Bruce glanced through the doorway. Pimental sat at his desk, staring vacantly at its unpolished surface. He looked as though he would rather have been anywhere but there. Bruce wondered why the department had hired the guy. He clearly had no interest in police work.

Pimental looked up as Temple and Stravenski arrived at his desk. "Hey, guys. What's up?"

"We got the rest of the lists from the Commonwealth," Temple said in a much too peppy voice. "There's only about twelve more for us to investigate."

Bruce cringed. As much as he didn't like Pimental's poor attitude, he hated morning people more. For someone who slept as little as Bruce did, "morning" extended to three in the afternoon.

"Yeah, because that last batch worked out so well for us," Pimental replied.

Stravenski grunted in agreement. He hadn't had much luck with his portion of the highway department's list of registered van users, either. The three of them had looked like fools and wasted the department's time and resources. Although Bruce wasn't held responsible for their inadequacies, he *felt* responsible. He'd given those clowns the go-ahead, and they'd come up with diddly squat.

Temple shrugged. "Well, these are our marching orders, like it or not."

"Who are the lists from?" Pimental asked.

"Department of Public Health, DCF, Department of Corrections… a few others. There are only a few names per list."

"Can I see them?"

Temple held the lists as though they were precious. He hesitated, sighed, then handed them to Pimental.

"Douglas Fournier," Pimental read aloud. "We can cross him off the list, and DEP, too, for that matter."

"Why's that?" Stravenski asked.

"I know Doug. Trust me, it's not him. And he's the only one on your lists from the Department of Environmental Protection, so we can scratch that department."

"Why?" Temple asked, sounding annoyed. "Just because you know the guy doesn't mean he's not a killer."

"No, Brian, the fact that the guy spends all his time attending church, volunteering, and generally trying to save the world from itself tells me he's not a killer. Doug is harmless, a 'Jesus freak,' as my friend would call him."

Bruce nearly sprayed coffee out his mouth. "Who's a Jesus freak?" he asked between coughs as he ran over to the officers, coffee splashing onto his hands.

"A friend of mine." Pimental sat up straight. "He's on one of the lists that we're using to investigate the murders."

Bruce looked at Temple. "Way to stay on top of this, Temple. Nice job."

Pimental's jaw dropped. Temple grinned with pride.

Bruce said, "I want to know where this Doug... what's his full name again?"

"Fournier," Pimental answered.

"Right. I want to know where he is and what he's doing twenty-four seven, starting immediately. Don't screw this one up, guys. I want to know everything and anything there is to know about him. Temple and you," Bruce said, pointing at Stravenski. "Find his van, and find it now! Pimental, in my office. You're going to tell me and Detective Beaudette everything you know about this Douglas Fournier."

CHAPTER 17

CRAIG'S PANIC SENT HIM BARRELING through brush, deep into the forest. He finally stopped to catch his breath at the edge of a brook. The soles of his feet were shredded, and his teeth jackhammered together from the cold. He had to get back to his car, or he would end up freezing to death.

Remaining under cover, he cut a wide circle around where he was pretty sure the house sat. Every now and then, he heard Carter or Ricardo call his name, their voices barely audible over the rumbling motors of the same ATVs Craig had wanted to try out earlier.

He picked up a branch. *I need to take one of them out, steal one of their four-wheelers. That's probably my best bet. I'm not sure how much more of the cold I can take. Just knock one on his ass and ride on out of here.* Craig needed to do something quickly before his body shut down from hypothermia or before he was spotted in his bright-white gi in a dead brown forest.

He told himself to calm down, think it through, and weigh his options. *Attack one of them and steal his ATV?* He shook his head. *Unless I get the jump on him, he'll probably run me down. Who knows what weapons they grabbed before heading out?*

"Why is this happening to me?" He almost started to cry before summoning his composure.

He considered sneaking back into the house and grabbing his keys or their keys, but that was too risky. He would have to break in after leaving the sparse cover for no cover. Plus, his keys might not be where he left them. He was running out of options. *Even if I make it to the road, they're guaranteed to spot me, and I can't keep traveling through these woods barefoot.* Desperation hit hard. *This is fucking crazy.*

Craig took a deep breath. *Well, one thing's certain. If I try to wait it out, I'll freeze to death. I need to keep moving, keep the blood circulating. The days are short this time of year. It'll be night soon and get a whole lot colder.*

He worked his way back to within fifty yards of the house. He could see down the western slope of Carter's property toward the lake beside the house. The sun, low in the sky, cast an eerie glow on the still, black water. Only a thin line of purple along the horizon separated the world from darkness.

Something across the lake caught his eye. It gave him his first semblance of hope since he'd escaped his former friend's grasp. *That light! That's another house!*

The shimmering light was faint but definitely real. A female voice yelled something. *Is she calling out to me? No, she can't be. Should I yell for help?* Craig shuddered. He knew that screaming would reveal his location. And she was all the way across the lake. Even if he could make her understand that he needed help, Carter and his crew would get to him first.

A dog barked and ran toward the woman. The pair retreated into the warm confines of their cozy country home, oblivious to the horror Craig faced and the monster that lived a few miles away. The light disappeared, taking with it that small semblance of hope he had fostered.

Then, Craig remembered something. *The kayaks! Where there's a farm, there's a phone.* Craig set his jaw and flexed his fingers. *I just need to get there. The shortest distance between two points is a straight line.* He listened for the sound of engines but heard nothing. *They must be too far away. Now's my chance!* He jogged down toward the beach. After a pause to listen and look around, he sprinted over to the first kayak. He dragged it the fifteen feet to the water then slid it in as quickly and as quietly as he could.

The noise from the kayak was nothing compared to the yelp he failed to suppress as his feet entered the icy liquid. Craig thought his feet had gone numb, but the cold sent tingly pain through his body like a jolt of electricity. It revitalized his sense of touch and reawakened his terror.

He hopped into the kayak, partially just to get out of the water. He sat as still as he could while shivering and listened intently for signs that his cry had been heard. Other than his own heavy breathing, he heard no sounds. He pulled up the oar, which fortunately was stashed down in the bottom of the boat. Pushing off the lake bottom, he propelled the vessel forward.

He'd only made it about ninety yards when he heard the sound of a motor. He drew in the paddle, letting the kayak drift. *Could they have heard my splashing over their engines?* He cursed himself for being so stupid.

He bent at the waist and put his chest to his knees. If he kept low in the seat, maybe they wouldn't see him. He spotted Doug and Ricardo pulling up to the beach on one of the four-wheelers. Carter followed closely on a dirt bike, still wearing his gi but sporting a helmet and sneakers. He parked beside Ricardo and Doug.

From their wild hand gestures, Craig guessed that Ricardo and Carter were arguing. *Probably about what to do with me.* He couldn't hear their words until the purring of their engines died.

"Tell him we were just fucking with him," Carter said.

"I got this," Ricardo said. He cupped his hands around his mouth and shouted to Craig. "What the hell are you doing? And why'd you break Carter's wall?"

"Fuck you, asshole!" Craig resumed paddling.

"Dude, you're acting crazy."

"I'm acting crazy? *I'm* acting crazy? You fuckers tried to *kill* me!"

"You're completely overreacting. We were only kidding. We knew you were paranoid about being followed, so we decided to play a joke on you. I admit it was a stupid idea. If we knew you were gonna freak out, we wouldn't have done it. But, Craig, you have to come back in, get out of this cold. You could be seriously hurt."

"That's fucked up, man. Joke or no joke, I'm not going anywhere near you guys."

"I'm sorry. You're right. It was a dumb joke. That's on us. If you want to leave, then fine. But shouldn't you take your car? I don't expect you to not be angry, but look at yourself. If you stay out there, you could die."

"I don't trust you. Leave me the hell alone." Craig had nearly reached the lake's center.

"You're going to freeze to death. Come in."

"You tried to kill me!"

"No, Craig, I didn't. Come on, man! How long have we been friends? I told you, it was a joke. Obviously, it was a bad one. But if we wanted to kill you, we wouldn't be wasting our time talking to you. Hell, we could have just shot you a long time ago. We could drive to the other side of the lake and wait for you there."

Ricardo paused, perhaps waiting for some acknowledgment. Craig said nothing.

"My point is," Ricardo continued, "no one wants to kill you. Carter's a little angry about what you did to his wall, but his insurance will cover it."

"Fuck Carter, and fuck his insurance!" Although he had no explanation for why his friend of twenty years would suddenly turn into a crazed maniac, Craig still didn't trust him. Ricardo's words made sense. At least they made more sense than the idea that one of his best friends wanted to kill him. Everyone said Craig was paranoid. Maybe it was true.

"Don't you see how silly this is?" Ricardo sounded sincere. "Craig, no bullshit. You could die out there. Don't you think you're being a bit irrational? You've been edgy lately with that whole van-following-you thing. This paranoia has to stop."

"I'm not fucking paranoid!" Craig was scared, but he was starting to feel foolish. *Am I? Here I am, out on a fucking kayak in the middle of December, freezing my ass off because I think one of my closest friends is trying to kill me. But he did try to kill me, didn't he? Choking is part of the sport, but he must have felt me tap, at least the second time.*

"Craig, come inside and get warm," Carter called. "You can take a hot shower."

Craig didn't respond. No one spoke or moved.

"All right, Craig. Be stubborn," Ricardo yelled. "We're going back inside. I already said I'm sorry. We're all worried about you. What more can I do? When you come to your senses, feel free to join us."

Ricardo, Carter, and Doug started their vehicles and rode up the beach toward the house, never looking back to see if he would follow. *Are they playing me? Or am I just being stupid? Rick's changed a lot this last year, but why would he try to kill me?*

Craig paddled farther out, not willing to risk his life on the word of a friend he could no longer trust. The adrenalin flowing through his body slowed, and the biting cold returned. He looked across the lake. He was barely past the midpoint.

"This is stupid! I'm freezing."

His feet were raw and freezing. He feared he would lose his toes if he didn't get inside soon. He stared across the lake. Even after he got to the opposite shore, he would have to trek another mile or two through thick woods before he made it to that farmhouse. *By then, my cock will be so frozen, I'll have to live with shrinkage for the rest of my life.* He glanced back at Carter's house. He saw no sign of Ricardo or the others. They weren't after him. They never had been.

I'm so fucking stupid. He turned around and rowed back toward Carter's house.

When he reached the shoreline, he braced himself for the step into the cold water. Fortunately, the pain wasn't as bad as he'd anticipated because his feet were pretty much numb. He pulled the end of the kayak onto land then stumbled up the slope to the house. Twilight had come and gone, and the whole area was shrouded in darkness. He was glad not to be plodding through woods and trespassing on some stranger's land. *What was I going to do when I got there? Call the cops on Ricardo?* The whole thing seemed silly. Still, he couldn't shake his doubts.

Ricardo, his longtime friend who had never harmed anyone, wouldn't try to kill him. There was no reason for it.

But Ricardo *had* changed. Not only had his sight improved, but he'd grown stronger and quicker since he'd first started training with Carter. Craig wondered if steroids had something to do with it. *'Roid rage might explain his intense chokehold.* He would never accuse his friend of illegal drug use and thought it better not to know. How, then, could he accuse him of attempted murder?

When he reached the house, he peered through a window. Ricardo, Carter, and Doug were sitting in the living room, drinking from mugs. Craig licked his chapped lips. He wanted one of those mugs. He limped around to the front door and waited until he wasn't panting so hard before ringing the doorbell.

"Who is it?" Doug snickered from behind the door.

"Come on. Open up."

"What's the secret password?"

"Are you four?"

"Are you four?" Doug mimicked. "Nope, I don't think that's the password. Hold on, let me ask Carter."

"Are you having fun?" Craig yelled.

"Carter, is 'are you four' the secret password?"

"Just let him in," Carter said.

Craig pounded on the door. "Give me my fucking keys already!"

"For God's sake, Doug, let him in," Ricardo said. "He's got to be as frozen as a Popsicle."

Finally, a voice of reason. The door swung open, and Doug stepped aside to let Craig in. But Craig didn't budge.

"See? No one is trying to kill you," Carter said, his arms out by his sides as he walked over to the door. Carter's smile seemed sincere, but Craig couldn't be sure.

He stayed on the porch. "Where's my stuff?"

"It's right there on the counter," Carter said, waving a hand. "Craig, you're a mess, and your feet may need medical attention. Why don't you get cleaned up so we can see the extent of the damage."

"I wouldn't need medical attention if it weren't for you three douchebags."

"Okay, we deserve that."

"You're damn right you do. Step back and let me grab my stuff. I'm leaving."

"If you don't mind, I'll get it for you," Carter said. "Blood and mud aren't easy to clean off the rug."

"Fine. Just get me my crap. My cell phone should be over there, too."

Carter walked to the kitchen counter and picked up Craig's gym bag. With his other hand, he scooped up the phone, wallet, and keys next to it. He strode back to the doorway. "Here you go," Carter said, handing the gym bag to Craig. "And the rest of your stuff."

Holding his bag in his right hand, Craig reached out with his left to grab his other items. Just as his keys were dropped into his hand, an excruciating pain shot through his left leg. He screamed and collapsed to the ground.

Carter had delivered a kick to Craig's kneecap. Craig tried to sit up, but all he could do was lie there, crying. His leg was shaped like a boomerang, bending in the wrong direction.

Carter took a step and sent another kick to Craig's ribcage. "That's for my wall." He turned to Ricardo and Doug. "Drag him into the garage. I need to clean up this mess. I mean, look at this doorstep. He tracked mud everywhere. He's not a very courteous houseguest, if you ask me."

Doug and Ricardo each grabbed Craig by an arm. He squealed as they dragged him, but he was in too much pain to put up any real struggle.

"We're doing this for your sake," Ricardo whispered. "You'll see. One day, you'll thank us."

Craig stared at the blurry ceiling. He couldn't see where they were taking him. But when he heard a vehicle door slide open, he cursed himself for missing the detail that could have saved him.

Oh God! He wasn't painting furniture. He was painting the fucking van! Panic jumbled his thoughts. Breathing became difficult. At last, the meaning became clear. Bile rose in his throat. He convulsed and threw up all over his chest.

As Ricardo and Doug hoisted him into the back of the van, Carter appeared behind them. His sinister smile had returned.

Give me one chance, and I'll rip that fucking smile right off your face, you son of a bitch, Craig wanted to say, but what came out sounded like a drunken slur. He tried to stay awake but only drifted closer to unconsciousness.

"Are we ready to go?" Doug asked.

"Not just yet," Carter said. "I still need to switch the plates. Once I'm done with that, you two go on ahead. I'll meet you there in a couple of hours."

CHAPTER 18

DETECTIVE MARKLIN'S STARE BORED HOLES in the back of Aaron's skull as he typed up a report. He cringed each time he made a typo, which was often with Marklin hovering over him like a prison rapist.

"Any update?" Marklin asked.

"We're working on it," Aaron said. *And we'd probably go a lot faster without you breathing down our necks.*

"It's been four hours."

"It's the weekend. He could be anywhere. We have someone watching the house and an APB out on the van. No one has reported in with anything."

"Well, time's being wasted. If this guy is our killer, he's due for another murder. Every second could matter."

Aaron hated being forced to work directly with his overbearing superior. Marklin had a point, but only if Doug was, in fact, the killer. He wondered what he'd said that could have given the detective that impression. He'd tried to dissuade Marklin from following up on his hunch. But Marklin wouldn't be swayed. Aaron needed evidence to prove him wrong.

So much for innocent until proven guilty. Doug was like a big teddy bear. In fact, he was kind of a sissy. From what Aaron had seen, Doug's wife had his balls locked up so tight, he couldn't piss without her say-so. *He can't be the monster we're looking for.*

But Aaron had to concede that he didn't really know Doug. They'd spent time together on many occasions, but they weren't exactly close. Their pseudo-relationship was a by-product of their separate friendships with Ricardo. Aaron knew Ricardo well, though, and he'd always vouched for Doug. *There's just no way Rick is friends with a serial killer. He's blind, but not stupid. He would have noticed something strange by now and mentioned it to me.*

Marklin had disagreed, saying something about serial killers hiding in plain sight, always trying to look normal… or some other bullshit. Aaron hadn't really been listening. What he thought didn't matter. Marklin was calling the shots, and Aaron was forced to assist. Marklin wanted immediate answers to questions Aaron couldn't answer, which only fueled his superior's impatience and irritability.

He's probably still mad about that whole blanket incident. Aaron recalled how Eliza Ramirez had been strewn across the garbage, discarded like the rest of the filth. The blanket was the least he could have done for her. He hoped Ricardo never found out about their investigation.

Marklin jabbed a finger at him. "Get a few more officers involved. This is priority one. You're on point for the time being, until you screw up. I want Fournier's phone records checked. I want to see his credit card statements. I want his trash examined for receipts, disposable phones, odd-shaped garden tools, duct tape, women's underwear… anything, I don't care. Just get it done."

Even if Doug was the killer, he wouldn't be dumb enough to buy his murder weapon on eBay with his MasterCard. Aaron rolled his eyes. "Do we have a search warrant for any of this?"

"Do whatever you have to do. Let me worry about the necessary warrants. He's your friend, isn't he? Invite yourself over and snoop around. Be a damn police officer, for God's sake. Did you even try calling him yet?"

"I don't have his number. He's more of a friend of a friend."

"So call your friend and ask him for Fournier's number. Make up some bullshit reason to meet him, then do some investigating. This shouldn't be so difficult."

I'm not completely stupid, thanks. "I already tried calling my friend." Aaron wasn't lying. He had tried calling Ricardo earlier, albeit on other matters, but Marklin didn't need to know that. "He's not answering. I left him a message to call me back. And no, I didn't tell him why I was calling." Aaron thought about Ricardo and Doug and their silly Bible studies, sitting around and singing "Kumbaya," praising some immaterial apostle and drinking Kool-Aid while... "Oh shit! I know exactly where they are."

"Better late than never, I suppose." Marklin raised one eyebrow. "Care to share?"

"Doug should be at this guy Carter's house. They were going to work out or something. Carter teaches martial arts."

"Now we're getting somewhere." For a second, Marklin looked as though he might smile. The second passed. "What's Carter's last name?" he asked gruffly.

"Don't know."

"Okay. Where does he live?"

"Don't know that, either."

Marklin's scowl returned.

Aaron tried to come up with something helpful. "Carter teaches judo or aikido or some other O in Somerset. I think it's the only dojo in town. If he's incorporated, I can look him up on the Internet. We could find his address that way."

"All right, get on it. I want an answer in two minutes. I'll grab my jacket." Marklin hurried off down the hallway, peeking through doorways and getting everyone's nerves up. The detective might have even gone into the women's restroom.

Aaron turned his attention to his computer. He found the dojo. The business was incorporated, and Carter had listed himself as its registered agent, complete with a Rehoboth mailing address.

Marklin returned. "Damn! Where's Detective Beaudette when I need her?" He frowned at Aaron. "Looks like you're my backup. If you know where we're going, let's go."

Bruce and Officer Pimental followed Officer Pamela Stevens, their liaison with the Rehoboth Police Department, to Carter Wainwright's secluded home. Bruce felt a little out of his skin. Rehoboth's farms and forests contrasted starkly with the city. At least in the slums of Fall River, he knew what to expect. In that rural seclusion, unseen by the rest of the world, anything could be hiding. He no longer had home-field advantage.

Pimental sat beside him in silence, looking as if he'd just swallowed coffee someone had pissed in. Bruce wasn't the least bit concerned how his investigation might impact the officer's personal life. He didn't care if the suspect was Pimental's college roommate, best friend, or even his father. The job, as it always had, came first.

When Bruce and Pimental arrived, Officer Stevens met them on the driveway and led them up the steep slope to the front door. She stepped aside and allowed Pimental to ring the bell.

A moment later, a man in a black T-shirt and plaid pajama bottoms opened the door. He flashed a million-dollar smile. "Hello, Officers. What can I do for you?" He did a double take when he spotted Officer Pimental. "Do I know you?"

"I'm Officer Aaron Pimental with the Fall River Police Department, and I'm a good friend of Ricardo Jimenez. We'd just like to ask you a few questions."

Bruce watched for signs of recognition in Pimental's face. If he knew Wainwright or even thought he might know him, Pimental did a fine job of hiding it.

"Sure thing, Aaron," Wainwright said. "Is it all right if I call you that? I feel like I already know you from all of the pictures Ricardo has at his house. You've known him for a long time?"

"Aaron's fine, and yes, Ricardo and I have been friends for many years."

Bruce coughed, hoping Pimental would take the hint and introduce him. He felt foolish standing there in silence as his officer and a potential witness carried on meaningless chitchat.

Pimental turned. "This is Officer Pamela Stevens and Detective Bruce Marklin. Detective Marklin leads—"

"Hello, Mr. Wainwright," Bruce interrupted, nudging his officer aside. "Do you know Douglas Fournier?"

"Yes, of course. He's a student of mine. Why do you ask? Is he okay?"

"Do you know where we might find him?"

"I'm afraid not. He and a few others were supposed to be here hours ago. I've tried calling them, but so far, there's been no answer. I figured something came up. Is everything all right?" Wainwright's concern seemed genuine.

"There's no need to worry," Pimental said. "We just want to talk to Doug."

With a look that would have made Hercules cower, Bruce said, "Stand down, Pimental." He wouldn't normally belittle an officer in front of a civilian or even another officer, but he needed to be the one to do the talking. Bruce turned back to Wainwright. "When was the last time you saw him?"

"I don't know, probably Tuesday at class. I teach jiu-jitsu a few nights a week in Somerset." Wainwright's brow wrinkled. "What's this all about, Detective? I can't imagine that Doug would be in some kind of trouble with the law."

"We can't discuss that. Your cooperation, however, is appreciated. Does Doug have a van?"

"Well, I don't think he owns one, but he sometimes drives one for work."

Bruce noticed that while they talked, Wainwright stayed framed in the doorway, effectively blocking any view inside. Bruce had made it a rule that whenever a witness or suspect tried to stop him from doing something, he would insist on doing it. "Do you mind if we come in?"

"Not at all. *Mi casa, su casa.*" Wainwright stepped aside.

Bruce nodded and led the other two officers into the foyer, which opened up into a sparsely but finely decorated living room. A white leather sofa and love seat stood on a pristine snow-white carpet. A crackling fireplace radiated warmth. Paintings that looked pricey splashed the walls with vibrant colors—reds and golds and oranges, a motionless inferno. The life they gave to the home seemed fabricated, false. The room reflected taste and refinement, but something else Bruce couldn't put his finger on. Something that made him shiver.

Wainwright smiled, an expression that also seemed fabricated. "Please, have a seat." He ushered them over to the couch. "Would you like some coffee?"

"No, thanks."

Pimental and Stevens sat, but Bruce remained standing.

"We won't take up too much more of your time," he said.

"Carter, you coming back to bed?" a woman called from deeper in the house.

Wainwright's face turned a pinkish hue from either anger or embarrassment. "Not just yet. I'll be there in a few minutes."

"Who's that?" Bruce asked. "Caught you at a bad time, have we?"

"My girlfriend. We were—"

"Say no more." Bruce had no interest in Wainwright's love life. Bruce had inventoried the entire room within seconds of entering. He could recall every item's placement with his eyes closed. His focus lingered on an oil canvas. "Do you know what that painting depicts?"

"Of course," Wainwright replied. "I bought it."

Bruce played dumb. "It's quite impressive. The use of color contrast and lighting is striking. What civilization does it represent?"

"How well do you know your Mesoamerican history, Detective?"

"How far back are we talking?" With thumb and forefinger on his chin, Bruce pretended to study the painting. "It looks maybe Mayan or Aztec."

"Quite right, Detective. The painting portrays the clash of two civilizations. More accurately, it shows the rise of one civilization and the fall of another and, with it, the end of the age of Mesoamerican gods." He pointed at a man dressed in sixteenth-century Spanish armor, sword in hand, climbing the ancient temple's steps. "That's Cortez, the conquistador credited with the downfall of the Aztec civilization. At the top of the temple is the last Aztec king, Moctezuma, painted in red: blood. The once-mighty king never understood Cortez's true intentions until it was too late. He makes his final stand on one of the twin temples, either Uitzilopoichtli or Tlaloc, where Mexico City is today."

"Wasn't that temple used for human sacrifice?" Bruce asked.

"It was. Aztec priests would open the chests of their victims with a stone knife and tear the hearts from their bodies." Wainwright's voice thrummed with too much enthusiasm. "They would raise the heart high, steaming it in the hot sun, an offering to Quetzalcoatl, their sun god. The steam represented the victim's life force, his soul more or less, set free to rise to the heavens. They believed that cosmic order could only be achieved through sacrifice and death. Chaos bred chaos in cyclic fashion, until in the end, the entire civilization was lost."

"Don't you mean slaughtered?" Officer Stevens asked. "If you ask me, the Spaniards did the world a favor by ridding it of those bloodthirsty murderers."

Wainwright shrugged. "Your point is well taken, but who are we to judge? Perhaps history merely did what it always does: substituted one evil for another. After all, the Spaniards were slaughtering entire races for gold in Mesoamerica, while torturing and killing in the name of Christianity through the Inquisition back home. To me, the painting serves as a constant reminder that no matter who we are or where we're from, we all have evil in our hearts that we must face and conquer. It's easy to recognize the darkness in others, but not so the darkness within ourselves."

"Well said." Bruce meant it. Despite all the red flags being waved in his face, he couldn't help but think he'd found a kindred spirit. "People say that change is the only constant. I believe there's another constant in this crazy world of ours: human nature. *Humanity* is the coldest of words. Its definition is at odds with our true nature—selfish, groveling, and pathetically immoral. As you might imagine, I see the depravity in humanity every day in my line of work. It will never change."

"Well, there are good people and bad people wherever you go." Wainwright chuckled. "But the reality is: I just like the painting and watch way too much History Channel. They have a special on Sparta this weekend that I'm dying to see. I'll probably have a painting of that by the end of next week."

"I don't suppose you practice human sacrifice in the name of your god?" Bruce had intended the joke to provoke a reaction. But if it had any effect on Wainwright, he couldn't spot it.

"I've never even so much as taken communion. Eating the body of Christ is kind of creepy, don't you think?"

"I take it you're not Catholic then?"

"Nope. No organized religion for me. It's just a means to control the masses. I'm sorry, but it's not for me."

"But aren't you part of Ricardo's Bible studies?" Pimental asked.

"I don't support *organized* religion. I didn't say I wasn't religious."

"That's ironic," Officer Stevens said. "The guy who owned this house before you was some kind of Liberian evangelist. He might have brought down the wrath of God on you if he'd heard you say that." She laughed. "Quite the character, he was."

Wainwright chuckled. "I don't know much about the previous owners. They did seem kind of... rigid, though. I doubt they would have approved of the addition I made to their house."

A man after my own heart. Bruce studied his host closely. *Educated and cynical. Still, the man raises too many suspicions.* He wondered how much more of the house Wainwright would let him see. "Now that you mention it," Bruce said, "I couldn't help but notice that unique structure. Is it some sort of pagoda?"

"Oh, that's my dojo. As I said, I teach jiu-jitsu and other forms of martial arts, sometimes here at the house. You're not going to report me to the zoning commission, are you?"

"May I see it? I'm a bit of a martial arts enthusiast myself," Bruce lied.

"Excellent. What discipline?"

"I did karate for many years as a kid," he lied again.

"We don't do too much of that. But if you're interested in practicing with us, here's my card." Wainwright pulled a plain business card from his pocket. His eyes shimmered as if he found the thought of a policeman practicing with him appetizing. He gestured to a hallway to the right of the living room. "The dojo's right this way."

As they walked through the house, Bruce took in as much of the interior as possible. Try as he might, he could find nothing out of the ordinary.

"Nice place you've got here, Carter," Pimental said as he brought up the rear.

"So I've been told." Wainwright stopped in front of a door and opened it. "And here we are."

"Damn!" Pimental blurted.

Bruce frowned, but he had to admit he was equally impressed. The dojo was magnificent, like something right out of a movie, as much a work of art as a place of exercise. With wooden walkways, bamboo blinds, and even a green slate stone *kamiza* with a Shinto shrine, it was perfect—except for the glaring hole in the wall.

"What happened over there?" Bruce asked.

"Yeah, that." Wainwright sneered. "We had a workout here, and some of the guys got a little too competitive. I told them to pay attention to where they were going, but two of them crashed right through the wall. Hopefully, my insurance will cover it."

"You should make the two guys pay for it," Pimental said.

"I know, right? It pisses me off. But I guess it's my own fault for bringing them here in the first place."

"You're lucky it wasn't Doug," Pimental said. "You'd have a much bigger hole. He might have taken your house down with him."

Wainwright's laugh seemed a bit forced. "That's true. Doug is a big one, isn't he?"

Bruce tuned out their conversation. His real interest was in the hole in the wall. He moved toward it to investigate.

"That will be fixed before our next class, should you decide to come," Wainwright said loudly.

"Huh?" Bruce turned, noticing Wainwright and the officers' stares. "Oh, right. Well, it was a pleasure meeting you, Mr. Wainwright." He hesitated. "Wainwright? What kind of name is that anyway? English?" He examined the man's face. With his Mediterranean features, he was a slightly darker version of Pat Boone. "I hope you don't find me rude for asking, but what ethnicity are you?"

"I don't know," Wainwright said, smiling almost as though he had expected the question. "I was adopted."

"Oh." Bruce had hoped to learn more about his host. He had a feeling he'd be back to Wainwright's home soon. "Well, we'll be off, then. Thanks for your assistance."

"If I can help, please give me a call. You have my card. I don't know what this is about, but I'd gladly vouch for Doug's character if it's in question."

Wainwright's feigned innocence was lost on Bruce, a man skeptical of all people and things. *Even the devil was an angel once.* "I'm sure you'll be hearing from us again. Thank you for your time." He turned to Pimental and Stevens. "Let's go."

As he got into his old Buick Skylark, Bruce's mind raced with speculation. "Here's his card," he said to Pimental. "Get me everything there is to know about this guy ASAP."

Here we are investigating what could be ritualistic human sacrifice, and I just happen to talk to a guy who has a painting that honors a dead race famous for it. All that research and investigation with no results, then this just falls into our laps. "Let this be a lesson to you, Pimental. Sometimes the toughest cases are solved with a mere stroke of luck."

Pimental didn't respond. Bruce was fairly certain the officer had no idea what he was talking about. Bruce reached for his phone and dialed his partner's number.

Jocelyn picked up on the second ring. "Bruce, where are you?"

"I'm looking into some new information on our case over at the house of Douglas Fournier's jiu-jitsu instructor. He has the most peculiar painting."

"What's his relationship to the case?"

"I'm not sure yet, but my gut tells me he's smack dab in the middle of it. Jocelyn, what do you know about the Aztecs?"

———————

After the officers left, Carter returned to his bedroom. He crawled into bed beside the beautiful naked woman who'd startled his houseguests with an expected call out from the darkness.

I'm lucky she didn't come out. I can't believe they didn't ask her to. He felt goose bumps rise on her skin as he caressed her arm.

She bit her lip, lust shining in her eyes, then nestled in closer against him. "What was that all about?"

"That was the police. I called them about the attempted break-in. I had told them to come by later in the week, since I don't expect them to find the guy. I guess they don't have enough to do because they came right over." *Uninvited, fucking pigs.* He wondered how Doug had managed to attract their attention.

"The police? Ugh! I tried to help them out with… the death of a friend of mine, and they all but treated me like I was the murderer."

"I know. They're useless." He sighed. "Still, I need to file a report for insurance purposes. I had to show them the dojo, but it's all taken care of now. I'm all yours, beautiful." *I'm glad they didn't ask to see the garage.*

She surely would have heard the gun go off, then I'd have four more bodies to clean up. This was sloppy... too sloppy. The police got too close too damn fast. Had they come an hour earlier, we all might be sitting in a jail cell right now. It's time to move on. He sighed deeply. *Too bad. I liked being Carter Wainwright.*

"Is something wrong?" she asked.

Carter shook it off. "No, honey. Sorry."

"Well, if there is, I know how to make you feel better." She reached down and put her hand on his cock, which hardened immediately.

"I bet you do, Maura."

CHAPTER 19

"**R**ICK, YOU'RE MY FRIEND, AREN'T you?" Tears streamed down Craig's cheeks. "Why would you do something like this to me?"

He'd awakened to find his wrists and ankles tied with nylon cord. Doug and Ricardo had taken every precaution. The binds were unnecessary, though; his swollen, misshapen leg made standing impossible. He wouldn't be walking out of there.

Ricardo stared down at him with reddened eyes. "I'm doing this *because* we're friends," Ricardo said.

"Why did you bring me here? Where are we? What's this all about?"

"We're in an old mill in Fall River, closed, not too far from the Quasar Fabrics factory. All our tools are here. It's a convenient location—"

"For killing people?"

Ricardo hung his head. "For redeeming them."

Craig was still in the dark on most things, but his failure to heed that raw gut instinct that had warned him of real—not imagined—danger manifested in a silent scream that forced his mouth open. Eyes clenched shut, he felt his breath hitch in his chest. *Why did I turn the kayak back around? I knew, damn it.* His eyelids pressed tighter still, squeezing droplets from their corners. *God, I'm so stupid.* He dug his nails into his palms. *I knew.* "You're him, aren't you? You're the one who's been killing all those people?"

"Sort of. We all are: me, Carter, Doug, and Kelly. There was one more of us, but she…"

"What? Did you kill her, too?"

"In a way. We failed her."

"And the van that I thought was following me?"

"That was Carter and Doug."

Tears sprang from his eyes. "Why?"

"I don't expect you to understand. We're doing this *for* you."

"For me? How is this helping me? Do I look like I want this?"

"I know how this sounds to an atheist, but we're going to save your soul from damnation."

"What?" Craig was astounded. "What if I don't want you to save me, Rick? Did that thought ever occur to you?"

"We know you don't. That's why this is necessary. If you won't give your soul to God willingly, then for your sake, we'll do it for you."

"Have you completely lost touch with reality? You can't be fucking serious."

"I'm sorry, Craig. I—"

"Ever hear of free will, asshole?"

"Yes. It's a misguided concept that leads many straight to hell. I'll miss you, but you should count yourself lucky. We can only do the Lord's work for so many. I'm happy to know that one day, because of what we do here, I'll see you again."

"Lucky?" Had he been free, Craig would have wrapped his fingers around Ricardo's neck and squeezed the life out of his former friend. But the slightest shift sent daggers of pain up his leg. "Rick, listen to me. I don't want to be saved, and I sure as hell don't want to die. This isn't you. What you're doing is wrong. We were both born and raised Catholic. God doesn't want you to do this. Listen to how crazy it sounds."

"First, I'm not Catholic. And second, I know how it sounds. Believe me, I was skeptical at first. They kept me tied up for days until I finally opened my eyes to what they'd been trying to show me all along. Faith is something you feel, and I've felt it. It's on a plane far higher than soulless logic."

"It's all a fairy tale, you moron! Make believe! Stuff you tell children to make sure they grow up right 'cause, God forbid, if they do anything not so squeaky clean and enjoy life, they'll be burned and tortured for all of eternity."

Ricardo set his jaw. "Carter has shown us God's plan. Look at me, Craig. I can see! How else can you explain that? Sure, my sight isn't perfect, but it gets better with every soul we save. When we take their hearts inside us, we grow stronger. We can actually feel it happening. Doug can probably bench close to six hundred pounds now. Kelly can complete a Rubik's cube in less than thirty seconds. Our growth is a sign of divine approval. Carter is his prophet, sent here to save the chosen few." He smiled. "You've been chosen."

Bile rose in Craig's throat. "So you're going to rip my heart out while I'm still breathing? And what do you mean 'take their hearts inside you'? Tell me that doesn't mean what I think it means. Are you planning on eating my heart? That's just twisted, man! And because of some insane delusion that you think it will make you see better? Who the fuck are you? Jeffrey Dahmer? Hannibal Lecter?"

"I don't appreciate those comparisons," Ricardo snapped. "Dahmer was mentally unstable, and Lecter is a fictional character. I don't *enjoy* eating hearts. They taste like rubbery liver, and we can't even cook them first. But it's necessary to save you, to absolve you of your sins and cleanse your soul in the eyes of God. We know for sure now that the soul resides within the heart. Carter has found a way... no, Carter has been taught by *God* the way to capture a soul and cleanse it so that it may kneel before our savior, pure and worthy, come Judgment Day. In other words, Craig, we're your ticket into heaven. But first, you've got to go through a little hell. So if you want to compare me to fictional characters, I'd prefer Michael Landon's character on *Highway to Heaven*. Tonight, I'm your guardian angel."

Craig began to realize that Ricardo, his friend for more than half his life, had truly gone over the edge. "I don't know what to say."

Ricardo grinned. "I know. It's a lot to take in, but—"

"You're totally fucking insane!"

Ricardo's smile vanished. "I guessed you might see it that way. In the end, though, you'll thank me."

"In the end, if you're right and there is a heaven and hell, you're gonna be the one burning."

"Why do you fight so hard to forsake him? His influence is all around us, in everything." He shook his head. "Aaron is the same way: stubborn, faithless. How else would you explain my ability to see?"

"Lots of carrots? Mitichlora-whatevers? I don't know, man. I'm no doctor. But I'm sure it has nothing to do with you being a cannibal."

Ricardo slapped his thighs. "I can see there's no reasoning with you. In light of our friendship—and I still consider you a good friend—I borrowed some of my mother's Valium for you to take before the ceremony begins. It won't take all the pain away, but it should lessen the sting. I'm sorry it has to be this way, Craig. We'll start as soon as Carter gets here, which should be any minute now." He held up a pill. "Open your mouth."

"Go fuck yourself."

Ricardo shrugged. "All right, your loss. Let me know if you change your mind."

Craig turned his head to face the wall. He'd already given up on trying to escape. He could barely move his arms, and his injured leg was useless.

He tried to hold back his tears while listening for the arrival of Carter. *If I yell for help, will anyone hear me? Would anyone care?* He didn't bother to try. All hope had been washed away with his blood and tears. "Give me the Valium."

His Chevelle's tires ground down on cracked pavement as it pulled into the lot. Carter's vehicle was perhaps not the subtlest, but the mill was secluded. Weeds sprouted through the cement. Huge black rats scurried back to their nests hidden somewhere in the dark, hollow spaces in the rotted wood or the lot's abutting tall grass. If anyone lived in the neighborhood, they'd yet to notice the activities taking place inside its deteriorated walls.

Or just turned a blind eye to it. He smiled and got out of the car, where he paused to draw in a breath of putrid air that hung wet and heavy from the moisture it sucked off the nearby river. *Home is where you hang your heart.* He chuckled quietly then headed inside.

Doug met him at the door. "Where have you been? He's been out most of this time, probably in shock, but still breathing. We had to bandage him up. His leg will turn gangrenous without medical attention."

"Like that's an issue. He'll be dead shortly." *And as for me, I've been dealing with police this evening, thanks to some bonehead mistake you made.* He stepped inside. "I had some cleaning up to do. I moved his car and yours into the garage, then I sealed that hole in my dojo wall. Last thing I need is some animal getting in there." Carter looked around the room. "Where are Kelly and Ricardo? Is everything all set?"

"They're both with Craig. He's prepped and ready to go. Ricardo's been talking to him. Don't worry, though. He's still on board."

"Good. I forgot his stuff in the car. Get everyone ready and light the furnace. I'll be right back."

He ran out to his car and grabbed Craig's navy-blue gym bag, along with his own bag. Upon returning, he threw Craig's bag and cell phone into the fired-up furnace. He slid Craig's wallet and keys into his own bag then walked into the kill room. Craig was out cold. Carter wasn't surprised. A man could only take so much pain and fear before his mind shut down.

Carter slapped Craig several times until the man opened his eyes. "Wake up, my friend," Carter said. "I wouldn't want you to miss this." He pulled on a pair of latex gloves and reached for the knife he kept on a nearby shelf. He kneeled next to Craig and whispered, "I'm going to enjoy this."

Glassy-eyed, Craig looked around the room like a dizzy drunk. Drool trickled out of one corner of his mouth. Carter raised the blade.

"Wait!" Ricardo shouted.

"Ricardo, we've been over this—"

"I know, but you're forgetting something."

Carter rolled his eyes, his back turned to the others so that they wouldn't notice. "Oh, I thought you guys had already done that." He slapped Craig again. "Hey, Craig, focus. What's wrong with this guy?"

"I gave him some Valium," Ricardo said.

"You *what*?" Carter growled then quickly got himself in check. *Why does somebody always have to ruin things? The look on his face won't be the same now. He'd better feel it, or this won't be nearly as fun.*

Carter pinched Craig's cheek like a grandmother adoring her grandchild. He wanted the man alert. "Craig, listen to me carefully. Do you have anything you'd like to confess before I kill you?" Carter smirked. *I wonder what I'll have to do when someone actually says yes loud enough for the others to hear it?*

Apparently finding a moment of coherence, Craig responded, "Fuck off."

"Suit yourself." *Defiant to the end. I like that.* Carter raised the blade and swiftly plunged it into Craig's chest. Blood squirted from the gash. Some of it landed on Carter's mouth. Carter quickly licked his lips.

Then, it was over. Craig died far too quickly for Carter's liking, almost instantaneously. He'd missed the heart on purpose, just as he always did. He loved the way his victims coughed up blood when he punctured a lung. If the others weren't watching, he probably would have started much lower and worked his way up, perhaps at the stomach. He continued his work, severing bone, muscle, arteries, and everything else composing the man's chest. Last, he began to carve out Craig's heart.

Killing Craig had been fun, but at best, it was like a premature ejaculation—it felt good, but it failed to satisfy. He would need to kill again soon.

Good thing I already have the next one lined up. He considered making her a solo job. The thought almost made him squeal with delight as he reached in and tore out Craig's heart. He held it high like a trophy, even though he felt as if he'd only won second place.

"Prepare the body for disposal," he ordered. "Divvy up the heart." He plopped the organ onto the operating table beside Craig's corpse. Not bothering to clean the streaks of blood from his face, Carter stared at his followers. He couldn't mask his sadism, so he played it off as religious zeal.

Sharon had seen him—the *real* him—and she'd killed herself because of it. The others ignored what their eyes perceived, apparently relying on the power they obtained through servitude as evidence of divine approval. Faith was a powerful weapon, particularly when it was backed by "miracles" science couldn't explain. Still, with the police bearing down on them, he was beginning to wish the others would follow Sharon's example. When he looked at his disciples, he saw three loose ends.

"We've done the Lord's bidding here," he said. "He will commend us for our actions."

Ricardo wept softly. Doug and Kelly stood on either side of him, patting his back.

Deciding it was best to just ignore Ricardo's grief, Carter went over and washed his hands and face in a bucket filled with bottled water. After disrobing down to his boxers, he threw his soiled clothes into the furnace. He put on a clean sweatshirt and jeans from his bag.

He turned to Doug. "Give me the box cutter."

"I'll do it," Ricardo said solemnly. He took the box cutter from Doug and walked over to the body to mark the wrists. "May God accept you into his grace, born again pure."

"Good, Ricardo." Carter put his arm around his acolyte to feign support.

The box cutter dropped from Ricardo's hand. Dust rose from the grimy floor where the tool landed. Ricardo put his head down and walked away.

While the others were watching Ricardo, Carter picked up the box cutter and slid it into his bag. "I'm going outside to get a jacket. I'll be right back. We should probably get something to wash these bloody shoeprints off the floor. Ajax usually does the trick. But that can wait. Burn your shoes before you leave, though. After he's clean, we'll need to get rid of his car. We can do that while we think of how to display him."

Carter carried his gym bag out to the van. *The cops will be looking into Mr. Carter Wainwright now.* He smirked. *But it will take them a while before they realize they're chasing a dead end. That should give me plenty of time.*

He opened the van's sliding door and got in. He pulled the box cutter and Craig's wallet from his bag, wiped both clean of prints with his shirttail, then slid the tool under the seat. Later, he would throw the wallet into Ricardo's trash barrel.

CHAPTER 20

On Christmas Eve, snow came down furiously. The scent of pine filled the air. Stockings hung over the fake fireplace. The cozy-quiet evening was reserved for the two of them.

Aaron drank eggnog while watching *A Christmas Story* for the forty-seventh time. *I wonder if Ralphie will shoot his eye out this time.* He laughed quietly to himself. Arianna, a New England native, stared out the window in awe, as if she had never seen snow before. Calypso, Aaron's golden retriever, nestled among the presents under the brightly lit tree. All was restful. All was perfect.

"Is it time?" Arianna asked, smiling eagerly as she hopped onto Aaron's lap.

"I told you, we can open presents whenever you want to."

Arianna's smile reminded Aaron of his youth, when the holidays brought excitement. Like the rest of life for him, Christmas had long ago lost its magic. He could never think of anything he wanted, anything that could fill the emptiness of his dull existence. The best one he could remember, though, was when Arianna got him the dog. He gave Calypso an appreciative look and returned to his movie.

"Party pooper." Arianna prodded him with her finger. "Come on! Where's your Christmas spirit?"

"I like Christmas," Aaron said. "I like the food and all those desserts that your mom makes."

Arianna ogled the presents under the tree. "Okay. Let's start!" The phone rang, but Arianna waved it off. "Let it ring, Aaron. We have more important business at hand."

"One second. We can't avoid our friends on Christmas." Aaron picked up the phone.

Arianna put on her pouty face, her upper lip tucked under her lower. He wondered if Arianna's clients ever saw that side of her, the good side, a side that he'd seen less and less since she'd become a lawyer.

He picked up the phone. "Hello?"

"Hey, Aaron. It's Ricardo."

"Hi, Rick!" Aaron didn't have to fake his enthusiasm. Unlike most things, Ricardo still mattered. "Merry Christmas!"

"Are you near a TV?" Ricardo asked, his tone grave. "Turn on Channel 6."

"Why? What's happened?" he asked as he reached for the remote. "Is everything okay?"

"You need to see this for yourself."

"Okay, I'm doing it." Aaron flipped through the channels one by one. The habit irritated Arianna, but she was far too busy shaking presents to notice.

When he reached Channel 6, his mouth dropped open. His mind and body numbed. A blue-and-gold wrapped present tumbled from Arianna's hands to the carpet. She covered her mouth with her hand.

"Ricardo, I'll call you back," Aaron choked out.

"Do you see what they—"

He hung up the phone and raised the volume on the television. The screen showed a picture of a smiling, happy Craig, while a newscaster spoke. "The sixth victim, whom sources confirm as Craig Sousa of Somerset, Massachusetts, was tied naked around a Christmas tree at Bridgewater Common. His heart had been removed in similar fashion to prior murders in the Bristol County area. In this highly trafficked, commercial district near Bridgewater State College, police are requesting that anyone with information that may lead to the capture of the unknown assailant come forward."

The camera moved to a middle-aged, uniformed police lieutenant. "At this time, we're advising people to stay inside and enjoy the holiday with their friends and families. The Bridgewater Police Department is cooperating with a number of state and local law enforcement agencies in a joint effort to find the perpetrator of this horrible act and bring him to justice."

A reporter offscreen asked the officer if the homicide was linked to the previous ones in the Fall River area.

"We are investigating every lead."

Aaron started to cry.

Arianna wrapped her arms around his neck. "I'm so sorry, honey," she whispered and gave him a soft kiss on the cheek.

A million thoughts ran through his mind. At last, he fixed on one. "Craig told me he was being followed, and I didn't believe him." His voice kept getting stuck in his throat.

"No, Aaron. This is not your fault. This is the doing of some twisted psychopath."

"But he—"

"Look at me."

He met her gaze and saw that she was crying, too. She kissed his forehead. He turned away.

"Let's not go through this again," Arianna said. "This is *not* your fault."

"I don't know. I feel like I could have done something if I just—"

"You didn't kill him. You didn't want him dead. You're not to blame. Only the killer is to blame. Understood?"

"I guess," he mumbled. Aaron didn't want to agree, but he knew the conversation would end badly for both of them if he didn't. Nothing she said made him feel any less responsible. His friend was dead, and he hadn't done anything to prevent it.

CHAPTER 21

THE POLICE FOLLOWED DOUG EVERYWHERE he went. Officers watched Carter Wainwright's home and business day and night, though he hadn't been seen in days. Detective Jocelyn Beaudette was as sure of their guilt as she was of her own name. The problem was: she didn't have enough proof.

After Craig Sousa's death, the killers had taken a break for a few weeks, perhaps to let the dust settle. Jocelyn and Bruce kept tabs on all the members of Carter Wainwright's jiu-jitsu classes and Friday-night Bible study. Every last one of them was a suspect, and she wanted to haul all of them in and see who she could break.

Since the gruesome Christmas display, most people stayed inside. Those brave enough to carry on with their everyday lives appeared on edge, suspicious of those around them. A heavy shroud of gloom fell over Fall River, and New Year's Day passed with little celebration.

All the while, Jocelyn worked. The circumstantial evidence was starting to add up. She just needed enough to obtain a search warrant so she could get a foot in the door. And once she got in, she would take down every last one of those killers. She hated them for their crimes and almost equally so for twisting her beliefs and the beliefs of so many good people. The religion she knew offered love and light, not what those lunatics professed.

Bruce made sure she did everything by the book. He insisted they go slow and take no risks that might jeopardize any future convictions. Phone records, bank statements, photographs, testimonial evidence from neighbors pertaining to the comings and goings of their suspects, and the like began to paint a picture in Jocelyn's mind. But the most damning evidence, especially the van sitting in his garage, pointed to Douglas Fournier. Then they discovered that Fournier had purchased a disposable phone with his Discover Card from a store at the Emerald Square Mall three days before Huntley's murder. The phone number matched that of the phone used to call Huntley on the night of his death. Finally, they were ready to present to a judge, and Bruce gave her the honor.

"We got it!" Jocelyn shouted, beaming as she ran out of the courtroom with the warrant in hand. "The judge was thrilled to sign this if it means getting our killers off the street. He gave me a lot of leeway, despite the fact that we have nothing solid linking Fournier to any of the crimes."

Bruce nodded. "People are getting desperate. There's a lot of pressure to arrest somebody. And it's not like we're empty-handed. That's a solid start, but not enough for a jury. Our motive is weak, too. Fournier has led an otherwise-normal life, a good upstanding Christian citizen—at least his adult life. I can't seem to find anything referencing his or his wife's upbringing, familial relationships… it's like they didn't have a childhood. Despite our theories on motive, even the Jehovah's Witnesses don't generally take a break from their door-to-door pamphlet pushing to knock off a few sinners. Why would Fournier suddenly go psycho?"

Jocelyn scratched her head. "You sound like you're not convinced we have the right guy."

"I *know* we have the right guy. I just wish we had more proof to show the rest of the world that we have the right guy. There are just still so many unanswered questions. As far as the van goes, we still have no corroboration on the license plate. Also, where is he killing them? What is he using to remove the hearts?"

Jocelyn wanted her case closed. She didn't need the explanation anymore, just a guilty party to charge, arrest, and if all went well, convict. "No matter. He hand-painted a van that doesn't even belong to him. Besides, the judge ruled that we have enough. What reasonable expectation of privacy can Fournier have in a state-owned vehicle, anyway?"

His expression softened. "The search warrant is great news. You've done far better than I could have." He extended his hand for a congratulatory shake.

Instead, Jocelyn leaned forward and kissed him on the cheek, her excitement getting the better of her. "Let's go. I'm going to enjoy serving this one."

After arranging for a couple of other officers to meet them, they drove to Fournier's Somerset residence. It was an ordinary middle-class home in all respects: raised ranch, gray with white shutters, wind chimes hanging near the door, a two-car driveway. Nothing about the place said "serial killer." A good killer's home rarely did.

They arrived just as Officers Pimental and Stravenski were pulling their squad car into the driveway. She would have loved to have Temple there, too, since he had been instrumental in the case, but it was his day off.

As she got out of the car, she heard Pimental complaining to Stravenski. "Making me serve a search warrant on a friend isn't cool. Is this Marklin's sick idea of a joke? Why does he need me here?"

"So do you think Fournier's going to be mad at you?" Stravenski asked with a smirk. "What are you going to do if he's the killer? Do you think you could shoot him?"

Jocelyn listened to Pimental's bitching, her frustration building. She glanced at Bruce, who was studying the house and didn't seem to be paying any attention to them. *A good thing, too, for your sake, Pimental.* Still, her patience had run dry. "Officer Pimental," she called, "serve the warrant."

Pimental shot her a look filled with disdain, but he walked up to Fournier's door and rang the bell. The door cracked open. A snarling snout with long, vicious-looking teeth forced its way through the opening. The nose belonged to a Rottweiler that managed to push out and lunge at Pimental.

Jocelyn laughed as Pimental jumped back, looking ready to run for the hills. The officer pretty much deserved that, in her opinion.

"Down, Molly!" a woman commanded as she wrenched the dog back into the house by its collar. "Back into your cage." In an instant, the dog was gone.

"Damn, Kelly!" Pimental struggled to compose himself. "I nearly pissed myself."

"Sorry about that. Molly's a big softie once you get to know her. She just gets excited around new people." Kelly Fournier looked past Pimental at Jocelyn and Bruce standing in the driveway with Stravenski. "What brings you here?" She wasn't an imposing figure at five-feet-nothing. But the stern way she set her jaw and scowled down her nose at Pimental made her look more vicious than Molly, and she probably had a far worse bite.

Pimental cringed a little. "I hate to say it, but I'm here on business. We have a search warrant for Doug's van."

Mrs. Fournier's face turned a sickly, milk-ish hue. "Doug!" she yelled and retreated into the house. "You'd better get out here. Aaron's here, and he says he's got a warrant."

A moment later, all two hundred ninety pounds of Douglas Fournier appeared in the doorway. He didn't look happy to see them. "What's this all about?" He towered over Pimental like Goliath over David.

Pimental raised one hand. "Calm down, big fella. I don't want to be here any more than you want me to be. We have a warrant to search your van. The sooner you let us do that, the sooner we can get out of here."

"What do you want with my van?"

"Some of us"—Pimental nodded toward Jocelyn—"think you may be involved in some rather unpleasant business."

Jocelyn frowned, making a mental note to deal with the officer later. His attitude was grossly unprofessional. If the police department weren't so short-handed, she would make sure he never worked another of her cases again. And to think she'd thought she was helping him to add a big collar to his name.

"Pimental," Bruce snapped, "what's the goddamn holdup?" He winked at Jocelyn.

She smiled back. *We'll see how much he likes having Bruce pulling his chain all the time.*

"Like I said," Pimental continued, "we have to toss your van. Then we'll be on our way. The warrant is for the van only, for tools and shit like that. So as soon as you open your garage, I can prove to them what I already know about you. I'm sorry about all this."

Fournier shook his head. "This isn't right, Aaron. But fine, I'll meet you guys in the garage."

He disappeared into the house, and a minute later, the garage rolled open. He stood inside with his arms crossed. His wife waited in the doorway connecting the garage to the house. Both seemed calm.

"Let me see the warrant," Fournier said.

Jocelyn walked up to him and slapped the document against his chest. She continued past him to the van's side door. "Is it unlocked?" she asked as she donned a pair of latex gloves.

Fournier fumbled around in his pocket, brought out his keys, and pushed a button on the fob. A double-beep emitted from the van. "It is now."

Bruce opened the sliding door and hopped in. Jocelyn went around to the passenger side, intending to start with the glove compartment.

A few seconds later, Bruce said, "Jocelyn, you're not going to believe this."

"What is it? You got something?"

"A disposable phone. Verizon." He pulled a crumpled sheet of paper from his pocket. "I'm checking the identification number... it matches!" He stuck his head out. "Stravenski, bring me an evidence bag."

Stravenski hustled over with the bag. Pimental hung back, staring at the scene.

Bruce dropped the phone into the bag. "Seal it and label it. Don't let it out of your sight."

Having found nothing of interest in the glove compartment, Jocelyn bent over to look under the passenger seat. She spotted something metal and slid her hand under the seat to pull it out. She stared at the box cutter in her hand for a second then yelled, "Pimental! Evidence bag."

While she waited for the reluctant officer, she looked over the seat at Bruce. "We'll need to do a full search of the van, including prints, back at the station."

Pimental arrived with the bag. She didn't trust him, so she took the bag out of his hands. "Pimental, step out of the garage and call the station for a tow." She dropped the tool into the bag and sealed it before passing it to Stravenski. "Label that, and keep it with the phone."

Bruce said, "You can have the honor."

Jocelyn grinned. "Thanks!" She walked around the van and approached Fournier, her hand resting on her holstered service weapon. "Douglas Fournier, you're under arrest for the murders of Paul Fernald, Eliza Ramirez, Benjamin Reinhart, Garrison Huntley, Peter Robillard, and Craig Sousa." She turned to Pimental, who looked as if he'd swallowed vomit. "Cuff him."

Pimental didn't move. Neither did Fournier.

"I said, cuff him," Jocelyn ordered.

Pimental shook his head. "Sorry," he muttered.

She wasn't certain whether he was apologizing to her or his friend, but she would bet it was meant for Fournier.

She recited the Miranda rights for the man, making sure to include and enunciate every word. Fortunately for Pimental, the bear-sized suspect didn't resist. The officer's hands shook as he cuffed the suspect. He walked Fournier to the police car and loaded him into the backseat.

CHAPTER 22

J OCELYN STARED AT HER SUSPECT through the two-way mirror. He'd killed all those people—she knew he had—but she couldn't detect the slightest sign of cruelty, hatred, or even madness. Douglas Fournier was a killer of the scariest kind, one who not only felt no guilt, but couldn't conceive of a reason why he should.

"He's not saying a word. Playing the tough guy, I suppose. Maybe he's smarter than he looks." She rubbed her forehead, hoping to massage away her stress. *Or maybe we're not as smart as we think.*

"Nevertheless, we need to get something out of him," Bruce said. "He's already used his phone call to contact an attorney. Still, he hasn't officially invoked his right to counsel. We're free to question him until he or his attorney puts a stop to it, not that it's doing us a whole lot of good."

Jocelyn's earlier optimism had become lost in a quagmire of red tape. She wondered if they'd been too eager in making their arrest. Sure, they had enough to charge Fournier, but she didn't know if it was enough for a prosecutor to make the charges stick. Getting Fournier down to the precinct had been the easy part. Keeping him there was turning out to be much harder.

Depending on the offense and the reasons for the hold, Massachusetts law required a prosecutor to make an independent decision on charges within so many hours of an arrest. If the prosecutor didn't charge

Fournier in the applicable time frame, the detectives would have to release him. The clock was ticking away as they scrambled to get lab results back for both fingerprint and DNA analysis on the seized items to be presented as evidence. Even on their best day, the lab rats could take up to a week on DNA results. While they waited for the lab and the indictment, they worked on Fournier.

"Let me talk to him. Maybe he prefers a woman's touch."

"You know how to be feminine?" Bruce teased.

"Sexist pig." Jocelyn feigned offense before heading into the interrogation room.

Fournier sat awkwardly, too big for the small aluminum chair, which bent beneath his weight. Every facet of his face was still, as if he weren't even breathing, a blank sheet empty of emotion. In his deadpan stare, Jocelyn saw nothing.

She tossed her jacket over the back of the chair opposite her suspect. "Would you like a smoke? Perhaps a glass of water?" Both offers were merely ploys to get a DNA sample. She and Bruce had been able to keep one piece of evidence secret: skin cells found underneath Eliza Ramirez's fingernails. Even power-washing her body and filing her nails had been insufficient to destroy the evidence completely. All Jocelyn needed was a match.

Fournier didn't respond.

No matter. Jocelyn knew the lab would find a DNA sample in the van. One hair was all they needed.

She'd been trained in the art of interrogation, but adopting a persona that was contrary to her own was not her forte. She slammed her palms onto the desk, doing her best to appear tough but in control. Her shirt was partially unbuttoned, exposing her cleavage when she bent at the waist. "We got you, you psychopath. We know all about your sick extracurricular activities."

She decided to take a chance. If she revealed a little information, maybe she would get a little in return, maybe even get a rise out of him or trick him into revealing the whole sordid story. "Tearing out hearts, sacrificing your victims to appease your god. Well, let me tell you something. God doesn't approve. He agrees with the rest of us that you're nothing but a worthless piece of shit. The only hope you have is to confess and turn over your co-conspirators. Then maybe, just maybe, we can convince the Commonwealth to cut you a deal. Otherwise, your size won't help you in prison. The cell blocks are loaded with plenty of guys your size and bigger. You can prepare yourself for the butt-raping of the century."

The threat of sodomy intimidated the hell out of the softer types, but Fournier didn't flinch. He raised his head slowly to meet Jocelyn's stare. His gaze cold, uncaring, he leaned back in his chair. Jocelyn couldn't read him. She wondered if he had any emotions to read.

Still, she pressed on. "Or maybe your friends will turn on you first. You think Carter Wainwright is going to stay loyal when we throw him to the wolves? You bet your ass he won't. He'll be gossiping like a teenage girl, and you'll be left squealing like a pig, *Deliverance* style. Maybe he'll be sweet and come visit you and your new boyfriend in prison. You can show him how big your asshole has gotten. Won't that be nice?"

Again, Jocelyn's attempts to rattle Fournier bore no fruit. The suspected murderer just looked away and sighed.

Well, nothing's sacred here. Let's kick it up a notch, see what makes him tick. "Or maybe he'll be off fucking your woman. How is the little wifey doing? Don't think for a moment we don't know she's involved."

Fournier jumped out of his seat, heaving like a gorilla as his face reddened. "Kelly has nothing to do with any of this!" he shouted. "You leave her out of it."

Jocelyn flinched but quickly recovered. She bit into her lower lip as a smile wormed across her face. At last, she'd found the chink in his armor. *This guy can be broken.*

But before she could continue to needle him, Fournier's rage subsided. He sat down slowly, the metal chair creaking beneath his weight. "You've had your fun. I'm not saying another word without my attorney present," he said through clenched teeth. He pressed his lips together, as if reminding himself to keep them shut.

"Your attorney can't do shit for you, so I suggest you start cooperating."

"I beg to differ," a voice said sharply behind her.

Jocelyn had been so focused on the interrogation that she hadn't heard the door open. Standing in the doorway was a woman in a sharp-looking business suit.

"Now, I'm sure you don't intend to continue interrogating my client after he's invoked his Fifth Amendment right to counsel, do you?"

Jocelyn glanced at Bruce, who entered the room behind the lawyer. "As he just now invoked that right, we've received no statements from Mr. Fournier." The woman's answer was evasive but accurate.

Defense lawyers. Soulless swine, the whole lot of them. Prosecutors were different. They performed a great public service. But the rest of them—and especially those money-grubbing private defense attorneys—were criminals representing criminals at a high price. *The worst of the worst.*

"Will you be formally charging my client?" the lawyer asked.

Jocelyn was at a loss for words. They had arrested him for the murders of six individuals, and they had handed over to the prosecutor everything they had. *Why hasn't he come back with charges yet?*

Sure, the detectives themselves had debated releasing Fournier, but they couldn't reach a definitive answer in order to cast their net around his cult. They had plenty of evidence against Fournier but didn't know if they could take down his accomplices.

Bruce wanted them all, not just the one. "Releasing this animal back into the wild may be our best course of action," he'd argued. "Now that he knows we're on to him, he might lead us to evidence or to the others in an attempt to cover his tracks. When he does, we'll be watching. With any luck, he'll make our case for us."

Jocelyn had disagreed. She always favored the bird-in-the-hand philosophy. "Or we could be letting a killer escape justice, or worse, he might get out and kill again. We could have him formally charged and arraigned in the morning. Maybe we'll get lucky, and the judge will deny bail."

Neither had budged, but if a decision had to be made, Jocelyn would defer to Bruce. But it appeared the Commonwealth was making their decision for him.

What could be taking her so long?

To her surprise, Bruce did an about-face. "Yes, Ms. Medeiros. We have already processed him and requested that he be formally charged. In all likelihood, we'll be transferring him to the Bristol County House of Corrections tomorrow morning. We thought we'd talk to him first, give him and you time to discuss his circumstances. We don't believe your client has acted alone. I'm sure the Commonwealth will take into consideration his cooperation should he implicate—"

"I told you," Fournier growled. "I've got nothing to say to you."

Medeiros smiled tightly. "Say nothing else, Doug. Let me handle this." She smoothed out her suit skirt. "I would like some time to talk with my client. Alone. I'll keep in mind your offer, but it seems premature without an indictment."

"Of course."

"Bruce, are you talking deal?" Jocelyn said. "We have enough to—"

"It's okay." Bruce grabbed her by the elbow and pulled her from the room, letting the door swing shut behind them.

Jocelyn shook her arm free. "We've got enough to put this guy away for life. He doesn't deserve a deal. You think the families of his victims would give him a deal? What if it were my husband he'd killed? My daughter? You just don't get it because you don't have a family."

Bruce's mouth dropped open.

Jocelyn immediately regretted what she's said. "Bruce, I'm so sorry. I... I wasn't thinking. I just got caught up in the moment."

He patted her arm in an awkward display of affection. "Don't even think twice about it. I get it. But you have to remember how these things work. We get him to roll on his accomplices, and we put away the whole damn lot. Fournier won't exactly walk away with a slap on the wrist. In fact, given the severity of the crimes, he's likely looking at life even with a deal. Maybe they'll offer him an extra pillow for his cart."

"Even that's more than the son of a bitch deserves." She let out a long breath. "Well, I suppose I should be happy—one scumbag off the streets. It's not like he's going anywhere. There's no way in hell he's gonna get bail. That's assuming we ever get an indictment. What gives? This is the most important case this area has seen in the last decade. We basically hand those pencil pushers a serial killer on a platter, and none of them over at the DA's office has the guts to prosecute it?"

Bruce stroked his chin. "Yeah, I don't like it. Something's not right. We've sent away many with less. This should be a no-brainer." He pulled his phone from his pocket. "Hang tight. I'll get to the bottom of this."

As her partner walked away, Jocelyn stared through the soundproofed room's window at the fancy-pants lawyer and her killer client. *He's gonna walk somehow. I can feel it. It doesn't make any sense.*

———————— •••• ————————

Aaron couldn't believe what he was hearing. He must not have heard her correctly. He *couldn't have* heard her correctly.

Arianna stared at the floor, unable to look him in the eye. She must have known her action wasn't going to go over well.

"You did *what*?" he shouted.

"This could be a huge break for me," Arianna countered sheepishly. "Don't you think you're overreacting?"

"Overreacting?" He paced the length of the kitchen. "Overreacting! Arianna, he may have murdered one of my best friends!"

"He needed a lawyer, and I'm the only one he knows. Besides, you said yourself that he couldn't have done it. You should be happy that I agreed to help him out. Plus, you know how much I want to open my own criminal law practice. And this is such a high-profile case! It could make me."

"Or it could break you," Aaron retorted. "Never mind what it'll do to us. Why didn't you discuss it with me first?"

"Because I knew what you'd say. I knew you'd be like... like... *this*."

"And how the fuck am I supposed to act, huh? My own girlfriend, sticking her nose where it doesn't belong. Don't you care at all what happened to Craig? Don't you give a shit about how I feel? Fuck!" He swiped his arm across the kitchen counter, spilling its contents onto the floor. Pens, notepads, the mail he'd brought in—all of it slid across the tiles. A newspaper stopped at Arianna's feet. He snorted. Doug's face was on the front page.

"You're scaring me," Arianna said flatly. She didn't sound scared.

If he hurt her, he knew he would regret it. But that didn't change the fact that at that moment, he was so full of rage and hate that he just wanted to grab her by the throat and—

He took a deep breath. *Not worth it, Aaron. Not worth it.* The roiling waters of his anger went from boil to simmer. *She pushes too far.* If he were honest with himself, Aaron had found it difficult to believe Doug was some heart-stealing psychopath plastering dead bodies around town.

152

But that was before his superiors had seized that van and everything in it. Since then, he didn't know what to think. And the only person he thought he could trust—aside from Ricardo—ups and joins Team Doug without even having the common decency to discuss it with him first.

"I'm taking the case. You can either deal with it or—"

"Or what?" Aaron pounded his fist on the table. He wanted to hit her. No, he wanted to *kill* her.

"Or leave," she replied softly.

He was tired of being depressed… of letting the world beat him down. He didn't feel like being life's toilet, always getting shit on. Anger felt so much better than melancholy. So much better. All that he dealt with alone, so many dark thoughts he kept bottled up inside. *Why should I be miserable alone? Why shouldn't I share it with those who make me miserable?*

Yes, anger was so much better.

Still, he'd never once laid a hand on Arianna. He rarely even raised his voice to her. *Is the unspoken tension between us finally rearing its ugly head?* He gritted his teeth. *Well, fuck it, and fuck her.*

"Fine! Your fucking ambition always comes before us, doesn't it? It always has, always will. Know this: if Doug is the killer and he gets to someone else, it's on your hands." Aaron charged toward the door. If Arianna hadn't stepped aside, he might have gone through her to reach it. He stormed out, slamming the door behind him.

CHAPTER 23

"They're watching us," Carter whispered as he pretended to demonstrate a throw on Doug, who had just been released from custody earlier in the day. Doug had thanked him for it, thinking he might have had a hand in it. Carter would have sooner tattooed a penis on his forehead than paid a penny of his own funds to bribe, cajole, or otherwise deter the DA's office from filing an indictment. "The Lord works in mysterious ways," was the only response he'd given, content to let Doug believe he'd helped. But *someone* had interfered, undamning he whom Carter had damned. He shrugged, willing to reap the benefits anyhow. His most useful pawn was back in play.

"I didn't think we should have class tonight, but I wanted it to appear like business as usual." Tuesday night always meant his jiu-jitsu instruction in Somerset. On that Tuesday, only Carter, Doug, Kelly, and Ricardo were there.

The patrol car parked in front of his Somerset dojo was so noticeable that it must have been intended. The officer in the driver's seat sipped coffee, staring at them through a window. Not wanting to raise suspicion, Carter had left the blinds open.

"First off," Carter said, "they probably have some of our phones tapped or are using listening devices. So let's keep it down. No more conversations on the phones or anywhere, if it can be helped." Carter realized he was overstating the local law enforcement's level of sophistication and technological savvy, but he wanted to stress the need for caution, even if that meant making his crew paranoid. "If we keep our heads and act normal, this will blow over. They've got nothing on us. Let's not give them anything."

"That's easy for you to say," Kelly said loudly. "Your vehicle wasn't impounded. And how was that box cutter left there anyway? Which one of us messed up that badly? Carter? Ricardo? I saw that bitch detective toss it in a plastic bag."

"Shhhh!" Carter hissed. *We have dissension in the ranks... it's too soon. I'd better keep up the harmony a little longer.* "Keep your voice down. If you remember, I never rode in the van that night. So let's not point fingers. I don't know how it ended up there. Are you even sure it's the same box cutter? Either way, if it was enough to pin something on us, the police would have done something about it by now."

"You keep saying *us*," Doug said. He'd lost weight and looked as though he hadn't slept. "Now, please don't think for a moment I don't appreciate you getting me out. I do, and so does Kelly. I don't know how you pulled it off. Those detectives were so mad when no one showed with an indictment. I thought the little vein in that one guy's forehead was gonna burst. But they will keep trying, so sticking around here just isn't smart. The cops didn't come to *your* house. They didn't haul you off to jail... or any of the rest of you, for that matter."

"What are you saying, Doug?" Carter feigned innocence yet again. The others didn't know that the police had also paid a visit to his home. They didn't know how much he wanted to scream out to the world, "Yes, I killed those people—them and many more. And I'm going to kill a whole lot more. I'll keep on killing until your gods shed tears of blood and your children would rather crawl back up their filthy mothers' crotches than face the world I create." *Well, maybe not quite all that.* "You're not alone in this. We're all with you, come what may. More importantly, *he* is with you. God will protect you. He'll protect us all."

Doug sighed. "Carter, I'm no Judas. You know I'm part of this team. I believe in the importance of our work. I always have. But I see Kelly's point. How does me rotting in jail best serve God or carry out our mission?"

"That's your fear talking," Carter said. "That fear will become your sin."

Carter knew exactly where to strike. He knew how to make Doug feel ashamed for placing his fears above his faith. Of all the group, Doug had always been the strongest in his faith. Carter would call on him to continue the task God had chosen for them. He stifled a smirk. *After all, God speaks through me.*

"Stay strong," Carter said. "It's natural to be afraid, but don't give in to it. Faith will guide you through."

"Carter's right," Doug said, reaching for his wife's hand. "His lips are God's mouthpiece; his words the Lord's gospel. Everything he has foreseen has come to fruition. If God has chosen to test us, then let us rise to the occasion." His voice softened, and his shoulders drooped. "I'm sorry I doubted."

Ricardo stepped over and put a hand on Doug's shoulder. "To give your life to God is the ultimate sacrifice for your faith. Jesus died on the cross for us. It was all part of God's divine plan. We must accept whatever he has in store for us."

"Oh, screw you, Ricardo," Kelly said. "Doug and I have been fighting this fight longer than you could possibly know. Your ass isn't on the line here."

Carter wondered if Kelly was losing faith or if he was just losing his control over her. A new influence competed for her attention: Doug's preservation. Doug had confided in him how he and Kelly had run once before, during that whole Waco fiasco, and how ashamed they'd been for doing so. Were there limits to how far Kelly would go when it meant her or her husband's necks were exposed? He considered the possibility of killing her when her tasks were complete.

Nah. The police will do it for me. But could he count on Kelly to finish his plan? *Killing her now is always an option. Might be a whole lot of fun, too.*

"Take it easy, hon," Doug said. "We're all under a lot of pressure. Turning on each other is exactly what the cops want us to do. Carter's right. We need to stay the course. Can't you see? Our resolve is being tested. Our very faith is being tested. Let's hear Carter out."

Carter smiled. "Thanks, Doug." He was a demon in sheep's clothing, and he knew how to wear the wool well. "Okay. Here's what I suggest. We have one more matter to settle. Meet me on Friday for—"

"But we were going to get out of here before then," Kelly whined, looking at Doug with pleading eyes. "You promised me."

"She's right, Carter," Doug said. "We don't know how this is going to play out. We saved up some money so we could take an extended vacation. But I don't need to run anymore. My faith is restored. I will see this thing through."

"Running would be like admitting guilt," Ricardo added. "They'll find you wherever you go, and you would probably be extradited."

"Since when did you become the fucking expert?" Kelly asked.

"Kelly, please, just let him talk," Doug said. "We're all friends here."

"You haven't told Aaron's girlfriend anything, have you?" Ricardo asked.

"She knows nothing," Doug said.

Ricardo grunted. "She could be trouble. Aaron hasn't mentioned anything to me about her taking you on as a client, so he probably wants nothing to do with it. Maybe he can be persuaded to help us, but I would only suggest that route as a last resort. Still, to have a cop on our side would obviously make things a whole lot easier."

"But, Rick, Aaron's an atheist," Doug said. "What are the odds of him seeing the light?"

"He won't be sympathetic to our cause; that's for sure. But you never know with him. I've known him almost twenty years, and I still can't guess when his odd sense of morality comes into play. But he's loyal to a fault. He'd put his friends before his job—I know it."

"In his eyes, what we do is murder." Doug sighed. "I agree. We probably shouldn't go down that road unless absolutely necessary. As far as either Aaron or Arianna knows, I'm as innocent as they come."

"And you *are* innocent," Carter said. *Well, foolishly ignorant, anyway.* "I think we're getting ahead of ourselves here. God has set forth one more task for us: an eighth chosen."

"Seventh," Ricardo said.

"Huh?" Carter's eyes widened. "Oh, yeah, right. Seventh." *Yeah, like the seventh sign of the apocalypse. I wonder if I could work that one in here.*

"But, Carter," Kelly said, "we have way too much attention on us to do another one."

"You worry too much, Kelly." Carter flashed his snake-oil grin. *And you're starting to piss me off. Maybe I'll make* you *the next chosen.* "Don't you feel his presence in our work? Isn't that enough to solidify your faith? After all that you've felt, after all that you've become, don't you believe? Don't fail us now. You're stronger than Sharon. I know it. You are God's chosen messenger. And he has one more message for you to deliver."

"Go on," Doug said. "Tell us about this seventh chosen."

"You needn't worry about the seventh. She'll be delivered to us on Friday. With her death, God's divinity will be exposed to all. Our hardships will be over. The Rapture is nearly upon us. Rejoice! We'll not only save her, but millions of others in the process." Carter was their prophet, their crutch, and their friend. They had faith in him, not the faith of the average churchgoer, but that of a zealot. That faith gave Carter all the power in the world over them. "This is our last task together, my friends. Don't falter merely because Lucifer has placed some adversity in our path. God will see us through, as he always has. He is always with us."

"Amen," the group said in unison.

"Yeah, but the police are always with me," Doug said. "How do I lose them?"

"Your backyard is fenced in, right?"

"Yeah."

"They can't have more than two cars watching your house. I'll bet they're too dumb to watch the back. We'll wait until after dark, say eight thirty. Go out to your backyard, hop the fence, and cross the property behind your house to get to the street. I'll be driving a silver Toyota Camry to avoid detection. I'll pick you up there." He turned to Kelly. "Both of you. You'll be there, right?"

Kelly looked to Doug for an answer, but he gave her none. "Yes," she said shakily.

"We'll then pick up Ricardo and head to the mill. Our seventh will be waiting there, prepped and ready."

"Who is it?" Ricardo asked.

"You'll see." Carter had something special planned for them, and the thought of it thrilled him. His groin flushed with blood. *I've outdone myself this time. If it all has to end here, we'll be going out with a bang.*

He met the eyes of each of his acolytes. They filled him with a greater sense of accomplishment and pride in his ability to craft an army to do his bidding. He'd given them all a taste for blood in the most literal sense. They were his pawns for as long as he chose to keep them. And when it came time, Carter would let them all hang. He felt nothing for them or their god. Religion was just a means to an end, and how successful it had turned out to be.

This flock will be missed. Such willing playmates—so faithful, so pliable. What is faith, anyway, but the ignorant searching for reasons, followers looking for a leader, a flock looking for its shepherd?

Faith is for the lemmings.

CHAPTER 24

AARON SWALLOWED HARD. "I CAN'T seem to find much on Carter Wainwright," he said. "As he told us, he's an orphan. He has no living family, adoptive or otherwise. No known business partners, associates, friends… well, none other than those we're already investigating." *My friends.* "Surveillance has been rough since Carter lives out in the boonies. We stick out like a sore thumb. He's a shut-in. Nobody knows anything about him, other than that he grew up around here under the care of his foster parents, Edward and Teresa Wainwright, then disappeared."

"Were the Wainwrights wealthy?" Marklin asked.

"They didn't leave Carter very much, if that's what you're asking."

"So then where did Carter get his money? It can't be from those classes he teaches."

"I checked his tax returns. He only claims income from the classes, and even that, only for the last two years or so. Maybe we can get him on tax evasion, like Al Capone."

"Pimental, you're about as useless as tits on a cow. Can you tell me anything that might aid our investigation?"

Tits on a bull. That's the expression. Tits on a cow are *useful. I wish I was at a titty bar.* Aaron squeezed his knee. *Focus, man.* "Well, the Wainwrights were old when they took in Carter. They passed away several years ago, leaving him as their only heir. They owned a house in Rockland. It was sold back in 1989, and it looks like Carter received the proceeds. That's when he disappeared. But the location got me thinking maybe Carter's old high school could tell me a few things about him. Or I could try the orphanage, Saint Vincent's Home here in Fall River. I figured what happened to Carter after high school might be more important, though."

"And what did the good people over at Rockland High tell you?" Marklin asked.

"With your permission, I was going to head over that way now to see if I can find anyone who might remember him and knows where he headed after graduation."

"Go for it. The next time I see you, you'd better have something for me."

Aaron gathered his things and headed out of the precinct. The drive out to Rockland High School began as a pleasant change, with no killers, no implicated friends, and best of all, no Marklin. Aaron welcomed the alone time until he rediscovered how much he despised his own company. A week had passed, and he still hadn't spoken to Arianna. Living back home with his parents was taking its toll.

He grabbed his cell phone then put it back down. He wanted to call Arianna, but he wouldn't do it. He loved her, but he rarely felt that she loved him anymore, and with every slight, he became more bitter and depressed. The quiet times—the long drives and lying awake in bed—were the hardest. He had too much time to think and too little to distract him from his own destructive thoughts of self-doubt, thoughts of self-hate, thoughts of self-harm... and thoughts of death.

The first time he'd felt that way was thirteen years ago, with the loss of a girlfriend he still loved and the ugly way things had ended between them. The memory of her... that day... threatened to surface. He resisted, using his mind like a blunt object battering the memory back down, but not before an image could break through. The rocks below him. The screams.

No! It was best to keep that memory buried. He had tried to do the right thing. *I was in the right,* he thought, scolding his brain for conjuring up such deceptive reminders.

"I was in the right..." His voice was low and sulky. "Wasn't I?"

His wrists burned with the heat of his shame. *Raquel.* The scars tingled. He swallowed the cry building in his throat and pressed his palms over his eyes. He could hear his own heartbeat pounding in his head. *I don't want to remember.*

Times are... what? Better now? Aaron choked back his sobs, buried them with the howling mad beast. He couldn't go through that pain again. He'd barely survived it. Only Ricardo watching over him had kept him from stepping over that edge again. He laughed at the irony, his own private joke. *Over the edge...*

He shook his head. *It wasn't just that. The second time was different.*

The second time he'd attempted suicide hadn't been because of a single incident but rather a combination of several factors, most of which were still woefully present. He'd never really recovered because there wasn't anything to recover from. He was just miserable, plain and simple, and it seemed he would always be so.

But did that stem from the first time? "Stop it, Aaron!" he screamed, slapping his hands against the steering wheel. Looking out the windows to see if anyone had seen his outburst, he muttered, "That was a long time ago. You've moved on. You've gotten so much better."

He adjusted in his seat, feeling the weight of his service pistol against his thigh. *And now I have a gun.*

When he pulled up to the high school, only a few cars remained in the lot. He parked, got out of his car, and headed straight to Principal Allison Mosher's office.

She stood when he entered and gave him a smile, the same type of smile she likely gave to parents of suspended delinquents: tight-lipped and oozing false concern. Still, she had that air of authority—or perhaps self-importance—about her: rigid stance, straight as a pole in her dark-blue suit, her librarian glasses perched high on a slightly upturned nose. She uncrossed her arms and extended a hand. "You must be Officer Pimental."

"That, I am." He shook her hand once, noticing a much tighter grip than his own. "I appreciate you meeting me on such short notice, Ms. Mosher."

"Please, call me Allison. I'm happy to help. I took the liberty of looking up the former student you requested. There isn't much, so I'm afraid I won't be too much help, after all."

"Well, anything you could tell me might be useful."

"Okay, I'll give you what I have." She opened a folder. "Carter Wainwright was an average student, decent grades. A few teachers who had him in class are still here. Most don't recall him, though. I wasn't the principal at that time." She pulled out a sheet of paper. "But I did find this. It's an evaluation from his guidance counselor, Vivian Burke."

Aaron held out his hand. "May I?"

"Well, I'm not supposed to let you look through this stuff, but I suppose it couldn't hurt." With a wink, she passed him the page.

"I won't tell if you won't." He looked over the evaluation.

The student is shy and introverted. He has no friends and keeps to himself the entire school day. His foster parents seem to be his only positive influences, and he speaks highly of them. He does not participate in sports, music lessons, or any afternoon clubs.

He has no plans beyond graduation. Personal opinion: I fear the deaths of his parents and the subsequent adoption may have severely—and permanently—affected his social skills and overall mental well-being. I have tried to talk to him, but he remains unresponsive to my attempts to get him to open up. Somebody needs to reach out to this boy, but I am afraid he will not let me be the one to do it.

Recommendation: psychological evaluation by a board-certified professional.

He handed the document back to Principal Mosher. "Thank you."

"You're welcome." She tucked the paper back in the folder. "I called Mrs. Burke to see if I could find out more for you."

"Any luck?"

"Yes, actually. She remembered Carter well. She called him a sweet boy, gentle but timid. She said she wrote this after several meetings with him at the request of teachers who were concerned for the boy's welfare. She said that when she looked at Carter, she saw a lost child, invisible to his peers."

"Were the parents brought in? Did he ever see a professional?"

"I don't know. I'm sure his parents were told. It's our practice to report abnormal social behavior to parents. What steps the parents took, if any, we don't know. Anyway, Mrs. Burke said that Carter never got into any trouble, so the whole thing was dropped."

"Is there anything else?"

"Not really. The rest of the documents are grade reports and a few other administrative documents. We have so many files like this. We only keep the bare essentials for each student."

"Do you have any pictures of Carter?"

"I have his yearbook picture, Class of 1998. I made a copy to show his teachers to jog their memories." She slipped a photo out of the folder and passed it to him.

Aaron stared down at the picture. "Th-This can't be right." The boy staring back at him made his stomach turn. The beast of his subconscious splintered its cage door. "Th-That's impossible."

The picture showed a boy of sixteen or seventeen who looked sad and dejected, even in still life. The vacant eyes seemed to float off the page, and they haunted Aaron, terrified him. *Why do I know that face?*

You know why, the beast inside answered. And it laughed.

"Is something wrong?" Principal Mosher asked.

"I-I'm sorry. I have to go. Thank you." Without asking if it was okay, he took the picture and hurried out of the office.

Back in his car, he picked up his cell phone then debated whether he should tell the detectives anything. They were chasing a ghost. Someone was a playing a game. Had to be. *That* boy had nothing to do with their case.

He breathed slowly through his nose, calming his nerves. *You're better now, remember?* The beast of his subconscious mocked and laughed again.

He growled, snatched up his phone, and dialed Marklin's number. "Detective?"

"What have you got for me?"

"Uh... I'm not sure... exactly." He couldn't keep the tremor from his voice. His forehead dripped with sweat. The perspiration ran down his back and made his armpits sticky. *Be calm. It has nothing to do with anything. Just one of those crazy coincidences. You know Carter.*

You do *know Carter, don't you?* The beast laughed.

"Pimental?"

Aaron focused, pushed the beast back in its cage. He was better. He had gotten better. He swallowed. "I don't think the guy we're investigating is Carter Wainwright."

"What are you talking about?"

"I just saw a picture of Carter Wainwright. His yearbook picture from high school. The Carter I know and who you met was dark haired and dark skinned. The Carter in this picture has blond hair, blue eyes, and pasty-white skin."

"Bring me that picture," Marklin said then hung up.

If he isn't Carter Wainwright, then who the hell is he? Aaron didn't think he wanted to know the answer. But one question troubled him most of all. *Where's the real Carter Wainwright?*

Try as he might to deny it, he was pretty sure he knew the answer to that question. And somewhere in the recesses of his mind, soft but sinister, the beast was still laughing.

CHAPTER 25

"**WHAT DO YOU MEAN, YOU** lost them?" Bruce was mad enough to hit somebody. "How does one 'lose' the equivalent of a two-ton gorilla, for Christ's sake?"

"Sir," Officer Angela Cusack said, "they ducked us. We heard them creep out their cellar door and proceeded to follow. We engaged them at—"

"Speak English, Cusack!"

"We saw them hop their back fence, and we went after them. But by the time we got over it, they were gone. We heard doors slam and tires screech, so there must have been somebody waiting for them at the street, like someone knew they'd be coming that way, over the fence and through their neighbor's yard. They must be up to something."

"You think, genius? I want all available cars responding to this immediately. We got half the country watching us, and you two just let our number-one suspect vanish!"

Seated across from him, Jocelyn raised an eyebrow. The matter called for action, not complaining.

He grumbled but tempered his anger. "Radio Captain Pelletier in Somerset and get his guys on it, too." Bruce's grumbling intensified. Something guttural, akin to a roar, passed his lips. "Fuck!" He slammed down his phone, turned, and punched the wall. His hand gave way before the plaster did. Blood trickled down his knuckles. "We should have never let that fucker walk! Something stinks like shit-stained shit over at the DA's office! Ugh!"

Jocelyn rose with the grace of a ballerina. She stepped out of his office. "All right, people!" she shouted. "Those of you not already assigned to a high-priority task, get out there and find Douglas Fournier. He is believed to be traveling with his wife and at least one other individual. Fournier is to be located only, with that location immediately reported to Detective Marklin or myself. He is not to be apprehended. I repeat, do not engage the suspect. Find him and report. And, people, be quick about it. That's all."

Bruce stepped out to stand beside her. "Stravenski!"

"Yes, Detective," Stravenski answered, springing to his feet.

"Get everyone here a picture of our suspect. Then, make sure you get a copy over to Somerset. We need everyone's cooperation in this manhunt."

"Officer Clemens," Jocelyn said. "You find out the makes, models, and plate numbers relating to all vehicles owned or registered by Carter Wainwright, address 8 Lakeside Avenue, Rehoboth. Get that information to all active cars, pronto."

"I'm on it." Officer Clemens hurried away.

CHAPTER 26

S*AVE ME!* A*ARON* T*RIED* T*O* yell, but his voice came out in bubbles. Someone or something was pulling him down. Skeletal hands tore at his clothes, clawed at his flesh, dragging him deep beneath the surface. A faint moon shimmered above, but its light was fading. Darkness spread around him and tried to swallow him. He reached up. *Somebody, please, take my hand!*

"Forgive me!" Aaron bolted upright, awakened by the sound of his own scream. Another nightmare, its details were quickly fading. The chill of the ocean remained.

A car honked outside, and he ran downstairs, where his mother waited with a brown lunch bag, likely filled with a ham sandwich and carrots, neither of which he liked. He ignored it and barreled out the door.

"Have fun at work!" his mother called as he jumped into the passenger seat of the police car. "Be safe."

"Dude, you're all wrinkled," Brian said. "I thought you had some important matter to take care of. Were you sleeping for the last hour?"

Aaron scoffed. "No."

"Who's that?" Brian asked, waving.

"That's my mom."

"I thought you said you needed to stop by *your* place," Brian said.

"Kind of lame that you're still living with your parents, isn't it? How old are you?"

"Ha, ha. Do you write your own material? Because you're way too fucking funny." *God, I hate this job.* "Anyway, I just separated from my girlfriend, and I needed a place to crash. This was... convenient."

"Oh." Brian grimaced. "I'm sorry. I didn't know. If you needed a place to stay, you could have called me."

Brian's straight-faced stare made him appear as though he were actually serious. Aaron found the offer disturbing. *Is Marklin's little errand bitch trying to bond with me? Yeah, living with him would be loads of fun. We could bake cookies for Grandma, suck off Marklin together, and still have time to get up bright and early for church on Sunday. We'd be a modern-day Felix and Oscar.* Aaron slouched in his seat. *Then again, living with my parents is double the Felixes. God, I'm so pathetic.*

"I appreciate the offer, Brian. But at least this way, I can get some bills paid off."

"That's cool. I just thought—"

Aaron's cell phone rang. He cringed. He still hadn't changed that awful ringtone. "Hello?"

"Aaron. It's Sven. Where the hell are you guys?"

"Dude, chill out. We just stopped to get a taco and—"

"Beaudette wants to know your status immediately. Aren't you guys listening to your scanner?"

Does anyone listen to that thing? Aaron didn't even know if it was on. "Like I was saying, we just got back to the car, and—"

"What about your portables?"

Aaron's portable radio was off, but when he glanced over at Brian, he was surprised to learn that Mr. By-the-Book's was, too. "Sven, why would we need those? We're in the car."

"Well, Fournier flew the coop. Everyone's looking for him."

"How long ago did this happen?"

"Only five or six minutes ago. Marklin wants him found and surveillance reestablished yesterday. He is pissed."

"Well, if I could go back to yesterday, it would be fairly easy to reestablish surveillance since we knew where Doug was then."

"Don't be an asshole. I'm just doing my job here."

"Sorry. Marklin just pisses me off."

"Yeah, well, you and me both, pal."

"But relax. You can tell Marklin that Officer Temple and I are heading over to Ricardo Jimenez's house to see if he knows anything." Aaron smirked. *Taking the initiative—that should appease everyone.* The detectives would think he was following up a lead, and he would get to enjoy some down time with Rick, maybe play some Xbox. He was thrilled that Ricardo's sight had improved enough to play again. *If Brian's good, maybe we'll even let him play a game or two.*

"Will do, Aaron," Sven said with a laugh. He'd been out on patrol with Aaron before. "Enjoy your Xbox." He hung up the phone.

"Aaron, we never got tacos," Brian said, stating the obvious.

Not yet, anyway. "No shit, Brian," Aaron responded, mildly annoyed. "I was covering our asses."

"What did he mean when he said to enjoy your Xbox?"

Aaron rolled his eyes. "Brian, shut up."

Brian frowned. "Well, we're going to your friend's place, aren't we?"

"What is this? Twenty fucking questions? Yes, Brian. We're going to my friend's place. He lives three miles from here. You need to relax already."

When they arrived, Ricardo was standing on his apartment steps, holding a bowling bag.

"Wait here," Aaron said to Brian as he parked. "I'll be right back." *Maybe. If I feel like it.* He walked over to Ricardo. "Going somewhere?"

"H-Hey, Aaron…" Ricardo shifted his feet, making the bag swing at his side. "What are you doing here?"

"I had some free time… sort of. You know how it goes. I figured I'd stop by and see what you were up to."

"Sorry, I'm going out. I'll be leaving any minute now." Ricardo chewed on the thumbnail of his free hand, his gaze shifting repeatedly up and down the street.

"Hey, are you okay? Did something happen?"

"Yeah, I'm fine. I'm going bowling, and now I feel bad for not inviting you."

"That's not it. Come on, Rick. What's up? Did Doug call you?"

"Why? You don't think he did it, do you?"

"Doug? Nah. He's about as normal as they come... more normal than us, anyway." Aaron laughed. "He's okay in my book. But, Rick, you should be wary of Carter. I don't trust that guy. I don't think he's who he says he is. Something about him and who he claims to be... it's all wrong. His name isn't even really Carter Wainwright." Aaron shoved his hands in his pockets and looked away. "There's something about him... like familiar, but all wrong. And something else, something I never told you, never knew how to tell you—"

"Is that so?" Ricardo seemed distracted, his focus constantly switching from Aaron to the street.

Aaron straightened and cleared his throat. "Anyway, Rick, you know me. I doubt I'd bust Doug even if he was the killer."

A Toyota Camry pulled up behind the patrol car.

"Well, here's your chance to prove it," Ricardo murmured.

The driver of the Camry opened his door and stepped out. It was Carter Wainwright.

"Carter! What are you doing?" Doug yelled from inside the car. "We need to get out of here!"

"Too late for that," Carter said. "Get the one in the police car," he ordered, keeping his eyes locked on Aaron.

Doug emerged from the Camry and walked toward the cruiser.

"Hey, Doug," Aaron said. "You've got the whole city looking for you." He laughed.

Carter's unnerving stare felt wrong—seriously wrong. Aaron tried to look through the tinted windows to see who else was in the car, but he couldn't see anything. His attention shifted back to Carter, then to Doug, who was getting closer to the patrol car.

Aaron unsnapped his holster and rested his palm on the grip of his service pistol. "Brian! Wake up, you idiot!"

Brian had been reclined in his seat, picking at a fingernail. He jolted upright. "Fuck!" He must have seen Doug approaching in his side mirror. He squirmed in his seat, probably going for his weapon.

Aaron sensed danger, but he couldn't be certain where it would come from first. They all seemed hostile, even Ricardo. The horror stretching Brian's eyes and mouth signaled the most imminent threat. Aaron had to act.

"Stay where you are, Doug," he said, taking a step forward.

Doug didn't stop. He loomed over the passenger-side window of the patrol car, his mountainous body casting an eerie shadow over the vehicle.

Aaron pulled his weapon out of the holster. "I said, don't move."

Doug drew back his arm and punched the cruiser's window. The force shattered the glass, and Doug's fist continued into Brian's head, whipping it to the side.

By the time Aaron had his weapon raised, he couldn't fire for fear of hitting his partner. He took a step closer. "I said *freeze*! Damn it, Doug!" His hand was trembling, making the barrel of his pistol shake. "Don't make me do this."

Doug's wrist and arm were badly cut, but if he noticed, he didn't show it. He pulled the door open with his left hand, grabbed Brian's shirt with his right, and pulled him from the patrol car.

Brian's back hit the street hard, a whoosh of air bursting out of him. Doug kneeled on his chest, pinning him down. Brian wheezed as he struggled to take in air. Soon, he would suffocate.

Aaron had a clear shot. He aimed, swallowed hard, and squeezed the trigger. Just as he fired, he tumbled to the ground. Someone had shoved him from behind.

Carter bent over and snatched Aaron's pistol from his hand. "Not my weapon of choice, but it'll do for now."

Aaron shot up to his feet, preparing to charge. Carter nonchalantly raised the pistol and aimed it at Aaron's forehead. Ricardo—the only person in a whole damn world suddenly gone crazy, the only one Aaron could still trust—stood behind Carter, holding that damned bowling bag and doing nothing.

"What the hell, man? Are you out of your fucking mind?" Aaron had no idea what he should do. His mind was racing. Then it hit him. "Shit, Doug. You really are *him*! Get off of my partner and lay down on the ground, right now! You, too, Carter."

Carter smiled like a politician. "But, Officer Pimental, I have your gun." He studied the pistol. "Such a crass way to kill someone. No... personality." He twirled it around his finger. "Do you want it back?" He held it out, butt first.

Aaron squinted. Expecting some trick, he stared at the offered pistol but did not take it.

"Here," Carter insisted, shoving the gun at his chest. "I don't need it. I have something much stronger on my side."

Behind him, Ricardo offered a low "Amen" as he moved to the right, away from Carter. Aaron snatched the gun and stepped back. He raised the weapon and aimed it at Carter.

Carter's smile broadened. In an instant, the smile was replaced with an expression of guileless innocence. His body sagged as if he alone carried all the burdens of the world. He raised his arms, palms up, and held them out as if he wanted to give Aaron a hug. "Ricardo, this has been foreseen. He's supposed to come with us. Today is his induction. Rejoice, for he is one of us."

"Shut the fuck up," Aaron said. "Stay where you are. I don't have any idea what bullshit you're going on about, but don't think for two seconds that I won't drop you where you stand, motherfucker. Get down on the ground. You and Doug are under arrest."

"Ricardo, trust in him," Carter continued. "He's led us here today. Aaron must come with us."

Aaron couldn't see where Ricardo was, but he didn't have time to worry about that. He had to keep his focus on Carter. "I said shut the fuck up, or I'll blow your goddamn head off!"

"Ricardo, you know what to do."

What is he saying? Ricardo? No fucking way! Aaron chanced a glance around to see where his friend was. Ricardo had moved until he was almost behind Aaron. "Rick, what's he babbling about?" Aaron asked. He saw movement out of the corner of his eye and turned his head back to see Doug finally getting off Brian, but his partner didn't move. He was either unconscious or dead. Either way, Aaron was on his own, unless Ricardo—

"I'm sorry it has to be this way," Ricardo said softly. "In a few hours, though, you'll understand."

"Rick, what—" A burning sensation at the small of his back dropped him to the ground, while the rest of him went cold and shuddered. He looked up to see Ricardo holding a stun gun.

"Give him a longer jolt," Carter said.

Ricardo bent over and hit Aaron with a second wave of pain.

"Put them in the car," Carter ordered.

"But there's no more room," Doug said.

"It has a trunk, doesn't it?"

CHAPTER 27

A ARON STARED AT A PINPOINT of light surrounded by darkness, an all-consuming black that had him lost in its bends and folds. That dot of light was his marker, the only thing that gave him bearing in the endless emptiness. But as a point of reference, it was too insignificant to afford him any sense of direction.

Still, it was all he had. The darkness was cold, and...

Something's here. He couldn't see them, but he knew both in his heart and his mind that he'd found the place where monsters dwelled. And one monster in particular.

He heard the laughter as if the mouth that made it were beside his ear. Hot breath made the hairs on his neck rise. He bolted for the light.

He seemed to cover miles in seconds. The light grew closer and larger at an alarming rate. He stopped and realized that the light was racing toward him. And he was suddenly more afraid of it than he was of the dark and all the beasts with their dripping fangs and sordid laughter.

Before he could react, the light smashed into him, enclosed him, and blinded him. He squeezed his eyes shut and heard a shrill cry of a—

A bird?

He squinted, and as his eyes adjusted, the brilliant white expanse gave way to a gorgeous blue: the sky, filled with rolling white clouds.

No. Rolling white caps. He was staring at the ocean, out in front of him and—his eyes followed the water toward his feet—below him.

Dizzying. Rocking forward, he feared he might fall into the waves. *Or am I already falling?*

"Is he dead?" The voice—a woman's voice that he knew well—was filled with agony and had the same effect on his heart.

He turned his head. Raquel Miranda stood beside him, as beautiful as he remembered. Her fingers bent like claws as she ran them down her tear-covered face. At that moment, he hated her, hated her as much as he'd ever loved her. *Maybe I should push her, too.* He raised his hands. *After all, this is all her fault!*

But he couldn't. He loved her. He did. He stepped toward her, arms outstretched. He tried to touch her, but she slapped his hands away. "Shhh, shhh. Please," he muttered.

"My God, Aaron, what have you done?" She paced back and forth, pulling at her hair, barely keeping clear of the ledge.

The enormity of his actions was beginning to set in. His hands trembled. "I... I don't know."

"Oh my God, Aaron! You killed him. You fucking killed him!"

"No, I... I didn't mean to! He came at me first. I was defending myself. You saw it."

"You pushed him! That's what I saw. You pushed him off the cliff! You weren't even supposed to be here." Snot ran from her nose, racing the tears down her face.

She was right, though. Aaron had no business being there, and what he'd done... he couldn't have. It must have been an accident. It had to have been. Self-defense, at the least. *And who could blame me?* He had been Raquel's boyfriend up until a few weeks ago, when their relationship had begun to spiral out of control. He clenched his teeth. *That was her fault, too.*

"He was just a friend, Aaron." Raquel started slapping at him.

He grabbed her wrists to stop her. Realizing he might be bruising her arms, he let go.

She cried out and fell to her knees. "Just a friend! Can't you understand that? We weren't doing anything. But you killed him anyway, all because you don't trust me, you jealous asshole. I never did anything. *He* never did anything. God, he was so shy and kind, wouldn't have hurt a fly. You didn't even know him, you… you… monster! What could he possibly have ever done to you?"

Aaron felt her strikes, both the physical and the mental. But each one seemed weaker, duller. He breathed in the clean air then stood a little straighter. "I did what I needed to do. For us."

Raquel looked up at him, wailed again, and curled into a ball.

"You're making a scene." He bent over and put his arms around her. She flinched at his touch, but he was gentle. He would be gentle. He lifted her to her feet. "I love you, Raquel. I don't want anybody to ruin what we have."

She beat her fists against his chest, but he just squeezed her tighter, willing her to love him again.

"What we *have*?" She sobbed into his shoulder then reared her head back and glared into his eyes. "Christ! We don't have anything. You've ruined that, Aaron. *You* did. Not him, not me, not anybody. Just you…" Raquel pushed off him and vomited violently over the edge of the cliff, into the water and rocks below, where her date had plummeted to his death only moments earlier.

The man's shriek, the sound of bone snapping against rock, the weak cries for help until he finally died—Aaron still heard those sounds in his ears, but he steeled himself against them. He moved to stand next to her.

Each crashing wave battered the fresh corpse against the cliff wall. The sight was probably making Raquel's upset stomach worse, but she deserved it. And that guy down below deserved his just rewards, too.

When her dry heaves stopped and she managed to catch her breath, she looked up at Aaron. Fear and horror had bleached her face, and he wondered if she would keep her cheating-whore mouth shut. And something else… his mind was working. Conniving. Seeking a way out.

Maybe I'll have to push her. He didn't think he could do it again. *Do what? Murder?* "That wasn't murder. That wasn't. That was a reset."

"You were smiling when you did it." She glared at him, and he realized he had spoken aloud. In her eyes, he saw more than fear. He saw hatred and revulsion.

"I was not. I'm not a murderer. That was self-defense." *And if I was smiling, it was only because I was taking out the trash.*

"You were. I'm going to the police." Raquel stood and slowly walked away on unsteady legs.

The Cliffwalks of Newport was a favorite spot for local lovers seeking a romantic evening. He knew why people went there. Hell, he'd taken Raquel there a few times. And each time had ended the same way: with his hands and other parts wherever he wanted them to be. Raquel had gone there with some asshole who thought he could just steal a girl he had no claim to. That asshole was the bad guy in all of this. Aaron sneered. *Bet she didn't expect this kind of excitement.*

He hurried to catch up to her. "How could you do this to me? To *us*?"

Raquel stopped. "You're sick. I hate you, Aaron—I hate you!" She started walking away again.

"You hate me?" Aaron was shocked. "After all I've done for you? Can't you see how much I care about you?"

Tears welled in his eyes, but with every step she took away from him, they became easier to hold back. The Cliffwalks were heavily patronized in the summer, but that cold, late-fall night, only those who sought privacy were out and about. Someone might have seen what had happened. Aaron could only hope luck had been on his side in that respect. But sooner or later, a jogger or perhaps another couple would pass by. He needed to get Raquel and himself out of there.

Aaron stomped up beside her. "Raquel!"

She cringed when he put his arm around her, but he held on. "Hey, babe, shhh. It's okay. Everything's okay. I'm sorry I yelled. I'm not going to hurt you." He kissed her temple. "I still love you. I always will. Let's just keep walking and pretend this never happened. Soon, it'll be like it never actually did."

"They'll catch you."

"Me? What did I do? The way I see it, you caused this. And I swear to you, Raquel, if you rat me out to the cops, I'll tell them you did it. That it was all planned—your idea, in fact. You're a sadistic killer who wanted to see if you could get away with it. You talked me into coming with you. I tried to stop you, but I was too late. There was nothing I could do." He smiled. "But I don't want that, babe, and you don't want that. Let's just chalk this up to the accident it was and move on. Can we do that, honey?"

"They'll never believe you." She tried to push away from him.

He didn't let her go. He would never let her go. "Maybe not, but I'd say the odds are in my favor." His confidence was growing despite the fact that the evidence of his crime still lay open for all to see a mere seventy feet below. "I have no history of violence. I'm the good, wholesome, all-American kid. Can you say the same? Do you want to take the chance?"

"I should've known you'd just keep getting worse. I should have left you a long time ago. If you didn't always threaten to kill yourself, I'd have left you a year ago. But I stayed because I felt bad, and I prayed you'd get better. You're not getting better, Aaron. You're worse, so much worse." She shuddered. "I should have let you kill yourself! Oh God, why did I ever have to meet you? I can't believe I fell in love with you."

"So you do love me!" Aaron smiled. That was all he wanted to hear. That made everything worthwhile. Things would be good again between them. He just had to be patient.

He walked her back to his car and drove her home.

When he pulled into her driveway, she jumped out before he could stop her. He reached for the handle to open his door, but it wouldn't budge.

"What the fuck?" He rattled the handle then pushed against the door, thinking it was jammed.

Raquel was climbing her front steps. *Don't let her get away. If she gets away, she's gone forever.* He dove into the passenger seat, but when he reached to open that door, he saw and heard the lock click into place.

"No..." He tried the handle then pounded his palms against the door. "No, no, no!"

Raquel was at her front door. When the door opened, her body blurred then dissipated as if she were no more than a wisp of smoke blown away by a breeze.

"Raquel, no. Don't—"

Aaron's eyes popped open. Tears were running down his cheeks. The words "leave me" haunted his mind then faded.

Frantic delusions and obsessive behavior had ruled his seventeen-year-old mind. Aaron had followed Raquel to the Cliffwalks, knowing full well he would find her with someone else. He remembered lunging forward, pushing Raquel's replacement for him off the long drop onto the rocks below. He could picture the guy's spine snapping on impact. But he couldn't remember making his body act, his mind giving his muscles the order to move and commit murder.

Afterward, the world seemed to spin a little faster on its axis. Aaron felt as though he were having an out-of-body experience. All he could do was watch from a distance as some force took control of his body. His first instinct had been to run, then his survival mindset kicked in. The only evidence of his crime were two witnesses: one alive and one dead or dying. Aaron could do little more to the latter, but the living needed extensive consideration. After all, he hadn't meant to kill the guy, and part of him truly believed it had been Raquel's fault. He'd never intended the guy to fall over the edge. At least, he couldn't remember forming that intent. He wasn't a murderer. He just wanted Raquel.

Later that night, Aaron hadn't been able to sleep. He kept envisioning the cops knocking down his door to take him away. But they didn't come for him that night. They didn't come the next night, either.

A few days later, a body washed up on First Beach. Aaron had never found out the guy's name, and the initial news report excluded it, perhaps because the police were unsure if the teenager had been a minor. Officers had found the boy's car nearby, a bottle of antidepressants in its glove compartment. They found no sign of a struggle, the paper said. No witnesses were interviewed. The death was written off as a suicide.

As the nights went by, Aaron still couldn't sleep. Thoughts of Raquel kept him restless. *Didn't she love him? Where did she go?* For a long time, he looked for her. Eventually, he gave up, but when he did, he gave up on life, too. He went into the bathroom and slashed his wrists.

Raquel was the first girl he'd loved, and like many foolish first lovers, Aaron thought it would last forever. It took three years to cope with the separation, three years to force the memories of her into the farthest reaches of his psyche. The guilt still remained, not for his crime but for driving her away.

The murder was much easier for him to deny, first through alcohol and later through prolonged indifference. He told himself over and over again that it was self-defense, until he believed it.

That ugly night in Newport was so long ago. He'd convinced himself it was part of another life, a former Aaron. He'd gotten better, the passions of youth having burned out with all his hopes and dreams. But the beast had only hibernated.

Lying in the pitch-black darkness, so utterly lost in the memory, he took a moment to realize he had no idea where he was. He tried to raise his hand to his face and found that he couldn't. They had been handcuffed behind his back. He opened his mouth to scream, but he'd been gagged. The smell of motor oil tinged with gasoline, along with a sense of motion, told him he was in the trunk of a car.

The carpet beneath his face was damp and chafing. He squirmed, looking for a means to escape, but he was trapped. He rolled onto his back. Someone was lying beside him. *Brian? Is he dead?*

Where are they taking us? Without knowing how long he'd been out, he couldn't guess how far they'd traveled.

Damn it, Rick! He brought his knee up quickly, underestimating the distance between it and the trunk lid. He squealed as his kneecap jarred against unyielding metal. *How could you do this to me?* He never expected loyalty from his other friends—not even from Arianna—but Ricardo wasn't like his other friends.

Aaron's fear left him. Anger filled the hole. He rolled back onto his belly. Inching his knees underneath his torso, he used all the power his legs could muster to push himself up against the lid. He slammed his back into the lid over and over again.

The trunk refused to open. Aaron rolled onto his side and drove his heels into the side panel as he yelled around the gag. After thirty seconds of his banging and muffled screaming, the vehicle stopped. He froze and listened. A door opened. Footsteps came toward him.

The trunk popped open, revealing the clear night sky. Driven by rage, he struggled to rise onto his knees, not to run away but to confront Ricardo. Doug swung a fist into Aaron's temple.

When Aaron came to again, his wrists and ankles were still bound, but duct tape had replaced the cuffs. He was no longer in a trunk. Someone had carried him inside. *But inside where?*

The nerve endings in the left side of his face awakened with brutal intensity, feeling as though he'd been blindsided with a baseball bat. Aaron couldn't imagine that much power in one punch. Pain shot along his collarbone like a colony of fire ants burrowing beneath the skin. He could only see a sliver out of his left eye, and he could feel the squishy, watery puffiness of swollen flesh each time he tried to open it more.

That motherfucker! Please tell me he didn't shatter my eye socket or detach a retina. I'll kill him.

Aaron worried about his eye, though he realized he should be more worried about his life. The prospect of death didn't faze him much. He'd craved death for so long, it was hard to get worked up when the reaper came knocking. All the painful parts that might precede it, those Aaron dreaded.

And at the hands of a friend? He chuckled then winced. *Only those you love can truly hurt you. I've done everything for him. I was always there when he needed me. And this is how the piece of shit repays me.*

The wall he faced was about six feet away. Patches of wallpaper had peeled back and curled like sunbaked worms dying on the pavement. He guessed he was in one of Fall River's countless old mills, long since abandoned except by vagrants, junkies, and the occasional serial killer.

He tried to turn his head to look around, but something barred his movement. Whoever had gagged him had been creative. Duct tape not only held in the gag, which tasted like a sweaty gym sock, but circled his head. His hands had been pulled through the back of the folding chair he sat on and bound to something he couldn't see. His neck offered little range of motion. With his left eye mostly useless, that side of the room was a blur.

Still, Aaron could tell he wasn't alone. He saw the hazy outline of a human leg a few feet to his left, covered in a standard-issue police uniform. *Brian. He's alive.* Quiet sobbing came from farther away.

"Aaron?" Brian whispered. "Are you awake?"

"Mmmph!"

"Oh, right," Brian said. "Still gagged. Well, my right eye is pretty messed up. You're coming in blurry. Your left eye looks pretty messed up, too. That Fournier packs a mean punch. Anyway, duct tape may be the all-purpose fixer-upper, but it doesn't stick too well to a pole that's rusty and chipping. Move around enough, and you'll peel the paint right off the pole and the tape with it. My head's almost free. Not to make you sick or anything, but they gagged me with a sock, and it didn't look all that clean. I'm assuming you got its mate."

Why did he have to tell me that? Aaron winced as his saliva dampened the cloth against his tongue.

"I'm trying to get my hands loose. I'm making progress." Brian's words were strained, his breathing heavy. "If I can just get it peeled a little more, I could wriggle free."

Aaron writhed and twisted. Searing pain, like a gazillion needles being stabbed through every pore in his body, met every movement. Tape stretched and peeled from his skin.

"Yes!" Brian hissed. "My arm is free."

A couple of minutes later, Aaron saw the leg move. When Brian next came into view, he was on his way to falling face-first onto the moldy floor. As he landed, black specks scurried away. Aaron shuffled his feet to scare the roaches away from him.

Brian climbed to his knees. Black grime smeared his cheek and covered his shirt. He must have forgotten to free his ankles before charging like the Light Brigade. "Jesus, Aaron, this must be where your boy Doug and company do it. There's dried blood everywhere! And look over there." Brian pointed.

Aaron turned his head as far to the right as he could and saw the end of a gurney. He let out a breath when he didn't see anyone lying on it.

"Oh God, this is blood!" Brian frantically wiped his hands on his pant legs. "There's someone else here. She's tied up over there."

Aaron tried to hop his seat around. To his surprise, it worked, and he saw a woman sitting in the back corner. Her hair was disheveled, and mascara streaked her face, but despite all that, she was striking.

"She's beautiful," Brian said, echoing Aaron's thought. "How could someone do that to her?"

Aaron rolled his good eye. If he could have spoken, he would have yelled at Brian to move his ass.

"It's going to be okay," Brian whispered to the woman. "I'm a cop. I'm going to get you out of here."

Aaron spotted an operating table across the room. On the tray below the table, something metallic shimmered in the flickering light of a lone candle. Grunting and nose-pointing, he alerted Brian to it.

Brian covered his mouth with one hand, his complexion turning pale. Limited by his bonds, he shuffled his knees back and forth two inches at a time. Inching through blood and grime, he moved steadily toward the table. He hesitated when he got close. "I could be corrupting evidence if I touch it. Should I leave it alone?"

Again, Brian was lucky Aaron couldn't speak. *If we live, we're all the evidence we need.* Aaron groaned. *Just pick the fucking thing up.*

Brian seemed to understand the meaning behind the groan. He grabbed a knife with a serrated blade and severed the duct tape around his ankles. Getting to his feet, knife in hand, Brian headed for the woman. He cut the tape from around her hands and calves then removed the ball gag from her mouth.

She stood and put her arms around him, resting her head on his chest. She didn't seem to mind the filth.

"What's your name?" he asked.

"Maura."

"I'm Brian, and that's Aaron," he said, pointing. "Wait right here." He pulled away from her. "I'm going to cut him free, then we'll all sneak out of here."

Maura nodded, and Brian headed toward Aaron. He circled behind the chair, out of Aaron's line of sight. Aaron felt a tug, then his head lurched forward, free from the tape. He could turn his head, but the movement sent pain shooting up his neck.

"Hold still," Brian said. "This may hurt a bit."

Aaron growled as the tape was torn from his face. Blood and stubble blotted its sticky side. "Thanks," he said, half serious and half sarcastic. "Now, get my arms and legs."

"Wait!" Brian froze, his head cocked toward the door. "Someone's coming." He picked up the stained sock, shoved it back into his mouth, and covered it with tape before Aaron could protest. Then he ran toward the doorway, standing off to the left so that when the door swung open, he would be behind it.

Brian! Aaron grunted into the gag. *Get me out of this fucking chair!*

Brian put his index finger over his lips and waved for Maura to join him. He raised the blade above his head as the door creaked open.

CHAPTER 28

"**A**NY WORD YET FROM TEMPLE and Pimental?" Bruce figured he must have asked the same question of every officer on duty at least twice.

"None, sir," Stravenski answered.

Bruce paced feverishly around the precinct floor. *Fournier is missing. Now, Pimental and Temple are missing. Is Pimental part of all this? He is friendly with the suspects.*

"Send a car around to Ricardo Jimenez's apartment. I want a status update from Pimental and Temple as soon as possible." A chill ran down Bruce's spine. *If they can still give a status update.*

Stravenski hustled off then returned a few minutes later. "Sir, Somerset officers were on-scene when I called. Neighbors had reported a disturbance at the Jimenez residence. No one was there when the officers arrived, but they did find Pimental's patrol car out front. Its passenger-side window had been shattered."

Bruce set his jaw. That nagging worry he usually buried in his subconscious moved to the forefront of his mind. "I want everyone working on this now! Wake them up if you have to. A couple of our own may be in trouble."

Aaron's eyes widened as the blade cut through the air. It traveled downward in a deadly arc, as if craving flesh. The knife swung toward the crevasse between Kelly's neck and her left shoulder.

Had Brian hit his mark, the stroke would surely have been deadly. But with almost superhuman reflexes, Doug caught and slowed Brian's arm. The blade sliced into Kelly's bicep instead.

She screamed and clutched her arm. Blood seeped through her fingers. The cut might need stitches, but it was hardly life-threatening.

Still clutching Brian's wrist, Doug glanced at her. "Are you okay?"

Before she could respond, Brian took the hulking beast's distraction as a second chance to strike. He drove his left knee into Doug's scrotum. The big man groaned and dropped to one knee, but he retained his hold on Brian.

Aaron shouted through his gag. *Get him, Brian. Kill that son of a bitch.*

Brian followed up with a left hook, hitting Doug's jaw and knocking his head back. Doug finally released Brian's arm.

Aaron began to hope. *It's him or us, Brian. Kill him!*

With his knife hand free, Brian slashed horizontally across Doug's chest, drawing enough blood to spatter the floor. Doug didn't even seem to feel it. Brian raised the blade again.

With one hand on the floor and his feet planted firmly under him, Doug looked like a defensive lineman going in for the sack. As Brian raised the knife again, Doug sacked him. Brian's head hit the floor hard, and the weapon dropped from his hand and slid across the wood.

With one hand grasping Brian's shirt and the other hand palming his face, Doug picked him up and ran the back of his head into the wall. Dust and plaster exploded in billowing clouds and ashen rain.

Aaron felt his chances for escape dwindle as Brian hung barely conscious against the dilapidated wall. Through the cracks between Doug's fingers, Aaron could see one of Brian's eyes rolling back in his head. Aaron struggled in his chair as Carter and Ricardo filed into the room.

Carter pointed at Maura. "Grab the girl."

Ricardo and Kelly ran over to her and subdued her quickly, despite her clawing and kicking. Kelly dug a pair of handcuffs out of her back pocket and chained Maura's hands behind her back. She swept Maura's feet out from under her with a single graceful motion of her leg, and

Maura crashed to the floor on her butt. Though she didn't appear hurt, she didn't try to stand.

"Looks like we have our first volunteer," Carter said, his face shining with sadistic pleasure. "Put him on the table."

Doug carried Brian by his neck over to the operating table. Brian clawed at Doug's tree-trunk arm and kicked his legs. Unaffected by the weak strikes, Doug slammed him down onto the table. Brian gasped for air, his attacker's powerful fingers still clenched around his throat.

"Guess it's time you guys earned your class participation grade," Carter said. "Hold him down."

Ricardo wrapped his arms around Brian's right leg, putting his weight on it to keep him in place. Kelly grabbed his other leg. Brian didn't stop kicking, but his motions were limited to slight bends at the knee and quick, totally useless jerks. His attackers seemed to be waiting for him to tire out.

Throughout the entire thing, Aaron had been struggling against the tape around his hands and ankles, but it didn't even seem to be loosening. He knew what was at stake: his life, his partner's life, and the life of a woman he did not know. But he could do nothing.

Brian continued fighting, scratching at Doug's hands. Doug let go of Brian's neck and clamped those powerful hands around Brian's arms. He slammed them against the table a few times. Aaron heard a crack, and Brian howled in pain. Afterward, his right arm hung limply off the side of the table.

Carter strode over and picked up the knife Brian had dropped. He brought it over and slid it underneath Brian's shirt. Brian's eyes widened, and he gasped. Carter just stood there, holding the knife in place.

Aaron could see the wickedness shimmering in the killer's eyes, glinting off the saliva on his teeth. *He's savoring it. Every second.*

Instead of pointing the knife down, Carter aimed it toward the ceiling and poked the tip of the blade through the cloth. He ran it along the button line of Brian's uniform. The sharp edge shredded the material with ease, exposing Brian's chest. Carter's eyes widened as he raised the knife.

Aaron fought harder against the tape. He screamed around his gag, but the sound came out as a whimper.

"Wait," Doug said. "Is he chosen? What is his sin? Does he need redeeming?"

Carter sneered at Doug. "The Lord chooses who we save, not me. After we finish here today, all will be revealed. The Lord will come again, this time as the Lion. Because of our deeds here, many more will follow Him. So I ask you all, help me get through this last task that He has set for us. Be patient and keep the faith."

"Doug's right, Carter," Ricardo said. "We can't save him without first knowing he needs saving and giving him a chance to confess. Otherwise, we would be no more than common killers. Our mission would mean nothing."

You are *no better than common killers. And you, Ricardo—you're something even worse.*

Carter lowered the knife to his side. "You both should be ashamed of yourselves. You're not questioning me but God Himself. Must I remind you of the Book of Job? What happened to Job when he questioned God?"

Aaron didn't understand the reference. Maybe the others didn't, either, because they just stared, expressionless.

Carter shook his head. "Fine, then. You will see his sins exposed just as I say, just as God has told me."

"Hey," Carter said harshly. He jabbed a finger between Brian's eyebrows. "Hey, you." He grabbed Brian's cheeks and squeezed, puckering his lips like a kissing fish. "Listen to me closely." Carter rested the blade on the skin of Brian's neck. "You might say your life depends on it."

Aaron gagged on the saliva pooling in the back of his throat and tried to cough. Carter flashed him a smile as though he had just remembered Aaron was sitting there. Carter's smile reminded Aaron of Trevor, the school bully, and the way he used to grin when he knocked Aaron's books out of his hands. Aaron had feared Trevor, but the olive-skinned devil looming over his partner was worse than any elementary school bully.

Carter gave Brian's face a light slap. "Officer Temple? Brian, is it?"

Brian glared up at the man without responding.

"Brian then," Carter said. "Are you a Christian?"

Brian took a moment to answer, as if expecting some trick. "Yes."

"What denomination?"

"Methodist."

"Do you participate in the practice of confession?"

Brian hesitated again. "Yes." The answer sounded like a question.

"Good. That'll make this go quicker. You have this opportunity to absolve yourself of your sins and declare your love for Our Father. Do you have anything you'd like to confess? Is there anything for which you'd like to be forgiven?"

From what Aaron knew of him, Brian was basically a saint. He'd probably never so much as taken a penny that wasn't his. Aaron bet the cop's life had been fairly ordinary. Brian had even become a police officer because he "wanted to help people." *What dirty, dark secrets could he possibly have to confess?* In a world full of evil, Brian was as sickeningly good as they came. Aaron just hoped Brian wasn't too good to lie to save his own hide… and maybe his partner's while he was at it.

"Yes!" Brian cried. "Yes, I have plenty to confess."

"Really?" Carter looked amused. The skepticism in his voice was clearly meant for his audience. He waited a bit, almost as if trying to impress Brian with his theatrics. "Well? What do you have to confess?"

Brian stuttered, no doubt searching his mind for something, *anything*, to confess. Finally, he spoke. "I would like to be forgiven for all the bad things I've ever done, for every sin I've committed."

Carter's mouth twisted into a wry smile. Aaron's heart sank. He knew Brian's words were about to be twisted somehow. No matter what his partner said, he was a dead man.

"Watch!" Carter said in a melodramatic tone. "Lucifer controls this poor man's soul. We must deliver it from evil." He sounded like a doomsday preacher from any number of low-budget movies.

Surely, he's overselling it. One of those people had to be able to see through him. But as Aaron examined the faces of Carter's minions, the rational sincerity he saw on each seemed so… *irrational*. The three of them followed the play with blank stares as if they were hypnotized by the shiny object in Carter's hand. *Not a brain cell among them.* Carter wasn't merely playing to the crowd. He was preaching to the choir.

"I confessed," Brian pleaded. "Isn't that what you wanted to hear?" Brian's eyes frantically searched the faces standing over him, likely seeing what Aaron had seen in them.

"See? The devil controls his voice," Carter said as the others leaned closer, apparently eager to find a reason to "save" Brian. "He tells us not the truth but rather what he thinks we want to hear. He lies to sway you from your task. The devil has forked this man's tongue. God has seen fit for us to save him, and that is what we must do."

Aaron lashed out with everything he had, desperate to free himself, sweating and grunting like an animal. The tape might have stretched a little, but it didn't break.

"You're nothing," Brian said. He spit at Carter's face, but most of it came back down onto his own cheek.

Carter cupped a hand around his ear. "What's that? I'm nothing?" He acted offended. "Do you think you're better than us?"

"I *know* I'm better than you," Brian said. "You guys are nothing but a sick bunch of sideshow freaks that history will soon forget. Your turn to die will come. One by one, you'll each march straight into hell."

"You see, my friends?" Carter smiled. "You see his wrath? You see his pride? You see the devil inside him?"

The other three nodded. If they doubted him, it didn't matter. They would follow.

"Well," Carter said as he raised the blade, "I say, be gone with the devil!" He drove his crude weapon into Brian's torso.

"No!" Maura screamed.

Aaron closed his eyes. He listened to his partner bellow for what seemed like an eternity. When the screaming finally stopped, he opened his eyes. He had to turn his head away from the ghastly scene. He looked at Maura, curled in a ball on the floor. He couldn't save her, either.

CHAPTER 29

JOCELYN HUSTLED INTO BRUCE'S OFFICE. Every second counted. "The neighbors say they saw a gray or silver Toyota Camry outside Ricardo Jimenez's home at approximately eight forty-five p.m. No one got a plate number, but I put out an APB anyway. Officer Reilly reported that she saw one drive by her on Davol Street around nine."

"Did she follow?" Bruce asked.

"She said she tried but lost them before she could even get close. They must have ducked behind one of the buildings in that area. Lots of abandoned factories over there, plenty of places to hide. I'll bet my ass that's where we'll find them." *But will we find them in time?* Jocelyn wasn't optimistic. A sighting of a Toyota Camry, one of thousands, was hardly something to get excited about. Pimental and Temple were probably already dead. *No. Don't think like that.* "If that was our guys, then we need to move on it."

Bruce nodded. "I'll have every officer we can spare sent to that location. On the off chance that it was them, I doubt they're still driving around or that they would be dumb enough to leave the vehicle out in the open."

"Well, even if Douglas Fournier isn't our killer, he's a criminal now. Three witnesses say a man matching his description assaulted a police officer at Jimenez's address. We have our people looking for him, his wife, Pimental, Temple, and Jimenez."

"What about Carter Wainwright?"

"Some of the witnesses said a fifth male was present. So yes, him, too. I had a car sent to his house. Of course, he wasn't home. No one's ever home." Jocelyn leaned closer and lowered her voice. "Bruce, there's something else. The officer sent over to Wainwright's peeked through the windows. He said the house looked empty, as though nobody lived there at all—no furniture, no stuff, no nothing."

"That's impossible. There's no way he could have moved all his crap—crap I saw with my own two eyes—out of there without someone noticing. He's been under surveillance twenty-four seven."

"I'm just telling you what the officer said." She frowned. "You think someone else is helping them?"

Bruce scowled. "I don't care if he's got a whole battalion of Christian crusaders helping him; I'm not letting this guy get away. I know he's part of it, and I'll get him sooner or later, preferably sooner. Right now, though, Temple and Pimental are our first priorities."

Jocelyn started buttoning her coat. "I'm not doing them any good sitting around here. I'm heading over there to help in the search. My gut's telling me they're there. You'll let me know if you hear anything?"

"I won't have to," Bruce said as he stood. "I'm coming with you."

Blood was everywhere. Its metallic taste seemed to float on the particles Aaron sucked through his gag.

Carter was carving up Brian's corpse. Blood sprayed onto the others' faces, but they didn't seem to notice or care.

Seeing Ricardo standing over the dead body, Aaron realized that he'd never truly known his best friend. *Or did I turn a blind eye? How could I not have seen this?*

A few minutes later, Carter held up Brian's heart like a trophy. "Move the body."

Doug picked up Brian's arms while Ricardo grabbed the ankles. They moved automatically, as if they had practiced.

"Where do you want us to put him?" Doug asked.

"Just throw it in the corner for now."

The pair walked to the corner with Brian's body dangling between them. There, they dropped it unceremoniously, like a bag of garbage. Aaron's eyes were tearing up, and he prayed his nose wouldn't get clogged.

Carter walked over to Maura and lifted her chin. She turned her head away, but he wrenched it back. He flashed a sinister smile. "Let's start on the girl," he said, never averting his eyes from her.

"What about him?" Ricardo pointed at Aaron.

Leave me out of this shit. But Aaron knew he wouldn't be so lucky. Even after seeing Brian flayed open in front of him, he still had difficulty believing Ricardo would allow him to be killed. Then he thought of Craig and how he'd been strung up like a Christmas tree ornament. *If Rick could do that to Craig, then I'm probably dead.*

He tried again to escape. The tape dug trenches into his skin, tightening around his wrists and cutting off circulation.

Carter flashed Aaron that same innocent smile. "He looks just fine where he is. He can wait his turn."

"His turn? You said he would be one of us."

The smile fell off Carter's face. "You're right, Ricardo. That's what I meant. I only thought that maybe we'd do Maura first then get to Aaron. But either way is fine. Let's make him part of the team, shall we?"

Knife in hand, Carter moved toward Aaron. Drops of Brian's blood fell from the blade like the first quiet raindrops before a storm. Ricardo, Doug, and Kelly followed. Ricardo was smiling.

Carter bent over and cut through the duct tape around Aaron's head. Without any semblance of delicacy, he ripped the tape from Aaron's mouth.

Aaron spat out the gag. "Yeah, Carter, you're a real bad ass with that knife while you got me all tied up. Let me out of this chair, and we'll see who the real tough guy is."

"All in good time, Aaron," Carter said. "You can relax. We aren't going to hurt you."

"Oh yeah? Then why am I tied up? And why is my eye swollen to the size of a grapefruit?" He looked at Doug. "And you, you fat fuck. You put a used sock in my mouth? You're next on my list."

"You're in no position to make threats," Doug answered.

"You're right. Killing a pussy like you would be too easy. Maybe I'll just take it out on Kelly. You know, angry-fuck her. It would probably be a hell of a lot better than what you've been giving her." Aaron knew he shouldn't be aggravating the situation, but rage and fear had taken over his brain.

Doug raised his hand. "Shut your mouth, Aaron, before I shut it for you."

"Yeah, maybe I'll fuck her up the ass. With a face like hers, yeesh! I don't know how you do it. Then again, it's not the face you fuck, but the fuck you face. You should—"

Doug cut him off with a punch hard enough to rock Aaron's head to the side, and his jaw almost popped out of its socket.

"Stop it, Doug!" Ricardo yelled. "He's pissed off because he doesn't understand. Weren't you the same way?"

"I don't think so. I had faith to begin with, unlike this pretender," Doug said. "I have faith that he'll come around, but until then, he's just another lost soul in need of salvation." Doug scowled but took a step back. "When he does come around, we will have converted the unconvertible, saved the unsavable. But until then, if he keeps talking about Kelly that way, I'm going to tear him apart."

"Bring it on." Aaron's words were a little slurred. The threat sounded tired and unconvincing, even to his own ears.

"Enough. We'll come back to him." Carter stepped between them. "I need to prepare the heart."

Aaron felt all the blood leave his face, and he renewed his struggles with the tape. He paused when he realized no one was headed his way to cut out his heart. They were all going back to Brian's table.

Standing beside the corpse, Carter held up Brian's heart like a trophy. Doug and Kelly stood on his right and Ricardo on his left. All three bowed their heads for a few seconds. When they raised them, Carter placed the organ on the edge of the table and cut it into chunks as if he were slicing a tomato for a salad. Each of them reached beneath the table and pulled out a bottle of water from the shelf underneath it.

No. Aaron shuddered. *They're not really going to eat it?* His stomach rumbled.

When Carter started chanting some kind of prayer, Aaron looked over at Maura and whispered, "Hey, now's your chance. Try to get out of here and get help."

The woman just sat there, staring at the wall across the room.

"Maura? Are you listening to me, Maura?"

"She's not going to stop this," Kelly responded.

Aaron stiffened like a child caught stealing cookies. Kelly glared at him as she reached for a piece of heart.

"Let his soul be one with ours," the four chanted in unison.

They all popped the heart chunks into their mouths. Feeling his last meal rise into his throat, Aaron tried to swallow it back down, but when he saw them chewing, he couldn't take it anymore. He leaned to the side and vomited onto the floor.

"That's disgusting," Carter said.

I'm disgusting? Aaron spat to get the last bit out of his mouth. "Rick, how could you eat that?"

"It's no joy to eat," Ricardo said, shrugging. "But it needs to be done. You'll see. The water helps it go down easier. After a while, you get used to it."

Get used to it? When the hell did Rick get used to it? He thought back to how he'd failed to listen to what he thought were Craig's paranoid delusions. *He'd at least seen something wrong in these guys. But I vouched for them. I told him they were all right. Some cop I turned out to be.*

"Please, Rick, you're my best friend. I'm begging you. Stop this." Aaron belched. Stomach acid burned in his throat.

Ricardo shook his head. "You don't understand. In this piece of heart resides a part of Brian's soul. When we take it inside us, we absorb it into our own. This way, his soul will be saved along with ours. So as brutal as our killing him may seem, we've actually done your friend a miracle."

Aaron's mouth dropped open, where it hung long enough for saliva to pool between his teeth and lower lip. "You have lost your freaking mind."

"Now you sound like Craig, and you called him an idiot."

"Well, even an idiot can be right about some things." Aaron looked away. He could hardly speak, choked up by his words and the memory of his failure. "He was right about you guys, right about a lot of things. You killed him. Now you plan on killing me. Doesn't that seem like an odd way to treat your friends?"

"Don't listen to him, Rick," Doug said. "He doesn't—"

"I know." Ricardo sighed. He tried on a smile, but there was little warmth in it. "You're not getting it, Aaron. This is a special day for me. Carter has prophesied that you don't need to die to be saved. God has shown him that. Once you take part in our ritual, you'll accept the Lord into your heart. You'll believe." He slapped his thigh. "You'll be one of us, Aaron! We aren't going to kill you. We want you to help us save his soul, and in doing so, you'll be saving your own."

He really believes this shit. Aaron swallowed hard, the bitter acid still lingering in the back of his throat. "You expect me to eat a piece of Brian's heart?"

"Exactly."

"No fucking way!" Aaron's outrage trumped his fear. "You guys go on with your fucked-up tea party without me. I'm not eating that shit, and I don't want to be part of your fucking cult. You might as well kill me now. Fucking nutjobs. For the record, *Satanists* practice human sacrifice, not Christians. Even I know that much."

"What do you know about religion?" Ricardo asked. "You haven't even been to a church since you were baptized, unless you count weddings."

"And funerals, but who's counting? I don't have to be a Christian to know that what you're doing ain't fucking Christian. Murdering people? Eating their hearts? That's barbaric. It may be all in a day's work for a Druid, an Aztec, some African shaman maybe, but it's not Christian."

"I guess there's only one way to convince you. I kind of knew you wouldn't have it any other way. You're stubborn to the end, just like Craig." Ricardo grabbed a chunk of heart and stormed toward Aaron.

"You're not putting that in my mouth!" Aaron decided he would bite the fingers off any sicko who tried to put that shit in his mouth.

"Doug, come give me a hand," Ricardo said.

The other man strode over and straddled Aaron's lap. He cupped Aaron's face, digging his fingers into his cheeks, attempting to pry his teeth apart. Aaron clenched his jaw and shook his head violently. With his other hand, Doug grabbed Aaron's lower lip and tugged so hard, Aaron thought he would rip it off. The pain caused his eyes to tear.

Aaron opened his mouth, thinking he could bite Doug's hand. As soon as his teeth separated, Doug stuck his thumb in Aaron's mouth. His teeth closed around the thick digit, and he bit down hard enough to draw blood. The big man didn't even seem to notice. He planted his free palm on Aaron's forehead and pushed his head back while his thumb fish-hooked Aaron's bottom teeth and forced his jaw open. Ricardo thrust the chunk of heart into Aaron's mouth.

Aaron could feel the meat on his tongue. The warm chunk tasted metallic with goopy parts the consistency of ketchup cooked over meatloaf. Doug released his jaw, but before Aaron could spit out the heart, a mammoth hand clamped over his mouth.

"Swallow it," Ricardo ordered.

Aaron shook his head. He used his tongue to block the unwanted bit from going down his throat.

"Swallow it." Ricardo rubbed Aaron's throat as if trying to get a dog to swallow a pill. "Swallow it, Aaron, or so help me God, I'll shove it down your throat myself." His voice took on a pleading note. "If you don't, we'll have to kill you. Is that what you want?"

Aaron remained resolute. At that moment, death was preferable. He clenched the piece of heart between his teeth as he struggled to breathe around Doug's massive hand.

"Fine. Have it your way." Ricardo waved a hand. "Doug, open his mouth again."

Doug grinned wickedly. "No problem." He pried open Aaron's jaw like a fearless gator wrestler atop a snapping beast.

As soon as his mouth was open, Aaron used his tongue to push the chunk out. It dribbled down his chin and landed on his chest.

Ricardo plucked it off. "Waste not, want not." He plunged his hand deep into Aaron's mouth, pushing the meat all the way to the back of his throat.

Aaron gagged, and whatever had been left in his stomach rose into his throat. Doug jerked Aaron's head back and covered his mouth with his free hand. The vomit ended up in Aaron's mouth with no way out.

"Swallow it or choke on it," Ricardo said. "You're running out of options."

Aaron fought to open his mouth and spew, but Doug tightened his grip even more. Streams forced their way out of Aaron's nose, burning his nostrils. Tears poured from his eyes. The taste was bad enough, but his air supply was dwindling. Eventually, he was forced to swallow. As soon as he did, Doug removed his hand from his mouth.

"There," Ricardo said. "That wasn't so bad, now was it?"

"Fuck you," Aaron said, gasping for air. The taste of bile still poisoned his mouth. He felt it might come bubbling back up at any moment. He wished it would.

"Give it a minute," Ricardo said, seeming almost giddy. "You're going to love this."

Aaron wheezed, still trying to catch his breath. "I swear to God, Rick, I'm going to kill you for that."

Ricardo grimaced. "You'll get over it shortly."

Aaron wondered if he'd somehow hurt *him*. "Not likely." He felt only one thing: a drive to get out of that chair and kick some ass, even if it meant sacrificing his own life.

Who would be first? Doug, for what he did to my eye, the sock, and that wonderful forced feeding I just had to put up with? Or Rick, my so-called best friend? Aaron felt his every muscle flexing as strength born from anger pulsed through him. *He's a fucking dead man.*

He slouched back in his chair. All his thoughts of revenge were useless without the means to enact them. All the willpower in the world made no difference. The tape held him firmly in place, and he was starting to realize that he would have no choice but to do what they said and get it over with. *They've won.*

He growled at the thought. No, he still had the will to fight. His anger saw to that—his anger... and something else. Something growing.

His captors were just standing there, watching him. They looked as though they were waiting for his next move, even though he was taped to a chair.

"What are you waiting for?" Aaron asked. "If you're going to kill me, why don't you just do it?"

"Do you feel it yet?" Ricardo asked.

"Feel what, asshole? The fucking human heart turning over and over again in my stomach? Trust me, I feel it. Are you happy?"

Ricardo turned to Carter. "I felt it almost instantly. What do you think his problem is?"

Carter smirked. "Maybe he has a slow metabolism." He waved

dismissively. "Be patient. I'm sure a lot is going through his head. He's probably too distracted to notice it beginning. It'll hit him, and when it does, it's going to hit him hard. Don't you remember your first time?"

"How could I forget it?"

"Hello? I'm right fucking here!" Aaron slammed his feet against the floor. "What's going to hit me? Huh, Rick, you fucking dickhead? Did you poison me? Drugs?" Aaron envisioned strange scenarios of illegal substances fed to him through sinister, maniacal, and undetectable methods. Through all his congested thoughts, he deciphered one bit of truth: he *was* starting to feel something.

Maybe it's just in my head. He trembled. *No, something strange is happening inside me.* "You prick! You did drug me! You are such a fucking coward, Rick." Aaron burst into tears. "I can't believe you'd turn on me like this."

"It isn't drugs," Ricardo said. "It's Brian's soul bonding with yours. Accept it into your heart."

"You're out of your mind! Completely whacko. Can't you see that? Going around feeding human hearts to people. What's wrong with you? All of you? And now this soul crap? Do I look like I'm dumb enough to believe that shit?"

"You will. I have faith in you even if you don't have faith in yourself."

"Now you sound like my girlfriend."

"Ex-girlfriend."

"Yeah, thanks for reminding me. Want to kick me a little more while I'm down? Hey, why not pour salt on my wounds, you sadistic—" Aaron froze. Something was causing tremendous strain on his heart, as if an invisible hand had reached through his chest and grabbed it, squeezed it hard, then released it. His blood pumped faster. *Am I having a heart attack?*

"What is it, Aaron?" Ricardo asked.

Instead, Carter responded. "His pupils are dilated, and he's starting to sweat. It's happening." He rubbed his hands together and smiled broadly.

Pain and energy coursed through Aaron's body. *What is this? Could it actually be Brian's soul?* He scoffed. *That's ridiculous. Whatever it is, though... so powerful. Some kind of instant steroid? I feel strong, alert. It feels so invigorating, so intense, so alive. I don't know what they gave me, but it was a mistake on their part. I feel like… like… now's my chance!*

With a mighty pull, Aaron wrenched his arms free of the tape. He fell forward, bringing his hands in front of him to avoid a face-first collision with the floor. Reaching down between his legs with one hand, he grabbed the tape around his ankles and tore through it as if it were nothing but wet cardboard. He leaped to his feet.

The motley crew of killers was just standing there, staring at him. Aaron had no idea why they weren't attacking, and he wasn't going to wait to find out. He grabbed the chair he'd been strapped to and threw it at Ricardo. The leg bounced off Ricardo's forehead and knocked him backward. He tripped over Maura, who was still huddled on the floor, and fell against Kelly. Doug tried to catch his wife and yank her out of Ricardo's way, but he only succeeded in pulling her over onto himself as they both went down.

Only Carter stood between Aaron and freedom. Ducking low, Aaron raced forward and rammed his shoulder into Carter's abdomen. The force of the impact sent Carter airborne into the wall beside the door.

Aaron opened the door and ran. A force unlike anything he'd ever felt compelled him forward. That force showed no sign of relenting. The feeling was nothing short of euphoric, something akin to bloodlust, but at the same time, insatiable.

He ran down dark corridors in a building that, if not already condemned, should have been. It was old and dead, unlike Aaron. He was alive, and for the first time in a long, long time, he was happy about that.

CHAPTER 30

CARTER SHOOK THE FUZZIES FROM his eyes.

Doug's giant melon head was right in front of him. "Are you okay?"

"I'm fine," Carter replied, getting to his feet.

Doug backed off a step. "Ricardo?"

"Yeah, I'm good. My head is pounding, but I'll live."

"Shouldn't we go after him?" Kelly asked.

As usual, in chimes the voice of reason. Why is the female so much smarter than these dim-witted men? Aaron's freedom could mean police outside their door in a matter of minutes. Still, Carter was confident that wasn't going to happen. "Relax. He isn't going anywhere." Carter made his voice sound cool and collected, even as he pressed his hand against his side, trying to mask the pain. *That's going to bruise.* "Even with his improved senses, he's never going to find the way out in the dark. He'll probably end up in the back room, wondering where to go next."

"You mean where we left all the stuff?" Kelly asked, crossing her arms.

"Don't worry. I incinerated most of it," Carter lied. He coughed. Blood filled his mouth, and he spit it onto the floor. "Damn. Who knew he could hit so hard?" He laughed, wiping blood from his lip with the back of his hand.

"He has the power of a redeemer now." Ricardo seemed pleased at first, but his expression soured. "Why does he still resist it?"

Carter gave him a smile. "He'll come around. I'll talk to him. He probably just needs to come to grips with the new sensations." *Unlike you idiots, he won't accept everything I tell him as gospel.*

"Should I come with you?" Ricardo asked.

Carter stared at his followers, and for a moment, he pitied them. They were so trusting, so loyal. The moment was soon lost, his pity forgotten. "We'll be back soon. You three stay here and prepare the girl." He picked up the knife by its bloodstained blade and handed it to Ricardo. "Do you think you can do this one? I'm not sure I'm still capable with this hurting Aaron put on me."

Ricardo stood tall. "It would be an honor."

"Good. Have her ready by the time I get back with Aaron." With that, Carter waved goodbye and walked out the door. He hated to give away a kill, but it seemed the smart play. He doubted he would ever see them again.

With every step Aaron took down the pitch-black hallway, he heard the patter of rat feet scurrying off in every direction. Once outside the kill room, he had run down a narrow hallway with windows. He thought about opening one and screaming for help, but he was pretty sure they were in a deserted area of town, and he didn't want to give away his position to any of the killers.

Peering through a window, he saw a parking lot far below, and at its edge, a rusty fence covered in weeds. The outline of the Braga Bridge ran along the horizon. He estimated he was about a half mile from the Taunton River.

The hallway ended at a massive loft, entirely dark except for two areas. The first was a starlit window at the far end. The second was a faint red glow emitting from a portion of the right wall. Aaron stared at the glow. *A neon sign?* An idea made him move a little faster. *Maybe it's an exit light!*

He crept toward the light. The floor creaked beneath his weight, threatening to give way. As he got closer, the room gradually brightened. The cold loft felt like a giant walk-in freezer. Until then, he'd been too distracted to notice the temperature. He shivered and pushed forward.

The source of the glow was the edge of a doorframe. Aaron grabbed the corroded doorknob and was surprised by its warmth. He twisted it and pulled open the door, slamming it against the opposite wall while he took cover around the frame. Warily, he edged to the left to peek inside.

The room was empty except for a few pieces of unfamiliar machinery. The source of the glow sat low to the ground, propped against the wall separating the room from the loft. It was a small antique furnace. Next to the furnace was a small folding table. His gun rested on the edge of it.

He smirked. *Things are looking up.* He walked over to the table and found the surface covered with his and Brian's equipment: both guns, nightsticks, belts, and—

Holy shit. They left the radios! They took the pepper spray, flashlights, and handcuffs with them, but left the radios and guns. He chuckled quietly as he belted up, strapping on his equipment as if he were going to work. In a way, he was. It crossed his mind that perhaps he was being lulled into a false sense of security. It was a blatantly dumb move by criminals who'd previously been so careful. *Maybe they'd just been lucky.*

His foot kicked something underneath the table. He looked down and saw a navy-blue gym bag and Ricardo's bowling bag. Without bothering to open them, Aaron opened the furnace, warmed his hands, and threw both bags in. "Motherfuckers," he said, snarling.

He checked both guns. They were loaded. He pulled back the hammers on both then holstered Brian's pistol. His weapon's familiar grip comfortably wrapped in his hand gave him courage. The feeling inside him had yet to subside. He wanted revenge.

He raised the radio and keyed the mic. "Dispatch, come in. This is Officer Pimental. Requesting backup and emergency paramedics immediately. Shots fired. Officer down. I repeat. Shots fired. Officer down." Of course, no shots had been fired. *Not yet.*

"Pimental!" an unfamiliar voice crackled back. "What's your twenty?"

"Not sure. Looks like an old textile mill not far from Battleship Cove. I can see the Braga Bridge through one of the windows, a mile away, tops." Aaron paused. He thought he heard something moving in the loft.

"Pimental?"

"Stay quiet for a second."

Aaron turned down the receiver volume. He heard a noise in the other room. It might have been rats, but he didn't want to take any chances. He keyed the radio and whispered, "I have to shut down. The perps are still on the premises. Bring everybody to the area. I'll wave you down from the street." *If I ever find the street.* He turned off the radio and hooked it to his belt.

Creeping toward the entrance, he halted by the doorway. Footsteps too big to be a rat's pounded the floor of the loft as if whoever made them wanted to be heard. Aaron shot a glance around the corner. A flashlight beam waggled around the room. He stepped back and listened carefully. He heard something else… *Whistling?*

The flashlight holder's position was easy enough to determine, but he couldn't know how many others there were. Charging out, guns blazing, would be foolhardy. On the other hand, he would be cornered if he stayed where he was.

Aaron took a deep breath and leaped from the room. He rolled into the darkness. The flashlight beam swerved in his direction.

"Stay where you are!" Aaron shouted. "I have a gun, and it's pointed right at you." *At least, I think it's pointing right at you.*

"Aaron. It's me. Carter. I'm unarmed, and I'm alone."

"Then you're an even bigger fool than I thought. Shine the light on your face."

Carter complied, squinting as the light shone beneath his chin.

"Put the flashlight down and roll it over to me."

"Aaron, that will probably break it."

"Then you'd better be fucking careful, huh?"

"There's no need for any of this—"

"Just give me the fucking flashlight already!"

Carter crouched and slid the flashlight along the floor. It landed less than a yard in front of Aaron's feet.

Aaron picked up the flashlight and quickly shined it around the room. Seeing no one else, he aimed it at Carter. "Raise your shirt and turn around. Slowly. Then, pull up each of your pants legs."

Carter did as Aaron asked.

As far as Aaron could tell, the man wasn't armed. "Put your hands on your head and leave them there. If you move, you're dead."

Aaron canvassed the room with the flashlight again. He held it steady to peer into each dark corner. When he was satisfied, he turned back to Carter. "How the fuck do you get out of this place?"

"There's a slight trick to it." He seemed awfully complacent, given the fact that circumstances were reversed, and he was the captive.

"Get over here. Stand by the window, where I can see you."

Keeping his fingers interlocked atop his head, Carter strolled toward the window. If his hands hadn't been raised, he might have looked as casual as a man walking through a park on a sunny day.

The man's calmness was unnerving. "You do realize that if help doesn't arrive soon, I'm going to shoot you? What makes you so fucking cheerful?"

"You're not going to shoot me, Aaron." Carter smiled, his teeth shining in the light. "You're like me now."

"Is that what you think? Is that what made you come looking for me unarmed? I have news for you, bud. I'm *nothing* like you. Any of you. I admit I don't know what I'm feeling, but I don't believe it's Brian's soul or any of that bullshit."

"Exactly. I said you are like *me* now, not them. They're puppets, 'lemmings' as I like to call them. You and I, we're so much better. We're capable of greatness."

Aaron raised his Glock to eye level. "You have thirty seconds to explain that." He was stalling until he heard sirens in case the others were lurking about. "Even then, I can't guarantee I won't blow a hole in your head the size of a softball."

"Easy. If I meant you harm, don't you think you would be dead already? Why would I come out here to talk to you like this? Why do you think I kept all your stuff sitting in there, waiting for you to grab it?"

"No one ever said you were smart." *Is he bluffing?* Carter seemed to be telling the truth. Something inside Aaron's gut confirmed it. Perhaps it was his partner's heart. "I don't know what your game is, but it isn't going to work. You now have twenty seconds."

"It *has* worked. The hardest part was getting you to eat the heart."

"Fifteen seconds," Aaron said. Conjuring images of his recent meal was not in Carter's best interests.

"Fine. You can't just go with it? You want an explanation? Let me explain it then. It's all about Type A and Type B personalities, those who take what they want in life and those who are... well, pussies. You were a pussy, Aaron. That's all going to change now."

"You're calling the guy pointing a gun at your face a pussy? How smart do you think that is?"

Carter waved a hand dismissively. "It didn't take much to convince your friends. Doug and Kelly were brainwashed into the cult mentality long before I came along, but even Ricardo was a more-than-willing participant."

"I told you, I don't believe in all that religious crap. Ten seconds."

"That makes two of us. I haven't believed in it since I was a little boy. My father would try to beat it into me, but with every lick of the belt, he was just beating it out."

"You don't expect me to feel sorry for you, do you?"

Carter laughed heartily. "Not at all. I love my life and everything about it. My point is only that I'm as faithless as you are, if not more so. I couldn't care less about God, Christianity, and all that other fairytale bullshit. I just used it to make good people do bad things. All in good fun, I suppose."

"You preyed on Ricardo's disability and his faith to trick him into murdering for your own selfish cause?"

"Well, I'd like to think there was more to it than that, but yes. There are people like me everywhere, and many of them are better organized than your narrow-minded police minds can comprehend. You cops are so inside the box, never seeing the broader scheme. Satanism, Neo-Nazism, racist or religious hate groups—whatever the preface, most are simply means to control, to conquer, and sometimes, to kill. I used the language of the Old Testament. I twisted the messages of the book of Joshua to suit my goals nicely. And each of my carefully selected followers took the bait. The pages of our history books are filled with visionaries like me, exploiting religion to obtain power, acquire dominion over land, control the masses, whatever. My goals are maybe a bit more humble than some, but I guess I'm no different."

Aaron shook his head. "I can't believe Rick bought into your bullshit."

Carter shrugged. "He wasn't that hard, but I lost two others along the way. Sharon Thomas killed herself. I was always wary of that one. She was too weak. But Garrison—you know him as 'victim number four'—he was a real bitch. 'Waah, waah, waah, I can't do this anymore.' That's all he'd say. It was just him and me at first. We killed three people the police haven't even found yet. They're buried... well, the location isn't important."

"Wait a second. The fourth victim, Garrison Huntley, was a murderer like you?"

"Yeah, pretty sweet, huh?" He frowned. "Well, he was a murderer, but not quite like me. I have... someone else in mind for that, someone I've had my eye on for a long time, though I'm sure he never knew it. You could say all this is as much *his* fault as it is mine. After all, he's the reason I came back home."

Aaron didn't care for the zealous gleam shining in Carter's eyes. *Are there even more of them?* But he needed to keep Carter talking, so he kept quiet.

"Anyway, Huntley was just another pawn. I tied him up and fed him one of my victims' hearts, just like Ricardo did to you. He was my first go at the religious angle. I never had a partner before. I made some mistakes, seeing how it all worked out poorly in the end... for him, anyway. I perfected my craft by the time I got to Ricardo. But I have to say, Doug is my crowning achievement. He's a perfectly trained attack dog."

Carter's brow furrowed. Perhaps he'd noticed Aaron's lack of enthusiasm. Then his eyes grew wide, and that zealous smile returned. "And get this! You know that woman in there? She was Garrison's selection. He seduced her like a pro. Made me proud. But then, can you believe he actually fell in love with the slut? Outrageous, right?"

Aaron didn't answer.

"Anyway, Garrison was married. 'Thou shalt not covet thy neighbor's wife,' yada, yada, yada. Once he was confirmed as an adulterer, my clan came around to my way of thinking. I hate loose ends. I had to use his four-year-old son as bait. Garrison knew he was dead as soon as he got into the van. It was dangerous letting his son go, though. But you know your friends... can't kill the innocent. I should have gutted the little tyke, but what can you do? The stupid cops never even thought to question him, and he'd seen everything!" Carter smirked. "No offense, Aaron."

"None taken."

"Well, you should have seen the little brat's face. 'Daddy! Daddy!' he cried. Ha! Try living down that memory, Junior."

"How?" Aaron asked, trying to keep the revulsion out of his voice. "How could you convince so many to do such unspeakable things? It's not possible." But Aaron knew it was. He couldn't deny what his eyes had seen. Or what his body still felt.

Carter beamed. "Finally, you're recognizing my achievements. How do cult leaders get their followers to commit mass suicide? True, I exceeded my wildest expectations. But you underestimate the power of faith because you have none. You also ignore what you're feeling inside. That feeling may not be divine, but it sure feels heavenly. You're a god among men now. And it only gets better. With that in my arsenal, it's not all that hard to believe how far a little education employed on impressionable minds can get you."

"You're disturbed. You know that, don't you? You'll get what's coming to you."

"From who? The police? They couldn't find their way out of a paper bag. They search for a motive, so desperate to find reason in what I do. So I stall them with a false one, make them follow leads that go nowhere. Sure, it may lead them to our mutual friends in there," Carter said, pointing behind himself, "but that's where it all ends." He winked. "You'll see to that, won't you, Aaron?"

The question caught him off guard. "Why in the world would I help you?"

"Oh, I can think of a reason or two." Carter giggled, actually giggled, as if he were a woozy child after an airplane spin. "I know things the police don't. Investigating Carter Wainwright will get them nowhere. I've set so many traps, so many red herrings."

"So what's the truth? What's all this for?"

"The truth? That's easy. I like killing people."

"And there it is," Aaron said. "All the experts with their psychological mumbo jumbo, spouting why people like you do what they do, and the reason is that simple. You're just plain fucked in the head. There's nothing magical about it. You're just fucking psycho."

Carter shrugged. "Well, I can't argue with that." He grinned. "But I can tell you this. It feels damn good to be me."

Sirens blared in the distance. *Keep him talking. Just a little longer.*

"So why bother with the hearts?" Part of Aaron knew the answer. He just didn't want to accept it. Energy surged through his muscles, and vitality coursed through his veins. Despite everything that evil man had put him through, Aaron was more alert, more ready for anything than he'd ever been. As if long-dormant brain matter had surged to life, his mind was sharp, focused. He knew the reasoning he kept coming back to sounded insane, so drugs seemed the most likely answer. He had been unconscious for a while. They could have drugged him. But if the power he felt was born from narcotics, he wondered how long it could last. And he wanted it to last.

"Come on, Aaron. Accept it," Carter said. "I can see it happening in you. I know you're feeling it, loving it."

Aaron shook his head, but his heart nodded its agreement. "What would possess you to do that? To actually rip out a man's heart and eat it?"

The sirens were much louder.

Carter glanced over his shoulder. "I should be going, but that's such a great question. Have you ever heard of Joshua Milton Blahyi?"

Aaron shook his head. "Who's that? Another victim?"

Carter laughed. "Blahyi was a high priest and leader of the Krahn tribe of Liberia. During the civil wars that plagued Liberia and Sierra Leone, he and his cohorts slaughtered thousands. Blahyi used to sacrifice children before going into battle. He would carve out their hearts and divide it into pieces for his men to eat."

"So because some crazy-ass motherfucker halfway around the world did that, you thought it would be a good idea to try it here? You're doing a lousy job of convincing me not to shoot you where you stand. I'd be a hero, and you… you'd just be dead." Yet, no matter how much he wanted to—and there was no denying that he did *want* to—Aaron didn't pull the trigger. He didn't care if Carter died. He just needed to know the truth of what he was feeling inside first.

"Let me finish," Carter said, sounding annoyed. "Blahyi explained everything. He talked of *juju*, a term used in Liberian black magic. It's an aura found in objects."

Aaron rolled his eyes. "An aura, huh?"

"I know what you're thinking. I didn't believe in that black magic nonsense, either. But I looked it up online, and I couldn't believe what I found. The ritual is real, and it's even practiced in America. So I figured, why not try it out? And when I did, I felt just like you do now: stronger, faster, smarter, able to conquer the world."

Aaron couldn't deny the strange energy festering inside. His shoulders heaved with each breath. His pulse thudded with a dull but rapid staccato, veins bulging in his arms. "What is it?"

"I don't know much more than you do. I choose to believe that, in a way, what you ate was part of Brian's soul, or at least the essence of his life. Call it a soul, life force, or even *juju*, the human heart has the strongest aura of all. In it resides whatever makes us exist and gives us energy, stored in a vessel and pumped out for use in moderation throughout our lifetimes. We take it from those we kill and consume it whole. It adds to ours, and we become stronger."

Aaron stared at him for a moment then burst into laughter.

Carter's jaw tightened. "Or it could just be a hormone that works like a steroid and improves brain and body functioning. It's certainly unique to the *human* heart, though. I've tried animals, but you don't want to hear about that. You can't cook it or let it sit too long, or whatever's inside… escapes. Who knows what it is? Who cares? It feels awesome, and it never goes away. I've heard LSD stays in your system forever, but this is so much better. It gets stronger the more you have."

Never goes away? It was a nice fantasy. Aaron couldn't help but smile, which made him feel dirty. He was trapped in a dark mill, being hunted by killers, and he'd been badly beaten. Yet he couldn't remember a time when he felt so healthy and grateful to be alive.

Staring at Carter in that light—a villain about six feet tall, one hundred eighty pounds, with short brown hair, brown eyes and a clean-cut look—he saw a man who looked strikingly familiar. Aaron gasped. He lowered his gun, confused and frightened. When he looked at Carter, he saw himself. *Drugged. I must be drugged.*

"It feels good to finally talk with someone about this, someone like me." Carter gave him a wink that made Aaron's stomach turn.

"I'm nothing like you," he said through gritted teeth. *Am I?* He wasn't so sure. His thoughts turned once again back to that day in Newport, the day he'd become something more than just a lovelorn teenager, the day he'd lost Raquel and a large portion of his humanity with her. He wondered if he'd ever gotten it back. He rubbed his eyes. Carter looked like Carter again.

"You are, Aaron. You may not realize it yet, but recruiting you was my goal all along. You're going to clean up my loose ends. You'll carry on my work here long after I'm gone."

"You're delusional." Aaron raised his service pistol and pointed it directly at Carter's pearly whites. *I know how to make him stop smiling.* "For what you did to me, Rick, Craig, and everyone else you've hurt or killed, I'm going to shoot you now." Aaron had no more reservations, no guilty conscience to plague him, no moral code standing in his way. His mind was made up. "Any last words?"

"You can't kill me." Carter backed up to the window, still smiling.

"The hell I can't!" Aaron pulled the trigger and kept pulling it, again and again, liking the power behind each squeeze. Liking the control over another's fate that he never could seem to obtain over his own.

Carter toppled backward, arms flailing. He crashed through the window, its wood pane splintering and its glass shattering.

Aaron didn't know how many bullets he'd fired, but he was sure it had been enough. More than one had hit its mark. He pulled Brian's pistol from his holster and replaced it with his own gun.

Backup should be here any second, but that woman may not have a second. She needs my help… and I need a little payback. He headed for the door. "Time to play hero."

CHAPTER 31

As soon as he heard the shots, Bruce was running. "It came from this way!"

Jocelyn, who was younger and faster, passed him up in seconds, with four officers at her heels. He lost sight of them as they turned a corner around some long-forgotten relic of the city's booming textile days. Dead leaves rustled across the pavement. Vermin scurried back into their burrows at the sound of the officers' footsteps.

As he took the corner, Bruce nearly plowed into his partner's back. "What the—"

Jocelyn placed a finger over her lips, then she pointed at the Toyota Camry parked beside a back entrance. "They're here."

She pulled her gun, and Bruce did the same. As they approached the door, broken glass crunched beneath his heels. Jocelyn tried the door and found it unlocked.

When they stepped inside, the area was pitch-black. The officers turned on their heavy flashlights, and Bruce got out his pocket Maglite. The smell of water-rotted wood laced with something sickeningly noxious accosted his nostrils.

A few steps down the hallway, a pounding on the floor above them drove Bruce into a crouch. He shined his light on the ceiling and lit up an intricate pattern of cobwebs. He ran the beam across the area until he spotted a section that had been cleared.

"There," he whispered, pointing at a trapdoor and the ladder that led up to it.

Aaron stood outside the slightly ajar door, feeling as though he could take on an army, kill every single one of them if he had to without so much as a second thought. And maybe even if he didn't have to.

He leaned to the side and peeked into the room. Maura had been laid out on the operating table. Her hands were cuffed awkwardly beneath her.

"Those were definitely gunshots," Kelly said as she paced in and out of his view.

"Maybe Carter had to shoot him," Doug said.

"Let's get out of here," she said.

"Fine. Are you coming, Ricardo?"

"I have to do the girl first." Ricardo reached for the knife next to Maura.

"Ricardo, there's no time—"

"He's right, Kelly," Doug interrupted. "We have to do the girl first."

Aaron kicked open the door. "Freeze!"

As he stepped inside, the door rebounded off the wall. He moved to get ahead of it then kicked it closed to make sure none of them could make a run for it.

Doug charged at Aaron like a bull at a matador. Aaron fired three shots before Doug was on him. All three shots had been good, turning Doug into Swiss cheese. But Doug barely slowed. Aaron needed more firepower, maybe a bazooka, to take down the big man.

Doug slammed into him, pancaking him on the floor. Aaron's head bounced, and a dull tone echoed through his skull. The gun flew from his hand. Doug's hands encircled Aaron's neck and squeezed.

Aaron clawed at Doug's cheeks, scratching until blood trickled down them. He wanted to scoop out the man's eyes with his thumbs if he could reach them, but they were out of range. He needed to find another weak spot quickly. Aaron dug his middle finger into a gushing bullet hole through Doug's collarbone.

Doug squealed in pain and grabbed Aaron's wrist with his right hand. Aaron took the opportunity to grasp Doug's ring finger on his left hand and pull it back until he heard a satisfying crack.

Doug screamed then drove his forearm into Aaron's face. Aaron moaned and reached up with a shaking hand to feel the smashed and bloody mess that had moments before been his nose. Waves of pain rocked his whole head.

What felt like bucketloads of blood flowed into the back of his throat, where it collected in a rapidly growing reservoir. If he didn't sit up, he would drown in it.

Police sirens blared nearby. Doug's hands again latched around Aaron's neck. The sirens became louder.

"Forget him!" Kelly shouted. "We have to go. Now!"

But Doug didn't let go, seemingly intent on strangling him. Aaron could feel his life slipping away.

"She's right, Doug," Ricardo said. "We need to leave. The police are coming."

"Doug!" Kelly yelled again. "Are you listening to me?"

Aaron felt consciousness leaving him. Black fog rolled into his peripheral vision. He groped at his waistband.

"He's nearly out," Doug said. "Let's get out of here." He raised his head and looked around the room. His grip loosened as he twisted from left to right.

Aaron coughed violently, trying to eject the blood in his throat and allow air back into his lungs.

"Kelly?" Doug called. He stood, planting one mammoth foot on each side of Aaron. "Kelly?"

Dizzy, his vision blurry, Aaron fumbled his holster open and pulled out Brian's service pistol. "Fuck you, Doug," Aaron whispered hoarsely. He pulled the trigger.

Doug cupped the side of his head, which was bleeding profusely, and backed away. He leaned against the wall then slid down until his ass rested on the floor.

Aaron sat up and looked around, swinging the pistol from left to right. Kelly had apparently deserted her husband, because the door was open, and she was nowhere to be seen. Ricardo was standing behind the table that held Maura.

Ricardo raised one hand. "Aaron, put the gun down and help me redeem her before it's too late... for her and for you."

"Rick, I don't want to shoot you... well, maybe just a little after what you put me through, but... put the knife down anyway. Or don't."

"No, Aaron. It's her fate and our destiny. We're saving her. All this is God's plan. We have done his work. He won't let you stop me."

"It's all lies, Rick. Carter told me so himself before I put him down."

"Carter's dead?" Ricardo asked, his voice wavering. "I don't believe you."

"You know me. When have I ever lied to you?"

He shook his head. "Anyway, it doesn't matter. I always knew it could end like this. All that matters is our mission. It's bigger than any one of us. There's just one more part to complete." Ricardo's other hand came up. He was holding the knife. He gripped it with both hands and slowly raised it over his head.

Maura squealed. She clenched her eyes shut, her body trembling so much that it sounded like a drum roll against the table.

"Don't do it, Rick." Aaron leveled his gun. "Last warning."

"You won't kill me." Ricardo smiled nervously. "We've been through a lot together, you and me. You can't kill me, just as I couldn't kill you. You're my closest friend."

"After what you did to me, after you *betrayed* me, you sick, sorry son of a bitch, what the hell makes you so sure about that?" Aaron seethed, finding it harder and harder to keep his anger in check. Ricardo *had* betrayed him. After all the years, everything they had been through, his best friend had turned his back on him, Tasered him, let Doug beat the shit out of him, and forced him to eat the raw, rubbery meat of Brian's heart. The last part, he was thinking he might be able to forgive, but the rest...

Ricardo's shoulders drooped, and he let out a long sigh. He placed the knife on the table. "Okay, Aaron. You win. In the end, you'll do what's right, and we'll have other opportunities."

"What's right is me putting a bullet through your skull. That's what's right!"

Ricardo snickered.

"What's so funny? You think this is funny? I can live with the beat-down you and your friends gave me. What I can't live with is the fact that the one person I trusted in this whole fucking world just took a big ol' shit on me. And you're fucking laughing?"

"It's nothing. Just irony, I guess. Can't you see? Everything we did *to* you was done *for* you. I didn't betray you. I—"

"You did this *for* me? For me! Your friend there"—he pointed at Doug—"almost killed me, while you stood there with your thumb up your ass. You would have let him do it. I can't believe it! You would have let him kill me!" Aaron raised the gun. "You know what, Ricardo. Fuck you. Fuck *you*!" He squeezed the trigger.

The bullet punctured Ricardo's forehead. He fell to the ground, knocking the knife onto the floor beside him.

Maura screamed, pulling at her restraints.

Aaron blinked repeatedly as he stared at the spot where his friend had been standing. He shook his head, trying to focus, to make sense of what had just happened. *Did I...? Could I...? No, the gun must have just gone off... or I tensed. Yeah, I tensed and squeezed the trigger by accident.*

Or... I killed him? The prospect wasn't nearly as horrifying as Aaron had expected it to be. In fact, he was surprised at just how okay with it he was. Better than okay even. It had to be shock or intoxication, though. He was sure they had drugged him. How would he feel tomorrow? Or next week? *Better not to think of it. Not now.*

He sneered. His so-called friend *had* tried to kill him. *So I killed him first. The bastard had it coming. For that matter, they all do.*

He twisted around and aimed the pistol at Doug, who was still slouched against the wall. The big man's eyes were glassy. He didn't appear to be an immediate threat.

Aaron mimed shooting him then blew imaginary smoke from the barrel of his pistol. "You're already dead. You just don't know it yet."

Aaron thought about how, in the movies, people always said crap like "revenge won't change anything." He was feeling pretty damn good. Justice was like smoking a joint, but vengeance... that was a high without rival. And topped with whatever drug or hormone his late friend had given him, revenge was pure bliss—for as long as it lasted, anyway. He never knew a high that didn't end with a low. *But Carter said it only gets stronger.*

The sound of a creaking hinge snapped him from his thoughts. The cavalry had arrived, and though the officers were undoubtedly trying to be quiet, he heard their movements as if they were in the next room. He went over to Maura, laid his gun on the table beside her, and took out the handcuff key he'd gotten from the furnace room. Once she was free, he helped her off the table.

On her feet, Maura pushed away from him and backed up against the table. She looked frightened, which would have been expected, except the expression was directed at him. She put her hands out in front of her as if warding him off.

He stepped toward her. "Maura?"

Maura grabbed the gun off the table and pointed it at him. "Stay back!" The gun shook in her grip.

Aaron frowned. "Maura... I saved your life." He eased closer to her. "It's okay. No one's going to hurt you. The police are here. I hear them coming."

She looked around the room then stared at Aaron. Finally, she lowered the weapon. He took the gun away from her with one hand and put his other arm around her. Hesitantly, she leaned against him. A moment later, she buried her face in his neck and let out a sob.

Aaron held her for a few seconds then let go when he heard footsteps approaching. Though it was most likely the police, he raised his gun and pointed it toward the door just in case.

"We have the building surrounded," Marklin yelled from the hallway. "Drop your weapons, and come out with your hands up."

Aaron smiled. *Maybe I can get away with one more shot.* He lowered his weapon. "This is Officer Aaron Pimental. The room is secure."

Detective Beaudette was the first to appear, gun raised high. She swung her gun toward Maura then lowered her weapon.

"She's not one of them," Aaron said. "She was going to be their next victim."

The other officers followed Marklin into the room. A couple looked a little green around the gills, and another put a hand up to his nose. Aaron realized it must stink pretty badly in there, but he had apparently grown used to the smell.

"Officer Temple?"

Aaron motioned toward the corner.

"Oh." Beaudette stared at Brian's body for several seconds. "Well," she said, composing herself, "thank goodness you're all right." She looked at Maura. Her hand flexed around the grip of her pistol, but she left it by her side.

"Then it looks like you're a hero." Beaudette's smile was genuine. "Great work, Officer Pimental." She saluted.

Hero? Sure, he knew saving the woman was the right thing to do, but Aaron hadn't truly seen himself as heroic. Revenge and anger had been his motives, not justice and morality. Given the right circumstances, anyone could be a hero... or a killer. And maybe the distinction was only a matter of perception.

"We've got a live one here!" Marklin shouted, his fingers pressed against Doug's wrist.

In an instant, seven officers surrounded Doug, each with their guns pointed at the bullet-ridden giant.

"Lie facedown on the floor and put your hands behind your back," Marklin ordered.

Doug remained sitting. He stared blankly, like a meth head who'd fried his brain.

Marklin gestured for the officers to move in. "You two... better make that you four, stand guard over him. If he so much as breathes in your direction, take him out. I'll call in the paramedics, though I'm not sure I want them to get here in time. Fucking cop killer." He spat and stepped away to use his radio.

"Jeez, Pimental," Beaudette said. "How many times did you shoot this guy?"

"Four... I think."

"And he's still breathing? I can't even get over a cold without days of rest, and this guy's calm as a cookie even missing half his face." She shrugged. "I suppose he's in shock."

"You two," Marklin said to Officers Clemens and Fortuna as he clipped his radio to his belt. "Go with him in the ambulance and stay with him until I get to the hospital."

Four gunshots rang out in the distance. After a brief silence, a series of blasts followed, as if someone had set off a line of firecrackers.

Marklin grabbed his radio. "What the hell is going on out there?"

Someone responded, "We had the Camry roadblocked. The suspect opened fire."

"Was it Wainwright?"

"No, sir. It's Fournier. The wife. We returned fire. She's dead."

"Any of ours hurt?"

"No, sir."

"Anyone else in the car?"

"No, sir."

"Roger that. Over."

Aaron turned to Marklin. "You needn't worry about Carter Wainwright."

"Oh yeah?" Marklin squinted. "Why's that?"

"Because he's dead. I shot him, and he fell out a window."

"Show me." Marklin gestured at Beaudette. "Come with us."

Aaron led the two detectives down a hallway and around an opening in the floor. *No wonder I couldn't find the way out. I was looking everywhere but down.*

Passing officers and lab technicians there to process the scene, they continued into the large room where Aaron and Carter had faced off. Portable fluorescent lanterns and flashlights illuminated the area. Aaron led them to what was left of the loft's window. Blood stained the glass shards that remained intact.

"I fired my weapon from over there." Aaron pointed. "Three times. I know I hit him at least once but probably with all three. He fell backward and crashed through the window."

Marklin poked his head out the window to examine the ground below. "You sure he fell out of this window?" Marklin asked, pulling his head back in.

"Positive." *Just look at the window. It's broken to bits. There's blood everywhere. It doesn't take a genius to figure it out.* "Why?"

Marklin grimaced. "Because there's no body down there."

"Impossible." Aaron ran to the window. They were four stories up. Carter Wainwright had to be down there. But when he looked, he saw no one, no matter how many times he blinked. "He went out the window…

at least I *think* he went out the window. It was dark, but... no, I'm sure of it. No one could have walked away from a fall like that."

Marklin raised his radio. "Jensen? Are you sure no one else was in Fournier's car?"

"Positive, sir."

"Did you check the trunk?"

"Yes, sir."

"Get everyone canvassing the area now. The suspect is Carter Wainwright. He is injured and believed to be on foot, still in the immediate vicinity. Detain anyone you see for questioning." He lowered his radio. "Let's go back into the other room. Pimental, I want you to walk us through everything that happened in there."

When they filed back into the room, a couple of techs had spread black powder over every surface. They were busy lifting prints. Someone had tossed a blanket over Doug, but he still just sat there, looking completely out of it.

Maura was standing in the far corner, talking to some of the officers. Aaron exchanged a glance with her. He was trying to listen in on her conversation when Marklin grabbed his arm.

"Okay, let's hear it."

Aaron started by telling them about the scene at Ricardo's house. He noticed that Maura was listening intently, as well as the two officers with her.

At one point, Marklin held up one hand and stepped closer to Aaron. "Are you... high? Your pupils are dilated, and you're sweating."

"They might have slipped me something." *Like a piece of Brian Temple's heart.*

Marklin huffed. "And you didn't think to mention that? You don't even really know what you saw, do you?" He jammed a finger at Aaron's face. "You fucked up this time. If we lose Wainwright, it will be your fault."

Beaudette cleared her throat, giving Marklin a look that was almost threatening.

Maura ran over and slammed her palms into Marklin's chest. "You fucking prick!"

Marklin's eyes widened. He started to stutter a response, but Maura spoke over him.

"He just went through hell." Fresh tears wet her cheeks. "While tied up, beaten and helpless, he had to watch his partner die. Then... it was so horrible... they forced him to eat a piece of his partner's heart."

Aaron grimaced. He had planned on leaving out that part. He knew it was only his imagination, but he swore he could feel the chunk of heart sliding around like a slug inside his stomach.

Marklin and Beaudette gawked at him with looks that blended shock, sympathy, and disgust.

"Even after all that, he managed to get free," Maura continued. "He came back for me. That monster"—she pointed at Ricardo's body—"was, uh, just about to stab me when your officer shot him. He saved my life."

"Maura—" Aaron started, blushing.

"No. Don't stop me." She jabbed her index finger into Marklin's chest. "I owe him everything, and so do you!"

"Ms. Fleurent—" Marklin began.

"You shut your damn mouth!" she screamed. "If it was all left to you, I'd be dead by now. 'Not his MO.' Isn't that what you said?"

"I'm sorry, Ms. Fleurent," Marklin whispered.

Beaudette touched the woman's arm, but Maura slapped her hand away. "Ms. Fleurent, you've been through a lot. Now it's our job to piece the rest of it together. Please come down to the precinct and fill out a statement, or better yet, come talk to me when you feel up to it, so we can close this matter out." She waved over one of the officers. "Officer Bradley, please take Ms. Fleurent to the ambulance for medical attention."

Maura flashed a smile at Aaron and cast Marklin a surly glare before she nodded and followed the officer out of the room.

Beaudette turned to Aaron. "You did well, Officer Pimental. Get yourself to the hospital, too. Your eye is going to need some attention, and your neck doesn't look so good, either. Afterward, get some rest and come into the precinct tomorrow, say two o'clock. A shooting and as many deaths as this, IA's gonna have a shitload of questions. But you'll get through. Bruce and I will have your back. Won't we, Bruce?"

"Huh?" Marklin seemed dazed from his scolding, but he let out an affirming grunt.

"After the questions and the psych exam and all the other red tape, take some time off and heal up, physically and mentally. Paid, of course. You let us know when you're ready to come back. I'll square it with the chief."

Aaron nodded. "Thanks, Detective. This is all… a lot to take in. I don't think I'm really processing any of it yet. But I'll head to the hospital as you say. Maybe I can hitch a ride with Maura if I—"

"The hell you will," Marklin interrupted.

Beaudette raised a hand to cut him off. "What Marklin means is that you have to stay away from Ms. Fleurent. She's a material witness to your shooting of at least two of the suspects. We'll need to take a full statement from her without any involvement from you to avoid the appearance of tampering."

"Tampering?"

"We know everything you did here was aboveboard, but it's best not to give IA any reason to question that. Those pricks don't mind eating their own. But like I said, we have your back."

Aaron frowned and left the room, not really sure how he was going to get anywhere or even what he would do next. He supposed he would go to the hospital, but his wounds were already feeling better.

Not see Maura? For some reason, that was sitting as well as a Drano in his stomach. Ricardo and Kelly were dead. Doug was on his way to the hospital and, if he survived, to prison for a life sentence. Carter had somehow defied all logic and disappeared. Still, a reign of terror had ended. He had done that. Yet, they questioned him and wouldn't let him see someone who might understand.

His eyes rolled back in his head as he was overcome by another surge of energy. He smiled, thinking about the new power inside him. Everything might actually be okay. But he craved more.

After hitching a ride from a fellow officer, Aaron ended up at his parents' place. His heart still thudded. It hadn't slowed since he'd killed Ricardo. Knowing sleep wouldn't come that night despite his fatigue, he got in his car.

Aimless driving landed him back at his house. Arianna's car was in the driveway. The glow of the TV through the bedroom window told him she might be still up. She wasn't one to pass out with the TV still on.

He drove up the street, pulled over to the curb, and picked up his phone. "Arianna?" He knew she had picked up, but she didn't answer him. "Look, I know you're mad, but I've had a really rough night. Can I come home?"

After a beat, Arianna said softly, "This isn't your home anymore."

"Babe, can we talk about this? Please?" Aaron's throat tightened. "I need you."

"You need me?" She huffed. "Well, you should have thought of that sometime in the eight years I gave you."

"Honey, I—"

The phone went dead. Aaron slammed his palms against the steering wheel. He thought about going in there anyway. After all, his name was on the lease, too. She had no right to turn him away.

Deep breaths. One... two... three...

When the rage subsided, leaving only contempt, he drove to a liquor store to pick up half a dozen nips of vodka to drink discreetly while he waited to be called at the hospital. He downed two on the drive over and stuck the rest in his pockets. After he was tended to and discharged, he went to the ICU. He learned from a nurse that Doug was already out of surgery.

Officer Fortuna guarded the door to his room. "Pimental!" He smiled and removed his hat as Aaron walked up, as if he were addressing someone of importance. "Way to go tonight! It's just a pity you didn't aim a little higher on this one." He laughed.

Aaron forced a smile. "Where's your partner?"

"He's got the shits." He raised his Styrofoam coffee cup. "Gets them every time he drinks this hospital gloop. I tell him to pick up a coffee on his way in, but does he? Noooo. 'I'm not paying five bucks for no Starby's,' he says. I'm not sure if he knows that that's not what it's called. So he spends half the night in the bathroom." He shook his head and whistled.

"And you partner is?"

"Matthews, that putz."

"How long do you have to babysit for?"

"Every night this week, playing next week by ear. Matthews, too." Fortuna yawned. "It's already boring the hell out of me."

"I got something to take the edge off that boredom, if you'd like." He pulled out one of the nips.

"Come on, Pimental. Why you gotta tempt me? You know we can't do that on shift."

"Who's gonna know?" Aaron peeked into the room. "That motherfucker is handcuffed to the bed. He ain't going anywhere."

Fortuna looked both ways down the hall then stepped closer to Aaron, his coffee cup between them. "Pour it in."

Aaron obliged. "Well, I'll let you get back to it. Maybe I'll stop by again for a visit."

"Why? To watch me sitting here, trying not to fall asleep?"

"Well, we wouldn't want that. Someone might want to get in there for a little payback."

"Now, I almost hope I do fall asleep. I tell you, if that cop killer never sees trial, I'd chalk that up as a win for the good guys."

CHAPTER 32

IN THE FEW DAYS SINCE they had closed the cases for all but one of Fall River's killer cultists, Jocelyn had been avoiding the press. That only seemed to encourage the reporters, who camped on her front lawn and called at all hours of the day and night. Even disconnecting the phone proved ineffective. They just knocked and rang the doorbell instead.

Exhausted, she plodded down the hall to Bruce's one-bedroom apartment. When she reached his door, a sense of accomplishment washed over her... until she tried to lift her tired arm to knock.

He opened the door with one hand, rubbing his eyes with the other. "Jocelyn?" Wearing sweat pants and a stained T-shirt, he reeked of stale potato chips. "Come on in."

As she stepped into his apartment, she realized just how little she knew about her partner. The shades were drawn over every window. Only square outlines of light were allowed to break through the dusty haze that thickened the air. Newspapers were strewn over the kitchen counter, while others were piled on the floor. He brushed a stack of unopened mail off a recliner then the crumbs that were hidden beneath it, the origin of which Jocelyn decided against guessing. Apparently satisfied the chair was presentable, he offered her a seat.

She plopped down, grateful to get off her feet. "Your place could use a woman's touch."

"How old-fashioned of you." He flicked on a lamp. "Why? You offering?"

"No." With the light on, Jocelyn got a better look at the place. The piles of pizza boxes and half-empty bottles of alcohol made the apartment look more like a dorm room than the lair of the brightest criminologist that side of the Taunton River. Not that there was much on the Fall River side of the Taunton River.

"Hey, the first wife got the house; the second got the money." He picked up a bottle of Scotch, sniffed the rim, then took a swig. "My third wife," he said, raising the bottle, "gets the rest."

He offered her the bottle, but she waved it away. After setting it down on the counter, he dropped onto the pleather couch. "Forgive the state of the place. I don't usually have visitors."

"You don't say? Anyway, sorry for barging in like this. I had to get out of that house. The press won't stop hounding us. Caitlyn and Steven can't sleep. I figured if I got out of there—"

"Then at least your family could get some rest. Makes sense, but then you came here?"

"Yeah, I know, out of the frying pan. Yet I didn't see any press here."

"That's because I did what you should have right off the bat. I talked to them." He scratched his thigh. "I'm old news."

Jocelyn frowned. "He's still out there."

"I know."

"I've got nothing. I don't even know where to begin looking. It's like he up and vanished."

"I know."

"How do you deal with it? You know, with letting one get away?"

"He hasn't gotten away yet. But I can't really say how I would handle it. I've never failed to make a collar in a case of this magnitude. Then again, I've never had a case of this magnitude."

"So what do we do?"

"We start beating down doors: neighbors, acquaintances, landlords, former owners of his properties, other properties in his name, tax records, bank records, credit cards, phone bills, DMV records. Hell, his connection to the real Carter Wainwright. We have tons to do. You know that."

"I just feel like... like he's already gone."

"Well, the funeral's in two days. With any luck, our killer will be there, so that's where we'll start."

———————•·•———————

"I saw your name and face all over today's paper," Arianna said. "You're a local hero... national, probably. I didn't realize when you asked to come over..."

"It's okay. I understand." Aaron left it at that. She had called him, so maybe there was something left, something they could salvage, maybe even rebuild...

"You seemed so collected in the interview I read. But I know you, Aaron. How are you really holding up?"

"Okay, I guess. Ricardo's death has been tough, obviously." Aaron choked up. "Probably more so since I caused it." His emotions had been a rollercoaster. One minute, the notion that he had killed his best friend, who happened to be a murderer, filled him with a sense of righteousness and even something akin to happiness and pride. The next, he was wallowing in grief, not so much for Ricardo's death, but for the hole it left in his own life.

He thought about how to swing Ricardo's execution—*no, no, that wasn't my fault, but tension and a hair trigger*—into a play for reconciliation. *Every girl's a sucker for a wounded puppy.*

The reporters had been slow to pick up on that little nuance to Aaron's fifteen minutes, that he'd been forced to kill his best friend. They kept calling, but they never pressed him about it. They simply asked whether he knew Ricardo. "Yes," was always his response, if he responded at all.

Aaron's fifteen minutes had stretched into an hour. The phone didn't stop ringing. Strangers appeared at his doorstep. Agents for major networks and talk show hosts sent gifts, along with exclusive interview requests. He turned them away. Fame was a novelty that wore thin quickly. Ricardo's death was hitting him hard.

Nevertheless, talking about the loss of his best friend to Arianna, his ex-girlfriend, was not his idea of cathartic. He wondered if she'd called out of concern or if she just wanted some juicy details. Still, he would say what he needed to say to get her back, or—

"I'm sorry. I know it must be hard for you. I'm still here for you, Aaron. I wouldn't have called if I wasn't. I'm still your friend if you want me to be." Arianna sounded sincere, as if she might even care. "The wake is tonight. Are you going?"

"Of course. Why wouldn't I be?"

"You think that's a good idea?"

Aaron's fingers tightened around the phone. "He was my best friend, damn it. You know that. He was misled. Nothing has changed how I feel about him. I want to pay my respects."

"Well, I talked to Brittney. She's not doing well. She's mad at you. The family isn't happy with you, either."

"I saved a woman's life!" What right did they have to judge him? Ricardo had died with the serial killers' weapon in his hand, about to add another victim to its death count. Maura Fleurent had survived, thanks to Aaron.

The headlines made him out to be a superstar, and even though Carter was nowhere to be found, Aaron was credited with putting an end to the killers' reign. There were already rumors he might get a promotion. But it was an empty victory. He had no one to share it with. In the eyes of those who'd once loved him, Aaron saw pity—or worse, contempt. Their gazes were accusatory, skeptical, and apathetic, as if he were the villain in all of it. He felt lowly and loathsome, a victim of his own unhappy circumstances. He wondered what they would have said if he'd let Ricardo live and Maura die.

"You did the right thing," Arianna said. "I don't question it. But try to see it from their perspective. Regardless of your reasons, you're still the guy who killed someone they loved."

"You sure know how to make a guy feel better."

"Sorry." Arianna remained quiet for a moment. "I can't understand why he did it. We've known him for years. He was so close to you, to all of us. He was a great friend and a great boyfriend to Brittney. He was never violent. Did you have any idea? Did he ever say anything that would help us understand why?"

"I don't know why he did it. Maybe he thought Carter was some kind of prophet. Maybe he thought Carter could make him see again. His eyes were improving, and I think Carter exploited that, saying it was some kind of miracle from God."

"What happened to him?"

"Carter? I shot him, and he fell out a four-story window. If he survived that, he couldn't have survived it well. He probably crawled into some hole to die." Aaron said it, but he no longer believed it. He'd experienced firsthand, and was still experiencing, the aftereffects of what they'd fed him.

"Well, I guess I'll see you tomorrow then. I have to visit Doug at the hospital."

Aaron tensed. "You're still representing him?"

"Everyone is entitled to legal representation, Aaron. Don't get self-righteous with me. There was a time when you would have thought the same thing. You and I, we were the same... once."

I'm nothing like you. I'm better than you.

"Besides," she said, "there are some interesting legal arguments here. What if Doug believed he was instructed by God to kill? Even if the instructions came through Carter, I may have a chance to argue some novel law in the state. Does that equate to legal insanity? I don't know, but it will certainly make headlines."

"Of course he's fucking insane!" Aaron took a few deep breaths to calm himself. "What about us, Ari?"

"There is no 'us.' It wasn't working, and we should have ended it sooner. I thought you agreed with that."

"Maybe I do, and maybe I don't. It doesn't make me love you any less."

"Don't do this," she said quietly.

"Do what?"

"Make it harder. I have to go. Save yourself and everyone else some heartache. Don't go tomorrow." She hung up the phone.

"Wait! I don't agree. I want you back. I need you back!" Aaron had wanted to say all that to her, but instead, he'd screamed it at dead air. He threw his brand-new phone across the room.

I'll be there.

He brooded in his chair for hours, losing track of time. When he snapped out of his rumination, he realized he was late. He cleaned up quickly and headed to the funeral home.

Standing at the entrance to the receiving room, Aaron stared at the oak box that held his best friend's remains. *Closed casket. No surprise there.*

He scanned the funeral home and saw a few familiar faces. Beaudette was seated in the back row, while Marklin loitered near the guest book. In a black suit, black tie, white shirt, and beat-up black loafers, Aaron had dressed the part of a mourning friend, but inside, his soul was dark. He felt only bitterness and betrayal. Solitude was making him rancorous. He needed to feel alive again.

Approaching the guest book, he nodded at Marklin, who nodded back. On the open page, he counted only twelve names—neither Beaudette nor Marklin had signed—but figured more people would be coming. Ricardo had so many friends.

He spotted Arianna sitting near someone he didn't know, her hand resting on his leg. *I see you, bitch. And I know you see me. Now I know why you didn't want me to come.* Aaron's rage grew, but he kept his cool. *This is neither the time nor the place.*

Forcing his attention to the front of the room, he let out a breath and a fraction of his rage with it. Ricardo's parents stood by the casket, teary-eyed as they greeted the straggling procession. The news had painted Ricardo as a crazed religious fanatic. Reporters cared little for the parts of Ricardo that made him human, the parts that those in attendance would miss.

To the right of Ricardo's parents, Brittney stood tall, dignified. Perhaps she'd shed so many tears that she had none left. The sadness, however, clung to her face, weighing down her skin so that it hung like old curtains.

For a moment, he felt humiliated. It occurred to him that maybe he'd wronged them all. The guilt passed quickly. No one would have to be there if Ricardo hadn't chosen to slaughter innocent people. *Choices have consequences.* He hated Ricardo for his.

Aaron moved toward the casket. Ricardo's older brother moved to block his path, and Aaron worried that things would get ugly.

"You've got some nerve," Benito said.

Brittney looked over at them. Warring emotions flashed across her face until she settled on one: revulsion. "I'll handle this."

Benito tensed, but he backed off, his cold stare fixed on Aaron.

"You're not welcome here," Brittney said.

"Brit, please," Aaron said. "He was my best friend."

"Just leave!"

The outburst attracted the attention of those nearby. She put on a thin, phony smile. "Aaron, you did what you had to do. We know that. But that doesn't change the fact that you took him from us. Right or wrong, we can't forgive you."

Dumbfounded, he stared at Brittney. Everyone had turned on him, and for what? Saving an innocent from a killer. *No good deed goes unpunished.*

"Please." Brittney's chin quivered. Maybe she still had some tears left in her, after all. "Just go."

Aaron turned and headed for the door. *Fuck it. He's dead anyway. They might as well all be dead. Who gives a damn? They sure as hell don't.* He walked out to his car and got in.

At least there's still one person left in this shitty world who appreciates me. He pulled his phone from his pocket and dialed. "Maura. This is Officer Pimental. Aaron."

"Hi, Aaron. How are you doing?" She sounded happy to hear from him. He was thankful for it.

"Not good. Can we get together sometime?"

"What for?"

"I want to talk about what happened."

After a beat, Maura responded, "I'm not so sure that's a good idea. I'm trying to move past it, to forget it if I can."

"Please. I don't have anyone else to talk to about it."

After a long silence, she whispered, "I appreciate everything you did for me, and I don't fault you for doing what you did—"

"What exactly is it you think I've done, Maura?"

"We both know he dropped the knife. You were tortured, terrified... after what they did to you, who could blame you, really?"

"He was going to stab you, Maura."

"I know. That's what I told them, too. Don't worry. I really should be going, though. I—"

"I saved your life."

Maura's sigh whistled through the receiver. "Are you seeing somebody? I mean, like a doctor? You should, after what you've been through. I am. I think it's worth—"

"I saved your life! Doesn't that mean anything to you?"

"It does, Aaron. I'll be forever grateful for what you did. But the truth is... you scare me. And I don't want to be around anyone that reminds me of those awful people. I'm sorry. I have to go."

"Don't you hang—"

The phone went dead.

CHAPTER 33

JOCELYN STRODE DOWN THE DIMLY lit checkered-tile hallway. The chipped walls were painted a cool blue with white baseboards that, in the pale-yellow light, resembled a chain-smoker's wallpaper. A nurse in pink scrubs looked up from the reception desk. Jocelyn flashed her badge and continued to the room.

"Good evening, Detective Beaudette," an officer said as he rose, tossing a paperback onto the chair behind him. The officer beside him jumped to his feet.

"At ease, soldiers," Jocelyn said, joking.

The officers smiled politely and returned to their seats on opposite sides of the doorframe.

Room 416 was a private room in an area of the hospital set apart for problem patients: the hostile, the rabid, the hopped-up on angel dust, and the criminally insane. It had one window, which offered a view of the wall of the adjacent building and a sullied alleyway. For the last week, the room had been occupied by Douglas Fournier.

"How's the ape doing?"

"He doesn't stir much," the officer on her right replied. "Actually, he's been quiet, mostly sleeping. When he's awake, he doesn't do much more than stare into space. It's kind of creepy, like he's shut himself off. Then again, he's lost a lot of blood. I don't know how many transfusions they've given him, but it was a lot."

Bruce caught up and joined her at the door.

"You good?" Jocelyn asked.

Bruce huffed. "My fucking Reese's Pieces got stuck. Now you'd expect that from the giant seventy-five-cent brownie or maybe even the Cheez-Its or Animal Crackers, but not from the damn Reese's Pieces. They come in a bag. They should never get stuck. All you gotta do is shake it just right…" He grunted as he tipped the machine, but it slipped out of his hands and back to its resting position. "Damn it!"

"We'll get you some when we're done here," Jocelyn said, trying to keep a straight face. Her partner sounded like a kindergartner who'd lost his recess, good practice for when Caitlyn got a little older. "Let's see if Fournier's more talkative this time." She opened the door.

Fournier was sitting up against the headboard. He was awake, wearing that thousand-yard stare the officer had described. He seemed unaware of their presence.

Jocelyn approached the bed. His upper body and face were partially bandaged, though the doctor had said his wounds were healing abnormally fast.

"Fournier?" When she got no response, she snapped her fingers in front of his eyes. "Fournier?"

"Go away," he murmured. "I have nothing to say to you."

"True," Jocelyn said. "You've got so few bargaining chips left. Ricardo Jimenez is dead. Your wife is dead. It's just a matter of time before we catch Carter Wainwright, if he isn't dead already. There's not much prosecutors could offer you at this point. You're no longer useful to anybody." She moved to stand in his line of sight. "Regardless, we thought you might want to talk to us. You must realize that we have you dead to rights. Plus, both your wife and Wainwright did abandon you back there, leaving you to take the rap for everything."

"So where's Carter Wainwright?" Bruce asked.

Fournier lowered his eyes. "My attorney has instructed me not to speak with you. Not that any of that matters now." He laughed, though there was no mirth in it.

"Well, if it doesn't matter, then why don't you just tell us where he went?" Bruce asked.

"Even if I did know, I wouldn't tell you. But I don't, so you're wasting your time."

"Why are you protecting him?" Jocelyn asked. "He sold you out." She was convinced Wainwright had purposely stashed evidence in Fournier's van to incriminate him. Maybe he had known the police were getting close, so he threw his lackeys to the wolves to save himself.

"Carter would never do such a thing."

"What makes you so sure? We had nothing on you guys," Jocelyn said. "Yet, lo and behold, we find a freshly painted van containing a phone used to contact one of the victims and the box cutter used to slice them up, all by dumb luck."

"So?"

"So it was too easy. We found a partial print on the box cutter—not yours, but Jimenez's. We went through his garbage and found Craig Sousa's wallet. If the lab results had come one day sooner, both Officer Temple and your buddies would still be alive today. You'd all be in prison, but alive. Any thoughts on why we found this evidence so easily?"

"We were sloppy."

"Yeah, that's what we thought, but given how meticulous your little club was, the misplaced evidence seemed awfully convenient... too good to be true. It was like you either wanted to be caught, or the evidence was planted without your knowledge. And you don't strike me as someone who wanted to get caught."

"And you think Carter planted it?" Fournier snorted. "Why would he do that? The closer you got to me, the closer you got to him. Why would he risk that?"

"I don't know, but why would you keep that cell phone? Not only is it damning evidence, but it's disposable. Why didn't you just throw it away?" Jocelyn crossed her arms, waiting for a response. When she didn't get one, she pressed the issue. "Almost all the evidence points to you. We stumbled on Wainwright in the process. We know his name isn't really Wainwright, but I'm guessing you weren't clued in to that."

"You're trying to get under my skin. It won't work. There's no rational reason for Carter to set me up."

Jocelyn smirked. *A guy who eats human hearts looking for rationality.* She saw right through his tough exterior. His confidence was shriveling as if the man himself were shrinking. More importantly, she'd planted a seed of doubt. "Maybe you were meant to be caught. Maybe you were supposed to be killed. What happened in that room? How did Officer Pimental escape? Why was his gun left for him?"

"Come on, Fournier," Bruce said. "With all the practice you guys had in kidnapping and killing people, how did Pimental get free? Pimental then shot and killed Jimenez and caused your wife to run out on you. You know her fate. Are you telling me that everything went according to plan?"

Fournier flinched. Any mention of his wife seemed to hit a nerve.

Jocelyn backed over to a chair and sat down. "Look, we're not here to harass you. You're already fucked as far as we're concerned. We just want some answers. It seems pretty damn convenient that Wainwright is free to party his ass off, while you're stuck here in police custody and all your friends and your wife are dead."

Fournier's face hardened. "I told you, I have no idea where he is."

"Okay, so you don't know where he is. Can you think of anything that might be useful?"

"Not really." He laughed. "You're never going to catch him. Quit wasting your time. He's too smart for you, always three steps ahead."

"Then we'll be four," Bruce said. "His smarts didn't help you out too much, did they?"

"I can die without fear or regret. Can you say the same? Are you prepared to face your maker?"

"If God has a beef with me," Bruce said, "I'm sure we'll take it up when the time comes. Until then, I'll sleep just fine."

Jocelyn stood again and stepped toward the door. "Bruce, this guy's a waste of time. He doesn't know anything."

"Is that true?" Bruce asked. "Are you really just the fall guy?"

Fournier kept silent.

"Enjoy this bed while you can," Bruce said, slapping the mattress. "Your next one won't be so comfortable. Let the officers outside know if you change your mind and feel like talking. Until then, heal up quickly, so we can get you to your new home."

They left Fournier to his thoughts. Jocelyn's comments about the evidence accumulating against him—and only him—would certainly fester. She prayed it would lead him to give up his elusive cohort.

Still, she walked from the hospital with a heavy mind and heavy feet. *Where are you, Carter Wainwright?*

CHAPTER 34

I T HAD BEEN OVER A week since Ricardo's death. Since the wake, Aaron had sat in his beanbag chair in his room, day in and day out, letting all the bad feelings fester and trying to forget the forbidden high and the excitement he'd felt while shooting Carter, Doug, and Ricardo. His mother's Himalayan cat, nestled dead center on his twin-sized bed, cast him a glare that said it was her room, that he'd forfeited it when he'd left home many years ago.

His old bedroom still looked the same as it had when he was in high school. Track trophies and posters for films and bands he could barely remember covered the walls. Pictures of the past surrounded him, pinned to bulletin boards or jammed in dusty frames—friendly faces belonging to people lost to him: a day at the beach with Raquel, their happiness apparent as they stood arm in arm for the camera; a trip to Six Flags with Craig, ecstatic to snag a photographic memento of himself, Aaron, and Batman; and a kayaking adventure with Ricardo at the mouth of the Coles River, with swells so high they had to struggle to avoid being dumped into the water.

He pulled his wallet from his pocket and retrieved a photograph of his favorite day: swimming with dolphins off the coast of Mexico with Arianna. He threw the picture, a forever-immortalized depiction of a happier and irretrievable time, onto the floor. Moments like those had helped Aaron keep it together. He could never return to them.

He pulled his pistol from the holster and rested its barrel against his temple. His finger slid onto the trigger. His phone rang. He lowered the gun and laid it on the floor. A tear rolled down his cheek. He stared at his phone's screen but didn't recognize the number.

He answered it anyway, desperate to hear a friendly voice, desperate to know he was no longer alone. "Hello?"

"Hi, Aaron." The voice was soft, shaking. "It's Maura."

Aaron sat up. "Hi, Maura. I was hoping you'd call. How have you been? Everything all right?"

"I'm... I'm fine. Listen—"

"You sure? You don't sound okay."

"Y-Yeah. Yes. It's just... cold here. Listen, could you come by tonight?"

Aaron cleared his throat. "Of course! Yes!" He couldn't help himself and had to ask, "Why the change of heart? I thought you didn't want to see me?"

"If you don't want to, I understand—"

"No, I want to. I'll be there." He hadn't showered in the last few days and was appalled when he sniffed his armpit. He checked the time. Six o'clock. "Is eight too late for you?" His mood dropped like an anchor when no response came. "Maura? You still there?"

"Nope. I mean, yes. That's fine. Eight's fine." Maura sounded nervous, as if the two were scheduling their first date. "I'll see you then." She hung up.

Aaron picked up his service pistol and held it with both hands. He examined its detail and envisioned the metal slug firing out of the barrel and splattering the insides of his head all over his old bedroom. He holstered it again and got to his feet.

"Not today, kitty," he said, scratching the Himalayan behind the ear. The cat opened one eye and stretched out its front paw, exposing its claws. Aaron shrugged. "You don't care much either way, do you?"

The cat went back to sleep. Aaron went into the bathroom for a long, hot shower and a much-needed shave.

During the twenty-minute drive to Seekonk, his spirits rose a bit. He was thankful to have someone to talk to again. He had so many things he wanted to ask her, but mostly, he wanted to know how she seemed to be moving on so easily so that he could move on, too, if that was possible. He knew one thing for sure: he wasn't going anywhere without his gun. He felt its weight tucked under his belt, hidden from sight by his shirttails.

As he pulled up to her house, he spotted a police cruiser. He got out and walked toward the marked car. "I'm Officer Aaron Pimental of the Fall River Police Department," he called out as he approached. "I'm visiting Ms. Fleurent."

He expected them to get out of the car, flash their lights, or call out to him. The officers didn't respond.

Aaron got closer and leaned down to peek in through the window. "Hello, I'm Officer—"

The car was empty. He looked around but didn't see anyone. *This isn't right. Something's wrong.*

Aaron opened the door and grabbed the radio handset. "This is Officer Aaron Pimental of the Fall River Police Department. I'm here at the residence of Maura Fleurent, 647 Everett Street. Your stationed officers are nowhere to be seen. Please send backup."

"Please repeat."

Aaron was too worried about Maura to waste time. "Officer down! Send backup to 647 Everett Street." He tossed the receiver aside. *He's here. It must be him!* He pulled out his service weapon then raced toward the house.

As he climbed the front steps, he could see that the front door was ajar, but it didn't appear to be broken. A washcloth and a small bottle lay on the carpet just inside the doorway. A strong odor emanated from the area. *Ammonia? Chloroform?*

He flicked on his flashlight and crossed his wrists so that the gun and flashlight beam pointed in the same direction. He took a step forward, and his foot squished into the carpet as if he'd stepped on a sponge. About five feet away, a uniformed officer lay on the floor. He went over and bent down to check for a pulse. Nothing.

He used his light to scan the rest of the living room. He didn't see the other officer, and he couldn't decide whether to search the rest of the house or wait for backup.

"I'm up here," Maura yelled. "Don't—"

Aaron hurried up the stairs. He paused at the top to check the hallway in each direction. Sounds of a struggle came from a room on the left. Gun ready, he stepped to the doorway and peered around it.

Maura was sitting on the bed, her wrists zip-tied around the headboard. She was gagged and crying. Her eyes met his, and she tried to scream something. Realizing she was trying to warn him, he ducked back out of the doorway.

Something hit him in the head from behind, and he slumped to the floor as his world went black.

———

An empty bottle of Scotch sat on the table, glinting under the dim ceiling light. Bruce swirled the last of the single malt in his glass as he pored over copies of all the reports and case files associated with Carter Wainwright's crew of killers.

His fingers ran across a photo of a young boy whose name happened to be Carter Wainwright but who looked nothing like the suspect Bruce's team pursued. *Plastic surgery?* Bruce scoffed. *Of course not. Maybe the name is just a coincidence. There has to be more than one Carter Wainwright out there.*

His gut told him otherwise. A suicide and a murder thirteen years apart might have seemed unrelated if not for the name. He ran a hand through his hair. He couldn't dismiss the name. *But what's the connection?*

His cell phone rang. "Marklin."

"Bruce!" Jocelyn shouted. "Something's going down at Fleurent's house. Pimental just called it in."

"Pimental? What's he doing there? Isn't there a car posted outside?"

"Yes, Seekonk police have had a patrol car there all week, but the officers aren't responding. I'm heading over there now."

"I'm on my way."

———

Aaron awoke to a hand slapping his face. Carter stood over him, holding a gun. Aaron probed his pounding head with his fingers and felt a gumball-sized bump.

"What the fuck did you hit me with?" Aaron asked.

"A billy club," Carter said, smiling. "It goes with the uniform." He tapped a rectangular pin affixed to his chest. "Like my name tag?"

Aaron squinted at it. He groaned and rolled his eyes when he realized it was his. He couldn't remember where or when he'd misplaced it, but its appearance on Carter's chest gave him a fairly good idea.

"I borrowed this from you. I hope you don't mind."

"Cut the crap, Carter. What do you want?"

"That depends."

"I thought you'd be long gone by now."

"I have a few things I'd like to wrap up first, Ms. Fleurent being one. You, another."

Aaron sat up. His eyes adjusted to the dark room, and he peered at Carter. He saw no signs of injury, no indication that the four-story fall or the shooting had ever occurred.

Could I have missed him? It was dark, but... no, there's no way I missed him. He's just covering up the wounds. Aaron shook his head. *He should be in a hospital or a cemetery by now.* "How in hell did you survive that fall?"

"I'm like a cat." Carter laughed. "I always land on my feet, not to mention the whole nine lives thing."

Aaron glanced at Maura, who was still tied to the bed. She didn't seem to be hurt.

"Are you going to kill us?" Aaron asked. He didn't find it strange that he wasn't the least bit afraid, just curious. He wondered why they weren't already dead.

"Her, yes. You, no. Not unless you force my hand." Carter's straightforward answer struck Aaron as coldly rational. He was like an Old West judge, choosing at whim which criminals would receive the death penalty.

"So where does that leave me?" Aaron didn't care anymore. Only hours earlier, he would have been more than happy to have done himself in.

"Don't you want to help me do it? Look at her, all splayed out for us." Carter waved a hand at Maura like a game show host revealing the grand prize. "Granted, I should kill you for shooting at me back at the mill, but I'm willing to forgive and forget if you are. Come on! It'll be fun. Given that you've already shot Doug, Ricardo, and me, not to mention your first, it's obvious you're developing a taste for it."

"My first? What are you talking about?"

"That's right. Newport wasn't your first. That was Mr. Fluffykins."

Aaron's eyes widened. "How do you know about that?"

"You'd be surprised how much I know about you, Aaron. Why'd you do it? Was it really over the *Star Wars* coloring book he chewed up? Or did it just feel good to wring that rabbit's neck with your own two hands?"

"Shut up. That was a long time ago. I—"

"And what about Franklin Ortiz? You remember him, don't you? Had to switch schools after that incident."

"Th-That wasn't my fault. He picked that fight."

"Oh, but you finished it, didn't you? Pushed him into traffic and told everyone it was an accident. That kid was lucky not to be in a wheelchair for life. Did Ricardo ever wonder why you didn't have any friends when you came to his high school?"

"That *was* an accident. How do you know all this?"

"That psychiatrist your parents made you see, she took thorough notes. The old crone's dead now—and no, not by my hand, unfortunately—but someone had to properly manage the disposal of all those juicy confidential records. Believe me, I could have taken all of them, and no one would have batted an eyelash."

Aaron slapped the floor and started to rise. "I should have shot you a hundred—"

"Ah-ah." Carter waggled his gun. "Slowly."

Biting back his anger, Aaron got to his feet. "But why? What do you want with me?"

"People like us, we're one in a million. I've never had a partner before, someone truly like me... at least not one that worked out or wasn't already well on his way to prison or the cemetery. I just want to do what I do, savor it, and move on to the next one, and that's a whole lot easier with someone watching your back."

"Don't you mean someone to take the fall for you?"

"And waste your potential? With our combined skills, we could look out for each other. We'd never get caught. Believe me, I've been at this for a long time. I know how to hunt, kill, and dispose of prey discreetly and professionally. It's the heart removal and consumption that adds more time and complexity to it, but now that I've experienced that, there's no way I'm giving it up. I know you want it, too. How empty your life must seem after having tasted that power and feeling like you can never taste it again. You can, Aaron. We could live our lives the way we want to live them, the way people like us were meant to live. It's simply Darwin's theory in action, survival of the fittest."

"Why do you think I'd even consider that? I tried to kill you once, and if you give me that gun back, I'll try again."

"Great. You need more time. I get it. Unfortunately, time is something we don't have right now. I know a killer when I see one. I've gone through a lot of effort for you here, taken a lot of risks. You should be more appreciative. I know what you are, and by now, you've got to feel it, as well. Tell me the truth. Were you coming here tonight to kill her, or were you just hoping to get lucky?"

The question was a slap in the face. *Why would I want to kill Maura?* He'd had thoughts of suicide, sure. But murder? Anyone he might have murdered had deserved it. Maura didn't deserve it.

He wanted to connect with her, with someone. "She's all I got left," he murmured, on the brink of tears.

Carter laughed. "Oh, I get it now. You're still clinging to that last bastion of humanity, personified in the form of Ms. Maura Fleurent. How delightful. Well, as a wise man once told me, '*Humanity* is the coldest of words.' What has it brought you? Nothing but pain and sorrow. Forsake it! Be something so much more." Carter tucked Aaron's gun into the back of his pants and unsheathed his survival knife.

"Stop preaching at me. I'm not one of your stupid lackeys."

"That's exactly what I've been trying to tell you. You just need help realizing your potential." He raised the knife. "I can help you with that. You won't need to do a thing."

Sirens blared in the distance. It sounded as though every cop car in Seekonk was on the way.

Carter sighed. "You just had to call them, didn't you? I guess this is her second lucky day. The third time's the charm, right?" He winked at Maura then turned back to Aaron. "Well, you're on your own. When you come to your senses, give me a sign. I'll find you." He walked toward the door.

"You're not going anywhere." Aaron leaped to his feet and charged. He crashed into Carter, and the momentum carried them into the wall. With both hands, he pinned Carter's left arm to the wall, the gun aimed at the ceiling.

Carter twisted around and threw a right hook that caused Aaron to stagger backward. "I don't have time for this!" He shrugged. "Not like I don't owe you one." He fired a single shot then bolted out of the room.

Aaron didn't pursue him. Blood ran between his fingers from a deep gash in his shoulder where the bullet had grazed him. He sat on the bed beside Maura. As he looked into her eyes, he saw a woman who was helpless and weak, the way he felt inside. She looked pathetic, a reflection of his own wretchedness. He didn't want to be feeble anymore.

He pulled his Swiss army knife from his pocket. As he leaned toward her, she flinched. He frowned. "I'm trying to help you." When the fear didn't leave her eyes, his hurt turned to anger.

He sneered and tore the gag out of her mouth. Grabbing her forearm, he gave it a yank. She winced and closed her eyes as he jabbed the blade at the zip-tie.

As soon as her hands were free, she rolled off the far side of the bed and backed away from him, gripping her right wrist with her left hand. Outside, tires screeched, and red and blue lights flashed through the window.

Maura continued to retreat until her back found the room's corner. "Those things he said, it's like he knows you."

"I'm not one of them, Maura." Aaron circled the bed. "You have to trust me."

"He said you killed people. There were others…"

He let out a nervous chuckle. "I didn't kill anybody. A rabbit when I was six. Let's just talk about this for a second." He raised his hands then realized he was still holding the pocketknife. After putting the knife on the windowsill, he took a long step toward her.

Outside, a bullhorn blared. "This is the police. We have you surrounded. Come out with your hands up."

"I don't know you," Maura whined. Tears streamed down her cheeks. "Get away from me."

"Maura, I—"

"I'll tell them. I'll tell them everything. If you don't step back, I swear to God I will."

Aaron sucked in a gulp of air. He put on a pained smile, full of clenched teeth. "Why would you say that? After all I've done—"

She pressed her back to the wall. "Stay the hell away from me!"

He reached for her, but she leapt toward the bed and scrambled over it on her hands and knees. She tumbled onto the floor on the other side. As she struggled to get back on her feet, Aaron jumped onto the bed and dove into her back. His momentum carried them forward, and he heard a bone-chilling crack as Maura's head collided with the corner of her dresser.

Aaron rolled off her. "Maura?" He crawled around to get a better look at what part of her might be injured.

The bullhorn sounded again. "Last chance. Come out with your hands up."

Maura moaned and raised her head. Slowly, she pushed herself up to her knees, her body swaying like a palm tree in a hurricane. Drool ran down her chin. Her eyes were half-rolled back in her sockets, the lids fluttering. Blood flowed from a large gash and matted her hair to her forehead.

"You were all I had left, Maura. I *saved* you. But you don't thank me. Instead, you reject me, just like everyone else." He reached out and ran his hand through the hair on the back of her head then closed his fist around a large clump. "I just wanted to talk to you. I wanted your help. Was that really too much to ask, after all the help I gave you?"

He pulled her head back. "I gave you your life, you bitch! And you threaten me?" He slammed her head forward against the dresser. "You refuse to see me?" He rammed her head into the dresser again. "You don't deserve your life, you fucking bitch!"

Over and over again, Aaron hammered Maura's head into that dresser. "You hear me? You don't deserve a goddamn thing!"

Thump. Thump. Thump.

The front door slammed. Footsteps thundered across the floor.

"Fuck. What do I do? What do I do? What do I *do*?" Blood coated his clothes, so much of it that he couldn't tell which blotches came from her head and which came from his shoulder. *And they won't be able to tell, either.*

An idea formed quickly, and he had to forcibly wipe the grin off his face. He sat cross-legged and cradled Maura's head across his wounded arm.

"Up here!" Beaudette shouted as she entered the bedroom. "Officer down!" Pointing her gun at each corner, she asked, "Wainwright?"

Aaron tried to inject a tremor into his voice. "Gone, I think, just before you got here."

Marklin rushed in. "My God, Pimental. What the hell happened?"

"Maura." The effort it took not to smile made him form a grimace he hoped would look as though he were fighting back tears. "She's dead."

"Fucking A, Jocelyn," Marklin said. "Three times we cross paths with Ms. Fleurent, and we still fail to protect her. I can see the lawsuits now."

"A woman's dead, Bruce," Beaudette said calmly. "And an officer needs our help."

"Yeah?" Marklin snapped. He turned to Aaron. "What the hell are you doing here, anyway? You know you aren't supposed to be here. She's already given her statement, but the matter has not been closed."

"She called me. Practically begged me to come by. She said she needed someone to talk to, and… I needed someone, too."

Two paramedics shuffled into the room. One checked Maura for a pulse and shook his head. They pulled her away from Aaron, who clung to her as if letting go meant losing himself. *If I'm not already lost.*

"Wait." Marklin said. "What's up with your arm?"

"Wainwright shot me."

"I think you better run through it from the beginning—that is, if you don't require immediate medical assistance."

"I'm okay." Aaron got up and sat on the bed. "As I said, I came by to see Maura. She seemed nervous, maybe even scared, when she called, so I thought maybe she was having nightmares or something. Now, I figure Carter must have forced her to call me to lure me here. Anyway, when I got here, I stopped by the cruiser out front to let them know who I am.

The car was empty, so I called it in. When I saw the front door open and one of the officers on the floor, I came inside."

"Why didn't you wait for backup?" Beaudette asked.

"I was worried about Maura."

Beaudette nodded, scribbling notes into a small pad. "Go on."

"I swept the first floor but didn't see anyone, so I went upstairs and swept there, too. Nothing. I pulled out my pocketknife—it's over there on the sill—and cut Maura free. I think she tried to warn me, but I couldn't tell what she was saying because she was gagged. I was reaching for the gag when Wainwright clubbed me in the back of the head." He winced as he touched the still-smarting wound. "I'm guessing he was hiding outside or something while I cleared the house. I must have blacked out for a minute, 'cause when I came to..." He lowered his eyes and cleared his throat. "When I came to, he was bashing her head against the dresser. My gun was gone. I got up and charged him, but he turned around and shot me."

"I heard the sirens then, and he must have, too, because he ran out of the room. I went over to check on Maura, but she was already dead."

"Why didn't he kill you?" Marklin asked.

Fuck. Aaron tried to hide his frustration for missing such an obvious point. "I don't know. Maybe he panicked."

"Maybe." Marklin stroked his chin. "Just seems odd that after you shot him back at the mill that he would let you live."

"Bruce, we can talk more about this down at the precinct," Beaudette said. "He really needs to get to the hospital."

Marklin narrowed his eyes at Aaron before nodding.

Aaron didn't like that look, but he'd told his story, and he just need to stick to it. *It's my word against hers, and she ain't talking.*

CHAPTER 35

THREE HOURS LATER, AARON STOOD in Doug's hospital room, a black ski mask hiding his face. Leather gloves covered his hands. He had already been discharged and sent home with a sling and a prescription for Percocet. No one would think he had returned.

He stared down at Doug. "Do you even see me? You look catatonic," he whispered. "How do you go to the bathroom with all this shit hooked up to you?"

As if breaking from a trance, Doug raised his head. "I knew you'd come. I've been waiting for you."

"Have you? Do you know why I'm here?"

He nodded. "To save me. The Lord knows about my doubts, my sadness without Kelly. You're here to take my sins away. You'll make me pure again. He told me you'd come. He came to me in a dream and told me that you would be my Saint Peter, opening the gates for me to enter the next world."

Feeling his mouth curl involuntarily, Aaron was glad for his mask. He wasn't going to question such an obvious gift. He'd acted on impulse by going there and had made it into the room by the sheer luck that Fortuna and Matthews hadn't noticed the flecks of broken Percocet in the coffee and brandy Aaron had shared with them. He didn't need all the painkillers the doctor had prescribed, anyway. In fact, he was already feeling considerably better.

Aaron had thought he would have to kill Doug quickly and quietly. He wasn't sure if he could extract the heart in time. But things were finally going his way, as if he should have been following that path all along. "Are you ready, then?"

Doug grabbed the bedrails. "I'm ready."

Aaron stepped back to the door and twisted the lock. His heart raced with nervous excitement. The nausea he had expected—and had once half-hoped for as proof of his humanity—did not materialize. He didn't care. He was already enjoying it, and he could hardly wait to feed. Doug had so much power in him, strength begging to be Aaron's.

"Here," he said, waving a dirty gym sock in Doug's face. "Put this in your mouth. I need you quiet if I'm going to finish... to save you uninterrupted."

Doug set his jaw. "There's no need. With God as my witness, I won't make a sound."

"Impossible."

"You feel the power of the righteous. You know what it can do."

Aaron stared at Doug, who didn't so much as blink. He dropped the sock and pulled his hatchet from an inside pocket of his jacket. "Sorry, Doug. I shouldn't have doubted you. Still, this won't be easy. This hatchet is all I have. I promise I'll make it quick."

Aside from the strained grip he had on the aluminum railings, Doug showed no sign of fear. He gave Aaron a nod then stared up at the ceiling. Aaron raised the hatchet but hesitated before swinging. He knew what he was doing was wrong. Doug wasn't like the others he'd killed. The others weren't planned. *There's no going back from this.*

"Do it," Doug said.

Aaron swung his arm with all his might. Then, he raised it and swung again. Hacking wildly at Doug's chest, he felt alive, adrenalin fueling his every stroke. He didn't want to stop and didn't think he could have even if he'd wanted to. He paused several times to wipe sweat and blood from his eyes.

He broke his promise: Doug's death was not quick. But Doug kept his. If the guards outside were listening, all they would have heard were the dull thumps of the hatchet against Doug's chest and the heavy breathing of both a murderer and his dying victim.

Once Doug stopped breathing and his blood quit pumping, things got easier. Aaron frantically shoved his hands into Doug's chest. Like a junkie in the throes of withdrawal, he had to have the heart, needed the high it offered. When he had both hands around the organ, he yanked hard, stumbling backward as it gave way.

This thing is huge! The heart was proportional to the rest of Doug. Aaron salivated, proud of his trophy. Blood oozed between Aaron's gloved fingers as he looked around the room for something suitable to carry the thing.

He spotted the bag with Doug's belongings, but he couldn't wait. He placed the heart on the bedside table and lopped off a piece. After thrusting the chunk into his mouth, he swallowed without bothering to chew.

He dumped Doug's clothes and shoes out of the bag and slid the remainder of the heart into it.

"How could this have happened?" Bruce stood over the body of the only person left who could have given him any insight into the whereabouts of Carter Wainwright.

Jocelyn crouched over the hatchet that had been used to slice up Douglas Fournier like an Easter ham. "What a fucking mess. Looks like our killer didn't care about his weapon." She straightened and walked over to the bed. Peering down into the open cavity of the victim's chest, she said, "No heart. That's not surprising these days. You think it was Wainwright?"

"If so, he had a busy night. First, the murder of Maura Fleurent, then this. And for what? Fournier wasn't telling us anything. Frankly, I'm surprised Wainwright didn't leave town for good last Friday."

"The officers posted outside said they didn't see anyone enter or exit the room. The only other possible entrance is through that window. We're on the fourth floor."

"So what did the killer do? Teleport in here? Are we hunting a ghost? I saw the crusties in the corners of that one officer's eyes. He was probably sleeping on the job. Who knows what the other one was doing? They're either lousy cops or corrupt. How could the perp chop up Fournier with a hatchet without alerting those two idiots? The blood spatters show that Fournier was alive when the attack began. I don't see a gag. He must have yelled loud enough to wake every patient in this hospital."

"Maybe he was drugged? He was one of Wainwright's goons. Maybe Wainwright had some pity and made it easier for him."

Bruce tapped the bedrail. "We'll know more when we get the blood results. For now, I'm not convinced this was Wainwright."

"Always the conspiracy theorist. Who was it, then? You think we missed a follower? Either way, the motive is the same: to silence Fournier."

"This just looks too sloppy—too sloppy to be Wainwright and too sloppy to be one of his followers." Bruce stared at the corpse for inspiration. "This seems foolhardy, not planned. Maybe even vengeful. We could have a vigilante looking to settle a score." He scanned his mind for anyone who might fit the profile. The many faces of Carter's victims, their friends, and their families processed through his computerlike brain, each discounted for one reason or another.

Of the few remaining who fit the bill, Aaron Pimental stuck out. He had both motive and opportunity. Hell, the officer had been discharged from the hospital less than an hour before Fournier's estimated time of death. Still, Bruce had seen the bullet wound in Pimental's arm. The physical labor involved in Fournier's death would have been a tremendous strain on someone in his condition. The ax strokes were strong and deep. *Still.* "Where did Pimental go tonight after he was discharged?"

Jocelyn put her hands on her hips and cocked her head. "You can't be serious."

"Why not? He's had a funny way of showing up wherever Wainwright does. He was friends with some of the killers. How do we know for sure he wasn't one of them all along?"

"Because he's been thrown in a trunk, badly beaten, forced to eat the heart of his partner, shot, and compelled to kill his best friend. Wainwright, on the other hand, would have been able to walk right up to Fournier without alarming him." She sighed. "You should lay off Pimental. He's been through enough."

Bruce stroked his chin. "Jocelyn, you are a great detective, but you'd be far better than I ever was or ever could be if you just killed off that last remaining bit of hopefulness for the human race you still cling to. Don't you think all that happened to him might screw with his head? How did he do on his psych eval?"

"He passed it. So either his psyche is just fine, or he knows what to say to pass it."

"When's he coming back to work? I'd like to give him my own test."

"The department is sending him to Orlando for a convention next week. He said he'd make a vacation out of it. I had him placed on light detail, traffic duty mostly, for when he gets back. I think he just needs to fill up his time, and he'll be all right."

"I'm going to order another psych eval immediately, before he goes down to Florida, citing Fleurent's death as the impetus. It's in his best interests, as well as ours."

"Okay, but let me handle it. You're about as delicate as a brick wall."

"Aren't you sweet?" Bruce smiled. "The guy's like a bad penny. Everywhere he goes, someone turns up dead. Florida better watch out."

"I admit the coincidences are... noteworthy. But considering his friendship with one or two members of the cult, isn't some coincidence to be expected?"

"In my mind, he's a suspect."

"Okay, but so is every friend or relative of each of the victims."

"Well, I agree that Wainwright is the prime suspect here, despite my gut feeling otherwise. So fair warning: I'll be watching Pimental. When he's on duty, I'm going to insist he be partnered up at all times, with his partner reporting to me after every shift."

"Hey, I'm not going to stop you. But as far as I'm concerned, Fournier's killer did the world a favor. So even if it was Pimental who killed Fournier, good for him."

"The laws apply equally to us all," Bruce said.

Jocelyn rolled her eyes. "What do you want to do about him?" she asked, jerking a thumb at Fournier's body.

"Have forensics do their thing. Bag the hatchet and the sock, sweep for prints, the usual."

CHAPTER 36

THE SUN WAS SHINING BRIGHTLY in Orlando, warm enough for shorts and T-shirts. It was a shame Aaron wouldn't be staying long enough to enjoy it.

The plane ride had consisted of a horde of little whining bastards screaming in his ear for three hours. Babies cried, toddlers puked, teenagers blasted iPods to no-talent bitch-boy bands, and fat, sweaty Hawaiian-shirt-wearing assholes engulfed Aaron in his coach-class bucket seat. It was the type of crowd that only Disney World could draw. *Yay, Disney.*

He arrived with a migraine and without the protection of his deodorant, which had completely melted off by the time the plane had flown over Newark. But as he exited the plane, his tension slowly slipped away.

Aaron took the monorail to the baggage claim, grabbed his lone suitcase, and jumped onto a shuttle to the rental car company hub in approximately thirty minutes. No hassles. No bosses. No killers. Nobody. He planned to head over to International Drive, sign in at the convention, grab his free gift bag filled with Chex Mix, pens, and stationery supporting the logos of various weapon manufacturers, then quickly be on his way.

He had work to do and a long drive ahead. A true test of his character stood before him. It was finally time to decide what kind of man he would be. His mind was sharp and focused, despite his recurring bouts with insomnia. His determination was his strength. His once-empty life was filled with new purpose. In a way, he had Carter to thank for that. He laughed at the irony.

Aaron had lost too much in his lifetime. A man's soul wasn't meant to bear such loss. Arianna had once accused him of being manic-depressive. The heightened sensations he currently felt made him wonder if that were true. But they came and went in sporadic flashes. He felt everything more but could hold it all in more easily.

Raquel, Ricardo, Arianna… each had left holes in him. He'd lost too much of himself, and he wanted it all back. He would take it back from those who'd taken it from him. They'd stolen his heart. It was time to return the favor.

"Reservation for Pimental," Aaron said as he approached the rental counter.

"Welcome to sunny Orlando, Mr. Pimental." The Hispanic gentleman smiled. "I'll just need your driver's license, a credit card, and proof of insurance."

Aaron handed over the requested documentation. "Do you have the vehicle I asked for?"

"Subaru Outback… yes, we have one on hold for you. It's the only one in the lot, actually. We don't get too many requests for those here." The salesperson entered information into the computer. "I see you want our unlimited miles plan?"

"That's correct."

"Not a problem." He click-clacked on the keyboard some more. "If you don't mind me asking, where will you be heading?"

Aaron shot the man a look that said, "Yes, I do mind you asking."

The salesman averted his eyes. "W-Well… um, off-roading with our vehicles is strictly prohibited, as is any beach driving. Please be sure to read the damage provisions in your contract."

Aaron drove straight to the Quality Inn on International Drive. He left his luggage in the rental car since he didn't see any need to unpack. He paid for the five nights he was supposed to be there, just in case. In his room, he set the alarm for six in the evening and crashed on the bed.

After those few hours of sleep uninterrupted by any kind of dreams, he felt refreshed. He splashed water on his face and headed out. He caught the tail end of rush hour but managed to get past Jacksonville and out of Florida just after dusk. He pressed on through the night, stopping only for gas and coffee. Not wanting to draw any attention, he kept his speed consistent at no more than five miles per hour over the speed limit.

He reached Virginia before sunrise and began counting down the one hundred seventy-nine miles of Interstate 95 North that he needed to pass before entering Maryland. He detested long hours behind the wheel, and he knew he would have to do it all over again in a day or two.

Morning rush hour around DC. He groaned. *That wasn't well planned.* He made it around DC, through the Fort McHenry Tunnel, then over the Woodrow Wilson Memorial Bridge into Delaware. He was well on his way to New Jersey by lunchtime.

He stopped at a rest area to grab Twinkies and a soda. His ass was sore from sitting, but his spirits were high. Over the course of the drive, he'd gone from air conditioning and short sleeves to defroster on high and a heavy jacket. He filled his gas tank for the final leg of his journey.

Before rolling into Atlantic City, he stopped at a Home Depot he spotted from the highway. There, he found everything he needed: duct tape, a power drill with a wide range of drill bits, and a miniature power saw. He paid in cash and got back on the road.

When he reached the city, he found a dive motel that took cash and asked no questions. After checking in under a fake name, he went to his dingy room and slept until morning.

When he got up, Aaron went about his day as if it were any other. He flipped on the TV to catch the news and brewed a pot of coffee in the cheap coffeemaker on the bathroom counter. After flipping through channels for almost an hour, he showered and shaved, brushed his teeth, dressed, packed up his things, and headed to the front desk to check out.

He took a deep breath as he plopped down behind the wheel of his rental car, then he turned the key in the ignition and headed to *her* place. The hesitation to act was gone. What he was doing felt right.

He'd looked up the house on the Internet using a computer in a library three counties away. The library did record his Internet usage, requiring an ID to sign in, but Aaron thought that if investigators ever got that far into their search for him, he would have already given them enough to hang him. The pictures had shown a small single-story house nestled on an acre of land bordered on two sides by wetlands. Most of the traversable land was flat and open, with few places to hide.

Driving by, he saw no cars in the driveway. *Good. She's not home.* He looked for a spot to park somewhere past the house, settling for a roadside spot on a nearby side street. He hoped anyone spotting it would assume the Subaru had stalled and he had left it to get out of the cold. He thought about moving the car off the road where the land sloped downward, but he didn't want to chance not being able to get it back up in the snow.

Grabbing his bag off the passenger seat, he got out of the car. As he walked briskly to the outskirts of the property, his boots squished into earth not yet frozen solid.

When he reached the perimeter of the yard, he headed straight for a large elm. From that vantage point, he had a clear view of the driveway and the side door. He zipped his jacket all the way up and lay on his stomach, letting his weight sink his body into the snow. His head would be partially visible from the driveway if someone were looking for it, but his dark hood might pass as an uncovered rock or some other part of the landscape.

An icy wind bit at his neck and howled through the branches overhead as he waited in the shadow of that tree. Snow blanketed everything and turned edges into hazy outlines. After what seemed like an hour, the time elongated by his miserableness, a car pulled into the driveway. He remained perfectly still while the occupants got out and headed into the house through the side door. Once they were inside, Aaron crept up to the window next to the door.

Raquel Bancroft walked across the kitchen, a bag of groceries in one hand and a baby on her opposite hip. Vanessa—Aaron had learned the four-year-old's name from combing through Raquel's social media sites—maneuvered around her mother and ran out of sight, carrying a stuffed penguin. Raquel plopped the bag of groceries on the kitchen counter then took the baby deeper into the house.

Aaron sidestepped to the door and twisted the handle. Just as he thought, she hadn't locked it. He moved inside and quietly closed the door behind him. Glancing around, he spotted a closed door that probably led to a pantry.

Raquel stepped into the hall, the baby no longer in her arms. Aaron froze, caught out in the open. She didn't look his way as she passed the kitchen doorway. A moment later, he heard a mattress squeak.

He put down his bag, counted to five, then moved into the hallway. Peeking around the corner, he saw Raquel lying on a bed with an arm draped over her eyes. He couldn't move, paralyzed by the waves of conflicting emotions flooding through him. Tears blurred his vision.

Hunger pushed him forward. Breaking his paralysis, he crossed the room in three long strides. He jumped on the bed and straddled her.

"Vanessa, let Mommy—"

Aaron jammed his gloved hand into her mouth. "It's been a long time." He settled his weight down on her. With his free hand, he pulled a screwdriver from his pocket.

Raquel grunted and bit down on his hand. She jerked her head violently, but the material was so thick Aaron only felt a slight pinch. He shuffled his knees up and over her arms, pinning them to the mattress. Raquel moaned and tried to scream, but Aaron dug his gloved hand in deeper.

"Stop your squirming and shut your mouth, or I'll puree your daughter and feed her to the baby." Aaron shoved the screwdriver into her nostril and scraped it along the inner wall.

She froze and stared up at him with wide eyes.

He pulled the screwdriver back but kept it in front of her face. "Good. You always knew how to listen. Just one of the many things I loved about you."

She squinted as if trying to figure out if she recognized him.

"I'm going to take my hand out of your mouth now. I'm not here for your kids, but if you try to scream or struggle or in any way cause me the slightest inconvenience, what I do to you will look like mercy compared to what I do to them. And I'll make you watch."

Raquel nodded. Aaron slowly drew his hand out of her mouth.

"How did you find me?" Raquel asked, sounding more angry than scared.

"Oh? You know who I am, then? I guess I won't be needing this."

Aaron tore off his ski mask and stuffed it into his jacket pocket. "I'm a cop now. With my training, it was ridiculously easy, plus all the crap you post on social media gave me anything I might need to know about your life. If only I knew then what I know now."

"What do you want?"

"Oh, I don't know." Aaron ran the screwdriver down her chin and along her sternum. He cupped her breast with his free hand. "I've got a surprise for you, Raquel Miranda, former love of my life."

"It's Bancroft now. I'm married, and my husband should be coming home at any minute."

"Nice try. Your husband works at one of the casinos and won't be home until after five, at the earliest. You've griped online about him having to work overtime too much. But it doesn't really matter. If he comes home, I'll just kill him, too."

Raquel gasped. "What do you want, Aaron? To kill me for something that happened half our lifetimes ago? Get on with it then. Just leave my children alone."

"Is this where he fucks you? Where you made those two beautiful children?" Aaron pulled his handcuffs from his back pocket. "Here's a little trick I learned from a new friend."

He slid his knee off Raquel's left arm and cuffed her wrist. She tried to strike him, but from her awkward vantage point, the attempt was feeble. He looped the cuff chain around a rung in the headboard then snapped the second loop around her other wrist.

After checking that she was secure, he got off her and stood by the bed to admire his success, the trophy that should have always been his.

"Please," she said, beginning to cry. "Please don't hurt my babies."

Lying in front of him helpless, she reminded Aaron of Maura. He wondered if he'd really wanted to kill Maura like Carter had said. He didn't think so, but recognizing what he'd become and considering his actions since leaving Seekonk that night, he wasn't so sure.

"This has been a long time coming," he said, grabbing Raquel's face by her cheeks. He leaned over and gently kissed her upper lip. He considered screwing her. She still looked as beautiful as she had that day in Newport, the last time he'd seen her. How he had lusted after her then. He could remember the sex vividly, so full of passion.

But raping her could cause him to leave more evidence, even if he could find a condom. But mostly, he felt that raping Raquel would somehow take away from the meaning of what he was doing, un-dignify it, make it seem cheap and petty. He was there for justice. Her crime had been to cause his heart immeasurable pain. Her punishment was delayed, but it still needed enforcing. And he was law enforcement.

Raquel stared up at him with glistening eyes. "Please," she whispered. "I have a family now."

"A family that should have been mine! Do you have any idea how much I loved you? I haven't been able to trust anyone completely since."

"Aaron, it was over ten years ago."

"And seeing you now makes it hurt just as much today as it did the day you left me. Why did you leave me?"

"You weren't right. You killed someone—"

"Oh, please. Don't use that as an excuse. You left me before that happened."

"Yes. I did. And I would have left you sooner had you not made me so afraid. You're sick, Aaron. You need help."

The sound of a baby's tearful cries came from down the hallway. Aaron turned toward the door.

"Please, don't hurt her," Raquel cried.

"What kind of sicko do you take me for?" Aaron snarled. "I would never hurt your baby."

Tears rolled down her cheeks. "Let me go, Aaron. You don't want to do this."

"Of course I want to do this. At one point, I might have agreed with you. Years of bitterness changed all that, always knowing you were the cause. I even tried to kill myself. Twice! Do you believe that? Eventually, memories of you faded, but the feelings of loneliness and loss never did. Why should I always have to feel like that while you can go on with your life, happy as a clam?"

"I had to leave everything I knew because of you. I started over, began a normal life. Even though that boy's face haunts my dreams to this day, I carry on. I live with the guilt and try my best to raise my daughters so they'll make better choices. I thought you had moved on, too. But when I saw your face in the news, associated with all those killings, something inside me told me that I'd see you again."

"I didn't kill those people."

"No, Carter Wainwright did. That's fucked up, Aaron. Carter Wainwright?"

"What are you—"

The pitter-patter of small feet was moving down the hallway, coming closer. He pulled a roll of duct tape from his jacket pocket and quickly ripped off a piece.

Slapping the tape over Raquel's mouth, he said, "Shush." He held the screwdriver behind his back and moved to block the view of the bed from the door.

Vanessa appeared in the doorway. "Mommy?"

"Hi, Vanessa," Aaron said, smiling. "I'm Jake, a friend of your mom. Your mommy's sleeping, but she'll be out in a minute."

"Tabitha's crying."

"Well, let's see what we can do about that." Aaron suddenly remembered he wasn't wearing his ski mask. *Now I have to kill the kid, too. No, I can't do that. She's just a little kid. I haven't fallen that far.*

He grabbed the girl, who let out a high-pitched squeal, and ran out into the hallway. Raquel started shaking the bed against the wall. The pounding headboard echoed throughout the house.

Ignoring the noise, Aaron bounced Vanessa in his arms as he carried her to a bedroom he was pretty sure was hers. He plopped her down on the edge of her bed and crouched in front of her. "Your mommy wants you to stay in here. She has a big surprise for you, but you gotta wait until she gets it ready, or you'll spoil it." Aaron hated lying to the little girl. He had no desire to hurt her, even if he had to hurt her mother.

"Have to," she blurted, sporting a grin short a few teeth.

"What?"

"You said 'gotta.' I say it too sometimes, but Mommy always says it's 'have to.'"

"You know what? You're right! How did you get to be so smart?"

Vanessa giggled.

"So will you promise to stay in here until your daddy comes and gets you?"

"I promise," she said, swinging her arms in the air for emphasis.

"You didn't have your fingers crossed now, did you?"

She giggled again. "Noooo."

"Okay, I believe you. Why don't you play with your toys while you wait? It might be a little while. But remember, if you come out, you won't get your surprise."

Vanessa nodded vigorously. Aaron exited the room, closing the door behind him.

He returned to Raquel. "That's one beautiful daughter you got there. Don't worry. She's in her room, completely unharmed. I asked her to wait there until her father comes home. She promised to do so. Let's just hope you didn't raise a liar." He patted her leg. "She's so happy, loving life. We were like that once, weren't we?"

He slapped his hands against his thighs. "Shall we get started? I'm going to kill you now. If it's any comfort, I promise not to hurt your children. Your husband will be fine, too, if he doesn't come home too early."

He grabbed the roll of duct tape again. Lifting Raquel's head, he wrapped the tape around and around enough times to lose track. Her heavy breathing whistled through her nose. "I'll be right back." He hurried back to the kitchen and picked up his bag.

When he returned, Raquel had stopped crying. She lay still, staring at the ceiling.

Aaron sifted through his bag and pulled out the mini buzz saw. He plugged it in then raised it to show it to Raquel, but she didn't react. She seemed to have come to terms with her fate, or at least realized that there wasn't anything she could do about it.

Tearing open her shirt, he exposed her breasts. He again considered raping her. But he couldn't. It wouldn't be the same, anyway.

He made quick work of opening her chest and pulling out the heart, suddenly finding no joy in prolonging it. The kill alone was enough, demanding with it a sense of power and control. But he didn't savor it nearly as much as he'd enjoyed killing Doug. Raquel's death was more about retribution, and he felt as though a part of him died with her.

The heart fulfilled his every expectation. He ate the entire thing while standing beside her corpse. Whatever he lost in killing Raquel was replaced tenfold when he took her heart inside him. Each bite was better than the next. Each swallow improved him instantly, both physically and mentally. He wondered how much he could progress. Could he become superhuman, like the characters in the comic books Craig used to read? He was determined to find out.

Throughout the entire operation, the baby cried. He wondered if she could sense the ill fate of her mother a few doors down.

He went to the refrigerator, where he found a row of baby bottles already prepared. He ran one under warm water for a few minutes then carried it into the baby's room.

He picked up the infant. "You're just hungry, aren't you?" he said, slipping the nipple into her mouth. "I'm sorry for what I did to your mother. Eventually, we all pay for our crimes. My time will come, too, I'm sure."

Minutes later, the baby gurgled up some milk. Aaron put the bottle on the dresser and wiped the infant's mouth with a clean section of his sleeve, careful not to get Raquel's blood in her mouth. He gently held her up to his chest and patted her back until she let out a loud burp.

He laid the baby back in her crib. Within moments, she was fast asleep. He thought maybe, if things had turned out a little differently, he could have been a good father. "Your father will be home soon to take care of you and your big sister," he said, leaning over the rail.

Back in Raquel's room, he changed into clean clothes from his bag. After gathering his tools and dirty clothes, he trekked back to the Subaru. The increasing snowfall quickly buried his tracks. The car needed some serious defrosting, and Aaron worried about being stranded so near the crime scene. But the car started, and he wiped the bulk of the snow off the windshield with his arm.

He put the car in gear and headed back to the highway to begin his long journey back to Florida.

CHAPTER 37

Jocelyn walked into Bruce's office. "That defense attorney is here to see us, the one who represented Fournier."

Bruce punched the keys of his keyboard harder and clenched his jaw. "I'm working here. I don't have time for that attorney's bullshit. I have nothing to say to her about Fournier's death. If she wants to file a claim on behalf of his family, if he still has one, that's between her and the Commonwealth. Far be it from me to stand in her way."

"That's not why she's here. I think she wants our help." Though it bruised Jocelyn's ego to admit she may have been wrong, she cleared her throat and said, "Something to do with Officer Pimental."

Bruce's fingers froze. He stared up at Jocelyn as if trying to read her then leaned back in his chair, his hands tucked behind his head. "Send her in."

Jocelyn nodded to Officer Clemens, who stood a few feet to her right—just far enough, she noted, to be out of Bruce's line of sight through his office window. Clemens hurried off.

"Any idea what this is about?" Bruce asked.

She shook her head. "Guess we'll find out soon enough."

"Is Pimental back yet?"

"From Florida, yes. He got back two days ago, but he said he needed another week off to recover. He'll be back on light duty next week."

"Do any of the officers know I'm looking into him or why that attorney's here?"

"Maybe Clemens, now. I'll make sure he stays quiet. I'm going to grab a coffee. Want one?"

"No thanks."

By the time Jocelyn returned to Bruce's office with coffee, a man and a woman occupied both of his guest chairs. She walked around the desk and stood behind Bruce, sipping her coffee as she took in the visitors.

The woman, Arianna Medeiros, didn't look nearly as smug and confident as she had the last time they'd met. The man, a morbidly obese fellow with bulldog jowls and droopy eyes, was unfamiliar.

Bruce stood, offering Jocelyn his chair. When she declined, he waved a hand toward their guests. "Detective Beaudette, you remember Attorney Medeiros?"

"Of course."

"The gentleman beside her is her brother, Seth Medeiros."

Jocelyn nodded. "What brings you two in to see us?"

Ms. Medeiros shifted in her seat. "As you probably know, I am—or I was, anyway—Aaron Pimental's girlfriend."

Jocelyn exchanged a look with Bruce. Up until recently, neither of them had taken much interest in Pimental, never mind his girlfriends, past or present. *He certainly keeps to an interesting circle.*

Bruce scratched his stubbled chin. "So let me get this straight. You represented an acquaintance of your boyfriend in a case involving his suspected murder of one of your boyfriend's friends, among other people?"

Seth glowered at them. "We want to stress *ex*-boyfriend."

Arianna touched her brother's arm then straightened, exhibiting a poise under pressure that Jocelyn couldn't help but admire. "It was... one of the many causes of problems between us."

"What brings you here today, Ms. Medeiros?" Jocelyn asked.

"I'm worried about Aaron."

"Aaron Pimental?"

"Yes."

"And what exactly has you worried?"

"Let me just say this first: I don't think Aaron had anything to do with that cult. And if you saw him after Craig's death... well, you wouldn't, either. But this whole thing has left him... I don't know... different. Angrier. More depressed. Unstable."

"Has he hurt you, Ms. Medeiros?" Bruce asked.

"No. Not physically. But there were times when I thought..." Arianna shuddered. "Anyway, he was extremely upset when I told him I was representing Doug, so much so that I thought if Doug actually had done it, there would be no need for a trial because Aaron might kill him first. And maybe me, too, if I helped Doug get away with it. So when I heard Doug was murdered, I..."

"It's okay, sis." Seth grabbed her hand. "Just tell them what you think and let them handle it as best they see fit."

She took a deep breath. "I think Aaron may have been involved."

Jocelyn noticed Bruce leaning forward. She had to work to keep herself from doing the same.

"What makes you think that?" Bruce asked.

"Oh, I don't have any evidence or anything like that. And I have no idea where he was the night Doug died. In fact, I would have just assumed Carter Wainwright had done it, except for what I saw on the news a few days ago."

"Do you mean what happened in Atlantic City?" Jocelyn's voice squeaked. That murder had caught their eyes, as well. The victim's heart had been removed.

Arianna nodded. "The paper said she was originally from this area, and she's the same age as Aaron. At first, I thought maybe I was jumping to conclusions. I'm no cop, but all signs seem to point to Carter. But I told Seth about it, and he keeps checking in on me, making me paranoid. He wanted me to come by and speak to you."

"So you don't know where Pimental was the night Fournier was murdered, but you do think he's capable of violence?" Bruce asked.

Arianna looked down at her hands and started to pick at a cuticle. At last, she said meekly, "That's right. He hated the fact that I represented Doug. He hated *me* for it. I'm scared."

"Murder's a serious accusation," Jocelyn said. "Have you had any recent contact with Pimental? Has he threatened you in any way? Called you or reached out to you?"

"No, none of that, but… I don't know." Arianna sighed. "I've never seen him hurt anyone. Maybe I'm just being silly. It's just that… I mean, it's weird, isn't it? That Aaron knows most of the killers and some of the victims? He was friends with a few of them."

Seth nodded. "Too many crazy coincidences, if you ask me. I wouldn't be surprised if Aaron was one of them and that's why they got away with it for as long as they did."

Jocelyn shook her head. "That doesn't sound right. Pimental shot Wainwright, saved that woman, and killed his best friend in doing so."

"I'm sorry," Arianna said. "I'm just shaken up. I mean… what if it *was* him?" Her face paled. She pushed back her bangs, tucking their ends around her ears. "Do you think he would come after me, too?"

"You may be worrying for nothing," Bruce said, "but why take chances? Keep your door locked. Don't go out alone. Don't even stay home alone, at least not until we catch whoever killed Fournier, or until we can clear Pimental. If you fear for your life, I'd also urge you to seek a restraining order."

"Is that it?" Seth rose. "That's all you can do for us?"

"Without more, there's not too much we can do. But you can sleep a little easier knowing we'll be monitoring his movements."

Seth leaned all his considerable girth over the desk. "That's not good enough. Can't you do something more? He works here, for crying out loud."

"We'll classify him as a person of interest and pull him in for questioning."

Seth grunted and stuck out his hand. Bruce rose and shook it, and Jocelyn walked over to do the same. Arianna gave them a curt nod before she and her brother left Bruce's office.

After they were gone, Jocelyn plopped down in the chair Seth had vacated. She squirmed to find that comfy spot, cringing at the seat's warmth. "Well? Aren't you going to say it?"

Bruce tapped his fingers on his desk. "Say what?"

"You know." She crinkled her nose. "I told you so."

"Despite what you may think, I didn't want to be right about this. A cop-turned-killer would make all of us look bad. As if we don't have enough problems trying to convince the neighborhood that not all of us are corrupt."

"Well, he certainly had motive to kill Fournier, *and* we had sent him to the hospital only hours before his death. Do you buy his story about the Fleurent scene?"

Bruce shook his head. "Something stinks like shit about that. This whole case stinks worse than all the septic tanks in Fall River. I mean, how did Wainwright just disappear? How did he empty his house right under our noses? I think there's another player here, an accessory at the least. He *must* have help. I might have suspected Fleurent if she hadn't wound up dead. Maybe Pimental's been in cahoots with Wainwright all along. Think about it. He says he shot Wainwright, who then fell out a window four stories, yet Wainwright wasn't lying on the ground dead. Not a single witness to that. Plus, Pimental seems to be everywhere Wainwright pops up lately." Bruce shook his head. "I wouldn't be surprised if Wainwright took off, and we've been dealing with one of his remaining stooges since."

Jocelyn chewed on that for a minute, then she held up a finger. "One, Pimental has access to crime scenes." She raised another finger. "Two, he can out-maneuver our surveillance if he knows our positions." Another finger. "Three, he can tamper with evidence. You're right. It's possible he's been an inside man all along. He was even the first responder to the Ramirez crime scene." She stared at the yellowing ceiling tiles. "Ugh! Then why would he save Fleurent, only to kill her later? Why would he kill his other partners in crime? None of this makes any sense."

"We'll prod him about it as soon as he gets back. If he is part of Wainwright's little gang, I don't want to tip him off that we're on to him. Not until we have what we need to hang him."

"What about this New Jersey killing? Different weapon, but the heart was missing. A copycat?"

"Maybe, but I don't think so." Bruce reached for his phone. "I'll contact the detective heading up the investigation over there. Something tells me that solving that case just may be the key to unlocking our own."

CHAPTER 38

BARELY THREE DAYS AFTER GETTING back from Florida, Aaron craved his next kill. It had been a week since he'd killed Raquel, and the memory of her taste still caused his mouth to water. Aaron drove down the snow-covered street parallel to his old house. He couldn't exactly pull into the driveway, though that would probably have raised less suspicion among the neighbors than if he kept driving around the block. He didn't want to draw attention to himself, a difficult feat in a part of town where everyone knew him.

He parked on a side street. After all, it had worked well enough the last time. "Last chance to turn back," he said to the empty car. Since he'd returned to Massachusetts, Aaron hadn't had any human contact except for when he'd called the department to request another week off.

If I do this, it will only be a short time before Marklin connects her to me. The prick was already suspicious even before he had reason to be.

Aaron climbed out and trudged through the snow to the row of bushes at the edge of his former yard. Scanning the house for signs of life, he saw no one. He entered the yard, another step toward certain damnation. Doug was excusable, but Raquel—and now Arianna? Ricardo and that boy so long ago? Yeah, he had killed them, too. The funny thing was he'd fought so hard to convince himself he hadn't pushed that boy off the cliff on purpose when admitting it, *accepting* it, might have saved him so much grief and heartache. He no longer cared. More than that, he embraced that side of himself.

He didn't bother with the front door, certain Arianna would have changed the locks. Every movement he made seemed loud against a still, quiet night. Whispers of his progression danced toward the ears of those who would listen. But if ears were listening, none heeded his approach.

Snow flurried around him, and he hoped it provided him cover. The night was dark. Overstuffed clouds blotted out the stars, but the snow reflected the streetlights' glow.

He pulled a black ski mask over his face, clenched his fists inside his black leather gloves, and scurried toward the bulkhead door, which had never been barred. To his fortune, Arianna hadn't thought to latch it. He pulled it open quickly but quietly then closed it behind him.

The door to the cellar was latched with a flimsy slide chain, which Aaron easily pried loose with a screwdriver. He made his way toward the stairs and began to climb. Each step was slower and softer, as he tried to avoid the creaky areas.

He heard scratching followed by whimpering. *Shit. Damn dog's gonna give me away.*

Footsteps came toward the door as he reached the top. He raised the screwdriver, holding the railing with his free hand in case Arianna tried to push him. *This isn't how or where I wanted it, but it'll have to do.*

"What is it, girl?" Arianna asked. "Wanna go outside? That's the wrong door, silly."

The dog barked once and panted. When Aaron heard the jingling of Calypso's leash, he knew he'd been spared. *That dog loves the snow.* He huffed. *She used to be my dog.*

"Caly, don't pull!" Arianna's voice was farther away.

A door creaked open, and a howling wind whipped through the house. The back door slammed, and Aaron made his move. He slipped into the house, ducking low under the windows. He chanced a peek out the bedroom window. Calypso was bounding across the yard. She dove into a snowdrift, her leash dragging behind her. He saw no sign of Arianna. But he did see something else.

"Fuck!" His tracks led across the backyard and over to the bulkhead door. *She must have seen them. She knows I'm here. She must have run.*

"Caly!"

Aaron froze. The back door opened. He heard the pitter-patter of feet and the jingle of Calypso's tags, followed by a wiping of human feet on the welcome mat. The dog beelined straight to him and appeared in the bedroom doorway.

"Hey, don't you want your treat?"

The dog's ears straightened. She looked back at the entrance then back at Aaron. A second later, she wagged her tail and trotted back to the kitchen.

Aaron smiled. Arianna liked to give Calypso those giant rawhide bones. That would keep the dog busy for a little while. After waiting three more minutes, he crept into the hall, passed the basement door, and stopped in the diagonal shadow created by the corner of the wall and the kitchen light beyond it.

Arianna stood at the kitchen sink, elbow deep in dishwater. She hummed while she scrubbed.

Aaron took a step toward her. *This is almost too easy.* He continued until he was only a few feet away.

Arianna drained the water and pulled off her gloves. When she reached for a dish towel, she froze.

The window. Of course. Even from where he stood, he could see his reflection clear as day. "Hello, Arianna. I've missed you."

She spun around. "What are you doing here?" she asked, shrinking back against the sink. "Leave now, and I won't call the cops."

"I *am* the cops."

"So you must know that you're breaking and entering. You need to leave. Now!" Her voice had gotten stronger, but it still cracked.

Aaron laughed. "Breaking and entering? I can live with that." More softly, he added, "You know I can't leave now."

She suddenly lunged toward him, bringing a hand out from behind her back. His head exploded with pain as she broke a plate over it. He stumbled and almost fell. Arianna lurched toward the phone on the end of the counter. She snatched it up just as he reached her. He grabbed her wrist and slammed her hand down on the counter. She yelped, and the phone fell out of her hand and slid across the floor.

Arianna jammed her other elbow into his stomach. When his breath came out in a whoosh, he bent over. She pulled her arm free and circled the table, heading back toward the sink. There, she pulled a butcher's knife from the rack.

"Interesting." Aaron picked up her phone and put it in his pocket.

Arianna glared at him. She shifted her weight back and forth between her feet, always keeping that knife out in front of her.

The wild look on her face made Aaron think of *The Shining*. "Here's Johnny," he said flatly and snickered.

"Come near me, and I swear I'll shove this knife so far into you, it'll come out the other side."

"That's the spirit! That's what I always loved about you. Hot-blooded Ari. No one could ever tell you what to do." He inched toward her, his hands held out in front of him. "But please, I'm asking nicely. Put the knife down, and we'll talk about this."

He reached her with one long stride. She thrust the knife toward him, and he jerked sideways. The blade slashed through the material of his jacket but never touched him. Before she could pull her arm back for another try, he punched her in the nose. Her head rocked back, blood pouring from her nostrils. She dropped the knife and brought her hands up to her face.

Aaron kicked the knife under the table. With the skill of a hockey player, Arianna checked him aside and ran. Caught off guard, he reached for her sweatshirt as she passed, but he came up short, grasping at air. He followed her into the living room.

As he rounded the corner of the doorway, she hit him in the head with something. Glass shattered. The broken remains of a flower vase sprinkled the rug. She began throwing things at him: a decorative pillow, magazines from the coffee table, and the television remote. When she tried to pick up the lamp, the cord wouldn't give, and it dropped harmlessly at her feet.

Aaron walked slowly, reveling in the hunt, knowing he would soon have his prey. He could already taste the warm blood of her heart smearing his lips. She flipped the coffee table toward him. The hard edge hit his shin just right, sending a quick jolt of pain through his leg like an electric shock.

Arianna raced past him, heading back to the kitchen. Aaron

recovered and came up behind her just as she was pulling another knife out of the block. He wrapped his arms around her, grabbing her wrists and slamming them onto the counter. She began to kick and scream, slamming her heels into Aaron's shins as he bear-hugged her off the ground.

He squeezed. *I need to stop fooling around. Somebody might have already called the cops.* He could feel her ribcage collapsing under his embrace. *Just some good old-fashioned domestic violence. Nothing to see here.*

Her long brown hair clung to his face. He leaned toward it, sniffing the clean smell of lavender on her scalp. She drove her head back into his nose.

"You bitch!" He staggered backward but held on.

She swung her heels back and up. Her right foot was blocked by his leg, but her left connected with his balls. Aaron squealed, releasing her as he bent over in pain. He coughed and cupped his genitals with one hand.

Arianna turned to run, but she tripped and went down hard on the tile floor. Though ready to vomit from the agony emanating from his crotch, Aaron lurched over and fell on top of her.

He grabbed a fistful of hair with his free hand and slammed her head on the floor. He repeated the move until she lay still. "I'm done playing around with you, bitch." He scowled as he punched her one more time for good measure.

CHAPTER 39

JOCELYN WAS AS FED UP as Bruce was, but the department had other cases and only so many resources to distribute among them. They wanted full-time surveillance on Pimental, but Bruce's request had been placed in a long queue. And while the brass dillydallied, yet another potential killer was given an opportunity to flee.

"If you want something done right, you've gotta do it yourself." Bruce threw on his coat and pushed his glasses up the bridge of his nose.

"We can put a couple officers on it," Jocelyn said.

"Like those two clowns who let the Fourniers slip by them? Or how about the idiots we had guarding Fournier's hospital room?"

Jocelyn frowned. "If I didn't know better, I'd swear half this precinct was on Wainwright's payroll." *I'm not sure I do know any better.*

Bruce grunted and turned up his collar, preparing for the harsh bite of the subzero wind. He exited his office.

"Wait." Jocelyn hurried after him, zipping up her coat. "I'll go with you." She slowed and suppressed a chill as they passed the two empty desks that had belonged to Temple and Pimental. *Bruce is right. Pimental's not coming back.* "What's the plan?"

"What I should have been doing from day one: I'm going to tail him. And when he slips up—and he will slip up—I'll be there to make sure he falls."

Jocelyn crossed her arms. "If he's got any skill as a cop, he'll spot you outside his place."

"I won't be going to his place. I'll be heading to *her* place. If he is our guy, Ms. Medeiros is the obvious next target." He held open one of the double doors leading to the reception area for Jocelyn then followed her through. "We've lost too many people to these psycho—"

"You!" A heavyset man barreled toward Bruce.

"Sir, we have to finish taking your report," an officer called after him.

Bruce waved off the officer. "Mr. Medeiros, what happened?"

"She's gone!" Seth blurted between wheezes. "He's got her—I just know it!"

"Easy," Jocelyn said. "Who's got who?"

"Who else? Aaron has my sister. Yes, that asshole I was just in here warning you about not even forty-eight hours ago has taken my sister. And it's all your damn fault."

"Okay, okay," Jocelyn said. "We want to help, but you need to calm down and tell us what you know."

Seth took three deep breaths. The purple of his face faded to a bright red. "I went by her house. I knocked a few times, tried the bell. No answer. So I let myself in. The place was trashed, the furniture tipped over and shit. I could tell there'd been a fight."

"When was this?"

Seth's nostrils flared. "Like twenty minutes ago. I came straight here."

"You said the place was trashed? And no one called us?"

Seth's eyes shimmered with tears. "This fucking city. Nobody lifts a hand to help nobody. That's why I got out. If you want something done right, you've gotta do it yourself."

She glanced at Bruce. "So I've heard."

Bruce asked, "Did you check the house for her? The whole house?"

"Not the whole house, but most of it. And I called her name a bunch. The dog came. That dog is always with her."

Bruce looked at Jocelyn. "She could still be there. She may be hurt."

She nodded. "Let's go. Mr. Medeiros, you can ride with us."

They ran out to Bruce's car and got in. Seth held his side and gasped for air, but he kept up and jumped in the back.

Bruce floored the pedal and flipped on his lights, while Jocelyn got on the radio and called for backup, pausing only long enough to get Arianna's address from Seth.

When she finished, she turned in her seat. "You holding up?"

Seth shook his head. "She's not there. He took her. We're wasting time."

"You may be right, but at least there, we stand a chance of finding her or some clue where he might have taken her. Do you have any idea where he could have taken her?"

"No, but I know where he lives."

Aaron let her howl for an hour or so. Spread out naked on top of an old workbench, her wrists and ankles bound, Arianna had no way of escaping. He wanted to wait for her spirit to break before going to her, but he couldn't. He walked over to her.

Arianna spat in his face. "Everyone will suspect you. I've told Seth, Brittney, and the detective in charge of the investigation... a Marlin or Macklin... all about you."

Aaron grinned. "Did you tell Reggie?" Yeah, he knew all about her new boyfriend and how quickly he'd entered the picture. They hadn't been hard to tail. He'd watched through slitted curtains with the aid of binoculars. The things he'd seen them do made his skin crawl.

Arianna didn't respond.

"Yeah, I figured they'd be looking into me after Raquel, but I thought I would have some time before they start piecing that one together. But since you opened your big mouth to all those people, I'm thinking time's short. After we're done here, I'll be gettin' while the gettin's good." He rubbed his hands together. "Do you know where we are?"

Her eyes rolled as she tried to look around the room. The glow from the portable lantern Aaron had placed near the table and the flashlight he carried were the room's only sources of light.

She swallowed hard. "Is th-this the place... the place where—"

"No." Aaron laughed. "But it is a mill. I sort of borrowed the idea from them, though I don't think they'll mind. It's a place where no one will hear you and no one will find you." She trembled. He liked that. "Just so you know, I was never a part of what they were doing, and I actually tried to stop it. I was a hero, but you, Brittney, everyone... you all kicked me to the curb. You didn't even care. You all looked at me like... like I was some kind of *monster*." He slammed his palm down on the table near her head.

Arianna closed her eyes. A tear trickled down her cheek. "That's not true, but even if it was, it's no excuse for killing people." Her mascara streaked down her face as her eyes rained harder. "And look at you now! You would actually do what they did? You would cut me open like that? At least Ricardo, as disillusioned as he was, believed he was saving people. There are no good intentions behind your plans. You *are* a monster."

Aaron laughed. "So happy I could finally live up to your expectations. But say what you will. I'm not crazy like them. It has nothing to do with your sins. I can't explain it to you. You'd have to experience it to understand."

Arianna was one of the average, while he stood so high above. She couldn't know without experiencing what the killers had each felt firsthand. No one could appreciate the thrill and virility that came with the consumption of Carter's delicacy without submitting themselves to atrocity.

"It's not easy to come to grips with," he said. "Trust me on that one. I could transform you like they did me, but by the time you came around, I'd be dead or in jail." He chuckled. "We're just two ships passing in the night."

"Aaron, you're not making any sense." Her words blended with sobs. "You need help. Let me go, and I'll help you."

Aaron shook his head. "I don't need help. For a long time, I did, but I never got it from you, from anybody. Not until Carter. Finally, I've found what I needed all along. For the first time that I can remember, life is good. I feel good. But I do need one more thing to be complete." He leaned over and kissed her forehead. "Tonight is about you and me. All of this—the setting, the quiet ambience, and the romantic atmosphere—it's all for dramatic effect. Kind of an homage, if you will. And who knows? Maybe I can take your soul to hell along with mine." He longed to feed, to feel that power surge inside him. "But personally, you hurt me. Real bad. I really just want to hurt you back."

Arianna screamed and called for help, over and over. Her cries were of no use. Still, he supposed she had to try. He crossed his arms and waited for her to finish. No one would save her. There were no heroes left in the world.

When she ran out of steam, he pulled out the knife he had tucked under the back of his belt. The blade was shaped like a scimitar, only thicker, and silver studs and spikes circled the grip. It looked like something from a cheesy sci-fi film, a postapocalyptic mutant's weapon. He held it up so she could see it. "It's amazing what one can find at a Florida flea market." He laughed. "I bought this beauty special just for you." He slid his thumb down the blade's edge. "Uh-oh. It's not that sharp."

Arianna squirmed and let out another hoarse cry for help. "Please, Aaron. Please don't do this."

His heart galloped. Her betrayal and abandonment still stung. He pictured her with her new boyfriend and hoped the guy was in love with her. That way, he would know how Aaron felt.

He raised the knife.

CHAPTER 40

ARIANNA MEDEIROS'S HOUSE HAD YIELDED no clues. Bruce and Jocelyn had searched it thoroughly. After dropping off Seth, they headed to Pimental's new address. Bruce drove through dark, empty streets. Half the streetlights were out, and the only people they passed were crouched in shadows, junkies needing fixes and those who would fix them.

Even though the circumstantial evidence was beginning to pile up, Bruce didn't think he would be able to get a warrant, especially at such a late hour. A stakeout was the best he could do, and he might get lucky and catch Pimental in some illegal act.

Without turning his head to look at Jocelyn, he said, "I have more details on that thing in Atlantic City…"

"What? And you're just now mentioning this?" Jocelyn said.

"I know. I should have told you back at the precinct, but I was so upset we didn't have surveillance placed on Medeiros's house that I just wanted to get over there fast. Turns out with good reason. Plus, you were busy following up on Wainwright. I thought maybe we'd—"

"Bruce, we're partners."

"I know. I'm sorry."

"Well?"

"Like the Wainwright kills, the heart was missing. Only this time, a power saw was used, and she was bound by standard-issue handcuffs."

"Fleurent was bound with handcuffs the second go-around, too, so I'd keep Wainwright on an equal playing field. We still need to investigate him for about ten or so murders, remember?"

"Well, I did some checking on Pimental anyway."

Jocelyn frowned. Bruce was pretty sure he knew what she was thinking. She certainly agreed Pimental needed to be investigated and particularly for Arianna's disappearance, if she had in fact disappeared, but their *known* guilty party was out there.

Better to focus on those we can still catch. "Why are you so reluctant to believe Pimental is part of all this?"

"Medeiros just reported his sister missing. It's only been a few hours. Maybe she just needed to get away from the craziness. And who knows who she might be seeing now? She could be anywhere, with anybody."

"You don't really believe that. And you saw the house. There was a struggle. The blood on the floor was a pretty obvious clue. So ruling out her just getting away for a while—what's your gut telling you?"

"It's just… I don't want to believe a cop could do all of those awful things. Not one of ours. Someone we know and have worked with for years."

"You know better."

"Sure. In my head. But…"

"It's like I told you. You'd go much farther than me in this job if you kill that bleeding heart of yours."

"Interesting choice of words."

Bruce sighed. "Well, consider this. Pimental flew to Orlando and paid for five nights at the Quality Inn on International Drive. After that, he spent two nights in Key West. Then he drove all the way to New Orleans for another couple of nights before driving back to Orlando, only to fly back here."

"New Orleans during Mardi Gras? Sounds like a fun vacation. So he was nowhere near Atlantic City."

"Jocelyn, Pimental is a cop. He put over two thousand miles on that rental car, driving the shit out of it in less than two weeks. Is that how most people spend their vacations? Also, the car he rented was a Subaru Outback, which he specifically requested. That's a vehicle that would be good in the snow."

"You're suggesting Pimental flew all the way down to Orlando just to drive back up here to Atlantic City to kill that woman?"

"Why did he drive to New Orleans? With today's gas prices, it's cheaper and faster to fly there."

"Maybe he prefers driving to flying. I don't know, Bruce. But he did check in, so he must've been there, right?"

"Unless he has an accomplice. Or maybe he got to Key West and New Orleans some other way, so he could account for all those extra miles he tacked on to the rental."

"Sounds far-fetched. Aren't you the one who always tells me the simplest answer is often the right answer?"

"I also tell you to follow your gut. I'm following mine."

"Even if we ignore all the obvious holes in your theory, you're still missing one critical element. What motive would Pimental have to drive all that way just to murder some housewife?"

"That's the million-dollar question. I found out that Raquel Bancroft was born and raised in Pimental's hometown of Somerset. She even graduated in the same high school class as he did, so it's no stretch to assume he knew her."

"That is an interesting coincidence." Jocelyn scratched her head and leaned forward. "Okay, you've got my attention. Let's get a couple of officers looking into it."

"Way ahead of you. In fact…" Bruce pulled to the curb and called the precinct. "It's Marklin. Get me Officer Holt." He wanted to keep dispatch free in case any emergencies came in, so he stayed off the radio. Also, Pimental might have a scanner. Bruce turned up the volume and put the phone on speaker.

"This is Holt."

"It's Marklin. How's that research going?"

"I talked to some of Raquel Bancroft's old friends, and I found out she had a creepy boyfriend right after high school. None of them seemed to have approved of her dating this guy. Care to guess his name?"

"Aaron Pimental," Bruce stated. He winked at Jocelyn.

"No, sir. Why? I'm sorry, sir. Does Officer Pimental know the deceased?"

"Never mind that. What was his name?"

"Well, they said she dated some waif of a guy, a pale, gloomy fellow. He was clinically depressed, they said, some loner who went to Rockland High School around the same time she was at Somerset High. He committed suicide while they were dating. He actually jumped off the Cliffwalks in Newport."

Bruce shared a look of disbelief with Jocelyn. *Things keep getting weirder and weirder.* "Well, what was his name?"

"They said his name was Carter Wainwright, sir."

An empty feeling surged up from the pit of his stomach. "Is that all?" he managed after a moment.

Officer Holt responded, "Well, when I showed them the picture of our Carter Wainwright, they all agreed it wasn't the guy they were talking about. They remember their Carter Wainwright being blond and fair-skinned."

Bruce had delayed investigation into the fate of the real Carter Wainwright, focusing instead on the individual who'd become him. With the new information, he was forced to stop and regroup. *How is Pimental connected to the dead woman or the real or fake Wainwright? Have I been wrong about all this?* He needed to focus, to connect the proverbial dots. But some dots were still missing. By the deepness of the grooves on Jocelyn's brow, she was equally perplexed.

Officer Holt cleared his throat. "There's one more thing, sir. I went to a few of the local libraries to search the newspapers for Wainwright's suicide. I checked paper after paper and found nothing—no obituary, no article. Nothing. I even called over to the *Newport Daily News* to see if they could help me. His name came up nowhere in their database. There's nothing about it anywhere, not even online. It's like the guy never existed. But two of the woman's friends knew the name. It couldn't be a coincidence, and they would have no reason to lie. It looks like someone went through a hell of a lot of trouble to eliminate records pertaining to Carter Wainwright."

Bruce grunted. "Good work, Officer Holt." *Everything comes full circle. Yet, I have nothing solid on Pimental, and I can't find Wainwright.* He had been certain he'd find a tie between Pimental and Bancroft. *But Wainwright and Bancroft?*

After ending the call, he pulled back onto the road. "Any ideas?"

Jocelyn shook her head. "I'm as surprised as you are on this one. I didn't expect that."

"Well, let's bring in Pimental. There's a lot I want to talk to him about."

When Bruce reached the address Seth had given them, he stared at the boarded-up fish market.

"This can't be right," Jocelyn said.

"Some of these places have apartments above them, but not this one. Could Medeiros have given us the wrong address?"

"Why would he give us the wrong address?" Jocelyn's eyes widened. "Stravenski! He partnered with him sometimes. He might know."

After struggling with dispatch for Stravenski's whereabouts, Bruce was eventually patched through to the officer's patrol car. He had Stravenski call his cell in case Pimental was listening. Stravenski called and told them that Pimental had been staying with his parents.

While Jocelyn requested backup, Bruce flicked on his lights and sped toward the new address.

Aaron had no idea how much time he had before Marklin and Beaudette would show up at his parents' house. But he couldn't sit around thinking about it. Arianna's overprotective brother or her idiot boyfriend would report her missing once they saw her house, if they hadn't already. And if she was telling the truth about blabbing to Marklin, it was time to leave.

He had to stop by his parents' house to pick up some stuff and get rid of any evidence he might have left. He would drive toward the coast, hide out in dive motels, then hop on the first plane he could find that would take him to some South American country that lacked extradition. There was nothing left for him in the States, anyway. He had cleaned out his savings account before his Florida trip. It wasn't much, but in some of the poorer countries, it could get him by for a long time.

At his parents' place, he grabbed his suitcase, which he'd kept packed for just such an emergency, along with his laptop and all the scraps of paper he'd written notes on while researching his victims. He crept downstairs quietly, trying not to wake his mother. He had left a note for her, so there was no need for a long goodbye or the bunch of questions she was sure to pepper him with. Backing up to the door while pulling his large suitcase, he reached behind him to twist the doorknob. He winced and froze when the door creaked open. After not hearing anything for a count of five, he turned to exit the house—and smacked into Seth Medeiros.

"Going somewhere, Aaron?"

Aaron staggered backward. He released his grip on his suitcase, and it rocked into an upright position. "Heading to Florida, remember?" he said, smiling nervously.

"I thought you already went." Seth stood in front of him, blocking his path. He held a double-barrel shotgun under one arm.

"You're confused." Aaron tried to steady his voice. "What's with the gun, Seth?"

"Where's my sister?"

"How the hell should I know? I haven't seen her in weeks."

Seth's jaw flexed. "I was supposed to see her tonight. She didn't answer my calls, and that ain't like her. I've been to her place, saw the mess. And it's like she up and disappeared. You know anything about that?"

"Seth, put the gun down and come inside. Let's talk about this."

"There's nothing to talk about. She's missing, and I know that you have everything to do with it."

"How do you know she didn't go away with her new boyfriend?"

"Aaron, I told you, I went by the house. I saw the mess. I've called her and everyone who knows her a half dozen times." He raised the barrel of the shotgun so that it pointed at Aaron's chest. "I warned her about you. Now I'm going to ask you one more time…"

Aaron moved his hand toward his pistol holstered at his side. He wondered if he could draw it before Seth pulled the trigger. Aaron's reflexes were better than ever, and maybe the shotgun wasn't loaded. Maybe Seth was just trying to scare him. *Maybe I should run back into the house.* But he knew better. No one could outrun a bullet.

"What do you think this is?" Seth snickered, glancing down at Aaron's hand. "The Wild West? I wouldn't do that if I were you."

"Seth, please. Let's be rational here." Aaron's hand slid closer to the holster.

"Move that hand again, and you won't be too happy with the results. For the last fucking time, where's my sister?"

Aaron's heart pounded, and sweat dripped from his forehead. "I don't know where she is!" He drew his gun.

The blast made his head ring. The buckshot felt like a thousand horseflies biting everywhere across his chest. The stinging was short-lived. True agony took its place, locking up his lungs as his feet swung up off the ground. He crashed down on the entryway floor, mind blurred by searing-hot pain.

The smoking barrel of Seth's shotgun lowered. After gaping at Aaron for a few seconds, apparently shocked that he'd actually shot him, he turned and trudged back to his car. Just as he reached it, an old Buick pulled in behind it.

"Don't move!" Beaudette yelled, thrusting her gun out the passenger window of Marklin's car.

Holding up one hand, Seth slowly crouched and laid the shotgun on the ground. He stood back up and raised both hands into the air.

Aaron laughed. It hurt to laugh. The fat fuck had actually done it, had avenged his sister. The detectives moved in on Seth as their backup pulled in. They cuffed him, patted him down, and ordered two officers to put him in the back of their cruiser.

Beaudette ran over to Aaron. She kicked his gun away from him. Marklin hung back, on his radio, probably calling for an ambulance. Aaron coughed up blood. It coated his teeth with a texture that reminded him of hummus. He tried to speak, but his words wouldn't form.

"Where is she?" Beaudette asked.

Aaron shook his head and smiled. "Too late..."

"Why?" Beaudette cried. "You were a damn hero. Does this whole fucking city lack a moral compass?"

Marklin came up behind her. "Yes. Now that you've learned that, you're going to make one hell of a detective."

Jocelyn balled her fists. "Who helped you? Were you working with Wainwright all along? Tell us, for your soul's sake!"

Aaron's eyes fluttered. *My soul...* He struggled to keep his eyes open.

The detectives stared down at him, no warmth or sympathy in theirs. He didn't care. Breathing became a chore, and he was ready to give up. He raised a trembling hand to his chest. With his last breath, he muttered, "Don't let it go to waste."

EPILOGUE

El Paso, TX. Seventeen months later.

"THE BIBLE TELLS US, 'JUDGE not, lest ye be judged.' Now, you all believe this to mean that you shouldn't judge your neighbors, your friends, your co-workers… that the Almighty is the only one with the authority to judge them. Am I right?"

The crowd mumbled softly in agreement. Well-dressed men and women sweated profusely in the late-summer heat, their asses sore from the hard oak slabs beneath them and their knees dusty from their bouts with the clay floor.

The preacher continued in a heavy Southern drawl. "And I say to you, no! That's not what the Almighty Lord Jesus Christ says to you through his glorious teachings. He wants you to judge thy neighbor, to judge him properly, so that you may be judged properly yourself, come Judgment Day. For one day, those who do not take action against the unfaithful and the sinners, those who do not take action while the Jews and adulterers and homosexuals are given free rein over our government, the media, our schools, and our children's innocence—well, I say to those of you among us, the Good Lord will not judge you kindly."

"Amen," the congregation said in unison.

"Rise with the Lord. Let the sinners swim in hell with Lucifer!"

The preacher slammed his palm onto the pulpit. It worked. His congregation was enthralled. They hung on his every word.

"Peace be with you, my brothers and sisters. Go with God." He smiled at his flock, so faithful, so malleable. They were like lemmings.

He was ready to begin anew.

ABOUT THE AUTHOR

In his head, Jason Parent lives in many places, but in the real world, he calls Southeastern Massachusetts his home. The region offers an abundance of settings for his writing and many wonderful places in which to write them. He currently resides with his cuddly corgi, Calypso.

In a prior life, Jason spent most of his time in front of a judge... as a civil litigator. When he tired of Latin phrases no one knew how to pronounce and explaining to people that real lawsuits are not started, tried, and finalized within the sixty-minute time-frame they see on TV, he traded in his cheap suits for flip-flops and designer stubble. The flops got repossessed the next day, and he's back in the legal field... sorta. But that's another story.

When he's not working, Jason likes to kayak, catch a movie, travel any place that will let him enter, and play just about any sport (except for the one with that ball tied to the pole thing where you basically just whack the ball until it twists in a knot or takes somebody's head off). And read and write, of course. He does that too sometimes.

www.ingramcontent.com/pod-product-compliance
Lightning Source LLC
Chambersburg PA
CBHW050713180626
46814CB00002B/421